HOUSE OF CRIMSON KISSES

A STEAMY VAMPIRE FANTASY ROMANCE

KINGDOM OF IMMORTAL LOVERS
BOOK TWO

RUBY ROE

House of Crimson Kisses - A Steamy Lesbian Fantasy Romance

First Published July 2024, by Ruby Roe, Atlas Black Publishing.

Cover design: Maria Spada

rubyroe.co.uk

SANGUI CITY
N
W
E
S
Castle Montague
HOUSE MONTAGUE TERRITORY
HOUSE BEAUMONT TERRITORY
Castle Beaumont
Sacred House of Blood
THE MIDNIGHT MARKET
PEACE TERRITORY
Sangui Canals
HUNTER ACADEMY TERRITORY
Hunter Academy
HOUSE ST CLAIR TERRITORY
Castle St Clair
Lantis Ocean

NOTE FOR READERS

This book is intended for adult (18+) audiences. It contains explicit lesbian sex scenes, considerable profanity and some violence. For full content warnings, please see author's website: rubyroe.co.uk.

This book is written in British English.

PLAYLIST

Make it Home - Dezi
Unstoppable (feat. Rånya) - Hidden Citizens
You Belong to Me - Ari Abdul
Monster - Chandler Leighton
Martyr - KiNG MALA
Vampire - Olivia Rodrigo
New Rules (Piano Acoustic) - Dua Lipa
Take Me to Church - Sofia Karlberg
How Villains Are Made - Madalen Duke
Adante in C Minor - Solo Piano - Nicholas Britell
Alive (feat. Jacob Banks) - Chase & Status
Middle Of The Night - Power-Haus, Tom Evans, Dramatic Violin
Like Me Better - Rosemary Joaquin
Fallout - UNSECRET, Neoni
Burn It All Down - League of Legends Music, PVRIS
I Will Rise (feat. ASHBY) - Steelfeather
Game Of Survival - Ruelle
You Put a Spell on Me - Austin Giorgio
Good Girl - Morganne
Ride It - Larissa Lambert, Jay Sean

You and I - Knives at Sea
Take You Home - Aaron Espe
Between Wind and Water - Hael
Eyes Shut - Years & Years
Balance - Lucy Spraggan
Face in the Crowd - Freya Ridings
What Could Have Been (from the series Arcane League of Legends) - Sting, Ray Chen
You Broke Me First - Tate McRae

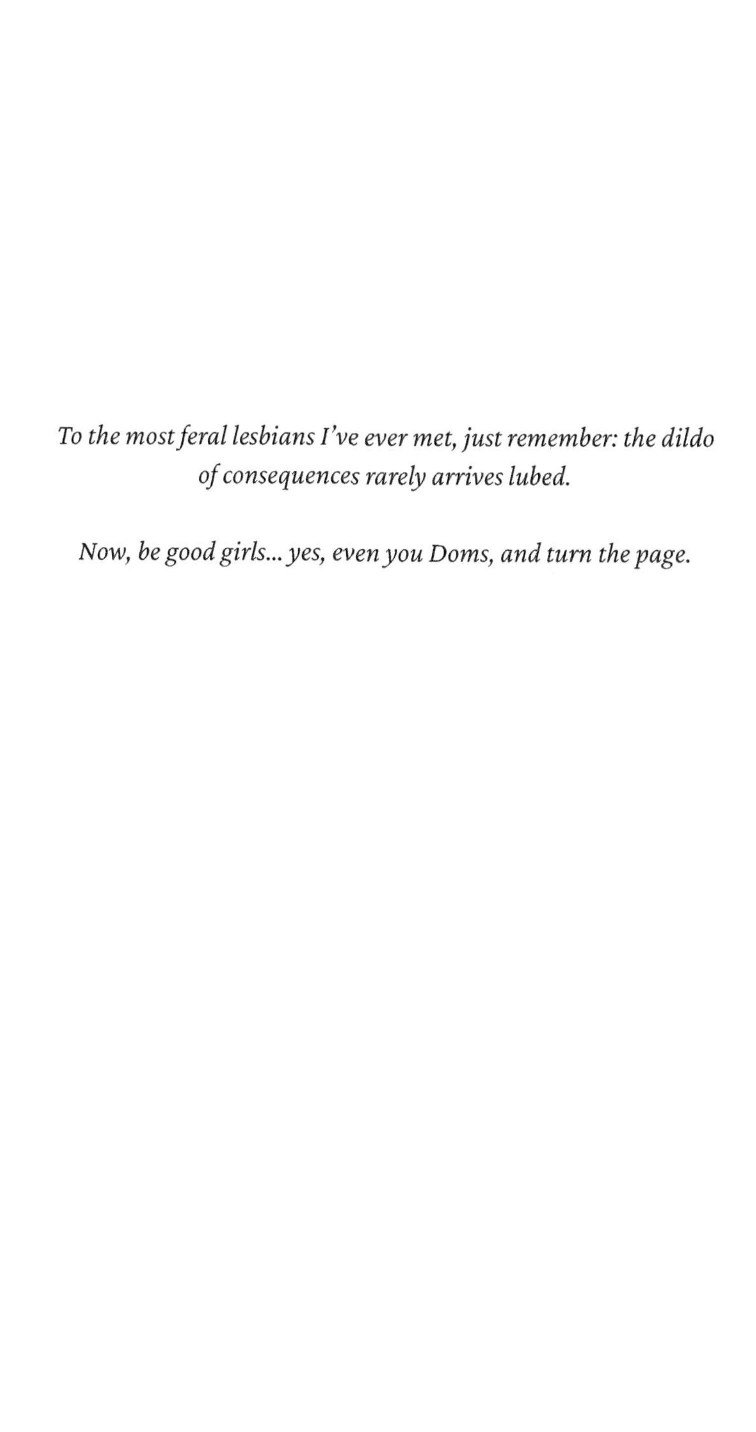

To the most feral lesbians I've ever met, just remember: the dildo of consequences rarely arrives lubed.

Now, be good girls... yes, even you Doms, and turn the page.

CHAPTER 1

OCTAVIA

I pride myself on many things: my exceptional taste in mansions, my ability to keep secrets, and my genuine love for my brother. I do not, however, derive any satisfaction from my mistakes. Of which, I have just made the mother of all fuck-ups.

"I had no choice," I mutter over and over as I pace the halls of Castle St Clair. My eyes shift to the corridor ceiling. I need to be gone. After I compelled her, Red fell asleep. But even a floor below is too close, so I make my way to the first floor.

Then again, is it really safe for me to leave her, given who she really is? What she really is?

I shuffle forward and back, indecision tearing me apart. I slap the wall between two portraits once, twice, ball my fist and punch it through the plasterboard. It hurts. I like it. The sharp heat in my knuckles travels up my arm right to my brain, and all my fragmented thoughts coalesce into clarity.

I should let her wake alone to ensure there's no risk of

me undoing the compulsion, because the temptation is there. The last thing I want is to endure Red having forgotten what I mean to her again. I make my way to the castle bar. It's closed. No one is in here, not even staff.

The room is sumptuous, with expensive chesterfield furniture and a black wood burner in the corner. The embers are molten and crumbling into ash. I dart around the back of the bar and pull a bottle of whisky off the optic.

Fuck using a glass. I'm going to drink the entire bottle. I can't believe I did it, especially after I swore to her I wouldn't compel her again.

But what fucking choice did I have? This is for her own safety. I skulk back into the corridor and make my way to the back door of my mother's castle.

I close it behind me and slide down the studded wood to slump in the doorway. I uncork the whisky and take an enormous gulp. It burns hot like the sun as it slides down my throat.

Good.

I deserve it.

"You look like shit..." Rumblegrit says in his raspy voice as he looks down at me. I grunt at him but remember the way Red treated Broodmire, the Whisper Club's goyle.

I sigh, push up onto my knees, and raise a finger in offer of a drop. His stone collar ruffles, and he opens his mouth, a smile he can't quite hide lifting the corner of his stony lips.

I push my finger onto his spike and allow not one, but four beads of blood to roll onto his tongue. He bristles, and I swear for a brief second the grey of his skin washes pink.

"Thank you," he says. "Most unusual."

"Perhaps I'm changing," I say.

"Do vampires change?"

"I thought not. But I've been wrong about a lot of things recently."

There's a scraping of stone against wood as he tilts his grey eyes down at me. He narrows his gaze. "You look like shit, and the whisky stinks like regret. What did you do?"

I sag back against the door and tickle him under his chin. "I broke a promise."

"And why would you do a thing like that?" he asks.

I smile up at him: a thin slip of a thing. But I stay silent because as much as he is ugly-cute, he's not my goyle, and I haven't forgotten what Mother did to that vampire responsible for the carriage attack. She was quick to temper. Quick to violence. That's not the mother I know, and I can't imagine my secrets would stay secret if I blabbed them to her goyle.

"Fine," he shrugs, as much as his half shoulders allow. "Keep your secrets. I have plenty of my own."

I frown. "Do you now?"

"You'd be surprised what the doors and walls hear, Ms Beaumont. We're always listening."

"Perhaps you already have my secret, then."

"Mmm, I can tell your heart is aching."

I huff at him. "You know nothing." But my hand wanders to rub my chest like it is aching.

"Blood can tell many a remarkable thing about a person. And I've tasted not one but four drops this eve."

In the distance, Sadie's snow-coloured hair drifts through the night breeze like eddies in a pond.

"Sadie," I say, surprising myself. We have a strange relationship, and I don't much want to be near her, but yet I'm drawn to call her over.

She halts as she levels with the gates into Mother's garden that heads out towards the entrance. She turns, looking this way and that. I must be obscured in the shadows under the porch, so I inch out and wave.

"Over here," I say and waft the whisky bottle I'm holding. Her face lights up. She waves hello and changes course, drifting over to me in her usual angelic way.

I take in her appearance as she draws close. She's wearing a long, flowing black dress, reminiscent of the style of outfits the blood monks in her church wear, albeit slinkier and more elegant. Her hair is wound into two braids either side of her head that join at the bottom of her skull to form one plait that drapes down her spine. She's tall like me, but her fair features and pale hair set her apart from all of us.

I don't bother standing up. Too miserable. Which is also why I called her over. Misery likes company, and I'm alone enough.

"I was having a drink here with Rumblegrit," I say.

She nods and leans down to kiss me on the forehead. Something she almost always does as a greeting. Only to me, though. I suppose that's the funny thing about siblings. We all have our unique ways of greeting each other or interacting with each other, and no two relationships are the same. Xavier and I are each other's favourites—to which that, *Hello, favourite,* is our usual greeting. Dahlia and Gabriel, though, are birth twins as well as vampire siblings. They speak in a language unique to them, all silent words and hard-to-decipher expressions. They can have entire conversations in silence. I used to be jealous until Dahlia turned out to be a bit of a cunt, at which point, I felt sorry for Gabriel instead.

I hold up the whisky bottle, but she leans over and tickles Rumblegrit under his chin. She dabs her finger on the spike, offering him a drop of blood. And I really do wonder whether I've been ignorant to the ways that everyone treats each other. It was a natural movement for Sadie to offer the goyle that kindness.

"I'm being treated this evening, it seems," he chuckles

out a deep rumbling crackle of a laugh—the origin of his name. His eyes roll back, and he yawns as the overdose of mine and Sadie's blood knocks him out. His lids drift shut, and he falls into a light slumber, his stone nostrils fluttering and emanating snuffles and snores.

I smile up at him and check myself. Gods, Octavia, what is wrong with you? He's a fucking gargoyle. He is not cute. You do not need to develop a soft spot.

"Drink?" I offer Sadie again, if for no other reason than to drag my mind away from itself.

Sadie takes the bottle out of my hand, and to my surprise, downs an enormous gulp. She hands it back and raises her hands to sign at me.

"You look like shit tonight," she says.

"Thanks," I huff. "I'm hearing that a lot."

"No offence, I'm worried about you," she says and touches my chin. Her fingers are warm and caring. This is the Sadie our siblings never see, and I wonder why she chose me to connect with. But then, why did I choose Xavier? Sometimes when you come from a big family, you resonate with certain siblings more than others. It's these softer moments that are almost enough to make me forget Sadie's dark side.

I lean into her touch and pull the bottle up to my mouth. I do not trust her. Not when I'm aware of what she's capable of. I've seen her slaughter villages for fun. Not in my territory, I might add. She knows I'd come for her. It's a reminder I need, though. Much as this is a lovely moment, we are still in competition with each other, and I don't trust anyone, not when it comes to winning the city and replacing Mother. I have got to change the face of this city for the people like me who have always been pushed to the edge. I need my home to be a home instead of a prison.

"I come bearing news," she signs at me.

"Oh?" I say, swigging from the bottle again and handing it back to her.

My chest aches. Pathetic, really. I fucked up and now what? I'm feeling things? Gods, I can't even be a proper vampire. I should be dead inside, not pining over a fucking human.

A human you've loved for three years.

She swigs and hands it back, and I decide to down the rest, dregs and all, to numb the... the sensation in my chest I'd rather not put a name to. I drop the bottle between my legs and rub my sternum.

Sadie's eyes drop to my hand. She narrows her gaze.

"You okay?" she signs.

I wave her off. There's no way I'm going to explain that I am pining after a hunter. I'll never live it down. She continues to squint at me as if trying to work out the issue, but explains the news she brings.

"Mother is pissed."

"Why?"

"Someone's won the last challenge," she says, her hands moving in a flurry of gestures.

It takes all of my control not to go vampire still. If I did, she would know I was suppressing something, hiding the fact I have more information than I should.

Instead, I embrace the pain in my chest, which seems to build. What the hell is wrong with me that emotional pain would manifest like this? Maybe I need to see a doctor or a vampire specialist. Red broke me.

"I see. Well, who won?" I say, trying to push as much rage into my voice as possible. I need to be convincing. Honestly, it doesn't take much to put the ire simmering in my gut at not being able to claim the win into my voice.

"That's the thing," Sadie signs. "The winner is staying silent."

I do my best impression of a frown and play dumb. "What do you mean? No one knows? Of course they do. Surely Mother checked the amulet?"

Sadie nods. "There's blood inside it. Someone found the dhampir and sealed their blood inside. It's the most beautiful thing in the city. One of us won but is choosing to keep it quiet."

Her eyes form slits as she tries to read my expression. Thankfully for me, my chest hurts enough that it's a distraction.

"Was it you?" she says.

I laugh, a sharp nasty thing. "Sadie, please. You know exactly how much I want to take over from Mother. Do you really think if I'd won a round, I'd be keeping that quiet?"

Some of the tension eases in her shoulders, and it makes me wonder exactly how much she wants to win. Did I discount her as a competitor too soon?

"True," she says. "I guess that means either Dahlia, Xavier or Gabriel's partner must be the dhampir. They'll need to keep an eye on them. The more trials we do, the closer we're going to get to discovering who it is... and the more danger they'll be in."

That makes me uncomfortable. I hadn't considered the consequence of protecting Red would mean putting others in danger. But if my siblings want to aid in protecting their hunter, that's their problem. They're all partnered with highly trained hunters who can protect themselves. They've all survived attacks so far. It will be fine. They will be fine.

Besides, I don't care. My priority is Red, always. If there's collateral damage along the way, too bad.

"That doesn't put Red out of danger, though," I say. "No one knows who the dhampir is, therefore attacks could come from anyone."

She shakes her head, her lips pressed thin. "The Festival of Blood is coming. With how high the political tensions are, it seems like a bad idea for the festival to happen."

"Slow down, too fast," I say.

She tuts at me and slows her signing down. I manage to catch everything the second time.

"Shit. When is it?"

"It's going to end up coinciding with the attempt on the boundary," she says.

I knead my temples. "Well, Mother will need to work with the Chief to put extra security on. Though it could work in our favour as a distraction."

Sadie nods. "That's true. I hadn't considered that. Well, I have business to attend to. If you find out which of them actually won, will you inform me?"

"Sure," I shrug, knowing exactly who won and the fact I'll never confess. She scans my face as if trying to find a lie.

I rub at my chest again, irritated at my weakness.

"What's up with that?" she gestures at my hand.

"Nothing. Just chest pains. Probably the stress of the competition and knowing I've lost another round."

"Is that so?" she signs, her eyebrow rising as she folds her arms.

"How is it you can still be sarcastic while totally silent?"

She laughs. It's a whispery sound, like clouds and summer daisies dancing in the wind.

"It doesn't appear to be stress to me," she says.

"What makes you say that?"

She shrugs and steps off the porch. "I have to get back to the church, but I'd monitor that if I were you. Almost looks like you bound yourself to someone, and they tried to leave you. But you wouldn't be stupid enough to do that, would you?" She steps away and outright winks at me as she turns around and saunters into the distance.

"No," I shout into the night as she disappears into the darkness. "I WOULDN'T, SADIE. THAT'S RIDICULOUS."

But she doesn't return. I watch her until she disappears, and then a nervous laugh bubbles up and spills out of me. I'm left cold, a reminder that Sadie has that effect on people. The occasional show of softness is not to be mistaken for anything other than the game she's currently playing. She's as ruthless as the rest of us, otherwise Mother wouldn't have adopted her. The night air wraps a chill around me as the knowledge that I did, in fact, bind myself to someone weighs heavy on me.

But Red wouldn't leave, right? We have a competition to compete in, and I'm not sure if she'll even remember we're bound at this point. Not after what I did.

Besides, she was asleep on the roof when I left her.

"I'd go and check if I were you," Rumblegrit says, scaring the life out of me.

"I thought you were asleep," I snap. "You better keep whatever you think you know to yourself or no more blood for you."

But I don't wait for his answer. I'm already up, shoving the door open and sprinting for the roof, my chest aching worse than ever.

She wouldn't leave. Even if I took her memories.

She can't.

But the sinking feeling in my gut and the pulling in my chest say something different.

I burst out onto the rooftop and slide to a halt.

Red's gone.

CHAPTER 2

Run little dhampir, I'll be here watching...

Waiting...

Octavia might have hidden your identity from everyone else, but not from me.

Never from me. I saw what Octavia did. What a delightful sacrifice she made for you, losing this round on purpose. Why, it's practically chivalrous.

I'll be observing you...

But don't worry that pretty little head of yours.

It's not what you think... I don't want you dead.

Not yet, anyway.

CHAPTER 3

RED

It took a monumental amount of self-control, but I let Octavia believe I'd fallen asleep. I waited, listening to her every movement. She paced for a while, waiting for me to fall asleep. And then she bent to kiss my knuckles. I wanted to yank my hand away.

I wanted to ball my fist and knock her out, quite frankly. But I did none of those things. I kept my eyes shut, forced my breathing to slow and deepen and I pretended to be asleep.

When her footsteps retreated, I swore I could hear her pacing in the corridor beneath the roof. I waited another five minutes, and when I figured the coast was clear, I shot up like a bolt and got the fuck out of there.

Which is why I'm now running through the castle.

How could she?

I scurry through the hallways as fast as I can, keeping my head down. The number of vampires in the mansion and the notoriety of these fucking trials mean I need to keep a low profile. No point hiding the fact my blood is warm. I find a cap and cloak on a rack by one of the side doors. I steal them both and shove them on.

And then, I run.

I run harder than I've ever run.

My feet pound over the cobbles, carrying me across Cordelia's courtyard, down the long avenue that leads up to the castle and into the underground tunnels beneath the base of the castle.

By the time I stop, my chest is killing me. I must have run hard enough to give myself a muscle spasm in my ribs. Gods, I assumed I was fitter than this. I'll have to work harder, go back to daily running.

I wait for a carriage to appear. This is the fastest way to get across the city and to the harbour where I can leave.

I need to get out of this city. I need to be away.

From her.

From the truth of what I am.

But more than anything, from what she did.

The carriage ride takes longer than I'd like, which means I sleep part of the day away. When I finally reach the harbour, I pay the carriage driver and head towards the underground tunnels beneath the docks. I have to pay the dock man in sketches and painting to keep my comings and goings quiet. He makes a note of what I owe him, and I head into the tunnels.

Fuck Octavia.

Fuck her forever. We are done. She broke the one promise I begged her to keep. She tried to compel me to forget everything we had and for fucking what? Because I'm the dhampir? How fucking could she?

It's only as the light dips and I enter the tunnels, the cool, damp air washing over me, that I realise...

She *tried* to compel me.

Tried.

It didn't work.

Fuck me, it didn't work. Why didn't it work? It should have. Not that I want to be compelled, but I am no different to any other human or hunter. We're all susceptible and she's admitted she did it before—the night she turned Amelia.

So why didn't it work?

I run through the possibilities. Maybe it's because I'm the dhampir? Or I'm meant to be. I won't be if I have anything to say about it. Would being a dhampir make me immune to compulsion? It would make me half vampire. That has to have some impact on the susceptibility of being compelled. That must be it.

Though, wait. Vampires can compel each other. Or rather, Octavia and Cordelia can because they're two of the original three—they're stronger than all the others—which makes this make even less sense.

I rub at my chest as I step into another carriage that will take me most of the way towards New Imperium—there's only one person I want to see right now. Part of me feels guilty for not going to Lincoln, but he's in too deep and too close to Dahlia right now that I'm not sure where we stand. It's too much of a risk. I'll have to walk part of the way to the city. Which wouldn't be a problem if my chest didn't hurt this much.

I spend the entire journey wondering what caused Octavia's compulsion to fail. What if she didn't mean it enough?

Who am I kidding? Octavia doesn't do anything without intention. I'm not going to defend her actions. She can go fuck herself.

The carriage driver deposits me about a kilometre away from the New Imperium border. It's a little further from here, but I should be in the city soon. I can't wait to see my bestie. Bella will calm me down. She'll know what to say to make it better.

I break into a run, deciding now is as good a time as any to bring up my cardio fitness. But before long, my chest is heaving, and I have to stop and catch my breath. Each time I stop, I get more irritated with myself.

What the hell is wrong with me? I can normally do a ten kilometre run without much difficulty. Why am I struggling today?

By the time I hit the city border, I'm dizzy. I slow even further as I meander through the tunnels and out into the heart of New Imperium. This is the new town, or I'm fairly sure it is. And if it is, Remy—Bella's girlfriend—lives close by. I could start by going there and seeing if Bella is with her.

I'm staggering now, my breath short. My chest is full of hot irons, stabbing and pulling at my lungs, my heart. I find the street Remy lives on a little by memory and a little by luck.

But I collapse to my knees, entirely winded, wondering if I can call Bella to come here, but... I'm not carrying the orb calling device that Remy made.

And that is my last thought as I bend forward, dropping to all fours and collapsing into darkness.

"Red, you silly cow, wake up," Bella's voice drifts into my consciousness along with the most potent and rancid scent I've ever had the displeasure of inhaling.

"What is…?" I mumble, but my words come out jumbled.

"She's had enough of that. Gods know I have, it's vile," Bella says.

"She needs to be fully conscious," another voice I recognise says. I can't place who it is, though.

My eyes flutter open. Bella's curvy body is bent over me. I cop an eyeful of her tits and I'm pretty sure I saw nipple.

"Mother of Blood, Bella," I say, shoving her back by the shoulders, trying to miss her cleavage. "What are you wearing?"

She glances down. "What? Remy and I were out for dinner."

"And you wear that for dinner?"

"Well, no," she shrugs, wrapping what I now see is a dressing gown tighter around her body, covering up the extremely skimpy lingerie I got an eyeful of.

"We finished dinner and were… having pudding… it was —" she starts.

"Please do not feel obligated to finish that sentence," I say, rubbing a hand over my face. I'm in an apartment. I glance around. There's a lot of glass and everything is clean and sharp, save for a messy office table in the corner with cogs and wires and a fuck ton of books.

Bella huffs at me and helps me up. Which is when I sort out who the other voice's owner is. "Quinn. Hey."

"How are you feeling?" she asks, waving a finger in my face and applying a daub of something gritty to my forehead.

I bat her hand away. Quinn and I aren't close like Bella and I are, but she's one of Remy's friends. They all work together for the crown in this city, and Quinn happens to be a rather excellent medic. No wonder she's here.

"I found you," Quinn says, running a hand through her hair. It's shaved on the sides but a mass of curls on top. "I called Bella down immediately. Scarlett's outside, guarding the building block."

"Where's the rest of your gang?" I ask.

"Remy got called out on a RuneNet server break-in. She owed a guy a favour. Stirling has stayed at the palace in Morrigan's place—because she should arrive at any moment."

A knock at the door startles me. Quinn dances off to open it as a kettle clicks off in the kitchen. Bella shuffles to the kitchen and clatters about. A minty smell drifts into the room and a moment later, she returns and hands me a piping hot mug of the minty brew.

Then she rubs my shoulder. "You're really shook up. What happened?"

"I fucked up, is the summary," I say, blowing cool air on the tea.

"What's going on?" Morrigan says, appearing from behind Quinn, who tuts at the tea and takes it out of my hand.

"Bella," Quinn whines.

Bella rolls her eyes. "It's only tea."

"It is not just tea." Quinn trots back to the kitchen, opening cupboards and making a racket before returning and handing me the now much cooler mug of tea. The colour has changed too, and it smells decidedly less appealing. I sigh and take a sip, and my mouth contorts at the bitterness.

"The fuck, Quinn?"

She laughs, "Drink it, and don't be a baby."

I do, and because it's cooler, I can take big gulps.

Morrigan pulls two chairs over from the dining room table. Quinn grabs the other one, but Bella pushes me up until there's space for her on the sofa. Then she takes my hand in hers and strokes the back of it as I slump against her.

"I asked you a question," Morrigan says, her tone a little clipped. I'd almost forgotten how in touch with her power she is. Morrigan is, to my knowledge, the single most powerful magician in this city. Her arms, neck, and legs and probably other parts of her are smothered in Collection tattoos—a sorcerer's marks that connect them to their buildings and enable them to wield magic. But aside from that, she's also a princess who will be queen and have control of the most powerful palace in the city, too. Essentially, she wears the don't-fuck-with-me-or-there-will-be-consequences type of pants. And aside from that, she reminds me a little of Octavia. She has the same dark-coloured hair, though Morrigan's is blunt across the fringe, and she wears a lot of black.

I take another gulp of tea. Each one I drink makes me a little brighter.

"We don't know yet," Bella says. "Give her a chance. Quinn called me and said she found Red collapsed at the end of our street. I called Stirling, who got in touch with you and Scarlett. And here we are."

"Why are you here?" Bella asks, patting my hand.

I frown at her and rub my chest. It still aches, though

considerably less. But worse, the hunger is gnawing at my gut. The rising need for a piece of her. I'm never drinking blood again. I yank myself out of my thoughts and focus on Bella.

"Did you not consider, oh, I don't know... putting some clothes on before welcoming me into the flat?" I say.

She pouts. "I sorely hope that if Quinn phoned you in the middle of the night and told you I was unconscious on your street that you'd drop everything and come running, too."

I open my mouth to remind her she flashed nip at me, but have to concede she's absolutely right. "You make a good point."

"Exactly," she says. "Now, what the hell are you doing here? I wasn't expecting you."

Between Quinn and Bella coming to my rescue, and the tea, which is now finished, I feel considerably better. The ache in my chest has eased almost completely.

"Okay, look. I realise I came here unannounced, and I owe you an explanation. But I need to get back to Sangui City before anyone comes looking for me. Is there any chance you can take me back to the tunnels and I'll tell you everything on the way?"

"Who's going to come looking for you?" Morrigan fixes me with her regal stare.

Suddenly I recall that vampires and magicians don't mix, and me coming here without explanation when Octavia knows who Bella is was probably an epic mistake.

I stand up. "Bella..."

Her eyes widen as she takes in my expression. "Okay, okay, fine. I'll throw on a tracksuit."

She rushes off to the bedroom and reappears in about twenty seconds flat.

A few minutes later, we're all on the street, Scarlett fifty feet ahead of us, scanning the street and darting this way and that. Morrigan, Quinn, Bella and I walk in a huddle, our voices low. Morrigan wears a cloak with an enormous hood that conceals most of her face, no doubt to hide from the public. Though it's the middle of the night, I hope no one will recognise her.

"Things have gotten... Mother of Blood, I don't even know where to begin," I say.

"How about at the start?" Quinn says.

So I do. I explain how there's a competition that the Chief agreed to run with Cordelia St Clair. I have to stop and explain a little of the vampire-hunter politics, but I get through everything, including the trials and telling them that whoever wins gets to run the city in the future.

I also tell them about how one of hunters is the dhampir who will bring magic back to our city. Though I don't tell them Octavia believes it's me.

My spiel ends, however, because Bella jumps in front of me as we reach a tunnel entrance, and I careen into her chest for the second time tonight. Thankfully, this time it's covered by a hoody.

Bella folds her arms. "Nice try. None of that explains why you're here, or why you collapsed."

I sigh and sag against a bench nestled under a lamp-post. Morrigan and Quinn sit next to me. Scarlett dives onto one end.

"You recall I hate vampires?" I start.

"To your very marrow," Bella confirms.

I lean forward, put my head in my hands. "Right. Turns out... I don't actually hate them all. Or at least, there's one specific vampire I don't entirely hate."

"Wait. What?" Bella shrieks. "You need to say a lot more, and quickly."

"It's complicated, and... there's more... I may have developed an addiction to blood."

I can't bear to look at them. Confessing makes my tongue taste bitter and my throat thick.

Bella's face pales, Quinn whistles, and Morrigan's eyebrows vanish up under her fringe.

Quinn touches my hand and pulls it away from my face. "I don't have extensive knowledge, but I know a bit about the physiology of hunters and vampires from my studies when I was an apprentice. The fae too. One thing that I never forgot is that the properties of vampire blood are..."

"Interesting?" I try to shrug it off with a laugh, but it comes out like a stifled cough.

"Did you fall for the vampire you were dosing from?" Morrigan asks, taking me by surprise.

I glance at Bella and then tear my eyes away and nod.

It makes Morrigan's lips purse. "I, too, have studied vampire physiology, history, anthropology and politics. You understand it's expected as part of my role?"

I wince as I say, "It gets worse."

Bella inhales a sharp breath. "I will actually drown you, Red, I swear to the gods. I will murder you, bring you back to life, and then murder you again for good measure. What have you done?"

Quinn's eyes flick a surreptitious glance at Morrigan. I suspect between the two of them, they already have the answer to that question.

"You bonded yourself to them, didn't you?" Quinn asks.

I nod meekly and keep my eyes low.

"I suspect the binding is why you collapsed. Where is she? This vampire you—" Morrigan cuts herself off and then kneels in front of me, gripping my shoulders. Her nails aren't sharp, but her fingers grip tight enough to shock me.

"Did you run? Please tell me she knows where you are, and you didn't run..."

"Morrigan, what is it? What the hell is wrong?" Bella says, her voice pitching up.

But it's Quinn who answers. "If she ran, that's why her chest was hurting. When you bind yourself to a vampire, you can't leave them. Like EVER."

"How could you bind yourself without knowing all the fucking consequences, Red?" Bella's pacing intensifies.

Morrigan pulls me to standing. "No wonder you collapsed. Your entire system is tied to hers. You need to leave. Now. You have a standing welcome because of what you did for this city, I'm not banishing you. But you can't be here like this. You need to leave right now before this vampire c—"

"Shit," I say, cutting her off. "I collapsed from the pain, straining the bond, I suspect, but now... Now, I'm better..."

"Which means..." Quinn says, her eyes darting in the direction of the tunnels.

Morrigan whirls around. "Scarlett! Get to the tun—" but the word is swallowed as I put my hand over her mouth.

It's too late. I sense her. It wasn't Quinn's tea, or at least it wasn't all the tea. I'm better because she came after me. Hunted me down like prey. Ironic, right? The hunter becomes the hunted. Oh Octavia, you should be proud.

"Sweet mother of fuck. There hasn't been a vampire in this city in centuries," Bella whispers.

"I'll leave," I say, releasing Morrigan and sprinting towards the tunnel entrance.

But I am too late because beneath the curve of the New Imperium tunnel arch, buried in the murky gloom, is the shadow of a vampire.

A vampire I recognise. A vampire whose blood calls to me, as if my hunger summoned her.

Her foot hovers in the light of a lamppost, waiting, no doubt, because she knows she'll cause shit if she steps onto the city grounds.

"Octavia, don—" I bark.

But she steps into the light as a set of Katana swords press against her neck and heart.

CHAPTER 4

OCTAVIA

"If you value breathing, I would advise you to remove that blade from my neck," I say.

"Thanks, but I'll keep it where it is," a woman snarls. "Move an inch, I dare you."

I sigh. It's deep and overly dramatic, but I need to demonstrate that no matter what this little magician assassin thinks she can do, I will do it faster and harder and end her quicker than she can blink.

"Need I remind you of the vampire-magician wars? It didn't end well for your kind," I say, my voice deep and full of threat.

The assassin sneers, "Funny, because I had an entirely different history lesson." She hitches the Katana sword closer to my neck, dangerously close to nicking the skin.

"Enough," Red says, bolting to the tunnel arch. "Scarlett, stop. Please. It's... this is complicated."

"Uncomplicate it," Scarlett says, not moving an inch.

"I'm getting bored with this," I say.

Red's eyes widen. She places a hand on Scarlett's wrist. "Octavia will behave, won't you?" she says, glaring at me.

"You're required in Sangui City," I say, ignoring the question. I'm not promising a damn thing.

"She's required to stay right the fuck here," a curvy girl wearing a strange baggy outfit says. The trousers are slung low on her hips, and she has lacy underwear underneath. Do magicians regularly walk around with their knickers out? What unusual attire.

"Bella. Gods. Everyone stop. It's going to be fine," Red says, now tugging on Scarlett's arm.

Bella thrusts a hand on her hip. Ah, now I recognise her. This is Red's friend. She's spoken about her several times over the years, but for obvious reasons, I've never met her.

"It's not fine," Bella says. "You ran away to New Imperium and then collapsed unconscious in the middle of the city alone."

That piques my interest, a quiet simmering heat sparks in my gut. "You collapsed?" I say, my jaw clenching.

"Not that you give a shit, but yes. I had chest pains and ended up collapsing, and Quinn found me."

Another girl appears now. Her hair is shorn to the scalp on the sides, and she has an array of tight-coiled hair on the top. I like the style. She holds an awkward hand up to indicate she was the finder of Red.

"Thank you for finding her," I say to Quinn.

She nods, presses her lips into a thin line at me. But her eyes bounce from me to Red to the rest of the group in a skittish motion.

Scarlett, still holding the swords at my neck and chest, hesitates at my gratitude. It's enough to make my move. I speed out of her grip and disarm her, knocking both swords out of her hands.

I'll give her credit, she's fast. I swing out of her fist

range and lunge forward, grabbing a short-handled blade out of her thigh strap.

There's a kerfuffle, a blur of fast feet, tangled limbs, and then a hot body squeezes between us. It's Red. Though Scarlett and I, both considerably taller than Red, are holding each other's throats around her head.

"ENOUGH," Bella says. "You look like a fucking sandwich all pressed together like that. Scarlett, stand down."

"I'll release her when she releases me," Scarlett says.

Wise move, clever little assassin.

"Fuck me," Red snaps. "You're as bad as each other. Right. Release together. In three. Two. One."

We do as she says and release each other simultaneously.

"Was that really so hard?" I sneer.

"Says the vampire in the magician's territory. Are you trying to incite a war?" Scarlett lurches forward but Red's hands land on her chest.

Protecting me, little hunter? How quaint.

Red kneads her forehead. "I'm taking her back. For all the bravado, Octavia is correct. I am required in this stupid competition that's partnered me with a drainer," Red sighs.

Drainer? I have to suppress a sigh. Alas, the compulsion has taken us back to hate. I knew it was coming and yet it doesn't make it sting any less.

"Then why did you come here? I didn't think I was seeing you until Morrigan's wedding," Bella asks.

"I..." Red hesitates, her brow furrows, the confusion of compulsion washing over her expression. "I guess I'm not sure. Something happened earlier that made me cross and then I don't... Maybe I drank too much and figured I'd go see my bestie."

Bella—the bestie—frowns, folding her arms under her

ample breasts and glares at Red. Oh dear, she doesn't buy the bullshit the compulsion is making you spew.

She's a good friend.

"Red..." I say, recognising that I need to get her out of here before the spots in her memory make her friend even more suspicious.

"Honestly, Bella, I'm totally fine. I drank wayyyy too much at the end of the challenge today, and I just missed you."

That softens Bella. She opens her arms, and Red flings herself into them. My jaw tightens so hard I'm sure I'll crack a fang. It's not that I'm jealous. She can hug whoever she wants, especially her best friends.

But... she is mine.

And mine alone.

And I don't like people touching what belongs to me.

I don't give a fuck who says that's toxic; I like my romance dark and intense and flavoured with the fieriest spice.

I glance at Scarlett, who hasn't taken her eyes off me this entire time. Her gaze is narrowed as she watches me watch Red. Assessing.

Perhaps I underestimated the magician.

"I should go," Red says, disentangling herself from Bella. "We'll have the winner announced in the morning, and it's going to take us all night to get back."

"Do you still have the orb Remy gave you?" Quinn asks.

Red nods.

"Good, use it. For anything. We're here for you," Quinn says.

Red says her goodbyes to Quinn and Scarlett and together we retreat into the shadows. The assassin-magician's eyes bore into my back long after we're out of sight.

We're silent for a long time.

She's keeping her distance, a good three feet of space between us.

So this is how it is.

Back to her hating me, hating vampires. Forgetting every time she's fallen for me. So strange that we can be bonded, and she doesn't even know.

It occurs to me that now I'm standing next to her, my chest has loosened. I feel... better? This must be the bond working. We are tied physically, mentally, and spiritually. This is going to make the fact she doesn't remember falling for me a lot more complicated.

How will we get through this? I pull a hand over my face, as if that will wipe away the frustration. I can't look at her. Instead, I glance anywhere, at anything but her. With each compulsion, each tearing of my heart, it gets harder.

The light in this tunnel is a pale rouge, like watered down blood. But the dark, rough walls make the air seem thick and moody. Ivy and vines grow up some of the tunnel walls, garrotting the lights that hang from the arched ceiling. I don't recall ever coming into the tunnels this far on foot.

We continue in silence, which means my mind continues to race.

What happens when the competition is over and she no longer wants to be anywhere near me? What if she tries to leave and accidentally kills herself because she strayed too far from me? But worse, what if this is the time she doesn't fall in love with me again?

Should I remove the compulsion?

No. That's stupid. I can't because if she accidentally let slip who she is... if I'm not with her. Gods forbid anything happen to her. The blood drains from my face as I grasp just how complicated this has become and that all of it is my fault.

Red jolts me out of my thoughts. "Don't make a habit of visiting New Imperium," she says as we trudge deeper into the tunnels. The gloom takes over, making it harder for her to see me, no doubt.

"I'll stop visiting New Imperium when you learn to stay put."

"Fuck you, Octavia, you don't own me."

"I think you'll find that you're my teammate. Which means you're mine to protect."

"I'm not an idiot. I don't need any drainers knowing where I'm going." She wipes her mouth.

God, this is déjà vu. She'd thrown things like this at me not two weeks ago. I wonder if it's me, if I'm quietly driving myself insane repeating the same mistakes over and over. Sure, the number of times I've expunged myself from her memories is limited. But the amount of memories I've taken? The number of mistakes I've hidden, hurts I've removed? She'd never forgive me if she knew. I can't keep doing this.

I sigh. "So we're back to drainer?"

"Did we ever leave it?" she snaps.

Fuck. Right. No, we didn't. Is this the time where I've overlaid the web so many times it all falls down? Can I even keep track of which memories are gone?

Mother of Blood. I rub my eyes, exhausted already. "I suppose not."

She turns away from me, hiding her expression. But she keeps wiping her mouth.

"Everything okay?" I ask.

"What's it to you?"

I grit my teeth. It's going to be a long night. "As my trial partner, it's of utmost importance to me you stay in good health. And frankly, you look terrible."

"And whose fault is that?" she snaps.

I tilt my head at her. "Explain."

She pauses one brief second and then flings her hand up. "Forget it. I'm just thirsty. Like really thirsty."

"If there's a carriage that passes, I'll stop them and ask for their water."

"Not. That thirst."

"Oh," I say. "Right. Your addiction."

She glares at me. "Don't call it that."

"Would you prefer I called it your teddy bear?"

She rolls her eyes at me.

"Well, I can assist you with this problem as well."

"I'd rather drink a dying vampire's blood than yours. Or did you forget you turned my sister?"

I groan. I can't help it. Amelia is going to kill me when I tell her she's going to have to break the news to her sister all over again.

"You have no choice. You're not drinking any other vampire's blood."

She rounds on me, shoves me against the tunnel wall. "Did you fucking hear me? You turned my sister. Why the hell would I drink your blood?"

She shoves and shoves. Something is... off. She's emanating a strange twist of emotions. I don't know if I can smell them or if they're inside me. The bond, perhaps. But they're visceral. She is visceral. The hot prickle of rage coats my flesh, the static tingle of irritation like pepper in the air. Confusion, disappointment.

Wait.

Disappointment?

I tilt my head, trying to examine her facial expression, to see if I can work out what's going on. Was this one time too many with compulsion? Have I actually broken her mind?

She's breathing hard as she pushes me against the wall.

"I hate you," she says, but the words are forced, like she's trying to hate me. And for the first time, I wonder whether my compulsion is faulty. Did I do it wrong? Has it only half taken?

Ridiculous. This is just like all the other times. Her head is telling her one thing, and her heart is saying something else. I narrow my eyes at her.

"I don't think you do," I say.

Her nostrils flare wide, her jaw tightens.

"See, I think you want my blood. You crave it."

"Fuck you, Octavia."

That makes me grin. "I'd love you to."

She pulls me off the wall and thrusts me back against it. I cock my head the other way, baring my neck, and lock eyes with her. This is what she wants. What she needs. I will always give her what she needs.

She steps into my personal space automatically. I raise a finger and draw it down my neck until it hovers over a juicy vein.

"Sure?" I say, tapping the risen thread of skin. This is our dance: the dare, the tease, the temptation. This is how it always starts. "Can't have my teammate in anything but the peak of physical health. Even if that means allowing the little hunter to dose herself into oblivion."

I dig my nail into my neck, threatening to pierce the skin. She rears back, her nostrils wide.

She looks up at me. "I do. Hate you, I mean. But this... I..."

We hold each other there, a million things passing between us. All of them unsaid. The air festers with everything we should confess, all our unspoken lies and promises, deceits and betrayals.

"Don't be ashamed. Take it," I whisper, pushing against my neck.

I swallow my next words, my throat aches with the need to purge them: take all of it. I'd give it all to you if it meant I could keep you.

Her face hardens like granite and steel and the coldest storm I've ever seen. And I know before she opens her mouth, I am well and truly screwed.

"What? Like you tried to take my memories?" she snarls.

Oh. Fuck.

CHAPTER 5

CORDELIA

One Thousand Years Ago

My horse gallops through the morning air, its nostrils flaring as I press my heels to his sides, urging him faster. I have to make it to Eleanor's apothecary because I can't go on not knowing whether she...

I push the thought away. I can't bear to ponder such awful things.

Air whistles past my ears, joining the scuffing of hooves against grass and mud as he flies across the fields.

"Yahh, yaahh," I shout, flicking the reins.

Finally, I make it to town. Frustrated, I slow the horse into a canter and then drop into a trot over the stone cobbles.

Better to be safe than not make it to Eleanor.

By the time we get to the other side of town, the sun is rising high in the sky. Morning warmth trickles over my skin. But it doesn't thaw the ice wrapped around my heart.

I spend my time singing a mantra, a prayer to the

witch-gods pleading with them to save Eleanor. Let her survive.

She has to.

Smoke is fizzling to a noisy steam that scatters through the air as I finally approach her street.

The anticipation makes my stomach drop when I reach her apothecary. I can't bring myself to look yet, so I tie the horse to a fence post and locate a bucket of water. Many stand abandoned by the townspeople who must have spent the night putting the fire out.

I put the bucket within the horse's reach, and he laps happily at the cool liquid. I rub his neck and give him a pat, cooing praise and whispers of, "Good boy, good boy."

I'm stalling because I don't want to face the horror behind me. I've carefully avoided staring at the cottage because I'm terrified of what I'll find, or rather what I won't.

I lean my forehead against the gelding's neck and inhale the musty straw and earthy scent that's unique to horses.

"Come on, Cordelia, we must do this. We must be strong and find our love," I breathe into his silken mane.

I give the horse one more pat, and then I turn and face the apothecary.

The sight drops me to my knees. It's all but smouldering embers.

There's no roof; the thatch has completely burned away. Half of the walls have collapsed, and everything is charred black.

I hold my mouth in my hands and let silent tears fall.

"Oh my gods, please... please have escaped."

I rock back and forth, hugging myself and wiping the tears away for what feels like an age. Finally, my courage returns, and I stand on shaking legs.

I edge forward until I almost trip over what I think is a piece of charred wood wrapped in what may have once been a sheet. There's the faintest hint of blue on an edge of the fabric, the only remaining colour left in the house. Everything else is black, charred coal or varying shades of soot.

I take another step and my ankle gives way. There's something under my foot. I bend down to pick it up and discover a ring. A ring Eleanor always wore. Bile climbs my throat. Please gods, I pray. The ring is gold, though part of it has warped from the heat. I suspect I could have a jeweller remould it or fix it enough it would be wearable. I slip it into my dress pocket. If she's gone, then at least I can keep a piece of her.

I step towards the house, and a wave of warmth hits me.

I frown, wondering why the apothecary is still hot when the fire is out. I step forward, my fingers inching towards the remnants of stone where the front door was.

A voice startles me, halting my progress.

"I wouldn't touch the stone, miss," a man says.

I swivel around to look at him. "Why not?" I say.

"It'll still be hot, you see. Fire's gone, but the stone holds the heat for a while. I wouldn't go inside either. Very dangerous. The remaining rafters will collapse, eventually. Wouldn't want a knock on the head, would you?"

"No, I suppose not. But I..."

His face is round and ruddy, but he seems very pleasant. "You looking for the healer that worked here?"

Worked. Past tense.

My heart spasms; my chest tightens. I'm not sure I can breathe. Everything blurs, and I'm convinced I'm going to pass out.

I can't do this. I can't find her dead.

He looks away, realising that I'm stricken with emotion.

"Sorry, miss, I didn't mean to upset you."

"Where—" I start, but I'm unable to finish the sentence.

The man nods at me as if he knows what I'm trying to ask. He comes up to me and takes my hand in his. "Such a tragedy. Awful thing to happen. I heard it was because of warring families."

I think I'm going to be sick. My stomach churns, rolling and frothing. What if her face has burned away and I can't tell if she's my Eleanor? My eyes sting and well with tears.

I tear my gaze away from him. "P-please... wh-where?" I stutter, unable to catch enough oxygen to give him a complete sentence. I just hope he knows what I'm after.

"I don't know what happened to her. But there were some firefighters that put the blaze out. They might help you."

"Who were they?"

"There's a station in the next village. Easy to find once you get there."

"Thank you!" I shout, already running back to the horse. I will not rest until I find her.

CHAPTER 6

RED

"What did you say?" Octavia says, her crimson eyes wide as full blood moons.

"You heard me." I'm snarling and growling, my whole body contorting under tensed muscles. But it's not the rage consuming me. This is happening involuntarily.

The addiction.

It's becoming completely unsustainable. I need to feed.

I mean, drink.

Fuck. What's wrong with me?

Octavia draws a sharp breath, and it brings me back to her. Her head is shaking in slow, steady, confused movements.

"It's... It's not possible," she says.

"What isn't, Octavia? It's not possible that you did the one thing I asked you *never* to do? Not possible that you stole my memories? Or tried, I should say. Tried to control me. To take my fucking free will and compel me into obedience? That's not possible? Because I assure you... you certainly tried."

She's stepped back. One foot, two. Her head still shaking, her pupils blown wide. Her bottom lip is dropped and gulping at the air like a fish.

"I don't understand?" she breathes.

"I do. I understand that you're a fucking traitor. You betrayed me. Broke my trust. And for what?"

That makes her snap to attention. Her face crumples into lines, and a simmering fury shivers through her expression.

"To protect you, Red. For the love of blood. Don't you get it? You're the fucking dhampir."

"And you think me not knowing that is going to help us? Are you naïve? In what world does me not knowing who I am help the situation? I'd be completely helpless. Entirely at the whims of your protection."

Something in her shatters. She shoves me back, gripping my shoulders. "Yes, and I'd give my life to protect you."

"YOU'RE ALREADY DEAD, OCTAVIA. You were born dead, for fucks sake."

She recoils. Her face crumpling.

Great. Now I feel bad. But as soon as I think it, I push it away. She doesn't get to make me feel guilty. She's the one who betrayed me.

"I did it to protect you. If you don't know... If no one knows, then I can keep the secret. No one can torture it out of me, and I can keep you safe." But she's no longer looking at me. She's examining the tunnel floor like there's a work of art on it instead of dusty cracked concrete.

I fold my arms. "I can look after myself. That's the point. You don't get to choose what I..." but my words fade as I cough.

My throat goes suddenly dry. The hunger in my belly is twisting and furling until I want to be sick. I buckle, bending over and gagging. Octavia reaches down to help me up. I shuck her off.

"Don't fucking touch me."

CHAPTER 7

OCTAVIA

Red smacks my arm away but stumbles forward, coughing and spluttering. She's withdrawing hard and needs to take my blood or we're going to have a problem.

The air shifts, something prickly sifts through the atmosphere, making my forearms rise with goosebumps.

"What?" Red says and then gags, bending over her knees again.

"Quiet," I say. And take a step to the side. I scan the tunnel left and right. Something is wrong. Someone is here.

"Get up. Move," I say, gripping her arm and dragging her forward as fast as she can stagger.

"Get your hands off me."

"Red—" I start, but a rushing wind steals my words away like secrets and shrouds, and then I'm knocked halfway up the tunnel by an immense blow to the ribs.

One moment I'm holding onto Red and the next I'm soaring through the tunnel, her body getting smaller and smaller in the distance.

I clatter to the floor, smashing my head against the concrete and bricks. My skull is cracked. I know by the immediate grey and black spots that smatter my vision and the sickness coiling in my gut. I lean over and puke.

I touch my hand to the back of my skull. It's definitely fractured. My fingers come away wet. I glance at them and groan. But the bone is already knitting back together. Someone is going to pay for that. I squint down the tunnel. Two men have Red, one on either side of her. She's hanging limply between them.

I'm up and using vampire speed to race down the tunnel towards her. No one gets to touch her or take her from me. I don't give a shit how pissed off she is with me. She's mine.

The vampires haul her up so her feet are no longer touching the ground. Shit, they're going to run her out of here.

No, you fucking don't.

I lean down, using my arms to pump my legs harder, faster. I have to reach her. My head throbs like a hammer striking an anvil. It makes my vision blurry as I finally get within touching distance. I don't slow down; I just barrel straight into the first vampire the way he did to me. I knock him flying as penance for what he did to me.

He clatters against the side of the tunnel in an almighty boom sounds as his head bounces off the tunnel wall.

"Put her down, and you get to live. Try to fight me, and I'll make it extremely painful for you." I say the words with a tangle of snarls and growls.

A mask covers his face. His entire body is hidden, so that the only pieces of him I can see are his eyes and his teeth.

One of his hands moves fast, whipping out a stake.

"A vampire with a stake? How original. How foolish," I say.

"Listen, love. You let me kill the little human hunter and we can all go home and be done for the day. Alright?"

"You touch a single hair on her head, and I will rip your balls from your crotch and feed them to you."

He laughs like I'm joking, but he has no idea.

Red murmurs, her head lifting. He must have knocked her out. I'm surprised he landed a punch. She doesn't normally drop her guard like that. Her need for blood must be greater than I thought. I will have to make her drink when this is over.

"Oct... Octavia," she breathes.

"It's okay, Red. Everything's going to be fine."

"Fine?" she snaps and hauls herself upright, to the vampire's surprise. He steps back, his eyes wide.

"What about this is fine? Yes, this fucking prick interrupted our argument, but that doesn't mean I'm okay with you. You fucking lied to me, Octavia. You broke the one promise you swore to keep to me."

Three things happen at once.

One, Red winks at me as she slides her hand down her hip and to a stake lodged in a concealed thigh pocket.

Two, the vampire I threw against the wall, gurgles and rolls onto his front, trying to stand up.

And three, the vampire in front of us reaches for Red as she ducks and I lurch forward, grabbing his throat.

Chaos erupts.

He throws himself forward, seeing me coming a split second before I can get a solid enough grip on his throat.

Red lurches forward, swinging up with her stake a second too late and punctures his shoulder instead of his heart.

"Fuck," she roars as she rolls and scrambles back to her feet.

Then it's an eruption of arms and fists and kicking as the second vampire races in to defend his brethren.

He focuses on me, swinging fist after foot after fist. I duck and throw my legs out, knocking his feet from under him. He flips his body, throwing himself upright before I can jump on top of him. And then the second vampire spins around Red's back to land a savage punch to my jaw, slamming me back.

I stagger several paces before leaping forward and jumping onto his torso, locking my legs around his arms so he can't move.

He swings about, trying to throw me off. He steps back, back, back until he crashes against the wall, crushing my legs. But I'm punching him hard and fast on his jaw, his eye, his nose over and over.

He's woozy and fading.

I'm going to win.

And then a blast of white-hot pain has me detached and falling to the ground.

"OCTAVIA," Red screams.

My vision whites out. I try to roll over, but my legs and arms aren't working. I'm paralysed. The vampire I was attacking sneers down at me, yanks the stake out of my spine and hauls me up by the throat.

As soon as it's out, the tingling sensation of nerves regrowing trickles through my body, but until I regain full movement, I'm defenceless. We're sitting ducks, especially because Red is now being held by the other vampire. Her face is bloodied, one of her arms hangs limp.

But she's done a serious amount of damage to the vampire too. She appears to have dislocated his shoulder, and he's limping. I glance down. There's a vomit-inducing amount of blood on the floor, but it doesn't appear to have come from her.

"Well, well, well, looks like we're at a standoff," the vampire holding me—let's call him Fucknut—says.

"What do you want?" Red says.

"Just you, pretty little thing," Fucknut replies.

"Take me instead," I say.

"Octavia, no." Red's eyes narrow, and I'm not sure if it's because she's defending me or wants to murder me instead. More feeling seeps into my limbs and body. My fingers twitch at my sides.

"We don't want you," Fucknut snarls.

I'm shunted forward as Fucknut slides his arm under my neck and pulls a stake out of his coat, resting it over my heart.

Red inhales, sharp and uneven, her eyes watery.

There's a moment of sheer silence where none of us move. The only thing I hear are the whirling, ragged breaths from Red as her shoulders heave up and down, up and down.

"I'll come with you," Red says.

"NO. No, you fucking won't," I shriek and shunt forward, but the stake the vampire is holding is sharp enough it pierces my chest.

Red hisses as a line of my blood dribbles down my clothes. I instantly stop, but Fucknut's grip is like steel. I stand there, blood leaking from my chest, knowing that Red is going to struggle harder the more of my blood that spills.

There must be something on the stake because my head feels woozy. I glance down and see the silver threaded like ribbons through the wood. But it's more than that. There must be some kind of potent herbs in the wood, too.

"Looks like we're in a stalemate," Fucknut's friend says.

"You can't stop me, Octavia," Red whispers, ignoring the vampires.

My heart is in my mouth, all I can hear is the roaring of blood in my ears. My stomach is so tight I think I'm going to be sick. I can't allow her to do this. I will not. She won't die for me. Not after what I've done to her. Not after how angry she is with me.

"I will not let you sacrifice yourself for me," I say.

"Oh, because you're the only one who gets to be a martyr?" she snaps.

"LADIES," Fucknut barks. "If you can stop fucking bickering for a second, I'll tell you how it's going to go. Red is going to come with us, and Octavia, you're going to sit here like a good little vampire bitch and let us leave, otherwise I'll make you watch as I pluck her eyes from her head and rip her arms off and slap you with them."

He pushes me forward as he pulls the stake out of my chest and his friend drags Red aside.

But just as suddenly, both vampires are on the floor, giant blades sticking out of their chests.

Red stares at me, open-mouthed. But I am equally confused.

"This wasn't me," I say.

"No. It was me," Scarlett, the magician assassin from New Imperium, says and steps out of the shadows.

Red drags Scarlett into her arms. "Mother of Blood, thank you, Scarlett."

Scarlett slides her arms around Red, a little stiff as she pats her on the back and holds my gaze.

She's right to check with me, too. My jaw is tight enough I may break a bone in my face. But I suppose this is only a natural reaction to someone having saved your life.

"Thank you, Scarlett," I say and incline my head. "But why are you here?"

Scarlett untangles herself from Red. "I came to make sure you got back to your own city. I can't afford Morrigan going off at me because I let a vampire into the city. You understand, I only followed you to make sure you left."

"Well, we did. And now we'll make it home too. I am in your debt."

Scarlett wrenches her long swords out of the hearts of the now desiccating vampires.

"It's a shame we can't question them. We need to know who is behind these attacks. Otherwise, none of us are going to make it to the end of the trials," Red says.

"I will leave you to it. I can see you're only a mile out from your city's border now. Will I see you at the wedding?" Scarlett says to Red.

She nods. "Bella asked me to go. As long as the trials are all done and dusted, I should be able to make it. Are you sure Morrigan and your sister are okay with me attending?"

I stiffen. I don't want Red in another city unguarded, especially at the moment.

Scarlett nods. "They'd love to you be there. It's the least they can do for all your help with Roman."

Roman? The magician blood bag in my club? Interesting.

"Octavia," Scarlett says, and then she surprises me and holds out her hand. "I misjudged you in assuming you were coming for my city, when I can see now you were coming for your heart."

I take her hand and shake it, and then she's off, sprinting down the tunnels back to New Imperium.

It's only Red and I left in the tunnels with the weight of everything we've done settling between us. I relax a little as Red looks up at me.

"We should talk," she says.

And then her expression hardens into steel and my stomach swirls with bile.

"This," she gestures at the vampires, "doesn't mean anything. Just because I didn't want you to die doesn't mean I forgive you."

And then she's off, marching down the tunnel back to Sangui City, and I'm left standing alone staring after her, wondering how the fuck I'm going to resolve any of this.

CHAPTER 8

RED

"Red, this isn't helpful," Octavia says as she catches up to me.

I managed to march quite a distance from Octavia before she caught up.

"Did you check the desiccating bodies for evidence?" I say, unable to keep the shittiness out of my tone.

"Yes, nothing, unfortunately. They were clean. We need to talk this out because we still have to work with each other to win the trials."

"You think I don't know that?" I say.

"Look, it changes things, you knowing who you are. But we're bound now. As far as I can tell, we're not going to be able to exist that far away from each other."

"Biggest regret of my life, knowing I'll have to spend the rest of it in the same fucking city as you. At least I know I'll be moving to the other side of it."

Her features harden, but she chooses to ignore that comment.

"I can still protect you, but we need to put it behind us."

"Put it behind us? Protect me?" I scoff. "Are you even sorry?" I say, scanning her face for a sign of regret.

I find nothing. "Oh my gods, you're not, are you?"

"If you're asking me whether I'd make the same choice again..." She falls silent, her mouth making fish shapes in the air.

I throw my hands up. Still, she doesn't answer.

"How could you hurt me like this?" I whisper, my voice cracking on the words.

I storm off, leaving her in the tunnel behind me, knowing full well that she's more than capable of catching up. But I'm dizzy. My arm is killing me where he tried to yank it out of its socket, and my head is fuzzy with a thirst no normal human should feel. I hate that I'm going to need to dose in order to get home. We tried withdrawals, lower doses but more consistent, and I hoped it would work. It hasn't. I'm worse than I have been in a long time, and I don't think it's just that I'm an entire day out from having had any blood.

I cough once, twice.

Everything goes dark.

I'm on the floor.

Octavia leans over me.

"Mother of Blood," she says, leaning down to give me a hand.

I smack it away and get up. "I'm fine."

"You collapsed."

"I'M FINE."

She kneads her temples like I'm the problem stressing her out.

"You're not even close to fine," she says, only this time it comes out through gritted teeth. She stabs her finger into her carotid. I lunge forward and pin her hand in place.

"Do not even think about pulling that nail out," I say.

"Red, you collapsed. Your skin is grey, you're sweating. If you don't dose, we're not getting out of this fucking tunnel let alone back to Sangui City."

"And if I do drink your blood? Then what? We fuck? Why would I fuck someone I hate?"

She snorts at me. "You've never had a problem doing that before."

I huff at her, release my grip, and wobble on my feet.

"For the love of my patience, take the dose before I have to carry you back to Sangui City unconscious..." she pauses, straightens up and then adds. "Please."

A sick curl of pleasure twists around my gut hearing her say please. I could make her beg me to take her blood.

"I'll take it if you answer one question."

"Anything," she says, keeping her finger wedged firmly in her neck.

"With the exception of the rooftop a day ago and the night Amelia was turned..." I start.

Octavia swallows hard, but she doesn't look away.

I take a step closer to her. I need to see her expression, read the micro movements, make sure she doesn't go vampire still and protect her truth from me. "Aside from those instances, have you ever taken my memories?"

She swallows once. Twice.

I shake my head.

"You fucking have. I knew it."

I spin on my heel and storm off. "We're done."

She chases after me, and I can sense the instant she pulls her finger off her neck. My mouth waters automatically. I wish it wouldn't, but I'd give just about anything to feast on her blood. The thought sickens me. How can I despise her so much and yet need a piece of her body so dearly? She must pat it dry because the exquisite scent of her blood dissipates in the air so fast, I barely taste the saliva buildup in my mouth.

"Red, wait."

"You don't get to 'Red wait' me anything. Give them back."

"What?" she says as she catches up.

"Give back the memories you stole," I bark and wipe my brow. I'm sweating harder now. My vision is dizzy. I lean against the tunnel. They're familiar now. We must be nearing home at last.

"I can't," she says.

"The fuck do you mean you can't? They're mine. GIVE. THEM. BACK."

Her jaw clenches, her eyes watery as she stands a little taller, steadying herself for whatever I can throw at her.

"No," she says. "I won't."

I scream and shove her back against the wall. "I FUCKING HATE YOU." I shout, and take a step but stumble, my vision smattered with grey.

"WELL, I FUCKING LOVE YOU," she bellows back.

"But you don't, because if you did, you'd give back what doesn't belong to you." Tears are falling. My hands ball into fists. I thump them against her chest with a weak rhythmic thudding. I don't want to hurt her, not really, not in this moment. But the movement eases the ache in my heart.

She folds her hands around my mine, pulling them off her chest. Then she brushes my shaggy locks behind my ear.

"It's because I love you that I took them." Her voice is soft now, patience ebbing through her tone.

I scoff against her chest. "If you really believe that, then you're more deluded than I imagined." I sway on my feet. The need to dose burns through me. I hate that it's true, but if I don't take some blood, I'm going to collapse.

"I know it, Red. I also know that if you don't feed, you're going to be unconscious within minutes."

"Feed? Don't call it that. I'm a human. An addict, perhaps, and I'm fucking *dosing*." I don't care that I made the same slip earlier, which makes me a hypocrite. I refuse to lose my humanity. It's dosing. I am not a vampire. I will *never* be a vampire.

"Okay, okay," she says, but she doesn't meet my eyes and that irritates me even more. Like she knows best? I am not the same as her. She looks away and tilts her head, her long, dark hair falling off her shoulder as she bares her neck to me.

"I don't... I don't want to take it like that. I'm not like you..." I say.

Octavia's lips purse. I'm being spiteful, but I don't give a shit. I don't want to be doing this.

"Listen, you can stand on your laurels later. Right now, you need to get as much of my blood in your system as you can, or you won't make the trip home. I've never seen you struggle like this."

This time, it's my molars grinding against each other. I open my mouth, run my tongue along the bottoms of my upper teeth. I swear they're sharpening. It's impossible. I am not a fucking vampire and I'm not a bloody dhampir either. Not yet, anyway. And maybe there's still a way I can stop this shit. Pass it to one of the other hunters. I don't want it.

I lean into her neck. Her smooth skin, despite being cold, sends heat radiating through my system. Her blood smells like iron and ice, like fires in winter and spices that warm your belly. I run my incisors along her artery, and Octavia shivers against me. I resent the fact that my pussy responds to her shiver.

"Is that disgust?" I ask, though I'm certain it's not.

"It's lust. I want you to take it." She pushes her neck down toward me and my body responds of its own accord. My eyes close, but cool tears roll down my cheeks. She might not find what I have to do disgusting, but I do. I hate myself. I hate her more for being here and coming after me instead of letting the bond sever so I could die in peace in these godsforsaken tunnels.

I lower my lips to her neck. I breathe deep, praying my stomach holds strong and the bile clawing at my throat doesn't make an appearance, and then I plunge into her skin. There's no resistance. I expected to struggle against her skin. But my teeth must be sharper because they sink into her flesh like a knife through cake.

Blood bubbles up into my mouth, smothering my tongue in the most delicious tasting substance I've ever had. Thick and warm. Sweet tones mixed with the tang of iron and beneath that an aged essence like rich wine that has me sucking on her neck like a kid with a milkshake.

The liquid heat warms me as it slides down my throat, yet its cool spiciness flows through my system. Then it drops, drops, drops and settles in my cunt.

My fingers grip Octavia's shoulders harder as a throbbing in tune with her heartbeat pulses in my pussy. My clit swells and vibrates against the fabric of my trousers, responding to the ingestion of her blood. This is the bit I was dreading.

My nails dig into her shoulders as I bite deep, pulling and sucking on her neck like it's my life force.

"Red," Octavia says.

But I'm not listening anymore. I am only consumption and blood and the raw rage bubbling in my chest. The tunnel has quietened to the sucking of my lips against her throat.

"RED," she says, louder this time.

I don't care. I need to drink it all. Drown in it.

Everything hazes over. A crimson veil drops over my vision. My throat is like liquid gold, my whole body alight with the electric bliss that is her life force. The more I take, the more connected I am to her. It's like I'm inside her, part of her, and it's intoxicating.

My entire system is eager, glowing, golden and glistening with power, energy and fury.

I am everywhere.

And then I'm not.

I blink up at Octavia from the damp tunnel floor.

"What the fuck was that?" Octavia says. "You were taking too much."

It starts with a tiny melodic tinkle. But it grows and blooms into a booming laugh. From laughter to hysterics. Huge wracking cackles spill from my chest. Tears streak my cheeks, only I'm not sure if they're of laughter or devastation. I smear them away, smudging her blood across my face with the moisture.

"What the hell was that?" she says, helping me to my feet.

"It was me, hungrier than I've ever been," I say, my eyes falling to her cleavage. Believe me when I say I want to drag my eyes away, but her blood is in my system now, a lot of it, and I can't tear them away.

"And now you're hungry for something else?" she says, wiping her thumb across my lips. She licks up the drop of her blood. My lips tingle at her touch, my body is hot with desire. Want. Lust.

I crave her.

Need her.

I try to push the desire away, fight to control my mind. There's a part of me deep down that loathes the fact I allowed myself to get like this. To succumb to an addiction that controls me when I've fought so hard against those who seek to control. It's pathetic. My mouth salivates at the thought of her pussy.

I want to spend the rest of the night wrapped in her. This desire is more intense than before. The fucking bond. As if it wants us to be near, to be one and united.

My body trembles, but not from thirst anymore, from an entirely different hunger. I can barely stand to stay dressed; I want to tear her out of her clothes and all the while, I fucking hate myself for it. I want to scour her out of my mind and soul and rid all my memories of her. And yet, that would make me just as bad as her.

The fucking irony.

Finally, I look up at her. "Yes, I want something else." Heat simmers in my eyes. Somewhere deep down, I'm aware of how pissed off I am.

"But you still hate me?" she purrs.

"With every cell in my body."

She leans against the tunnel wall. The ivy vines are overgrown here. She licks her lips and holds my gaze. "Then I suppose you need to punish me, don't you? Will that make you feel better?"

She's practically electric with anticipation. I swear I can detect her sweet scent in the air. The faintest hint of lust between her legs. But how could I? I don't have her vampire senses. Was I too hasty in wanting to be rid of this dhampir fate? Maybe there are upsides.

Her eyes glow a sultry crimson, and finally, I get it. "You want to be punished for what you've done," I say.

She sucks in her bottom lip and stares up at me from between her bangs. Her eyelashes practically flutter.

"Punishing you won't make it go away."

"But it might make you feel better because that is what you want to do, isn't it? Punish me?"

I shake my head, knowing she's right. "You're some kind of fucked up."

"Coming from the human who just drank my blood straight from my neck? I think we make a fine pair. And we're bonded now. So I know exactly how much you want me. Exactly how much you hate me, and exactly how much you *want* to punish me. Why don't we stop fucking lying and give each other what we need?" She grips my crotch.

My entire body flexes, urging me to back away. To do the sensible thing.

Sadly, I don't. "Turn around. I don't want to look at you while I punish you."

She sucks in a breath, her mouth dropping open as her eyes glimmer. I lower my tone. Thread command through it.

"Take your trousers off. Now."

She acquiesces and drops them next to her.

"Underwear too," I say.

She slides her lace underwear off.

"Hands on the wall. Tell me how many memories you took?" I say, my voice scathing.

"Wh—"

"How many?"

"A lot."

"Fine. If you can't quantify it, then how many times. Let's start there."

"I... I don't know. Five? Six? Seven, ten times?" she says, her voice hitching up a notch.

"We'll start with seven. One smack for every time you stole from me. Now. What is your safe word?" I say.

"Villain."

"Good. Now bend forward."

She does, pushing her arse out as she's bent in half, her head level with her arms.

"Are you ready?" I ask. "Because this will be a punishment."

"Y—" she starts as I land a slap in the centre of her arse cheek.

"Count."

"One," she says, already panting.

I pull my hand back and swing again, harder this time, and collide with her soft flesh.

She gasps, "Two."

I slap again. And again, it's harder than the last.

"Three," she whimpers. I slide my hand over the reddening skin and then I slip between her legs. She's wet and soaking her thighs.

"If you take the punishment like a good girl, then I'm going to take care of this," I say and draw a finger through her excitement. Her legs shake, her breathing hitches faster.

But I also increase the ferocity of the smacks. She's right, a part of me needs this. Needs to make her pay for what she's done to me. And with each smack, I'm a little less furious, a little less vindictive.

"Four," I say as I bring my hand down on her arse. This time it hurts enough to sting my palm. But there's something in the stinging sensation that threads through my body and wipes every emotion away.

I don't know how we're going to continue when this is over, because I'm never drinking her blood again. Never touching her, fucking her or being near her unless it's under duress.

She can break the bond. This was a terrible mistake.

How can I ever be with someone who has lied and betrayed me? Who took a piece of me without my permission?

"More," Octavia says. "Harder."

"Did I tell you to speak?" I snap, and I pull my hand

back and slap harder still. The sound rings around the tunnel, echoing off the walls. "Five."

She shunts forward this time, almost slipping off the wall. She makes a strangled sound, something between a gasp and a moan.

"I need..." she starts.

"What do you need?"

"To... to touch myself," she pants.

"No. Now spread your legs." I reach up and break a thick branch of ivy off the bush. I tug all the leaves off and then brandish it. Flicking this way and that. The swish of the branch cuts through the air, making a whipping sound that has Octavia jerking around to see what it is.

"I said face the wall or I'll make it eight."

She does, and I bend to slide my head between her open thighs, inhaling the sweet scent of her soaked pussy. I inch toward her clit. I can practically taste her sweetness.

"You don't get to come, you don't get to touch yourself, until I decide you can." My words brush against her folds.

She whimpers, the heat from my face pooling around her pussy. Then I'm gone and standing up again. It's cruel. But this is a punishment for a reason.

Her fingers grip the tunnel wall harder. She's electric. The worse the punishment gets, the more her mind is slipping from reality into total submission.

I stand up against her bare arse, wishing I had a strap-on to fuck the punishment into her. Later, I decide.

Wait, no. Never. I shake my head, trying to steady my own grip on reality.

While this is helping, one fucking scene and one punishment does not rectify what she's done. There won't be any 'love making' ever again.

I step away from her arse, pull the vine branch back and whip it down on her red skin.

"Six!" She screams it this time.

She's gasping as a red line blooms across her skin. I rub her cheeks, moving my hand in slow circles, changing the pressure to ease the soreness.

"Do you need to use your safe word?" I ask.

She shakes her head and pushes her arse out towards me, offering herself.

"More," she breathes.

But her legs are shaking, and her shoulders move in a more erratic motion. She's had enough, and the sight of that makes all the heat in me bleed away. I didn't mean to push so hard; seeing her this close to breaking fucks up my head. I step back and drop the branch.

"What are you doing? Finish this," Octavia says.

I can't do it anymore.

"Red..."

I'm dissolving.

"What do you need, Red?" She cups my jaw, her fingers tender, and draws me close, brushing her lips against mine. I close my eyes as she leans her forehead against me.

"It still hurts," I say, rubbing my chest, and then I'm crying. Nothing makes sense. How can all of me and none of me want her at the same time?

She pulls me in tight, kissing everywhere. My hand finds its way between our embrace to her pussy, slipping through her slick centre. I know this, her, her body. It's a comfort because it feels like home. I just wish it didn't make my chest tight and the air hard to breathe. I guess even dosing can't remove heartache.

My fingers glide between her folds.

She's drenched.

Good.

I shove two rough fingers right into her.

"Fuck," she says.

This isn't healthy. I should stop, but how can I when there's a part of her that still makes everything feel better? I pull myself together and lean into her ear.

"You're going to take what I give you, and you're not going to make a fucking sound. Do you understand?"

She nods. I thrust, slow and deep at first. She whimpers beneath her hair. She's breathing through her nose, the heavy, strained chest movements a sign she's pressed her lips together. Good. At least she can take these instructions.

I speed up, thrusting faster and harder. Her back rocks against the tunnel wall as I drive inside her and stroke her clit.

"Fuck," she gasps as I draw circles over her nub. I release her.

"I told you not a sound. Do you need to be punished again?" I say and withdraw my fingers, hovering at her entrance, circling and only slipping the tip inside. She wriggles and pants against me.

"Something you want to say?" I ask.

"I can't hold it in anymore," she says.

"The only thing on your lips better be my fucking name, Octavia, or I swear to gods, your next punishment will be so much worse."

I drive into her, thrusting hard as I return to circling her clit and winding her body tighter.

I crouch between her legs. My fingers push up into her as I slide my tongue over her cunt. I drive harder.

Harder.

Harder.

"Fuck, Red," she pants, her head tilting back against the tunnel's stone. Her hips grind against my mouth as I lap at her pussy. I thrust soft, hard, soft. Over and over, my tongue mimicking the pace until she's panting and breathless. Her fingers wind through my hair, gripping tight as she rams her cunt into my mouth.

I keep pumping into her until she twitches, her body jerking and wild where it was rhythmic. “Shit, I’m going to… oh gods.”

And then she spills over the edge with a blissful, wordless moan. Her pussy clenches, and a rushing liquid pours out, squirting all over my face as her body comes undone.

CHAPTER 9

CORDELIA

One Thousand Years Ago

I untether the horse, jump back on and nudge him in the ribs. He jerks forward straight into a trot. I dig a little harder, and he shifts into a canter. The next village is an hour's ride away. I shan't waste any more time.

The sun is high in the sky by the time I reach the village, and I'm exhausted. My backside aches, and I haven't slept at all since yesterday and only a few fitful hours before the men came into Eleanor's house.

Alas, I also don't remember the last time I took any form of sustenance. I must stop and drink a little before I have a dizzy spell.

But I can't wait. I have to find the firefighters.

There's a little market in the middle of the village, so I approach the first seller, who's hollering about vegetables.

He's a rugged-looking chap, his cheeks and nose ruddy from always being outdoors, I suspect.

"Alright, miss?"

"I don't suppose you've encountered any firefighters in your village?"

"Yes, miss, there's a station of sorts. They do training on the other side of the village. Can I interest you in some fruit?"

I go to leave, but I'm awash with guilt because I asked for something from him and provided nothing in return. I hand over a small silver coin, and he passes me an apple as rosy as his cheeks.

My lips sink over the flesh, and I take a bite, instantly perking up. My tummy gurgles in protest, but I eat half of it and then give the rest to my horse.

"You need a name, don't you, boy?" I say. "Rather wish I'd bothered to check with the stables before I took you. I'll call you Teddy." The colour of his coat reminds me of a bear Mama gave me as a child.

I pat his neck as he chomps on the apple before sucking it entirely into his mouth.

Finally, after what seems like a millennium, I find the station the market man was talking about.

It's nestled in the most adorable and picturesque part of the village. Little grey stone cottages with thatched roofs and gardens bursting with potted plants and lush shrubs line the main road and side streets.

Among them sits a larger, squarer building where several men are training in the courtyard. Some hoist buckets of water and run with them up and down the expanse. Others lift logs or unfold ladders and scurry up them to the building's second-floor window.

I tie up Teddy on the outer gate, and I make my way into the yard.

"Excuse me," I say.

One man, a rather muscular fellow, turns and cocks his head at me. "Corr, what's a pretty little thing like you doing here?" he says.

Another, a man on the ladder, whistles a swit-swoo sound. It takes quite the effort of self-control for me not to roll my eyes at him.

"I'm looking for the men who attended to the dhampir healer's house yesterday. It was on fire."

"Ah, yes, quite tragic that. It was a beautiful house."

Tragic? My stomach turns in on itself and the mouthfuls of apple threaten to spill out and onto the cobbled yard.

"You alright there, miss? You're a little pale."

I pat my stomach and raise a hand to cover my mouth as I swallow down the urge to be sick.

Another man, shorter and blonder, appears at the first's shoulder.

"How can we help, miss? I'm Deyrn and this is Alanin."

"I'd like to know if the woman who was inside the house is alive."

Deyrn glances at Alanin. The way their expressions soften makes another round of bile crawl up the back of my throat. I can't do this. I can't hear the words I'm dreading.

"We... It's, ahh... Would you like a cup of tea, miss? Something to help the nerves? We don't have much here, like, but a cuppa we can do," Deyrn says.

"Thank you, no. That's kind of you, but I'd rather be on my way. I must find her, you see."

"Right, oh," Deyrn continues. "In that case, we can't tell you what became of her. But she weren't looking too good when we pulled her out. A lot of smoke inhalation. Some of her skin was burned up real good, and honestly, it looked like she'd been beaten, too."

"We weren't too hopeful of her survival, truth be

known," Alanin adds. Deyrn elbows him in the ribs. Alanin shrugs like he has no idea of how inconsiderate he's been.

My eyes water. Every time I hear more news of her, it breaks another piece of my heart. I can't take this. I need someone to tell me if she's dead or if she survived.

"Where did she go? Who took her after you pulled her out?" I ask, my voice barely above a whisper.

"Aye," Deyrn says. "To a village a few miles away. It's got more medical facilities there. Specialist dhampirs and the like. We couldn't do nothing for her. I can't tell you if she lived, but if she did, then it's because of them. Best in the world there."

"Thank you. What's the name of the village? How do I get there?"

"It's about a day's ride in that direction. Follow the coastline. Make your way to the water's edge. Use the cliff as a guide and you'll eventually see the forest in the distance. The village is in the heart of it."

"Thank you," I say.

And with that, I'm back on Teddy, cantering towards the ocean. I make it to the cliff. The wind is refreshing. It almost feels like it's washing away all the awful things I've been churning over, all the worries, all the fears I have that she's gone.

The sun sets as the forest comes into focus on the horizon. It's further inland than I am now and while it seems close, I know it's still several hours' ride away. The horse is foamy around the mouth. His belly is wet and salty, and I know the pair of us need to rest. So I begin looking for somewhere to stop for the night. I weave back inland, heading towards the trees. We roam long enough that the ocean becomes a brackish marsh and then a river. I regret not purchasing more food, but at least the horse can feed and drink river water.

Eventually, he eats his fill and settles on the grass near me. I nestle against a boulder, trying to gather any warmth they soaked up from the sun. Eventually, I close my eyes for a few hours of fitful sleep.

CHAPTER 10

RED

Despite what happened in the tunnels, Octavia and I haven't said a word to each other during the entire carriage ride. We caught one as soon as we could and have been racing towards Castle St Clair. The terrain underneath the wheels evens out. We must be near the castle station. I decide to break the silence.

"What happened in the tunnels can't happen again."

Octavia glances up at me, her face falling. "I... oh, I see."

"We're not good for each other."

"You're wrong," she says.

"Am I?"

"All I've ever done is try to protect you. Try to do what's best for you." She runs a hand through her hair.

"What you've done is martyr yourself, Octavia, because you'd rather sacrifice yourself and put yourself in pain than admit someone loves you. Someone thinks you're enough."

Her expression goes blank.

"See? You can't even face the fact that no matter how

fucked off I am with you, I am still here. Still choosing you and you are refusing to do the right thing. Why can't you do the thing that will save us and give me my memories back?"

"I..." she starts. But I already know she's not going to do what I want. My chest tightens, and I tear my gaze away from her.

"How do you expect me to be with someone who won't tell me the truth?" I say as the carriage slows; we must be pulling into the station.

"I can't. You don't understand," she whines.

I hitch off the seat and lean forward, taking her hands in mine as I kneel at her feet.

"Then make me. Explain it so I do understand, because the way I see it, you're the one breaking us apart."

She pulls her fingers out of mine and stares out of the carriage window. "We're here."

"Mother of Blood, Octavia," I whisper, and I step out of the carriage. Octavia is behind me in a blink.

I press my lips into a thin line. My nostrils flare. "I'm not going to run. Not again."

"You promise?"

I nod. "I understand we can't be too far from each other. But... I don't want to be near you right now. You're going to have to accept that I need space. Or we break the b—"

Octavia holds her hand up to interrupt me.

"Impossible. One doesn't break a bond, and the answer would be no, even if I could break it."

"Then you need to give me space."

She stands a little straighter, her brow furrows, her lips thin. Something I can't read washes through her eyes, and then her face morphs and becomes devoid of emotion.

"As you wish," she gives me a curt nod and walks off towards the castle door.

I slump against the carriage and wipe my face. My mind is racing with a maelstrom of thoughts. Octavia tickles Rumblegrit under the chin before depositing what seems like more than a required offering of blood and slides the mansion door shut behind her. Even that confuses me. She never used to treat the gargoyles with kindness; she's changing for the better. And while I breathe easier now she's away from me, the space hasn't made me feel any better. Our connection is soul deep, and it's not just the swirling confusion but the tug of hurt in the bond that consumes me.

I am pissed, disappointed and a million other things, yet I still want to be near her, with her. It's twisting me up inside.

Is this love? Is this healthy?

I don't think I can be with someone who lies to me like this. Someone who betrays me. She holds all the power because she took it from me. How can I be with someone like that when she stands for everything I hate?

I don't want to be trapped inside another building after spending the last few hours in the carriage, so I meander around the castle grounds. My feet carry me past the stables. That's when I notice Sadie. I stiffen. She makes me uneasy.

I think it's the calmness that pervades her entire being despite the horror stories of her past. Screaming herself mute night after night until she lost her voice. They say the scar that Cordelia has on her cheek was from a bite Sadie gave her.

One horse whinnies as Sadie passes the stable. She turns to face the animal, staring it right in the eye. The horse clops back, raising its head and dropping it in a rhythmic motion. It neighs and then goes quiet.

All the while, Sadie hasn't moved. She's staring the

horse down like a lion to its prey. She's vampire still, her eyes locked onto the horse.

A line of goosebumps shivers over my arms as I watch her interact with the animal. Exactly what kind of game is she playing? Gods, there's something mildly unhinged about her.

Eventually, the horse sticks its head back over the stable door, and she unfreezes and pats its velvety nose.

She wraps her arms around its neck and leans into its ear almost like she's whispering to it. I shift foot to foot, and a twig snaps underneath my feet. Sadie stands bolt upright and turns to find me. It makes me feel like a trespasser.

Her eyes lock onto mine and narrow. She's motionless, yet an ocean of darkness swims in her expression. It makes me wonder what's truly beneath the surface.

I edge away. But she's already charging across the yard towards me, her gaze fixed on me the way it was on the horse. I shiver.

I glance at the path I came down. I could turn back, probably should. Instead, I step towards her.

Why the hell I would want to be caught near a St Clair on my own, at night, when they're my competition, I've no clue. But here we are.

She halts. Waits for me to come to her, fucking entitled. Just like the rest of the St Clair's. Why should they come to you when you can go to them?

But regardless, I step toward her. She stares at me the whole time, patiently waiting for me to reach her.

"Hi," I wave, knowing that she uses sign.

"Hi," she waves. Her expression is open, friendly. The opposite of what it was facing that horse. I wonder if it's a ruse, whether she's waiting for me to turn my back so she can drain me and eliminate the competition?

"Shouldn't you be with Octavia in the castle?" she says. Or I think she does. My signing is a little lacklustre. It's been a while since one of my students spoke in sign.

I take a second to process what she said.

"Ah. Yes. I, umm... I have to get back to her, you're right."

Her eyes narrow further at me. She doesn't buy the bullshit I'm selling. It occurs to me then that she works in the church, with the spirit, with the fibre of our beings, and that perhaps she could give me back the memories Octavia stole.

"Can I ask you an answer?" I sign.

She frowns at me.

I try again. "Can. I. Ask. You. An. Answer?"

She smirks. "You mean question?" she signs correctly.

"Shit. Yes. A question," I half say half gesture as I mimic her hand movements. Signing is coming back to me now.

"Sure," she shrugs.

"In the church, you guys focus on spirit stuff, right?" I ask.

She bites her lip as if trying to suppress a smirk. "Yes, we do spirit stuff."

"Gods, sorry, I'm not being very polite. What I mean is, do you work with people's minds?"

"Sort of," she signs.

"Could you tell if someone's memories have been messed with?"

That earns me a tilt of her head as she examines my expression. "Yes. Do you mean compulsion?"

I shake my head, not understanding the word.

She rolls her eyes at me and signs slower. "Com-pul-sion."

"Yes. That. Can you help someone get them back?"

She folds her arms, making me wait while she decides

whether to tell me what I want to know. She pauses long enough I shift on the spot, uncomfortable with the silence. But as I drag my gaze from her, she unclasps her hands and answers.

"Yes, I can tell what has happened to a mind, what damage has been done and get the memories back, though it is much more reliable and better for the person in question to have the original vampire who took them give them back to them. Now, tell me why you want this information."

That's a lot of signing, and she doesn't speak slowly, so I take a hot second to interpret what she said.

"Nothing in particular," I say, deciding it's quicker to speak and let her do the signing.

She huffs at me, and her fingers fly again. "I guess I have nothing to tell you then." She turns away, her flowing black dress drifting in the night breeze.

"Wait."

"Something you want to share?" she signs.

I grit my teeth. No. I look away. She touches my chin, tilts it up to face her. She's tall like Octavia.

"Don't come to me asking for help and then lie to me." Her expression is cold enough to crack bones and freeze summers.

I swallow hard. Decide to change the topic.

"I wondered if there was ever an occasion when memory wipes and compulsions don't work?"

She laughs. It's whispery and indignant. "Only one I can think of..." she steps back smiling, but instead of making her face radiate joy and light, it makes her face dark and sinister. Like a void sucking in everything, every emotion, every secret, all light and love.

I shiver, and she lets go of my chin. But the cool press of her thumb lingers.

“Wh-what’s the only occasion?” I ask, not at all sure I want the answer.

“Bonding. A piece of our soul binds to a piece of the person’s we bond to. Magic that controls in this way doesn’t work on one’s bonded.”

“Other magic might?”

She shrugs. “Healing, perhaps. Maybe magic from other cities. Why? You haven’t found yourself recently bonded... *have you?*”

She leans in, drawing out the signed gestures on the last words.

“Obviously not,” I roll my eyes, sending every ounce of will I have to my heart, praying it doesn’t betray me by speeding up. She holds my gaze for an agonising amount of time before recoiling and sighing.

“To answer your original question, I can both check your memories and give them back...”

My lips purse. “But you’re not going to?”

She shakes her head at me. “No.”

“Why not? I’m willing to make a deal. I’m sure there’s something I can offer you.”

She scans my face. “Oh, there is. But I am also sure that whatever I ask for will be a price you’re not willing to pay.”

“You don’t know that... Not unless you ask.”

She smiles, and this time it makes her eyes glint like the beady orbs of ravens.

“I am certain you won’t be willing, because I only ask for the most impossible things to give. Otherwise, what’s the point of making a deal?”

Psycho.

She wipes her hands down her dress and says, “Good evening, Red. See you at the awards ceremony.”

She waves a willowy hand at me and then speeds off

into the night and darkness. The mountains and forests swallow her.

I have to bite back an insult. What a bitch. She can help me, but won't? Fucking St Clair's are all the same. Twisted fucks.

I should never have gotten involved with any of them.

CHAPTER 11

RED

I spend some time in the gardens, but it isn't the same as truly being free. The bond is like a splinter, an ever-present niggling. An irritation I can't quite reach to scratch.

What's worse is Octavia has sent a vampire guard to watch over me. I sense his presence. He's kept to the shadows and given me as much space as he can, but it's obvious enough that I raise my hand in greeting. He nods in return, but the damage is done.

I stumble upon the castle bar and find it full of people drinking. Nobles cluster in groups, and the odd hunter stands or lounges, too. Everyone's gathering for the awarding ceremony for the amulet challenge, I suspect. I've no idea how this is going to go because Octavia and I haven't claimed the win. We won't be, either. It's not something we've outwardly discussed, but that's exactly why I've come to find her. We need to talk before we walk in there to an ambush.

Gabriel has his feet curled under him, a book on his lap and another open in his hand. Keir scrawls in a notebook quietly next to him. Lincoln sits opposite them chatting to Talulla; he smiles at me, but it doesn't meet his eyes. I'm not sure when we fell out. It's like the last couple of weeks have driven a wedge between us that neither of us asked for but nor do we know how to get rid of it.

There was a time when I'd walk into a room and he'd jump out of his seat and ruffle my hair, and we'd scheme our next joint training session or night out or prank on the Academy kids. Now he stays rigid in his seat. His eyes dart to Dahlia like he's seeking reassurance. What's happened to you, Lincoln?

I follow his gaze and spot Dahlia with Xavier and Octavia at the bar, laughing and drinking together. They're such an odd family. To loathe each other with such contempt one moment and then be laughing and slapping each other on the back the next.

"Red, darling," Xavier says, clearly a little inebriated. He opens his arms to me, and I outright frown at him.

"How much has he had?" I mouth to Dahlia.

"Too much." She smirks.

"What happened to him?"

Octavia opens her mouth and then shrugs. "Found him like this."

"My fault," Dahlia says. "Consoling each other."

"More," Xavier says, throwing his arms up and at the barman.

"Why the hell not?" Dahlia says and slaps Xavier on the back. He pitches forward violently.

"Gods, Dah, go easy on me. You forget how strong you are."

"Stop being a pussy and neck this," she says and hands shots around. Octavia and I politely decline. We don't have time for this. I need to clarify the story with Octavia before we walk in and screw everything up.

"We need to talk. Somewhere private," I say.

She nods and leaves Xavier and Dahlia at the bar. We find a small, secluded room somewhere on the floor above the main ballroom.

"What's wrong?"

"What's our story? What are we saying when we go in there? They're expecting a winner to be announced and we can't... You've made that perfectly clear with your actions."

Octavia rubs at her forehead. "Are you going to make everything an argument?"

"That depends on whether you're going to insist on taking my memories away repeatedly."

"It was a one-time thing." She practically growls the words.

"Was it? So you've forgotten the tunnels, and the fact you told me there were other times? Like the ones you're refusing to give back? Ironic." I snort.

"Mother of Blood, give me patience. You have no idea what you're talking about, Red. Why can't you trust me that I'm doing this for both of us?"

"Trust you? TRUST YOU?"

She snaps. "This isn't getting us anywhere. We are going to sacrifice the round. We'll still be in second place, I hope. And then everything relies on the next round. As long as we don't fuck up the next trial, we will be fine. It's a lot of pressure. But we'll win the next one and pick up the points we need."

"And what if we're not in second place? What if we don't win the next trial?"

Her face hardens. "We have to. Everything relies on the next trial, Red. To protect you, we sacrifice this round, but the next one is vital."

I shake my head. "The risk is too great. What if Cordelia takes points away from us as a punishment for not giving her a winner? I need that cure for Amelia. I have to win."

"I need to win as much as you do, or I'm never going to belong in this city. You think I don't want this just as much as you? I already have plans drawn up for how I'm going to shape Sangui City. There's so much I can do. I can bring equality, peace, stop the constant civil fighting between hunters and vampires. I can make those on the periphery feel wanted."

I take her hand. "Then we claim the win we deserve and put ourselves in the lead."

She flings her hand out of mine. "WE CAN'T. Don't you get it? This whole thing is about finding the fucking dhampir. Finding you, for fuck's sake."

"What if it's not me?"

She glares at me.

"Okay, fine. But what if there's a way to give it to one of the others? What if I can get rid of it?"

She shakes her head. "You might not want this responsibility, but it is yours. And you're going to have to face that reality if you want to get through this. But that's why I'm trying to buy you time. If we give up your identity now before you've fully transitioned into this new dhampir, before we know what you're capable of and what it really means, all we're doing is putting you in danger."

"Danger? You do realise I'm a hunter? I am more than capable of keeping myself safe?"

"Who had to run into the sun, pull you into their house and feed you half their blood to save your life?"

"Wow, Octavia. Low blow," I snarl.

She huffs at me and starts pacing around the little room we're in.

"We should never have bonded," I say before I can stop myself.

She stops dead. Turns to me. "Don't say that. That is the second time you've expressed regret, and each time it's like a knife wound." She pokes her chest.

I snort. "Why? It's the fucking truth. Oh, and by the way. The reason you can't compel me anymore is because of the bond. A piece of your soul is attached to mine. So I suppose that's one good thing to come out of this. I'm no longer subject to your whims anymore. You can't control me the way you do everyone else."

"It's not about control, Red. I was trying to protect you."

"I can protect myself. It wasn't your fucking decision to make."

"GODS," she shouts. I don't think I've ever seen her truly lose her temper.

I shake my head. "What are you hiding from me?"

"Nothing you want to know. Be careful what secrets you uncover, Red. Not all of them are truths you want to hear."

"Don't you get it? If you don't tell me, we're never going to fix this."

She smiles, soft. But it never reaches her eyes. And instead of resolving the fucking issue, she changes the subject.

"We need to come up with an item we tried to get into the amulet. Otherwise, when everyone else tells them the thing they tested, we're going to be screwed. Cordelia is going to be pissed that there's no winner."

Irritation flares in my gut, but she's right. This is why I dragged her from the bar. So I comply, and we brainstorm ideas for items that seem logical and believable enough we would have thought to test them. We settle on the most plausible thing we can think of.

One of Cordelia's staff appears in the doorway. "You're required," she says.

We follow her down several hallways, tracing our steps back the way we came, when I stop suddenly. Outside the castle window is a mob of people.

"What's going on?" I ask.

The staff member glances at the floor. "Don't worry, miss. Lady St Clair is on top of the protesters. They're anti-cure folks. But they caught word of the awards ceremony this evening. There are vampires out there patrolling and monitoring it, and the Chief sent a few hunters out too."

"I see," I say and glance back outside. There's an uncomfortable number of placards and signs being brandished with words like:

Fuck the dhampir.

No dhampir, no cure.

I swallow hard and try to ignore the chills nestling inside my stomach.

Octavia gives me a pinched, I-told-you-so look.

We traipse after the staff member until we re-enter the ballroom that is becoming increasingly familiar to me. Though each time it looks a little different.

Today, the floor is chequered black and white flagstone tiles. It's beautiful and ornate. Some areas have larger tile patterns and others have smaller tiles. It makes for an almost hypnotic atmosphere, a sort of illusion and warping of time and space and reality, and I see now that's all this is. One giant game. And I'm no longer sure if we're the players or being played.

Above us hang two enormous crystal chandeliers. The candles standing in a ring are black, but the wax dripping down their stems is red and looks like blood drops.

Gabriel, Sadie and Dahlia sit at a table near the front, drinking goblets of blood and talking in hushed tones.

My stomach coils. Hunger gnaws at my insides. I hate that I can't recognise which hunger I have anymore.

A heavy hand lands on my shoulder. I whirl around.

"Chief, hey," I say.

"Hello, Red. Can I have a moment?" she asks.

"Sure." I follow her out towards a balcony on the other side of the ballroom. She opens the door, and we slip into the night.

"What's up?" I ask.

"I just wondered whether you'd unearthed anything yet? It's been a few days since our talk at the Academy, and I wanted to know how your progress was going digging up any dirt?"

I shrug. "Honestly, the trials have taken up so much of our time and energy, I haven't had a chance to snoop. But anything I have found hasn't been worthy of bringing to you."

"Everything is worthy, Red."

I don't think the Chief needs to know I've mostly spent my spare time dosing and fucking.

"We're all trying to uncover who's behind the attacks."

"I thought that was resolved with the execution at the last awards ceremony."

I narrow my eyes at her. "There was another attempt. And he didn't confess to the first one. So there's something else at play."

The Chief stiffens and nods. "Good work. I told you everything was relevant. Any sign of which of you hunters is the dhampir yet?"

I hesitate, wondering if now is the time to confess, but we're surrounded by vampires.

She continues before I decide.

"We need to know so we can put extra protection in place around them."

There's a knock at the window before I can answer.

Amelia's head bobs in the window, waving maniacally at me.

"I should see what's wrong with her," I say to the Chief. "If anything comes up, I'll let you know."

I leave the Chief and head inside, dragging Amelia back towards the food table.

"Hey," Amelia says.

"Hey yourself," I say.

"Can I have a word?" she asks.

I glare at her. "Well, you just interrupted another conversation I am now not having, so, yeah, you have my attention. What's up?"

I glance at the balcony and then the stage. It doesn't look like they're about to start yet. I pluck a chicken leg off the food table and gnaw on it. Predictably, it doesn't hit the right spot. I find Octavia as I leave the room, and she narrows her eyes at me like she can tell there's an issue. I'm not sure if I love the bond for this connection or hate that I can't keep anything to myself.

"What's up?" I say to Amelia as I take another bite of chicken.

She looks down, her feet all shifty. "I, umm... I want you to know that I don't blame you."

"Blame me? For what?" I say, chowing down and tearing more chunks of chicken off the leg bone.

Her neck contorts. It's like she wants to say something and can't.

"You alright?"

"Fucksake. Yes. Look. I wanted to tell you that I don't blame you for Mum and Dad leaving us. Okay? You were late the night she died, and I know you've worried over the years that if you'd got there sooner, you could have stopped it. But you couldn't, okay?"

My chest tightens, and my eyes sting. This isn't the time to discuss this. I try to find words, but my throat is thick with memories. How does she know this? We've never really spoken about that night. Not like this. I was young, but old enough to be an excuse for Mother to leave work. I was meant to get her from the club she was working at because she'd donated too many times already that week. The worst bit is, I don't even remember why I was late now. And that, more than anything, haunts me. It's my fault she died, I know that, and so does Amelia.

I frown at her. "Really odd time to bring this up," I say, finally finding words.

She flaps her hands at me. "Yeah, well. It's been on my mind since the ni—"

Her voice cuts off and her eyes nearly pop out of her head.

"You are being very weird tonight. Is everything okay?"

Her cheeks turn red, and I'm not sure if she's livid or embarrassed or what.

Someone calls the room to attention.

"We need to go in," I say and rub her arm before depositing the now clean chicken bone in a bin and heading into the ballroom. I edge around the outside of the room to where the buffet is and take more chicken and potatoes. Then I take a seat on one of the rounded ballroom tables. They're as grand as the rest of the room, with flowers bending and bleeding like the chandeliers. Servers place wine on the table. It's a deep red and looks far too close to the colour of blood for my liking. Next, they wheel in barrels and caskets of blood. From what I can see, a variety of blood types all flavoured with different emotions—jealousy, fear, joy—are deposited on the table.

I inhale the chicken and potatoes, but when I'm done, I am struck with that increasingly familiar sensation: physically full, yet hungry. It's like the addiction has shifted. It used to be more of a craving. Like when you've had a delicious Sunday roast but you're still craving sugar at the end. Except it wasn't sugar I was craving. Now it's more like I'm ravenous, starved even.

Octavia comes and sits beside me now I'm finished eating.

"You okay?" she says.

It's childish, but I bite at her. "Oh, you care now, do you?"

"Is this how it's going to be?" She sighs.

"Until you give me my memories back, yes."

She shakes her head at me. "You don't know what you're asking."

"Don't patronise me. I want what's already mine."

The ballroom fills fast. Hunters grab plates of food, and vampires tend to the metal casks and barrels of blood. One vampire turns on the faucet and fills their goblet. Beneath the barrel of that cask in particular is a low fire, more embers than anything, but it keeps the cask and the blood inside at body temperature, I suspect.

Octavia draws her own goblet to her mouth, and I twitch.

"What?" she says and takes a sip.

"Is that off?" I ask.

"The blood?" She frowns and looks at the goblet. "No? Why?"

"It stinks. It's so strong."

"Smells fine to me." She downs the rest of it, saving me from having to smell it.

"Wait, are you thirsty already?" she says.

My eyes skirt the crowd to make sure no one is listening or understanding the context, and then I nod because, yes, I really am and now is not a good time for that. Her eyes widen, but before we can discuss it, the Chief and Cordelia enter the room side by side. They walk so close together that if you hadn't been told their history of hatred, you'd think they were firm friends. Everyone grows quiet. Xavier sits with us alongside Talulla. Amelia is at another table, a couple of rows in front. Lincoln and Dahlia are at the front, near the stage. Gabriel and Keir are on the same table as Lincoln, though Gabriel doesn't seem interested in anything other than the book he's flicking through.

Octavia's hand slides under the table and inches over my thigh and between my legs. The long tablecloth hides her arm from view as she grins at me, her eyes glimmering under the chandelier light.

Acutely aware that Xavier is mere inches away, I mouth the words, "We are not doing this here. And definitely not now." I give her the most potent "What the fuck are you doing" stare I can muster. But my skin has already broken out in goosebumps.

She grins, her eyes rolling over my arms.

"Octavia," I growl under my breath.

"Still pissed with me?" she says.

I nod.

"Then I will spend eternity making it up to you." She slides her nail up my crotch, making a small incision in my trousers.

Mother of Blood, I should stop her. I really should. I hate her for what she's done. And yet, this isn't even the bond. It's me. She's like a drug and I am already an addict. She's hurt me, and yet I come back for more because every time she touches me, I melt. I want to feel her, fuck her, come on her fingers.

My head might be furious, but my heart doesn't want to be away from her.

"Orgasms can't right a wrong," I mouth.

"Maybe not, but they don't hurt either."

I have no arguments left.

My thighs inch out, stretching the hole in my trousers. I inwardly cuss myself for being a traitor to myself.

She slides a finger up my pussy and finds my clit, and I jerk upwards as she hits the spot.

"Everything alright?" Xavier says.

I nod. But keep my mouth firmly closed. He turns back to face the stage.

"Not a sound," Octavia mouths at me in silence.

"Good evening, vampires, nobles, hunters, friends, family, humans," Cordelia says.

The Chief steps into the middle of the stage next to her. I will never get over the sight of them allied. It makes me wonder if Octavia is right. If there is potential in her dream of unifying the city under one rule. One welcoming city for everyone, no matter their race or species or beliefs. One city where she and I and everyone else would belong.

The Chief takes over. "It is our great pleasure to announce the end of the second trial, the amulet trial." Her hands open and rise in the air, gesturing to the amulet hovering above the stage.

She glances at Cordelia to continue. "As you all remember from the opening ceremony, each team had to pick the most beautiful item in the city and present it to the amulet. The amulet would accept only the most beautiful item and seal it inside."

Octavia's finger slides down my increasingly wet slit.

Fuck her. How dare she make me this wet. How dare she know exactly how to fuck me in the way I want and need.

The Chief lowers her hands, and the amulet floats down through the air to hover above the lectern. Cordelia grasps it and turns to the audience.

Octavia's finger circles my entrance. My breathing increases. Xavier's gaze snaps to Octavia. He must be able to smell my excitement.

He raises his brows at her and then mouths, "Really?"

"What?" She shrugs.

My cheeks flame hot with shame and excitement because he knows exactly what we're doing. My pussy throbs. I should note that neither of them acknowledges me in this conversation. In fact, Octavia leans forward to rest her other elbow on the table and her chin in her hand like I don't even exist. Fuck. The fact she's ignoring me while she pushes her finger inside my pussy drives me fucking wild. I have to swallow down the yelp of excitement.

"This. Doesn't. Mean. Anything." I pant as quietly as I can.

"I know," she whispers.

Cordelia finishes examining the amulet and turns back to the audience. "I can confirm that the amulet has chosen one of the offerings. It has sealed an item inside of its protective casing."

The audience draws in a collective gasp and then a round of oohs and ahhs follow. It allows me a moment to pant audibly and for it to sound like everyone else. Which promptly makes Octavia slide another finger inside me.

Fuck. Me.

She moves agonisingly slow, her fingers drawing in and out of my slickness. The hole in my trousers is only small, so she doesn't have a lot of room to manoeuvre, but that doesn't seem to stop her.

"Would the winners of this round please now step forward," the Chief says.

There's a shuffling of movement as the audience full of humans, hunters and vampires alike all glance around to search for who will stand up and claim their prize.

There's a couple of muffled coughs, and the temperature in the room rises—and not just because Octavia is fucking me under the table.

"Come now," Cordelia says, a slight hitch in pitch in her voice. "Present yourselves."

No one moves and the room descends into silence, no one even reaches for a drink glass. I grit my teeth and clench down on Octavia's fingers and prevent her from moving. There's so little sound and I am so fucking wet that everyone will hear what we're doing.

She curls her fingers until she finds my G-spot.

Oh gods.

She doesn't need to move in and out. She curls her finger and rubs over that glorious spot that has heat flushing my cheeks and me struggling to control my breathing and sit still.

"We have other things to be doing this evening. Children?" Cordelia says.

"Hunters?" the Chief calls.

But still, there's nothing. No movement, no sound, no one claims the win. It's a mutiny against the process, against the trials. This is not how she expected it to go. It wasn't in her plan—well, mine either.

The Chief's expression changes, shifting and morphing. The lines of her porcelain face harden, her expression narrows, a seething tremor rumbles through her eyes. Someone is going to suffer as a result of our keeping the win a secret.

"What is going on?" Cordelia snaps. "Come forward at once."

The room breaks out into murmurs and the chatter of growing confusion. I release Octavia's fingers, and she continues fucking me, harder, faster now. I grip the table with one hand and try to keep my face as neutral as I can.

But I'm so close. I'm going to spill over. She thrusts harder. Shifts her arm position to keep her body motionless and only the feverish movements of her wrist and fingers under the table would give us away.

My pussy clenches and relaxes as I climb higher.

Xavier shifts in his seat, clearly aware of exactly what is going on. Octavia looks at me, stares me right in the eye and mouths, "Do you want to come?"

I nod feverishly. My nipples are so hard against the fabric of my sports bra, every nod of my head ignites a tiny sizzle of pleasure that goes straight to my pussy.

"Eyes on me," she whispers.

Xavier turns around, raises an eyebrow at the pair of us as Octavia breathes, "Come for me."

I do, my mouth falls open, my pussy tightens around her and because I can't draw attention to myself, the orgasm races deep, rushes around my body and washes through my entire system.

Slowly, Octavia pulls her fingers out of my cunt, and I have to take a shuddered breath in order to calm myself down. My cheeks are rosy as heat crawls up my neck.

Xavier shakes his head at the pair of us, his nose pinching.

"What?" Octavia says and then smiles at me as she slides the fingers she buried inside me into her mouth. She pushes them all the way into her mouth and sucks them clean. The sight of it nearly makes me come again.

"Lesbians," Xavier huffs, looking disgusted and amused all at once.

"This is unacceptable," Cordelia says, slapping the lectern in frustration. "Children. On stage immediately."

"Hunters. You too," the Chief says and touches Cordelia's lower back, guiding her away from the lectern. My eyes narrow. Octavia catches sight of the movement too. Xavier turns to us, a deep frown running through his brow. An odd expression for a man whose porcelain features rarely crack.

"We should talk about this later. Something is going on. Mother was too quick to anger when she executed that vampire for the carriage attack," she whispers.

Xavier and I nod.

Octavia slides her chair back and I join her, grateful she didn't make too much of a cut in my trousers' crotch. I make a minor adjustment and walk with my legs close together up towards the stage.

We meet everyone on stage and stand in an awkward cluster of bodies. Cordelia guides Sadie to the front.

"Sadie," Cordelia says. "What did you try?"

"Blood. I took it from the Church of Blood," she signs.

"Gabriel? Keir?" the Chief asks, encouraging them to come forward.

"The most prized possession in the city, a book. The oldest one in our possession, it's said to have segments written by the Mother of Blood herself," Keir says.

"I see," Cordelia says. "And neither of you had any success?"

"The amulet refused to change size for us," Gabriel says.

"It spat the blood out," Sadie signs.

Cordelia grows increasingly irritated. Loose strands of her hair fluff out, making her seem harried and wild.

"Xavier, what about you?" the Chief says.

He shrugs, "I tried to give it the memory of my turning. I am the most beautiful vampire in the city. I thought for sure it would acknowledge me."

His words are a little slurred, like he's been drinking for hours. But he puts just enough snark and arrogance in his tone that Cordelia outright rolls her eyes at him.

"Fine. That leaves Red and Octavia. What did you two try?"

My mouth runs dry.

CHAPTER 12

OCTAVIA

There's a pause as Mother stares at me, waiting for me to confess. I glance at the ballroom and all the eyes on me, and I pray to the Mother of Blood that she buys the lie.

"We tried a shaving from a mansion: Castle St Clair, specifically," I say.

Mother's eyes narrow to pins, their prick hot and scratchy on my skin. "Why did you do that?"

I want to shout at her. How dare she question me? She didn't question the others.

"Because we believe that magic is the most beautiful element our city offers. Where does magic come from? And which castle is arguably the most powerful?"

"Castle St Clair." Mother presses her lips shut, but she gives me a nod of acceptance. Then a muscle in her jaw ticks.

She turns to the lectern.

"This displeases me. Someone is lying. Either one of my children or one of the hunters."

The Chief places her hand on Mother's wrist. "Or we have a winner in our midst that is not part of the trials."

Mother's eyes glance at where they touch, and I bristle. I scan both their faces but can't work out what's between them. By their expressions, it's hatred and yet there is a familiarity between them I cannot place. Are all enemies like this?

"Well," Mother says, pulling her hand away. "As of right now, I'm not sure which."

There's a murmuring in the crowd. Disquiet threatening to unfurl around the ballroom. The Chief folds her arms.

"What about the dhampir?" someone in the audience shouts.

"It's clear that the dhampir has awakened," the Chief says.

"And why's that?" Lady Netterley, one of Mother's pet nobles, says from the round table in front of the stage.

"Because..." The Chief starts and then unfolds her arms and takes the amulet from Mother. Their fingers brush as the Chief yanks the amulet away. That is far more like the enemy interaction I expect, and yet, something... something is going on that I cannot understand. I zero my focus in on the pair of them, watching every movement. My attention has been on Mother's movements since she executed that vampire right before the trial of beauty, but I'm still missing something.

The Chief holds the amulet up to a chandelier and twists it this way and that. She whispers a few words to the amulet and the crystal green liquid in the centre brightens to a pinpoint so sharp that I have to squint to stop it, making my eyes ache.

It shoots a beam of light upwards. Hovering in the eerie green shaft of light is the projection of a single bead of blood. I go still, suppressing the tremors threatening my body. I cannot let them discover us.

The Chief straightens and points at the shaft of light and projection of the blood drop. She whispers more words, and the blood expands, its composition appearing in the air before us.

"This is no vampire's blood. It is not hunter nor human, nor the blood of the dhampirs of old. No. I can only conclude that is a bead of blood from the new dhampir. Ladies, gentlemen, vampires, hunters and friends. We may not have identified who the dhampir is, but someone knows. I'd bet its someone in this room. Or perhaps the dhampir knows who they are and used the trial as a cover to get confirmation."

"Why don't we have magic back, then?" One of the Chief's hunters yells from a table at the back of the ballroom.

The Chief glances at Mother, who indicates she'll take this one. "The process of becoming a dhampir is more complicated than just awakening and discovering who they are."

She steps up to the lectern as if she's about to give an academy lecture. "The dhampir must embrace their power. They must transition into the powerful being they are destined to be. The Chief and I believe this will be a new breed, something different from the dhampirs from our history. This time they will be both healer and vampire."

Red pales.

"And if they don't transition?" someone in the crowd asks.

Cordelia slowly nods at the audience as if approving of the question. "First, they transition, then they unlock the door and cross the threshold. And when they return, so too will all of our magic. And if they don't, then... well, I can't say for sure..."

The Chief glances at her and nudges her with her elbow.

"Fine. If they don't fully transition, it's our suspicion that they'll die."

Red swallows hard beside me. I dig my fingers so hard into the palms of my hands I feel the skin splitting and resealing as I release the pressure. I can't afford to let Red smell my blood while we're on stage.

Lord Netterley stands up at the front table.

"Lord Netterley, something to say?" Mother says.

"When you say transition. You mean into a vampire?"

Mother shakes her head. "Half. The prophecy indicates that this new type of dhampir will be a true hybrid of vampire and witch: 'Blood of the night, a child of two worlds' embrace, A dhampir born, a dhampir turned. The heir to unlock this sacred space.' As they are currently human, they'll need to embrace their vampire side and allow themselves to turn."

Lord Netterley shifts on the spot, then a nasty sneer crosses his face. "Then I would like to offer my house as a host. To whomever you are, the most gracious dhampir. I offer you the blood and services of House Netterley. Let me open my arms and home to you. I am certain you'll need a noble vampire lineage, and as the first to offer, I do hope you'll see that it is my family that values you most."

The sneer reaches all the way to the ends of his impeccably groomed hair as he scans the ballroom, laying his eyes upon the other nobles in the room.

A hiss rips around the room as several vampires and several more hunters gasp. That was a bold move from Netterley. I glance at Red. This is quickly becoming a political minefield. There are protesters outside desperate for the cure not to be released. And yet in here, the vampires are welcoming the dhampir like family. A dhampir that is half hunter—the very thing they've hated for a millennium.

And it's now that I see Red's point. They are opening their arms not because they welcome the cure, but because they seek to control it, or more accurately, control her.

Lady Woodley stands next. "I too, offer my name, my blood, and my services. House Woodley would be honoured to have you as part of our family."

The hypocritical bitch. I swear that was who Dahlia said was supporting Mother's efforts to push back the hunter territory.

Noise erupts then. Offerings from a dozen different vampire families, until Mother bellows across the audience for everyone to be quiet.

It's only then I notice the only people to speak were vampires. Which is when a hunter I don't recognise stands. She's an elderly woman, but one in uniform and looking very much like she belongs on a political council. Perhaps a hunter elder, then?

"Yes?" the Chief says.

"Surely, if the dhampir is human currently—and a hunter, no less—then that makes them more hunter than vampire. In which case, I offer Hawk Battalion as their family. Vampires do not deserve the honour of claiming the dhampir. It is from hunter blood that the dhampir derives, and therefore, I am presuming they will reside in the Hunter Academy territory once they have fully transitioned."

Three vampires all sitting at the closest tables to the elder hunter stand up. Two of them snarling. The guards at the back of the room step forward. Two hunters and two vampires, the hunters have their hands on their stakes.

This will not end well.

Another greying hunter stands, again in uniform. She has several pips on her shoulder epaulettes, so I'm assuming she's someone fairly senior.

"I too offer Eagle Battalion."

"Fuck," the Chief mumbles.

Mother glances at her, and then raises her hands out to the ballroom. "ENOUGH. The dhampir is likely in this room, likely on this stage, and we do not need them to see the petty desires we harbour. This person is a free agent in this city. They do not have to align with any hunter or vampire house. And if they were to, I should imagine they would choose either the Chief or the St Clair family, given our highest-ranking statuses."

That doesn't go down well at all. I've heard enough. I glance at Xavier, who, while still inebriated, is skirting his gaze feverishly between all the shouting vampires and hunters in the room, trying to take stock of the political mood and how to make everyone friends again, I suspect.

"We need to get out of here," I say to Red and Xavier under my breath.

Mother tries to shout for silence, but there are now hunters and vampire nobles bellowing at each other across the room.

"Mother," I bark. She spins to face me. "I'm getting these guys out of here. This is dangerous."

She nods and says to all of us, "The next trial is the trial of spirit. Your instructions will come to you shortly."

She turns to the Chief, and they nod at each other and descend the stage to assuage the political discord.

I march out of the ballroom, my hand clamped around Red's wrist, Xavier trundling behind us.

"What are we doing? I want a drink," Xavier says.

"You need to sober up. Go get Amelia and meet us in the corridor. We're going to the carriage tunnels," I bark and grab his arm, too, yanking them both down the corridor. Red is sweating, her skin is clammy and greenish.

This isn't right, she's too hungry. Too needy for my blood. If the pace she's wanting to drink at continues to increase, I may not be able to satiate her, and that makes my insides burn like nothing else. But more than that, her hunger is far deeper than what's normal for an addiction.

Xavier returns with Amelia in tow, right as Red wobbles on her feet. Fucksake, we need to get blood in her fast, but not in Castle St Clair. Not where everyone can witness it.

"Xavier, get down to the carriage tunnel and get one ready for us. I'll carry her the rest of the way."

He speeds off in the direction of the tunnels. I bend my knees and sling Red over my shoulder.

"The fucth uuu doinnn," she mumbles into my shoulder and then proceeds to whack my back. "Lethhhh me donnn."

I ignore her and race after Xavier, albeit slightly slower. Amelia speeds along behind me.

Xavier, Amelia, Red and I climb into a carriage, and I pay the man double to get us there extra quick. He shoots us into the tunnels, driving the horses aggressively as he veers under the city as the afternoon dwindles and dusk approaches.

Red tries to stay awake but she ends up nodding like a rocking horse and eventually falls asleep on my shoulder.

Xavier, thank the Mother of Blood, sobers up. His brow furrows, and he glances at Red. "She doesn't look too hot."

"No," I shake my head.

"What's wrong with her?"

I grit my teeth. I wasn't going to remove the compulsion, but at this point I'm not sure who I trust? Perhaps no one? But how can I do this alone? I need a team around me, a confidante and unfortunately, Red is declining the closer she gets to transitioning. This is terrifying. I've never had to rely on anyone. I've never had people around me who liked me enough I could rely on them.

Xavier takes the decision away from me. "It's her, isn't it?" he says.

Amelia glances between Red and Xavier, her eyes widening. "No..."

Red rolls over, little snuffling snores emanating from her nose.

I sigh, "Look at me, Xavier."

He frowns but does as he's told. "Remember, Xavier St Clair. Remember what I took from you. Remember what you did, the sacrifice you made, but most of all, remember who she is."

He goes vampire still for a moment, his gaze glossing over, and then he shakes himself free of the remaining vestiges of the compulsion.

He glances at Red, then Amelia, and then at me. "We have a problem," he says.

"Yes. We do. It's going to become increasingly obvious it's her, and I'm not sure how to protect her from what's coming."

"It's more than that. Did you not just witness the political unrest at Mother's? It's not just the increasing protests from the public and the fact there's such division in the city. The vampires offering their houses will cause unrest between the nobles. It means that all the hunters, not only the ones in the trials, will be under increasing scrutiny. And the alliances between vampire families will be tested. Let alone hunter politics. What happened in the ballroom... it's concerning."

Amelia chews on her lip. "Wait. Wait. So, my sister is the...?

"Quiet," I snap a little too harshly. "But yes."

"Fuck," Amelia breathes.

"Quite," Xavier adds.

Amelia's eyes go distant. "Our mother used to have some residual magic. She could do little party tricks. I was always useless, but Red picked up some forging skills." She turns to Xavier. "You don't seem surprised. You already knew?"

"I did. I worked it out after she saved my life. Gave me some blood after Dahlia stabbed me with some kind of poisoned blade. If she hadn't let me drink her blood, I'd have died."

"Oh," Amelia says and then is quiet for a while before her head pops up. "The blood in the amulet..."

"Is Red's," I confirm.

"Gods," Amelia leans back on the carriage seating, her expression drawn.

"I tried to compel her memories away shortly after I realised. I compelled Xavier's, so that I was the only one who knew. It was a mistake. But aside from that, it didn't work, anyway. We..."

Amelia's eyes nearly bulge right out of her head.

"Mother of Blood, you bonded?"

"We did. She tried to leave Sangui and ran to her friends in New Imperium. Nearly killed herself stretching the bond like that. But I fear the bond has sped things up a little. She's grown increasingly thirsty."

"This is a lot to catch up on," Amelia says. "Do you not think we should tell her about—" Her throat tenses. Her words cut off, just as they should. At least the compulsion still works on her.

Xavier's eyes dart between Amelia and me.

"No. I do not think telling her anything else will help. What we need to do is to find the person who attacked Red on my grounds."

“Talulla was attacked too,” Xavier says.

“Don’t act like you’re concerned about a piece of ass.”

He shrugs. “Perhaps not, but you owe me two bottles of Sangui Cupa for bedding her before the first trial. Or did you forget our little bet?”

I had, in fact, forgotten that bet. But I always pay my debts. Debt is what got Xavier adopted in the first place.

He was orphaned young, and rather than being taken into the Sangui care system, he took to the streets, and we all know how those stories go. But Xavier had one thing to his advantage. He was beautiful. One of the club owners back then took him under his wing, put him on the door to attract the ladies into his club. Unfortunately for Xavier, ladies’ nights weren’t the only thing the club ran. He got addicted to the casino nights. It was the appeal of wealth, you see. In his eyes, it was everything he wasn’t. Everything he’d never had. He was good too, for a while, until he wasn’t. Isn’t that just the story of every gambler? One losing streak led to another, and then he was indebted to the club owners.

Luckily for him, Mother attended one night and saw his potential, so she bought his debt. He was twenty-one. She made him work it off the first four years, until, like Gabriel and Dahlia, she turned him against his will at twenty-five. The least harrowing of all our stories, I think.

“Well, I agree too,” Amelia says. “We could try to torture the information out of them...”

I cock my head at her. “Since when are you the dark one in the room?”

“It’s not a bad idea, though,” Xavier agrees.

I frown.

“You have a suspect?” Amelia asks. Red shifts and rolls over again, a bead of sweat on her brow.

“No. But I suspect Mother. I think she has something

else at play here. She was quick to kill the vampire responsible for the carriage attack. Yet he was adamant he didn't do the first set. There was no reason for him to lie. Which means it was someone else. Who has the most to gain from the cure not being retrieved?"

"Mother?" Xavier asks.

I shrug. "Maybe, maybe not. But I don't buy the retirement line at all. Though I have no evidence to support her being behind those attacks."

"Why would she be if she was the one organising the trials and wanting to open the door and get the cure in the first place?" Amelia says.

"Unless she's hiding in plain sight?" Xavier adds.

"Fine. I'm in. I'll help however you need. I'm thinking I should try the church and maybe the library? If you guys focus on the attacks, I'll focus on Red, see what I can dig up about her condition. Cordelia said she's a new style of dhampir, but there might be something in the old grimoires."

Xavier nods, "Good idea. And in the meantime, what are we going to do with her?" His eyes fall to Red, who is now in a fitful sleep.

"I'm going to leave a few vials of my blood with Amelia. Unfortunately, I think we're going to have to increase the amount of blood she's given."

"But you won't allow her to feed from another vampire? If you give up too much without feeding regularly, you'll weaken yourself. What happens if there's a physical trial of some sort? They've been far too intellectual to date. We can't afford you to be in a weakened state if that does happen."

"What else would you have me do? Not feed her?" I say a little too abruptly.

He leans back in the carriage seat, rubbing a thumb

along his chiselled jaw. He pulls his fingers through his hair and when he glances up at me again, I dislike what I see.

I press my lips together.

"You suspect it's going to get worse? That your blood is going to have a decreasing impact?"

I nod, and it makes Xavier's eyes widen.

"You've worked it out, too, haven't you? That's why you suggested leaving vials with me?" Amelia says.

"We can't afford for Red to be in a weakened state, either. What the hell is going on?" Xavier says, glancing at her restless body.

"It's just a theory at the moment. Perhaps you'll find something to back it up, Amelia."

"What's the theory?" she asks.

"It was something Mother said in the ballroom. That the dhampir will be a true hybrid and that they have to embrace their vampire side..." I say a little too loudly. My words hover in the air, thick with unsaid realisation.

"Oh, fuck," Amelia says and a second later, Xavier groans.

"She's not going to like it," he says.

"That much *is evident.*" This time I can't help the little snarl that rips from my chest.

Red wakes, sitting up and rubbing her eyes. "Where are we?" she says and coughs, struggling.

"Thirsty?" Xavier asks.

"Yeah, but... umm. I..."

"Come here," I say, saving her the embarrassment of having to answer. I hold out my arm, and she slides back into my embrace.

She seems smaller at this moment. More fragile and I hate it. The Red I know is strong, fierce, angry, but she's weakening without what she really needs.

Xavier clears his throat. "I know who you are... what you are."

"Me too," Amelia says.

Red's eyes snap up to him and then flick feverishly between all three of us.

"Xavier is going to help us," I say.

"And you trust him?" Red asks.

Xavier glares at me, but I discover, in this moment, that I truly do.

"He was willing to sacrifice his memories for you. I trust him with your life because he owes you his."

"If you're curious, I've actually known longer than anyone," he purrs.

"How?" Red says, her throat dry and crackling.

"Your blood. When you helped heal me in the amulet challenge, I took your blood and knew it was the most beautiful thing I'd ever experienced. If I weren't so injured and in such shock at the exquisite taste of your blood, I may have had a problem controlling myself. You are quite the delicate morsel."

"Xavier," I snarl. His eyes have gone dewy.

"Sorry," he says, breaking out of the memory. "I do apologise. That was impolite. I will, for the record, just reiterate that you have my word of secrecy. It might interest you to know I was the one who told Octavia about your blood. And as a result, you weren't the only one Octavia compelled. She's only just given me my memories back. My point is, you saved my life. I will help to save yours."

The carriage slows to a halt as we reach the underbelly of the Whisper Club. Xavier helps Red down and out of the carriage. She leans on his arm as he guides her through the club and up towards my office.

Erin waves at me .

"Could you send word to Rhea Nightfall that I'll be visiting?" I ask.

Rhea works in a border town between our city and the next. Gods, I hate that fucking city. It's run by seven fae mafia families. Awful place it is. No one has any morals, everyone's a fucking villain and none of them can see that their city is going to corrupt itself to death if they don't get a grip. But I suppose you can't save everyone.

Rhea, though, has good standing with all the families. She's a mediator of sorts. She also has ears everywhere in this city. So if anyone knows what's going on with the hunter attacks, it will be her.

Erin vanishes, and I return to my office. Amelia is sitting on a chair with one leg crossed over the other, her foot tapping as she sips from a blood bag she hasn't even bothered to pour into a glass. Xavier leans against the back wall, his expression stiff, like he's trying to calculate something unfathomable.

Red is scrunching her nose at the bag and turning a sickly shade of green.

Fuck me.

"One. Drink," I say to Red.

I slide my fingernail down my wrist and cut until the vein bursts and blood wells up. Red is lightening quick and sinks her increasingly sharp teeth into my wrist.

My pussy reacts immediately. This is not going to be helpful. I inhale, trying to force calm through my body. Forcing myself to think about hairy legs and decomposing corpses and anything disgusting so I don't think about how fucking wet I'm getting, how every pull of her mouth against my veins makes my breathing rougher, my clit pulse harder.

"Fuck!" I yank my arm away. "That has to be enough."

Red doesn't look even half satiated, but the colour has dropped back into her skin and the sweating has eased.

"You okay?" I ask.

She nods. "I may need to go to the er... well, somewhere private."

"I use a bedroom in the back when I can't be bothered to return home. You'll find what you need in there. But first we need to talk."

Red shifts in her seat, glaring at me hard. But I'm well aware of her need. I have the same one pulsing between my legs. She repositions her trousers and then nods at me to continue.

"Your hunger is increasing," I say.

Amelia stops drinking and scrunches up the blood bag, chucking it in the bin under my desk.

"What does that mean?" she says.

"Xavier, check the door, send Frank away, make sure Erin is at the end of the corridor, and tell her no one is to disturb us."

He speeds out the door and is back in ten seconds flat. Red is skittish. Her eyes drop to my wrist and then Amelia's blood bag in the bin.

Amelia catches Red's movement and fidgets. No one says anything.

"Alright, I've had enough. What aren't you telling me?" Red asks.

Amelia puts her head in her hands. "And feeding her more vampire blood won't help? How much have you given her? What if Xavier and I—"

"No. In terms of vampire blood, it's mine and only mine," I snap.

Red's eyes narrow to slits. "What do you mean in terms of vampire blood? What other blood is—"

She cuts herself off. Her gaze drops to the bin where

Amelia just threw the blood bag. She gets up suddenly, shoving the chair she was sitting on away.

"No. Absolutely fucking not. No way. Never," she says, pacing the office.

Xavier's nostrils flare as wide as his eyes. Amelia is wearing a grimace I'm not sure she'll ever remove it's so deeply engrained in her features. This is what we feared.

"Amelia, this is on you. You're going to have to convince her. Otherwise... well, I don't want to experience the consequences."

"We'll talk. And then I'll head off and do the research," Amelia says.

"We have a little time until the next trial. I'm taking Xavier to see a contact I know and hunt down the people attacking the hunters. And especially the vampire who attacked Red on Castle Beaumont grounds. We need to find out who he's working for. In the meantime, I am entrusting your sister to you. Her life is in your hands."

"I won't let you down."

"I am fucking here. And since she is MY baby sister, I'll be doing the looking after, thanks. I'm fine now I've had some of your blood. Save for the raging horn I'm currently experiencing. I'll come with you," Red says.

"Gross," Amelia cringes.

I don't care what Red thinks she needs; she needs to rest. "You're staying put, and you're going to talk to your sister. Xavier and I won't be long. This room. Those of us here now... I..."

I pause because what I have to say is so alien I'm not sure I've ever uttered words like it.

"I need you. I am placing my trust in you, and I... I don't think I can do this without you. And honestly, that is terrifying for me, and I don't know how to process it but... This is me asking you to please help me."

Red's mouth falls open, her face softens, and I swear I want to leap across the room and shred her clothes from her. But she's still furious with me, and I can't keep fucking her under tables for my own pleasure. She's right. We do have to sort things between us.

Amelia lowers herself to one knee. "I pledge myself to House Beaumont."

"Wow, Tave. You're really growing," Xavier says.

"Go fuck yourself, Xavier," I say, rolling my eyes.

But to my surprise, he also lowers himself to his knee, and it takes my breath away. He picks my hand up and kisses my knuckles.

"I love you, and we both know I'm not responsible enough to run this city. And honestly? I think you will make a fine leader. I pledge myself to House Beaumont."

I rub my throat, feeling… I'm not sure how to describe the swirling in my stomach. It's a new sensation. My eyes sting. I feel rather out of sorts.

Xavier continues. "I'll make you a deal. I'll bow out of the competition in all but name. Mother would slaughter me for actually giving up. But you can count on me as part of your team. I've no doubt Dahlia and Gabe are making a similar deal, anyway."

Red's mouth hangs lower, Amelia smiles from her position on the floor. I can't breathe. I'm not sure I've ever had anyone swear fealty like this. Certainly not an offer of unconditional support like this. It makes me believe for the first time that I can run this city. If I can get two people to pledge their allegiance, perhaps I can convince the city, too. My eyes sting. I think… if I'm not very much mistaken, that this might well be the first time I've ever truly felt… accepted. For me. As me.

But I also know Xavier. "Alright, but what will it cost

me?" I say, my voice barely above a whisper as I try to suppress the tremble.

"So crass, Tave. Straight for the balls, as always," Xavier says.

"Am I wrong?"

He sniffs. "No."

That, at least, reassures me a little that even though he's on his knee, I'm not having a complete mental breakdown. This is actually happening.

"The cost?"

"A position of power without too much responsibility. One I can come and go from. Publicly seen powerful; privately, I'll handle some of the finer negotiations for you. Consider me your right-hand man, and we'll call my life, loyalty, and love yours."

I meet Red's eyes from across the room, and even though the fury still bubbles under her skin, she's smiling at me, like she too is proud.

"You have your deal, Xavier St Clair."

He kisses my knuckles, sealing his pledge with a kiss, and I pull him up off the floor.

"Now. Come. We have business to attend to. Amelia. You know what you need to do."

Red's expression turns thunderous. But I don't have time to argue, and I am in no position to convince her that if she doesn't drink human blood, she's going to die, and all this will be for nothing.

For the first time in my life, I'm relying on someone else to do that, and it's fucking terrifying.

CHAPTER 13

You're all pathetic.

You think you're winning and getting closer to the dhampir.

But I know who actually put that drop of blood in the amulet.

There's so much betrayal in this ballroom and none of you can see it.

Backstabbing. Lies. There's a traitor right under your noses and you're too busy in-fighting to see.

Well, don't worry.

My time is coming, and when it does, you'll be too busy warring with each other to see what's been here all along. And that is when I'll end things for real.

CHAPTER 14

RED

Octavia rushes out of the office in a blur, Xavier speeding off after her. I've taken a step forward without even realising it.

Amelia appears suddenly, standing in front of me.

It takes me a second to realise her arm is against my chest. Slowly, I lower my eyes to her arm. It's an iron bar, wedged firm against my ribs. That, too, takes a second to process. I used to be the strong one, the responsible one. The one who did the looking after. What is this strange reversal?

I slide my eyes up to meet Amelia's. There's a flicker of hesitation where, I suspect, she remembers she's the younger. But it doesn't stop her. She remains a steel wall blocking my way.

"You're not going after her," she says.

There comes a strange moment in life with one's siblings. The same moment when you mentally separate from your parents and discover they are fallible mortals like you.

This is that moment with Amelia. I've spent years looking after her, caring for her and dutifully playing the role of mother to her. I made sacrifices to ensure she was cared for and had everything she needed. There's nothing I wouldn't do for her.

And even though this isn't a betrayal, it's a line in the sand that she's crossed. Amelia has proven that she'll go against my will. What I don't understand is when we grew apart.

The hierarchy in our family is shifting.

In this moment, she is stronger than me. I am weak; I am lost. I am shaking from the shock of her movement.

"I—" she starts, sensing that something between us has snapped. But she doesn't move her arm.

My body tightens, wanting to cry or slap her. Make her understand that she can't do this to me. She can't just grow up and leave me.

Fuck.

I back away from her arm. I slump down in the chair.

"I'm sorry," she says, but she can't bring herself to look at me.

"It wasn't because Oct—"

"Just stop," I say. "It's fine."

It's really not fine. But how can I tell her I feel more like her mother in this moment than her sister?

I decide that instead of holding back, if she really has grown up, I owe her this truth.

I lean forward, resting my elbows on my knees and my head in my hands. "I've looked after you for so long I forgot you were my sister and not my daughter, I guess. And yes, there's only a few years between us. But I..."

"You gave up your youth to let me keep mine," she says and slides to her knees, nestling her head between my arms and onto my knees. "You won't admit it, but it's because you blame yourself for what happened to Mum. It wasn't your fault. You were young, too."

Suddenly she's the little sister she always was. I stroke her hair, brushing the locks fallen loose from her blonde bun behind her ears.

"I didn't mean to treat you like a child. I realise we're both adults. But I put myself in that position because you had no one else, and I thought it was my responsibility to give you some semblance of a mother and then all this shit..."

"I love you, Red," she says. "Thank you... for everything you did for me."

I lean down and kiss the top of her head. "I'd give it all up again, over and over, if it meant you got to have a childhood."

"That's the thing. You don't need to keep giving things up anymore. I'm grown now. We both are. Neither of us are tweens living in Oriana's back room. We're fine. We're coping. We're okay."

She lifts her head off my knees and pulls my hands into hers.

"We should talk about..." her eyes go to Octavia's bin. The one holding an empty blood bag.

I yank my hands out of hers.

"What's the alternative?" she says, her voice pleading.

"There's always another way," I say.

"Red, please. Just do this for me."

"I... I can't," I say, tearing my gaze away from hers.

"Please? Don't you get it? If you don't drink it, you could die."

"Don't fucking do that. Don't guilt trip me. I won't do it. There's no way I'm drinking human blood, Amelia. I am not becoming the monster that took everything from us."

"Half the monster," she says. "And lest you forget, you fell for one of those monsters too."

I glare at her. "And where's the line? Did you lose all your morals when you became a vampire? Where's your humanity?"

"Then what about the cure? You want me to take it so badly, and yet you're resisting becoming the one thing that will secure it."

"Yeah," I huff, looking her up and down. "I can see we need the cure more than ever."

"Oh, go fuck yourself, Red. How dare you! I'm being pragmatic here. You want a chance to fix this city? Fix the wrongs that were done to us? Done to so many others? Then you have no choice but to drink the blood."

"THEN I'LL BE AS BAD AS THEM." I fling my arm out towards Octavia's office window. The curtains are closed, but the meaning is the same. Them in the club. The vampires. The ones in power.

"That may be so, but you'll have a pure heart and all the power in the world to fix it."

"Well, maybe that is the fucking problem. No one should have that much power."

"Say that when this city is safe, and no more humans die needlessly. Say that when we have a taxable blood system—I bet you haven't even let Octavia tell you about those plans, have you? Or the fact she wants to up the pay rates so that there's enough willing donors that no vampire ever starves, and no human ever dies. Isn't that worth becoming half the monster you fear so much? Isn't that worth holding the power so you can do something good with it?"

That floors me. I knew this meant a lot to Octavia, but I hadn't imagined she'd already thought it through so much.

That she had plans and ideas solidifying into place, real tangible ways of making her dream come true.

I glance up at Amelia. "What if I can't? What if I take that power and I'm no better than Cordelia? Than everyone who has ever come before?"

Amelia sniffs. "You're being a coward. What would Mum say?"

"Don't you dare use her name against me."

She shakes her head and then freezes. It's such a sudden movement. My skin prickles.

"What's wrong?" I ask.

Her head snaps to face the door. "Someone's injured in the club. A lot of blood. They're coming here."

The door is flung open, and Erin comes barrelling in, holding the body of a limp man. Blood is pouring out of him, splattering on the floor like juice.

I instantly feel sick and hungry and deeply fucking confused. Amelia's eyes widen as she takes in my expression. She wipes a hand over her mouth with a feverish swipe, and it takes me a second to figure out she's miming about me. I close my mouth, running my tongue along my teeth. Whoa, they're sharp. Way sharper than they should be.

Fuck. What is happening to me?

"Let me help," I say. "Amelia. Rags, sheets. Get some O negative blood from the stocks. He needs a transfusion. I need the first aid kit. Lay him there. Do we have a vampire medic in the club?" I say to Erin, pointing at the sofa.

"Not tonight. There normally is at least one vampire who will donate in case of emergencies, but the designated one on duty tonight had to leave."

Amelia is off and back before he's even on the sofa. I breathe through my mouth and not my nose. The last thing any of us need is for me to lose my head at the first scent of blood.

"Erin, get vodka, the purest you can get."

I shred his shirt and find the gash in his stomach. It's a stab wound. Amelia hands me the blood and a first aid kit as Erin returns with the vodka. I pour it over his stomach, and he shrieks. I hand the bottle to him, and he guzzles.

"Erin, knock him out."

"What?" the man shrieks. But Erin lands a brutal blow to his jaw and his head falls slack.

I slide my fingers inside his stomach and feel around. Lincoln and I had to take an advanced field medics course before we could get our officer ranks. I rack my mind trying to find the right knowledge. My fingers glide around his fat cells and deeper skin layers until I punch through into his abdomen.

I fumble for his organs. I'm not trained enough to be confident, but it doesn't seem like there's anything seriously cut.

My fingers grow warm. They tingle at the tips, and as I pull them out, the blood flow slows.

"What the fuck?"

"What's wrong?" Erin says.

"What?" I snap my head up. "Nothing. Nothing. Get me sheets and shred them. We need to pack his wound and apply pressure."

She darts off and grabs the sheets Amelia brought. She shreds them into sets of strips, and then Amelia speeds them over to me.

"What's wrong?" she whispers under her breath.

"I'll tell you in a minute." I apply pressure to his wound and focus on trying to get the blood flow stemmed. When I pull the first bloody rag off, I move my fingers over the wound. They tingle again. I pull them off his skin, confused, but when I look back down the wound is still bleeding, though it's no longer pouring blood out in long ribbons, it's more of a lazy ooze.

Amelia lets out a little gasp as I glance up at her. "Do it again," she breathes.

So I do. I run my fingers over his stomach and focus my thoughts on healthy, smooth skin. I picture a thin silvery scar and when I pull my fingers away, nothing else happens. The tingle doesn't return. And from all the expended effort, I am now ravenous.

"I can't," I whisper. "That's all I've got. There's nothing else."

"You did good, Red. Even if you don't have enough power yet to fully heal a person, you did amazing." She squeezes my shoulder and I lean into her arm.

But I buckle over, holding my stomach, cutting the celebration short.

The craving for blood is sapping the energy from my every cell. It claws at my insides. Knives stab my consciousness. I'm not sure if I want to be sick or sink my teeth into the same man I just saved. The wound is still a nasty gash, but there's only a trickle of blood left. Still, it takes everything in me not to lean down and lick the red thread off his stomach. I gag at the thought and stumble back. I can't get anywhere near him. My head is all over the place.

What kind of fucked up is this?

"Bandage him," I say. "Wrap them around his stomach. Pull tight. We need the pressure to seal the rest of the wound. I need... I need a minute."

I stagger to Octavia's worktable, pick up the vial of blood that she gave Amelia, and head to the bathroom at the back of the office. I close the door and flip open the vial, downing the entire thing.

I don't care if they wanted me to ration it and have a

drop or two every couple of hours. I need the entire thing right the fuck now before I do something I regret.

I let the vial clatter to the basin and lean over it, breathing heavy. When my head stops spinning, I stare at myself in the mirror. I'm not even sure I recognise who is looking back anymore. My face is pale. Paler than normal and my skin sallow, my cheeks gaunt. When did I prioritise blood over food? Aside from the awards ceremony, I can't remember the last time I ate a decent meal.

I run the tap and hesitate. Blood smothers my fingers and hands. I turn my fingers this way and that. It would be easy to taste it. Lick a drop off and see what it was like. But if I do that, it's a slippery road and I'm not sure I want to know where it leads.

I bring two fingers to my nose and sniff. It's rich, and potent enough my mouth fills with saliva. It's the most divine thing I've ever smelt. Like summer evenings and fires and s'mores. I open my mouth, my tongue skitters over my bottom lip, but I can't bring myself to do it.

I shove my hand under the tap, cursing myself internally for even hesitating. The fuck, Red. Of course, I'm not going to drink human blood. I'm a hunter. I'm better than this.

I do not have to be any fucking dhampir. I'm sure one of the other hunters can take the role. It doesn't have to be me.

I wash the blood off and decide to get in the shower. Octavia's blood is now in my system, and I need to appease the ache between my legs. I survived earlier, but I am not going to survive this. I'll be a puddle on the floor and completely useless.

I barely have to touch myself before I'm coming. But it's not enough, so I slip my hands between my legs and rub at a frenetic pace. I slide to the floor and use both hands, shoving two rough fingers inside and letting my other hand ravish my clit. My eyes close and I think of Octavia, imagine her sat on my face, grinding the pleasure out of me. I savour the sweet taste of her excitement and I come again with the thought of my tongue between her folds, my fingers inside her. When I'm spent, I climb out of the shower, dress, and I head back into the office.

But it's silent. The type of silent that's deafening.

"What?" I ask, my cheeks reddening as I wonder if they heard me masturbating in the shower.

The man sits up on the sofa; the colour has returned to his cheeks. Erin has removed the blood transfusion bag, and his stomach is bandaged and strapped up. He looks... basically fine.

"How the hell is he upright?" I say.

"He healed fast," Erin says.

Amelia is giving me the side eye because she knows exactly why he's better. Fuck. I wonder if that's why I needed more blood. Did he drain me of... of what? A millennium of lost dhampir magic? Well, good. Maybe I'll stop transitioning. Hopefully, I gave him everything and he can be the fucking dhampir.

I shake my head, pull my hand down over my face. I need to get a grip and confront the reality that what just happened means no matter how much I keep hoping, I've already started to transition, and I really don't want to think about the consequences of that.

"Erin, will you give us a moment?" Amelia says, her eyes darkening as I think she's come to the same conclusion I have, and this situation getting outside of this room isn't good for anyone.

Erin nods her assent and leaves. Amelia turns to the man.

Her voice drops an octave as she rounds on him. "What happened to you?" she purrs, her voice like liquid silk.

I have to shake myself to stay fully conscious. Damn Amelia, you have changed.

"Stabbed, glass bottle got smashed. It was an accident to be fair, but my blood got spilled on the dancefloor, and several vampires weren't expecting it and it sent them into a blood lust. It was bad until they got a grip of themselves and alerted Erin. That's how I ended up in here."

"And what do you remember of how you got fixed?" Amelia says.

His eyes glide across the room to me. "I... I don't know how you did it, miss. But it was definitely you. I was unconscious, but it was like a sheet of golden energy coming out from a point near my belly. It was glistening and warm and like... I don't know. What I imagine heaven to be, I guess."

"I see," Amelia says.

She glances over her shoulder at me, and I nod my head.

I am a hypocrite. I can't believe I am furious with Octavia and yet, I'm agreeing to let Amelia compel him. But what choice do I have? If she doesn't, then he's going to know or at least work out who I am fairly quickly, and then word will get out. Until this whole situation is under control and the door is open, I can't let anyone know who I...

I can't bring myself to say the words. It doesn't have to be me. I don't want the power. Someone else needs to take it.

Amelia takes a step towards him. He hesitates, his eyebrows cinch together. "What's going on?"

"Red? Tell me to do it..." Amelia starts.

"Do it." I exhale, and a coil of bitter sickness climbs up my throat. Is it possible to hate yourself more than I do right now? I slump into a chair, wondering how I got this far from my moral compass.

Amelia stares into his eyes. "Forget what happened here

tonight. Forget that you were stabbed. You fell onto something sharp on your way home, and the club doorman helped patch you up. You never saw me or Red. In fact, you don't even know who we are."

His eyes go hazy, distant and glazed, and then he snaps out of it.

"I need to go home," he mutters, getting up off the sofa and walking out of the office.

I sag against the chair, and Amelia turns to me.

"You see now? You see what you could be capable of? How many people you could save? All you need to do is drink the fucking blood."

CHAPTER 15

OCTAVIA

Xavier and I stand in the club's rear exit doorway waiting. Both of us nestle in the shadows of the porch.

One breath. Two.

"Good evening, Lady Beaumont," Broodmire says.

"Good evening. If anyone asks whether you saw us, you didn't. You've no idea where we've gone. Can you do that for us?" I ask.

He inclines his head, so I tickle his chin until his mouth opens and deposit three drops of blood as a thank you.

"Most generous," he says and settles himself down for a nap.

"Do you know where we're going?" Xavier says.

I nod. "Edge of the city there's a safe house. It's a neutral point between this city and the fae's. Rhea uses this house in the middle of the forest as a mediation point. Rhea works there most of the time, but even if she's not in, someone will be. It's manned twenty-four seven and they'll be able to reach her."

"In that case, after you, favourite."

I glance at my watch. The sun should be setting in thirty seconds. I hesitate and risk leaning out past the porch. The sun is low enough that the last dregs of hot light are dipping below the horizon, and I don't get anything more than a mild hiss.

"Ready?" I say.

"Born ready, Tave," Xavier says, and he leans forward, placing one foot in front of the other.

I glance back out, no hiss, no burn. But Xavier is younger than I am, so I wait another minute to be sure. The sky is a glossy mirage of oranges, burnt reds and ochre colours. They're shifting like molten lava into pinks and purples. It's the kind of sunset promises are made under and...

"In three," I say.

Xavier stiffens like he's going to race me.

"Two." This time, I bend into a racing start position.

Ahh, sibling rivalry. Adrenaline flutters in my belly. The kind of hot dancing breeze that races across skin and burrows into my bones. The kind of high that tells me he wants to play.

He tilts his head to look at me. "Last one to City Edge Point buys the drinks tonight." He grins, showing his fangs, and I am so ready to show the little twerp what an extra five hundred years looks like.

"One," he says. And then he bolts like lightning.

"Mother fucker," I shriek. But I'm already sprinting to catch him.

I don't lose.

I haven't run like this in years. Maybe a decade. The wind whips my hair so hard it leaves little sting marks on my back and spine like needles.

Harder and harder I push my legs. We have miles to run.

Though it's easy enough for us when we have the ability to move so fast, we eat up three miles before I even catch up to him.

But I do... Catch up to him, that is.

And then I kick his leg out from under him and he barks a laugh as he rolls headfirst over and onto a grassy park area.

But I don't have time to get much of a lead. He's up and on his feet with his longer legs giving him the advantage that no amount of years or power give me.

It's an even race, but I am faster.

Just.

We reach City Edge Point neck and neck. I lean forward, pumping my arms harder, faster. We're both stretching forward, our fingers straining for the lamppost. But I manage to brush the skin of the lamppost a millisecond before he does.

"Fuck," he says, careening to the ground and rolling to slow himself down. It takes me a second to stop running too.

"Well played, Octavia," he pants, bending over forward and retching.

I join him and leave a little bit of sick on the pavement.

He slaps me on the back. "We need to do less shagging and more cardio."

I laugh hard enough I'm sick again. I wholeheartedly agree with him. "Except we won't," I say.

"Not a fucking chance. Right. Beers on me tonight. Where are we going from here?"

We meander down several narrow alleyways. The city shifts in appearance this far out of the centre. While our city has a distinct border, the next city has spread out. It's a sprawling area with seven distinct regions. One for each of the ruling families. Because of the sprawl, there are scattered villages and towns that aren't quite in their jurisdiction but not really in ours either. The villagers live a little like us and a little like them.

No one pays them much attention, and they don't really bother or cause trouble for us. But these villages and towns make for excellent neutral ground.

We pass out of Sangui City's border and into a forest area heading for a specific village. Finding Rhea takes longer than I'd like because I can't remember the exact road the cottage is on. I have to edge my way through the forest, trying to recognise buildings and the landscape. At this point, running would get us lost.

Eventually I find it; a little cottage nestled in a set of about ten other houses, three of which are set above the ground. We're stood outside when my back prickles.

I scan the trees looking for someone, and I find nothing. But the scents of cinnamon, mint, and smoke drift on the air.

"Octavia Beaumont, as I live and breathe. What's it been? Four? Five years?"

"Rhea Nightfall," I say grinning. "Son of a bitch, where are you?"

She drops down from a tree less than fifteen feet from us; she was utterly cloaked in the shadows of the night, and I'd missed her.

I never miss a threat, and she really is a threat. Gods dammit. She's getting good.

"What can I do for you?" she says and takes a puff of her cigarillo. She blows several rings of smoke and then taps the cigarette out on the tree trunk.

"I need your help."

She tilts her head. "Help is expensive."

I smile. "I expected nothing less."

"Then come, friend. Let us have a drink and discuss what help you need."

Xavier and I enter the cottage, and she guides us to her office. Rhea is as tall as me, though her body is far more toned. I have to remind myself not to stare at her ears and the strange point they have at the tip. They poke out from her shorn hair. Most of the fae I've encountered have long hair, but Rhea never was one to follow the rules.

She leads us into her office and Xavier whistles.

"Gods. There must be a hundred ways to murder a man in here."

Rhea laughs as she takes a seat behind her desk and kicks her legs up on it. She pulls an ashtray back towards her and opens a fresh packet of cigarillos. She knocks the bottom of the packet and yanks one out, shoving it in on the edge of her lips.

She lights up and then pulls in a deep drag. "Three hundred and eighty-six weapons. Seven hundred different poisons, sixty-nine different types of bullets and I dare say more than a few things I can't confess to owning. Doesn't matter whether you're a fucking vampire, fae, magician, demon, shifter or any other fucking species. If you're living and breathing, I got a way to kill you in this office."

"And you're friends with this woman?" Xavier says, his eyes startled.

Rhea huffs a laugh and takes another drag on her cigarillo. "Being friends with me is better than the alternative... no?"

I glance around the room. Each wall is filled floor to ceiling with shelves and display cabinets. Each of them rammed with equipment, weapons, arrays of jars and vials and herbs and gods know what.

She leans back in her chair and gestures for us to sit in

the seats on the other side of the table. "By all means, make yourself at home."

Xavier glances at me, giving me a look of, *are you sure about this?* I wave him off. I'm absolutely sure.

"Sit down, boy," Rhea says.

He does, rather promptly, and it makes me laugh, which I turn into a snuffled cough when Xavier glares at me.

"Now, what can I do for you, Octavia?"

"We're looking for information."

"Information is expensive," she replies.

"Everything with you is expensive."

She smiles at me; her face is more lined than the last time I saw her. Her hair a little greyer. She must have aged fifteen years in the five it's been since we last met. But fae don't age like humans. Their long lifespans often rival vampires—we get killed before they die of old age. I still remember her when she first came to the safe house three hundred years ago. Rhea was never allowed in the field. She was born with bones that didn't form properly in one of her feet, which meant she couldn't run fast enough to pass the fitness tests. You can't be in the army or an assassin if you can't escape. So, she became a trainer instead—the most brutal and respected of them all, no less. And I dare say an equally accomplished assassin in her own ways. I've watched her career progress with pride over the years. Besides, I've known her to take enough lives that I would rather stay friends.

Especially because she's less of a guns-and-arrows killer, and more of an up close and personal one. The kind that would shove a knife in your femoral artery and vanish before you even knew she was there.

Hence the collection of weapons. She reasoned that if she couldn't get away, she'd perfect taking the life instead.

That's why she's always been good for off-books jobs.

No one actually knows how accomplished she is because she's not a registered part of the fae army.

The office door creeps open and a woman in her mid-thirties sticks her head around the door.

"Hey boss, where's that report? The new client that needs... oh," she stops herself.

"Evening, Orion. File is in the cabinet in the end office. This is Octavia, one of the original three vampires. I dare say you'll have dealings with her eventually."

"Octavia," the fae woman says, inclining her head. "I'm Orion Isles." Orion's hair reminds me of Sadie's, white as snow, but her eyes are breathtaking. They're the colour of autumn leaves, auburn and chestnut and a hint of orange.

"Nice to meet you, Orion. This is Xavier, my brother."

"I'll leave you to it," Orion says and walks out of the office.

"She's like no one you'll ever meet. The most incredible killer. Now. Tell me, how can I help?"

"Information on a series of attacks that are targeting hunters in the city. You know anything about that?" Xavier says.

Her fingers trail over a brown file on her desk. "No," she says as her eyes snap up to meet mine.

Xavier leans forward ready to have a go at her, but I put my hand on his leg.

Rhea always says no to every job. You might think that counterintuitive, seeing as she needs jobs to pay the bills.

But it's a test. I've seen her do this to a couple of clients that have come in while I was visiting.

She likes to assess how much her clients really want murder on their conscience. I don't need murder today. But I guess the habit is ingrained.

Her fingers pull open the file and push a piece of paper

towards us. "Well, maybe I do, as it happens. It's your lucky day."

Xavier leans forward and takes the paper. But she pulls it back.

"Payment first," she says closing the file again.

"What do you want?" I ask.

"At the moment, nothing. Let's call it a favour at some point in the future."

"I dislike having debts around my neck, Rhea."

She presses her lips together. "Unfortunately for you, you're the one asking, and I do have the information you need. So, agree or get out."

"Fine. But I know what you fae are like. For clarity, I agree to a favour of equal magnitude and not an ounce more."

Her expression narrows, but she smiles. "I always liked you, Beaumont."

We shake hands, and she gives the piece of paper back to Xavier.

"A gang?" he says, scepticism leaching through his words.

"Of vampires. Yes. Ones for hire who are good at keeping their mouths shut. You're not the only one sniffing around for information."

"What's that supposed to mean?" I ask.

She shrugs. "One favour, one piece of information. You'll find the gang in the west of the city, not far from here, as it happens."

"Thank you," Xavier says.

"Good seeing you, Rhea," I say.

She stubs her cigarette out and flicks open the lid tapping the base for another.

"Those things will kill you," I say.

She huffs out a raspy laugh. "With the business I'm in,

there's always someone trying to kill me."

Turns out, this particular gang of vampires is rather dense when off duty. There's a group of six vampires built like castles sat around a metal fire barrel spit-roasting a keg of blood.

"Gods, could you be any more uncouth," Xavier says.

"Could they be any more obvious?" I shake my head. "There is six of them, though."

"Oh darling, you'll be fine, you're a savage when you want to be."

I crack my neck, let my fangs drop, "Hold my jacket."

My plan is to drop two of them before they figure out what's going on. If I can do that, I shouldn't have too much trouble taking on the rest. They might look like athletic enthusiasts, but they're young—which means they'll be weak and probably reckless.

I sprint across the field, hand out, nails sharp and ready to slice. I draw my hand across the first vampire's neck, slashing his throat and use the momentum to grip and rip. His head pings off, and unfortunately for me, drops straight into the barrel, causing the fire to spray sparks everywhere.

The three vampires the other side of the barrel spring up. But I'm already on the back of the second, my nails sunk into the underside of his chin, which I clench and rip, tearing his jaw clean off.

He collapses to the floor; I leap off his back and land with my foot in what's left of his face. Stamping down, I squish my foot into the ground, squelching through what's left of his neck. Then I reach down, punch my fist through his rib cage and pull his heart out. A sweet smile forming on my lips as I chuck the heart on the fire and use my other leg to kick the severed body away, makes the other vampires take one look at me and scarper.

The vampire still sat down is the one I have my eyes set on. The one who, given his stature and the brief flash of his eyes I remember from that night, is the one I want.

He stands, his eyes widen and then my luck runs out because he too runs.

It takes another ten minutes of chasing this motherfucker through the park to hunt him down. I'm quietly cussing Xavier for the race earlier this evening because my energy is spent.

Thankfully, the lazy arsehole decides to get off his pretty little backside and help.

The vampire tears across the field towards a copse of trees. I catch the flash of Xavier's movement right as the vampire cocks his head over his shoulder to glance at me.

As he breaches the woody area, he goes flying and careens headfirst into a thick tree. I skid to a halt and pick up his bleeding carcass.

I drag his leaden body by the scruff of his shirt towards Xavier. The shirt rips, the seams splitting under the pressure of his body weight. That's when I see Xavier found something that looks like old, discarded rope and tied it between two trees.

"Are you going to help or are you going to stand there watching?" I snap.

"I thought I was the pretty face? I helped." He gestures at the rope the vampire tripped over. "You have vampire. What's the problem?" He examines his nails all the while leaning against a tree, and my blood boils.

"Xavier," I bark.

"What? Come on, you didn't expect me to actually do any real work did you?"

"I swear on the Mother of Blood if you don't get the fuck over here and help me sprint this body across the city, I will tell Mother who actually b—"

"—Fine," he sighs, dramatic and exaggerated, then flicks his hair back as if this is a great endeavour. He sidles over to me and then turns his nose up at the unconscious vampire.

"It smells."

"Yes, well, he was drunk, and then he got a serious head injury. What do you expect?"

"Here's the drug Rhea gave you." Xavier hands me a heavy-duty needle.

I stick it in the vampire's neck.

Xavier's nose wrinkles. "He's probably going to piss his pants or defecate. There was enough drug in that dose to sink an elephant. Now. Come the fuck on, Xavier, before we end up ashing ourselves because dawn breaks?"

He picks up the man's arm and a leg while I pick up the other arm and leg, and then we run. We're slower than we were at dusk, but nonetheless, we make it to the Whisper Club in good time, and we only have to change paths twice to avoid being seen, thank the Mother of Blood.

The club seems to behave itself and know that we need shelter because the door appears the minute we step into the Midnight Market. I shove the door open, placing my finger on Broodmire's spike.

"Should I ask?" he says.

"No, get Erin." His eyes roll shut and however he sends messages, it gets across because Erin appears, panting, a few moments later.

She's covered in blood.

"What the fuck?"

"There was an incident earlier. But it's all sorted."

"Fine. Clear the dungeon. Make sure no one is in there and that the back corridor is clear too. We need to interrogate him."

She sprints off, her booted feet clapping against the tiles. She's back just as the vampire we're carrying starts to stir.

"All clear, I left a chair and silver chains. I can tie him if you want, or I put gloves in there too for you," Erin says.

"You've done more than enough. Thank you, Erin, we will take it from here," Xavier says.

We race past her and drop the vampire into the seat. I put on the gloves and chain him to the chair. This son of a bitch isn't going anywhere.

The club's dungeon is gloomy but not like Mother's castle dungeons, which are all cold stone cobbles, iron bars and damp puddles. This is mostly a clean space. Grey walls, and plain, empty rooms. No clocks, no windows, and a muted light that is continuous no matter the time of day.

Xavier picks up a piece of plastic from the back of the room and prods the vampire's cheek.

"Oi," the vampire says, biting and tearing at the plastic, only to realise he's tied up. "What the fuck?" he hisses. And then the panic sets in.

He tries leaping up and down and writhing his body around, but the chair is bolted to the floor, and he is chained to the chair. This motherfucker is going nowhere.

Erin knocks on the door and hands Xavier and I a goblet of blood each.

"Ooh, my favourite," Xavier says.

"Essence of hope and essence of despair. Gods, Erin, you're more twisted than I thought. You're going to make a wonderful vampire."

The chained vampire growls as the scent of blood drifts into the air.

I thank her and place the goblets just out of his reach.

“Only good boys get blood,” I say.

“Bad boys get bloody,” Xavier continues and swings his fist at the vampire’s face, landing a savage blow that makes his head recoil backwards and a splatter of blood spray onto both Xavier and the floor.

“Annnnd I’m done. Do you know how expensive this shirt is?”

I roll my eyes at Xavier.

The vampire groans as his head lolls forward, his eyes drooping in their sockets.

“My, my, Xavier, have you been in the gym? I don’t think I’ve ever seen you land a blow like that.”

He shrugs. “Have to keep this body in exquisite shape somehow.”

“What the fuck do you want?” the captive vampire says.

“Your name, first,” Xavier answers.

It’s a tactic of course. Rhea already told us his name is Drax Clayborne, but he doesn’t know that. We need him to acquiesce, so he understands who is in charge here and that fighting is futile.

“Fuck you,” Drax says.

I laugh.

“Okay, fine,” Xavier says. “One more won’t hurt.” He lands another vicious punch to Drax’s jaw. This time, he’s knocked out for a solid minute before he rouses back to consciousness.

I pick up the goblet of hope Erin gave us, and I hold it just in front of Drax’s nose. Close enough to smell the sumptuous liquid, but an inch too far to actually drink it and heal himself.

“Name,” I say.

He growls under his chest. "Drax Clayborne."

"Good," I say and edge the cup to his lip so he can take a sip of blood. "That wasn't so hard, was it? Now. Who are you working for?" I say and withdraw the cup after only a single sip. His tongue skitters over his lips trying to mop up every morsel of blood. The split in his lip mats back together.

He stays silent. I tut at him, "Come now, Drax, do you really want to make this harder than it needs to be?"

I slide my finger over his healed lip and down underneath his chin, resting it against a pulpy bit of flesh.

"I'd answer her if I were you," Xavier says, leaning against the back wall.

"I work for... none of your fucking business," he says.

I snarl and then I punch my finger through the pulp of his chin and up into his mouth. He screams and screams, and I ignore it as his blood spills down my finger.

I yank him forward by his chin and lean into his face.

"Now you listen to me, you spineless sack of shit. You are going to tell me exactly what I want to know, or I am going to make this..." I wiggle my finger around the flesh and muscle of his mouth making him scream all over again, "look like child's play. I know a lot of fun ways to make you bleed, cry and beg for desiccation. But I'd rather not get blood all over this outfit. Play nice, and I'll give you the rest of this blood so you can heal, hmm?"

He nods, gently, wincing the entire time.

There's a rustling at the door and Amelia's face appears.

"Evening, boss," she says, her eyes bright.

"I'm busy," I say without breaking eye contact with the piece of shit in front of me.

"I can see that, but I think I am going to head to the library," she says.

That gets my attention. "Good."

She lingers in the door, shifting from foot to foot.

"What is it, Amelia?" Xavier sings.

"Things seems to have... er... progressed."

"Progressed how?" I say never removing my eyes from Drax's.

"There are talents developing."

Xavier kicks off the wall, as interested as I am.

Amelia continues. "I think we need to find out as much about the umm... condition as possible. We need to know how..." she pauses and glances at Xavier and then the vampire in the chair. "Things will develop."

I pull out of the vampire's chin and suck the remnants of his blood off my finger.

"Good thinking. Take Xavier. He can be helpful when he wants to be. Bring Red down here before you go. I think she earned the right to have a little fun."

Amelia raises her eyebrow but vanishes to a serenade of the vampire's screams: sharp and hollow, sweet and deep.

I close my eyes and listen to the rattling of the chair, the trickle of his piss hitting the floor and the shrieking pleas of each and every beg.

Delicious.

CHAPTER 16

CORDELIA

One Thousand Years Ago

The closer I get to finding my Eleanor, the further she feels from me, and the less hope I hold. I swear on the witch-gods that time rather misbehaves itself. Elongating and stretching into an ever more expansive test.

I find myself screaming into the air, at whoever will listen. I want to crawl out of my skin. I want to burn the heavens down for taking her from me.

One moment I am cantering across a field, and the next I am sobbing into Teddy's neck, pleading with him to keep her alive.

It is a form of torture I've never experienced, the not knowing. It is a sadistic thing, allowing my imagination to hope and pray one minute, concocting elaborate escapes for her from the cottage. The next, the burning roof and building flashes in my mind's eye, knowing there was no chance she got out.

But still. I cannot give up. I shan't. Not until I see her body or have her lips on mine again.

After what has seemed like three legions and a lifetime, I enter the village the man told me about. It's different from the heart of the city. Far greener and lush with fields, garden plots, shrubs and planters. There are cottages and bungalows everywhere I cast an eye, but each of them wears a shroud of green like a coat and scarf.

I slow Teddy down to a walk and hop down, deciding to walk him through the village as the houses are all so close together that the path between them is more like a city alley. Bungalow doors sit opposite each other, nestled safe under their porches which hang with leafy greens, colourful flowers and swollen fruit. Some of the doors are perched above a set of three steps, each one smothered in potted plants and urns. The path is twisty, I keep expecting it to widen out into a large open square like it would in the city, but it doesn't, it just keeps twisting and bending around more cottages. Occasionally, there's a split off and the cottages continue to fan out down one of these narrow tracks, but all huddled close together.

There are no road signs, no street labels to tell me where I am. My chest tightens, the well of tears rising to meet my lids. I wobble on my feet, leaning against Teddy, wishing he could tell me to keep going, wishing he could find me some food or anything to keep me journeying.

I desperately don't want to stop, but I have no idea where I am, no idea where Eleanor could be. I am at my wits end.

I slacken the reins and slump onto the step of the nearest cottage and put my head in my hands.

"Come on, Cordelia, you've come this far, you can't quit now. Eleanor wouldn't quit. She would go to the ends of the earth for you. Now you need to do the same."

The door behind me creaks open, and I startle, leaping out of the way of the hunched-over old lady.

"Sorry dear, didn't mean to disturb you," she says, smiling at me with a set of extremely white teeth that don't seem to match her wisened appearance.

"No, I apologise, it was most rude of me to sit here uninvited."

"You're perfectly okay, my love. Steps are for stepping on and sitting on, I don't see that you're doing any harm at all. I say, you look a little worse for wear."

Her watery blue eyes wash over my appearance. It's only now that I glance down and examine myself, I see that she's correct.

Oh dear. I stand up and examine my reflection in her window.

My dress is filthy, dirt smudges and stains cover my skirts. A burn hole mars the top layer, and several rips perforate the skirts. There's even one section where the fabric hangs on by a thread.

My arms and skin are just as vile. Black grime is caked under my fingernails and several are chipped, broken or ragged. My hair has more or less fully escaped from its bun, there's only one clip left holding strands on the left side. A layer of muck coats my face, which makes my skin appear darker than usual. The only evidence that I am pale complexioned are the shadowy streaks left behind by long-dried tears.

I look like I've been abducted and dropped into horse manure. I probably smell the same, given the amount of time I've spent with Teddy.

"Oh my, would you like to come and get cleaned up, dear? I can make you some food and a cup of tea with herbs, it will have you feeling proper in no time."

"That's kind of you, but no. I wonder whether I might trouble you for some information though?"

"Of course," she says, hesitating the slightest bit as she looks at me, as though she can't imagine why I would want to continue to look the way I do.

"How can I help?"

"I'm looking for a woman... well, maybe a body, I'm not really sure. But she would have been bought here a few days ago, burned, maybe. But definitely injured. She would have been taken to specialists, I guess. Do you have healers in this village? Perhaps some that know how to treat burn victims?"

"Oh yes, dear. We have plenty of healers here. This is the healer village, all here practice or are training. Each cottage houses a different specialist."

I instantly brighten. "Truly? Could you take me to the burns specialist please?"

She nods as a fluffy white cat appears between her legs. "Naughty Herbert, get back inside. You know you're not allowed out here." She shoos him inside and then hovers in the doorway, picking up a key and a bag that looks like it's for collecting plants.

"I'm off to the forest to collect supplies, but I'll point you in the direction." She grabs some cutters and then locks up.

She leads me down several winding paths, all of which look identical. All of them cobbled, with as many plants and twisting green vines coating the cottage fronts as every other street. The only difference between any of them are the brightly painted windows and ledges. Each house is adorned with a colour so bright it practically glows. It makes them look like toy houses in a child's playroom.

"May I ask, why each house has a different colour? In

the city, we tend to have areas where everyone's buildings either match or blend in."

She nods, sage and knowing. Her back is so hunched I'm not sure how she can see which direction she's going in, but perhaps her feet have memory and guide her the same way they have for years.

"The colours represent the family's magic and specialism. There," she points as we reach a T-junction. Down the left, the houses abruptly stop about thirty metres in, and the forest begins. To the right, the houses wind in the same way they have done along all the other paths we've trodden.

"The orange house at the end. If you find yourself bending around the corner you've gone too far."

"Thank you so much," I say. "How can I ever repay you?"

She smiles, "I used to be in love the way you are now. My wife died a long time ago now, your smile and knowing I helped you find her is enough."

She gives me a toothy grin, and then she's shuffling left towards the forest. I call out after her to say thank you, but she waves me off and much as I feel impolite, I cannot wait any longer. It has taken all of my strength to make it this far, and I need to face the truth. I need to find out whether Eleanor is still alive.

By the time I have Teddy tied up to the stone wall outside the cottage, I already have more tears streaking my cheeks.

What if she is dead? What if I've come all this way and it's too late? My hand shakes as I raise my fist to the door knocker.

It's a strange little thing in the shape of a creature, a gargoyle, I guess. I rather like it; I wonder whether I could have one in the city. I go to pick up the ring hanging from its mouth when it opens its eyes and I shriek.

I stumble back off the step and nearly roll my ankle.

"What on earth?" I say as I pick myself up.

"Whath your problem? No coming in unleth you pay," the strange door monster says.

"What... what are you?" I say, brushing my dress down and scrambling back up the steps.

"I have no money to give," I shrug, trying to look apologetic. It's not quite the truth, but I need to save the coin I have for room and board.

"I donth wanth no money."

"Then what will you ask of me?"

"A fingle drop of blood." He opens his mouth and sticks out his tongue. There's a little spike on the end of it.

A drop of blood doesn't seem like much to offer if Eleanor is inside. Besides, I know that she uses blood in her magic anyway. This is probably their currency.

"Sure," I reach out and press my finger on his tongue. His hackles bristle, I swear a wash of colour flutters over his cheeks, and then when he's satisfied the door opens.

As I step inside, I gasp and glance back at the cottage opposite, which is of a similar size.

The inside of this cottage does not match the outside at all. It's an enormous sweeping corridor that stretches further than I can see. There are dozens of people milling about, most of them in uniform. There are people being wheeled around on stretchers and in chairs on wheels.

"May I help you, miss?" a man, behind what I assume is a reception desk, says.

"Umm. I'm looking for a woman who would have been brought here a couple of days ago. She was badly burned. Her name is Eleanor."

"Eleanor? Hmm." He scratches his beard; it's neatly trimmed and a little orange like the windows outside.

"I ain't got no Eleanor, but I got a Jane Doe."

"Jane Doe? Her name is Eleanor," I reiterate, urging him to check his records again.

"Aye, but Jane Doe means we don't know her name. Either dead on arrival with no identification or unconscious with no identification."

My stomach rolls hearing that. Bile claws at the back of my throat, my stomach threatening to expel itself. I swallow hard.

"May I check if it's her?"

"We don't normally let visitors in without proper identifications or being family members."

"Please?" I say, and I cannot prevent the desperation from spilling from my lips. I get on my knees, clasp my hands together. "Please sir, I will do anything. I possess coin. I can give it to you. Anything so long as I can check it's her?"

He presses his lips together, thinning them. "Just this once. Follow the corridor down there, third turn on the left. Second door. Any trouble, tell them I sent you."

I glance at his name badge, committing his name and the instructions to memory.

This is it. This is the moment I get to see her.

I run, not walk my way towards her door, leaping out of the way of uniformed staff and those assisting patients.

When I reach the room, there's a healer woman standing outside. She wears an orange apron and carries a basket of herbs and jars.

I stand there gawping at the basket. Two words scream through my head.

If she's carrying healing supplies in, then, then...

“She’s alive,” I whisper, mimicking the words pounding in my brain. I collapse to the floor.

“She’s alive?” I say again and grab the legs of the healer. I sob into her legs. If she startles, then she doesn’t show it. She politely pops the basket down on the table outside the room and disentangles herself from me.

“Beg your pardon, miss, but I need me legs back. Is everything okay?” she says, patting my hand.

“I do apologise... it’s...,” I wipe my face, my breathing hiccuping back to normal. “The woman in there, is she... she’s alive, right?”

Her face lines, deep grooves carving into the curve of her eyes. As she pulls me up, I discern she’s older than I thought. But the expression she’s wearing does nothing to reassure my waning confidence.

“She’s... she’s alive, though? Your...” I scratch my head trying to remember the name. “Jane Doe?”

“I think it’s best I show you.”

She pushes open the door and my world crashes down.

There, under a sheet of white fabric, lies a motionless body. I rush to her side. Her brown locks are flat and lank, so unlike the shiny, tousled waves I love.

I scan down her body, rest my eyes on her chest.

And that is when the tears begin.

Her chest rises and falls. Slow and steady and deep. But it does move.

She’s alive.

“Here, miss,” the healer says and hands me a rag.

“Her name... it’s Eleanor Randall.”

“Thank you, now we can contact her family, I’ll bet they’re proper concerned that she’s missing.”

I’m so caught up in finally finding Eleanor that her words don’t hit me until she’s already by the door.

“Wait. Please.”

The healer stops and grabs the basket she popped on the table outside. "Don't worry miss, I need to apply her herbs and pastes, I'm here for a bit."

She brings the basket back in and pulls two stools to the side of her bed. "Do you want to help me?"

"I'm sorry, I didn't catch your name?"

"It's Trudy, miss."

"Well, Trudy, are you sure I won't hurt her?"

"No, miss. She's in a deep sleep, you see."

I swallow hard. "What kind of deep sleep? Will she wake up?"

The healer's eyes fall away from mine. "We're not sure. We managed to fix up her skin. It was mangled, she had several broken bones. But flesh and bone, that's easy to fix. It's the insides that take work. And she's been on her own. We didn't know who to contact to support her..."

"I'm here now. I'm her support. I'm not going anywhere until she's better."

I slide my hand into hers, gripping it both tight and gently, fearful of letting go, fearful of hurting her.

"We need to contact her family though, so if you got any information, I'd appreciate it..."

I glance away. Of course, I know her family. Every nobleman and woman in this region of the world knows the Randalls, but do I want to tell her that? Do I want them here?

No.

Gods forbid they found me with Eleanor and blamed me for what happened. I need her awake before I can give the healers that information. She has to come back to me first before her family take her from me all over again.

"I'll endeavour to remember," I say.

She purses her lips at me. "It's okay if you're lovers... I

don't mind. But it's best and proper that we tell her family... Perhaps tomorrow, hmm?"

I say nothing else. My heart breaks into ever smaller pieces.

The healer hands me a green paste, "Here, pop this on her chest, in the middle, a little to the left. And another on the right, above her breast there, and the same on the other breast."

My cheeks instantly heat as she asks me to smother this stodgy green paste that smells a little like mint and a little like lavender all over her chest.

"What is it?"

"It's Sanatio, a healing plant from another city. Miracle worker if you ask me. It's what cleared her burns and mended her bones. It is working on the insides but..."

"But not her heart?" I whisper.

"Not yet, something tells me she was waiting for something else. A reason perhaps... to keep living."

Trudy gets up and totters to the door. "I'm guessing you'll be staying, miss?"

I nod.

"Right, I'll get clean linens brought for you and show you to the showers later."

"Thank you," I say.

Then she's gone, and I clasp Eleanor's hand tighter and lay my head on the edge of the bed, silent tears of gratitude flowing.

"Come back to me, Eleanor. Please? I found you, so you have to come back to me now."

And there, crouched on a stool, I fall soundly asleep for the first time in days.

CHAPTER 17

OCTAVIA

By the time Red appears in the doorway, Drax is looking worse for wear. I've beaten him hard enough that his vampire healing is failing. His face is swollen and bruised. His nose is broken and definitely not repairing. He's lost a finger, has a busted kneecap and has fallen unconscious more than once.

I'm rather pleased with myself. I drank the goblet of despair-infused blood, of course. It was a delightful accompaniment to torture. And I wafted the hope under his nose every break in the beating I gave him.

Red leans against the doorway and I melt. Drax just became boring. Red must be able to tell seeing her has an effect on me because she tuts.

"What? You don't like being appreciated?" I say.

"From a liar and a betrayer? Not really."

My nostrils flare. "Come on, I thought we were going to try to work past this. I thought the tunnel—"

"I told you in the carriage, memories or nothing. Who is this sorry ass motherfucker, anyway?"

"This is the fool who attacked you on my castle grounds."

Red's eyes widen. "A gift?"

"A gift, for my love." She ignores the last bit, so I continue. "He was just telling me that he doesn't know who he's employed by. But that his contact comes from Castle St Clair."

"So, there's a mole?"

I nod. "With a very obvious suspect."

She prods the vampire, who groans at her. His head rolls up and lolls back down on his other shoulder.

"Gods, Octavia, he's still alive."

"That can be rectified," I say, selecting a stake from the pile of tools and torture devices Erin scrounged up for me.

"Octavia. For Blood's sake. You can't gift me a half-dead vampire and a stake and think it's an apology."

"Well, it seemed like a good idea. He hurt you. I hurt him. That's how it works."

Red pulls her hand over her eyes. "That is not how it works. If you mean your apology, if you truly want me to forgive you, then you have to give my memories back."

My throat constricts. I can't. That's the problem. I can't give them back to her because I promised I wouldn't.

She was the one who made me swear I'd never return them. But I'm beginning to wonder whether I can keep the oath if it means losing her, especially now we're bonded.

If I give them back, if I tell her everything else that happened the night Amelia was turned, she'll hate me more and then I really will lose her for good. She'll blame me for everything that's happened.

I can't do it.

I can't give them back knowing that withholding them is the only way I might get to keep her. I'm on a knife's edge. Either way, I may lose her, but at least this way there's a chance. If I return them, I know she will leave.

I won't take that risk. She will have to continue hating me, and I will continue praying that she'll come around.

"Consider it a make-up gift. I thought you'd like to torture him. Perhaps I should have gone one step further..."

I lean down, grab his arm, and wrench it until the slick squelching of flesh rings through the air and his arm detaches from his torso.

Red and I are immediately sprayed with arterial blood. Our clothes, bodies and faces are smothered in the liquid.

I lay the arm flat across both my hands and present it to her like a dog with a bone.

"Mother of Blood," Red says, exasperated.

"What? Those hands hurt you. Bruised you and marked your skin. And I swore I would hunt him down and tear him limb from limb. Or something similar. I'm following up on my promise."

"Following up with one promise does not make up for the breaking of another," she says, taking the arm out of my hands, swinging it back and slapping the vampire in the face with it.

Fuck, that was hot.

I stand a little straighter, adjust my crotch.

"But it certainly makes me feel better." She proceeds to beat him half to death again with his own hand. "And this is for my fucking ribs, and this is for my jaw and my eye. And this, you piece of shit, is because I feel like it." She wallops him over and over and over.

And all the while, my cheeks grow hotter and hotter, my knickers slicker and slicker.

I don't think I've ever been so turned on.

She's feral.

She swings his arm and slams it into his face repeatedly

until she drops it on the floor, the hand half hanging off, and proceeds to jump onto his lap, punching his face, splattering blood, bone and muscle on the walls, floor and both of us.

His torso has stopped spraying so much arterial blood. He's done for. The desiccation will start any moment if he doesn't get any blood, and I'm not about to give him any.

"Enough," I say. "He's had enough."

She can't hear me. She's lost herself in her rage, funnelling it all into him.

"Red," I bark. "He's not me. You can't attack him and make the pain of me keeping your memories go away."

She screams in frustration and lands a punch to his jaw that has his head rocking back. Then she's up and staring at me, her shoulders heaving. That's when I notice the tears streaking her cheeks.

I glance back at the vampire, now one armed, his face a bloodied mess. The state of him makes the curling need to punish him for hurting Red subside. He looks pathetic, all broken and bleeding in the chair. I need to put him out of his misery.

I punch my hand into his chest and grip his heart. His head comes up, his remaining hand grabbing my wrist, his eyes wide.

"You shouldn't have touched her," I say, and then I yank his heart from his chest. It's already desiccating by the time it's in my hand and presented to Red.

She looks down at it, her nose wrinkled. "Thanks?" she says, but her words are snuffly. She wipes her bloodied hand across her face, smearing the tears with blood.

She wobbles on her feet.

"Didn't Amelia give you blood?" I ask.

"Yes, I took it."

I replay her words. "It? As in, all of it?"

She nods.

"On top of the blood I gave you in the tunnel? And what you took from my wrist in the office?" I ask and take a step back. The heart rolls out of my hand.

"I did something. It wasn't really healing. But it wasn't not healing either."

"The situation Erin mentioned?"

Red nods. Fuck. Amelia was right to go to the library. We do need to know exactly what this transition is going to do to her.

I'm not going to be able to keep up her feeding needs at this rate. She's drinking like a newly turned vampire, and they are insatiable.

We're not even going to be able to keep this secret from the rest of the teams or Mother at this rate, either. Shit. Heat pools in the room. Her eyes go from wet and watery to deep and hungry.

"How long ago did you take it?" I ask.

"Not long."

I see.

She takes a step towards me, and I know where this is going, and it hurts. I want to fuck her, gods, I'd fuck her every day, every night. But even I can recognise when this is bad for us. And yet... it doesn't stop me wanting her.

She steps into my personal space and looks up at me.

"I want to forgive you," she breathes.

"But you can't?" I say.

She looks away, her eyes trailing the now desiccating heart. "I don't know."

"And yet you want me anyway?"

"We're completely fucked up," she says. "I know you want me too. I know you're fighting taking me right here in this room. I feel it here," she presses two fingers over my heart.

I close my eyes. It's true. I want her more than I want blood.

I'd kill for her, maim for her. Hell, I'd burn every last vampire in Sangui City for her. But what she's asking... for me to break a promise I made to her, *for* her? Which her am I indebted to?

Is it better for her to love me because of a lie, or hate me because of the truth?

When I open my eyes, her lips are millimetres from mine. She brushes them across my skin, soft, needing.

Her caress is filled with many things. The agony of the lies between us, the electricity of surging want. The bond, the blood in her system.

"This is all I can give you right now," she says.

And so I take it. Knowing that it's all fucked up and that eventually this will come crashing down. But I'd rather have her wrapped in a lie now than lose her forever later.

I crush my lips to hers. She hops up into my arms, wrapping her legs around me.

We kiss and spin until I push her up against the wall. I slide my finger to her crotch and slit her trousers. Again. This is all too familiar, but if she must insist on wearing clothes that prevent me from touching her, what does she expect? I stretch the fabric, shredding it in two and then slide my finger between her folds.

She breaks the kiss to throw her head back, rocking her hips, begging me to give her more.

I do. I give her everything, starting with her clit, rubbing gentle circles and rhythmic brushing motions over and over until she's on my lips with a bruising kiss against my mouth.

My fingers find her entrance. She's soaked. I ache to taste her. I bring a second finger to her hole and push both in at once.

She groans against me, into me.

She sucks my tongue into her mouth, holding me in place, giggling until I pull away and free myself.

"Dirty little blood sluts who misbehave like that, who think they're in control, get punished," I say.

"Yeah?" she says, her eyes fluttering under her lashes, and then sucks my lip into her mouth and bites down.

I hiss as her increasingly sharp teeth make little puncture wounds, and she practically comes from the taste of my liquid iron spilling into her mouth.

"Red, I'm warning you. Continue to be a brat and I will punish you."

She bites harder. Sinking her teeth in deep enough I stagger back, nearly taking us both out as I slip on the desiccating heart and stumble over the arm Red dropped.

She laughs as she releases me and draws a long lick over the wound on my chin. It's already healed, though.

She giggles into another kiss and grips hold of me as I try to right myself.

Eventually, I'm on steady feet and speed us out of the dungeon. As the door swings shut behind us, I recognise we probably shouldn't have been fucking next to a tortured vampire carcass anyway.

But then again, that's the price to pay for touching what is mine.

I rush her up to my office and shut the door on Frank, shouting at him not to let us be disturbed.

"Clothes off," I say as I race around my office desk and pull out the strap-on I used to fuck her last time we were in the club.

I pull the office wall curtains open, knowing damn well that the club goers are about to see her pretty pink pussy pushed up against the wall as I fuck her into oblivion.

"You know you're not the only one who's pissed off,

Red. I have feelings too. There are things I can't tell you that are fucking me up just as much."

"Punish me then. Punish me the way I punished you."

I stride over to her, buckling the straps, dildo in one hand, a knife in the other.

"What are you going to do with that?" she asks, her eyes glistening.

I bring the point of the blade under her chin, press it lightly. It only makes a slight depression in her skin.

"I am never letting you go, Red. I don't care how angry you are with me. I will make you love me again."

She drags her eyes away from mine. "You can't make someone love you, Octavia, any more than you can control everything around you. That's not how it works."

I grit my teeth and drag the blade down the centre of her chest. It is sharp enough to slide through her clothes and shred them in one swift motion without touching her skin.

She gasps and leans into the pressure as her shirt pops open along with her sports bra.

I brush my hand along the clothing until I expose her nipple. The pink bud hardens in the air. I glance up, locking my eyes on hers.

"What are we doing?" she says.

"We're fucking everything up," I answer.

"Are we going to survive this?"

"I hope so, I really do. Because I can't imagine a world where you aren't mine. And I don't think I'm willing to give you up, even if you try to leave me."

I move fast, vampire-fast. I slice all of her clothes from her body before her eyelids flutter shut in a blink.

She's standing there completely naked and bared for me. Her breathing is heavy and rapid. Breasts rising and falling with the movement. Her cheeks still have the remnants of vampire blood and the rivulets of tears that flowed through it streaking her skin.

"What do you need?" I ask.

"I need you to remind me, Octavia. Remind me why I'm yours. Why I should love you."

My patience snaps. "Turn around," I demand.

She does, and a short, sharp breath escapes as she clocks the curtains are open, and the office can be viewed from below. In reality, most of the club goers will be too drunk, too intoxicated or too busy fucking each other to notice us up here, but when did reality ever ruin the power play of sex?

"Hands on the window," I say.

She presses them up against the glass, her heart rate already increasing.

"Safe word," I ask.

"Elysium."

"Good. Mine is villain." Only when I say the word this time, there's a weight to it. A weight that I am carrying. The way I keep making the same mistakes, keep playing her villain over and over. Was she right in the tunnel? Am I martyring myself for her?

Is that not what someone in love should do? Martyr themselves for those they adore, even if it means they suffer?

I strip, pulling my clothes off and letting them drop to the floor. With each item, Red's shoulders rise and fall faster.

I take a bottle of lube from the desk and deposit a load on the end of the strap-on that goes inside me. I push it into myself and flip on the switch for both ends, and then I press myself against her back.

She squeaks, not expecting the vibrations. And then sticks her arse out.

But I'm not having that. She isn't leading this. This is about her pleasure, and I'll deliver that to her exactly how I please.

I step forward, pressing her against the glass.

"It's cold," she squeals.

I press harder against her, wishing I could see her breasts plastered against the glass.

I knock her feet out until there's room for the dildo and notch it at her entrance.

She moans, the vibrations teasing her entrance. I grin as her eyes shut and she bites her bottom lip.

I shunt the cock in right up to the hilt, then I drag it out real slow and gentle. Her fingers claw at the glass like she's trying to find purchase. But there's nothing to hold on to.

"Octavia?"

"Yes?"

"Don't be gentle," she says, and a tear runs down her cheek.

It's almost enough to carve me in two. I know she suffers with the same jagged pull of emotions.

I grab her chin and guide her round until she looks at me.

"I don't want to hurt you."

"You already have," she says.

My mouth goes dry. I wish I could explain to her that it was her desperation that made me take them. She pleaded with me and made me promise not to give them back.

But how do you make someone understand that in their lowest moment, they broke their own beliefs?

Red finally looks at me. "Until you give me back those memories, you can't make it go away... So I need you to make me feel something else. Anything else..."

"Okay, Verity," I whisper. "Okay."

I thrust hard and deep, and she rocks against the window. Her eyes squeeze shut as I drive the shaft into her.

Again and again.

I drag the cock out and pump in.

Over.

And over.

And over.

Her body bangs against the glass. As I thrust, she moans a melody against the muffled beat of the club music.

"Harder," she pleads.

"I can't," I whine, knowing I'm losing the power in this scene.

"Then bite me," she says and shoves back off the window, making me stumble back.

The dynamic has switched.

She marches towards me, her whole physique radiating authority, power.

"Sit in the chair." She points at my high-backed throne, and I do as I'm told, recognising that I've relinquished the dominance to her.

Red climbs onto my lap. She grips my chin, tilting it exactly where she wants it.

"I—" I say.

"Quiet," she says, and her nails dig into my cheeks. It stings. She glares at me, a searing heat boring into me.

"How can I love you and hate you all at once?" She kisses me. It's vicious and hard and angry. All lips and tongue and nails digging into my cheeks. The pinch of her nails turns into a burn as a dribble of blood oozes out from beneath her fingers.

She releases me and slides her tongue into my mouth, lowering herself onto the cock. I thrust up into her. I might be in a sub role now, but it's still her orgasm I'm chasing.

She bounces on my lap, her teeth grazing my neck.

"Do it," I say.

I don't have to ask twice. She sinks her sharp little dhampir teeth into my throat. And then she rolls her neck to the side, making way for me to bite her.

I kiss her milk-white skin and line up with her artery. It's intoxicating. I can smell her blood even without piercing the skin, but I'm not sure I should bite her.

She pulls her teeth out of my throat and looks up at me. My blood covers her lips, her teeth, it's smeared down her throat.

If she's going to drink human blood, someone is going to have to teach her to do it neatly and tidily.

"Bite me," she says again.

Her eyes are harried and wild. She's not in her right mind.

"No," I whisper, barely able to look at her.

"Octavia," she says aghast, "fucking bite me."

And once again, the dynamic shifts between us. Switch. Switch. Switch.

Calm, quiet, with all the power that I am and that I have, I respond. "No."

She stops grinding against me, her eyes turning dark. "I said, bite me." Her hands dig into my collarbone where she was using me as an anchor.

"No."

She pulls me forward and shoves me back into the chair. "BITE ME."

I pick her up, speed her across the room and back against the wall, slamming her back into the glass.

"No."

She's sobbing now, as I let her slide down the wall until she's standing. I kneel, nudge her legs apart and draw my tongue down her slit.

"Please. Just bite me," she pleads, the tears coming hard and fast now.

I slip two fingers inside her and curl my tongue around her clit. I won't bite her because that's not what she needs right now. What she needs is to come and to hate me and to let me fuck the orgasm out of her. So that is what I'll give her.

I lap at her clit, flicking my tongue faster and faster. She's close. It doesn't take long until her pussy clenches against my fingers.

She's gasping and still pleading with me and slapping at my shoulders, pulling at my hair, begging me to bite her.

But I don't. I continue to worship her instead. I may have caused her heart to hurt, but I won't do the same to her body. Not tonight, anyway.

Her pussy tightens. I curl my fingers up, slide deeper into her, and then she spills over.

Panting my name.

I pull out of her, and she sinks into my arms.

"I'm sorry," I say. "I'm so, so fucking sorry."

She whimpers as I cradle her. We stay like that for a long, long time until she falls asleep, nestled safe against my heart.

Where she belongs.

Where she will always belong, no matter how much she hates me.

CHAPTER 18

RED

I leave Octavia at dawn. She took me back to Castle Beaumont before the sun rose, and then she disappeared to handle castle business. I snuck out, but I'm not running. I have something I need to do today.

Would Octavia kill me if she found out? Absolutely. Do I have to go, anyway? One hundred percent.

I'm getting weaker. I don't understand it, but a lot of truths came out last night, especially after Amelia intimated that I'd have to drink human blood at some point. But I refuse. No matter how sick I get, I'm not doing it. I'm sure I can control the cravings if I just drink more vampire blood. My only concern is that as far as I can remember, the old dhampir's didn't actually drink blood, they just used it in spell work. And I don't like what my gut is saying about that. No part of me wants to be a vampire and definitely not half of one.

Maybe Amelia will dig something up in her research. I sneak into the tunnels and find the carriage station under

Octavia's castle, then take the fastest carriage I can across the city and to the Hunter Academy.

I nap for most of the trip, but when we finally pull onto Academy grounds, it feels like a lifetime ago since I was here, when in reality it's been barely two weeks. The carriage drops me off a little after lunch. I'm not fully nocturnal yet, despite keeping to Octavia's schedule, which means there are still times I find myself awake at the wrong time or sleeping when I shouldn't.

But today isn't about that. Today is about doing the right thing. Doing the thing I'm paid to do; the thing I've trained most of my life for. I couldn't let go of how genuine the Chief's expression was when we were on the balcony. How much she wanted to protect us hunters.

And protecting the hunters, protecting the Academy, and being loyal to those who raised me—that's ultimately why I agreed to enter the trials, right?

I pay the carriage driver what he's owed and a few extra coins to keep his mouth shut.

My assumption is that if I'm within the city bounds, and my intention isn't to run, then whatever this bond is between Octavia and me shouldn't give me too much hassle. It only caused an issue when I left the city. I'm sure intention is everything. The bond taught me that much, at least. And so far, so good. No chest pain. No twinges. It makes me wonder whether I could venture further if my intention is to return to her when I'm done. It also makes me wonder if I had enough intention of wanting to break the bond, would it actually snap—something tells me I'm not that lucky. But if she doesn't give my memories back, it might be something I test.

I walk through the courtyard and external training grounds in the front of the Academy to find the first- and second-years going at a hardcore self-defence training session in the sun.

"Morning, Red," they shout.

I wave as I traipse past them, but I don't have time to stop and chat. I'm on a mission to get in, see the Chief, and get back to Octavia before sundown.

The Academy looms tall above me today, the pale, sandy turrets reaching into the cloudy sky. I'm about to step inside the giant oak door when it swings open, and the Chief appears right in front of me.

Goosebumps fleck over my arms.

"Oh," I say. "You're exactly who I was coming to see."

She beams at me, her bright blue eyes sparkling in the lunchtime sun. "How fortunate. And good morning to you too, Red. Office? Or will a walk suffice?"

"Walls have ears. A walk makes sense."

She guides the way, leading me through the foyer, and out through the inner courtyard and to the back of the grounds where there are several sports fields, permanent obstacle courses and outdoor gym equipment installations.

We take to the sports fields and walk a wide perimeter. When we're far enough away from the building and any students, she nudges me.

"Tell me, how are you finding the trials? I apologise you got partnered with Octavia. I recall you asked me to prevent it, but in the end, we decided in the name of fairness to pick randomly."

I pat her on the arm. "It's fine. I'm a big girl. I can deal with it. How are you coping? We haven't had a chance to talk about the fact Cordelia essentially cornered you into stepping down as Chief."

The Chief stiffens under my touch, so I release her. She glances at me, tentative, her shoulders sagging.

"Honestly? I don't want to retire. This job, this life even. It's all I've ever known. But if stepping down enables us to win... to truly rid this world of vampires, then I'll do whatever it takes."

I tilt my head at her. "You can't really believe that."

I want the cure for my sister, but hearing the way she phrased that, so clear cut—she wants to rid the world of a species? That's... genocide. I hate vampires. But as soon as I consider it, I catch myself in the lie. I don't hate them all. I hate the actions of a few... But even then, I wouldn't wish a genocide on an entire species. The Chief can't mean that.

"Believe what?"

"That we're going to rid the world of vampires. What if they don't want to be cured?" I ask.

She huffs at me as we round the corner and walk down the long edge of the field. A bird swoops down and plucks a worm, or perhaps it's a twig, from the field and flies off into the trees.

"Red, they are the scourge of the Earth. They're unnatural and they must be stopped. Perhaps I was a little excessive in my wording. I'll admit that was wrong of me. But they do need to be stopped."

"Even those that aren't hurting anyone?"

She glances at me; her face wrinkled with confusion. "Red, that's literally why we exist. To stop them and protect humans. Think about it. What vampire hasn't hurt someone? They don't come into existence without draining a human."

I narrow my eyes at her. "I'll accept that, but equally though, what hunter hasn't killed?"

She shrugs. "Only vampires though."

I open my mouth to argue, but she's not listening. She's stuck in her ways, in the hatred for the other species. If I recall myself of even a couple of weeks ago, that's exactly who I was, what I thought.

But spending time with Octavia, really getting to understand her as a person and not the mask she lets the world see, has made me realise they're not all bad. Xavier too. Can't say the same for Dahlia and Gabriel. But something tells me not all vampires are bad.

And then there's Amelia. Has she changed? A little, I guess. She's grown up, she's more independent. Hell, she's even a little more responsible. In a way, this has done her good. That's not something I ever thought I'd say.

But if we had more willing donors? More safety measures? What if Octavia is right and that a city of cohabitation and cooperation is the way for all of us to live safe and happy?

"So you're going to cure every vampire in the city, even if they refuse?" I ask, my voice quiet.

"I think we will need to create a persuasive campaign to convince the vampires so that we don't have to force them. But, before we get to any of that, finding the dhampir is first. It's why finding them is so important, because without them, there is no cure. No opening the door. And on that note, any updates? Have you found anything out by being in close proximity to the vampires? What about speaking to the other hunters?"

"Yes, in fact, that's why I came back. I can't stay long. But I wanted to tell you that we captured the vampire who tried to attack me while I was in Castle Beaumont."

"And?" she says, suddenly brighter and more alert than I've seen her all afternoon.

"And we... It wasn't pretty. We had to push him pretty hard to get even a shred of information."

"What did you discover?"

"That, in truth, he didn't know who had hired him. A proxy, no doubt covering for whoever, actually commissioned him. But he was fairly sure they had come from Castle St Clair."

That makes her stop dead. Her face pales.

"Cordelia?" she whispers.

"We can't be certain of that. It could be anyone in Castle St Clair, but it would certainly suggest her as the most likely candidate."

"Then why did she bother setting up the trials in the first place? Why not let the boundary swallow the door and take the cure with it?"

"I have no idea, but whatever is going on isn't going to spell good news for us," I say as we round another corner on the field and have to duck under a few tree branches that are hanging low. I make a mental note to tell security to get the groundskeepers out to trim them.

The Chief scratches her head. "Why send other vampires to attack? She's the oldest and strongest of them all. Why not do it herself?"

"She's far too well known. Someone would identify her. That's a suicide mission and one that will wreck her reputation. But if she looks like she's trying to be supportive..."

The puzzle pieces lock into place and this suddenly feels like exactly what she's doing. I continue. "If she publicly appears to support the cure and work with the hunters, then she'll be buying in the human vote, swaying them to her way of thinking. And then no one will question that it's her trying to stop it."

"You don't think she wants to retire any more than I do?" the Chief asks.

"You said it yourself last time we spoke. What do leaders on the way out do?"

The Chief's lips part. "They burn it all down."

"Exactly. If there's a threat to her position of power,

then either she secures her place as leader of the city, or she burns it all to the ground."

We walk in silence for a while, both of us mulling over all the things we said, the options for how we progress, the security threats we're under.

I'm not sure if it's the tension rising off the Chief or if it's actually a chilly afternoon, but the air around us cools. The Chief halts.

"We need to find the dhampir," she says.

I go rigid. Stress leaks through my shoulders, stiffening my spine. I try to force myself to relax, but the Chief must notice because she turns to me. Her eyes narrow.

"It's important. Whoever it is, is one of us. It's our job to protect them. It's literally your job as head of security to keep them safe."

My eyes drop to the floor. Because I do carry a secret and it is heavy. But I am trying to protect the dhampir—to protect me.

"Oh, Red...You know something, don't you, sweetie?"

"No. I—"

She rounds on me, her face soft. Despite her gentle tone, her warm ocean-coloured eyes, there's something uneasy nestled in my gut. A gnawing I can't get rid of.

"Well, even if you haven't identified who the dhampir is, I know you well enough to recognise when there's something you're not telling me... is everything okay?"

She slings her arm over my shoulder and rubs my back. It reminds me of when I was young and training and the way she always cared for all the trainees. It was instinctive mothering. She was always there when we needed geeing up, a cuddle and a cry, or the praise we hungered after. She knew what to do as if she were our mother.

I came here to tell her about the vampire we tortured

and the fact that I'm pretty sure Cordelia is trying to kill all the hunters.

Not to confess that I am actually the dhampir.

But what harm can telling her do? She's the Chief, for Blood's sake. She's the one that sent me on a mission to go undercover and bring back intel. The Chief has always been and will always be on my team.

All she wants is to keep me safe.

My mind races back to Octavia, and how she was willing to take my memories to make sure no one would ever find out who I was. The fact that she doesn't trust anyone. And yet she is the one who took not just my memories but her brother's.

She did it to protect me, but there is a line between doing a bad thing for the right reason and actually playing a villain. I think she's the former, but if you truly had a good heart, wouldn't you give the memories back? Or is the villain Octavia says she plays for me who she actually is?

Octavia is worried, but really... who am I meant to trust? A vampire or the hunter who's looked after me my whole life?

"Red? What is it?" the Chief says more urgently this time.

I have a decision to make. Who can I trust? Who do I trust more? Who's never lied to me?

The Chief or Octavia?

My gut swirls as I realise there's only one obvious choice.

"I know who the dhampir is," I say.

And the Chief's complexion pales, her blue eyes glimmer like ocean droplets in the lunchtime sun and she smiles for the first time since I stepped onto Academy grounds.

CHAPTER 19

Sneaking out, Red?

Tricky, tricky.

Looks like you're letting your hunter skills go. I followed you, and you didn't even notice.

I wonder if you'll notice when I pull the rug out from under you?

I wonder if you'll figure out before it's too late what I have planned for Cordelia.

Dear, Red. None of this is even about you.

But then, collateral damage is a part of war.

And you, sweet thing, will be collateral damage.

CHAPTER 20

RED

The whole carriage ride back to Octavia's mansion, I second guess everything. It's in part the time and space to think and partly because I am famished. I need to drink. I should probably eat human food, too. But I am consumed by the need to drink.

The carriage rocks me side to side as the horses clip-clop under the city and I fight wave after wave of exhaustion. My head told me to tell her. She's the Chief. What else could she want other than to protect me? Regardless of the fact Cordelia has cornered her into retiring, she wants the best for us hunters.

"I'm the dhampir, Chief," I said, and her mouth fell open. I swore for a brief second, as her eyes drooped, there was a flash of sadness. But then her expression hardened, and she grabbed me by the shoulders.

"Listen to me. We have to keep this secret, okay?"

I nod and she continued.

"You can't tell anyone. Especially none of the vampires."

"But, Octavia—"

"Especially not her. This is between you and me. We have to do everything we can to protect you. There will be vampires and hunters alike from both sides of the political divide over the cure coming for you, and I want you kept safe. What you're going to do... bringing back magic... it's a gift, Red. You are going to change the face of our city, and I want nothing getting in the way of that."

Her tone was so serious. Her eyes bored into me; her nails dug into my arms as she spoke.

"Okay. I get it," I said.

"So we're agreed? We're keeping this just between you and me? Our little secret? I'll send additional security for you."

"No. You can't. Not if you want to keep it a secret. It would be too obvious that it was me. And even if you sent it to all the hunters at this stage, it would be suspicious. The best thing to do is to continue pretending we don't know who it is."

She released me, folded her arms and pressed her lips shut as she thought.

"Okay," she nodded. "I agree. Oh, Red. I am so proud of you. I'm just sorry you had to be the one to take on the burden."

The horses whinny outside the carriage, and it pulls me out of my reverie. A shiver of hunger crawls over my skin, making my stomach turn. I wipe my hands over my face, forcing myself to concentrate.

It was odd telling her. I thought I'd feel a weight lift off my shoulders, but instead, I came away with a worm in my gut. Something I can't place my finger on. She was polite, outwardly supportive. And yet... and yet... something.

I'm still thinking about it as the carriage comes to a halt. The sun has gifted its last liquid rays to the horizon as my hand presses a drop of blood over the gargoyle's tongue and the door swings open for me.

I slide inside, grateful I made it before anyone was awake. First job is to find Octavia or a vial of her blood. I can't wait much longer. I'm already dizzy.

I meander through the corridors, my skin prickling like I'm being watched. The atmosphere is odd, sharp and cold all at once.

I veer down a main hallway as a breeze rushes past me and makes me blink. As my eyes open, Octavia is in front of me, staring at me in a way that makes me shiver. I bite down the shocked scream and take a step back.

"Oct—"

"Where have you been?" she cuts me off.

"Don't be rude. I was out."

Her eyes narrow to vicious little slits. "Where?"

I thrust a hand on my hip and glare up at her. "You don't own me, Octavia."

"Is that so?" There's a snarl under her words as she grabs for my wrist and hauls me down the rest of the corridor and into the empty bar.

"Oi, let go of me," I say, staggering after her. "And I'm hungry. Where are the vials you store of your blood?"

"We don't keep secrets from each other," she snaps.

"I think you'll find we do," I say back, putting as much snark and brat into my tone as I can.

She shoves me against the side of the bar and snarls. "Don't. Test. Me."

"Or what?"

She picks me up by the arse and shoves me atop the bar so my legs are dangling over the end, and then she pushes me until I lay flat on it. This could work. Sex could definitely work. If I wind her up enough, it'll be a distraction.

"Or you get punished. Now. Where were you?"

She slices her wrist and lets a few drops dribble onto my lips. I lick them up, swiping my tongue this way and that. I reach up to grab her wrist, but she pulls away.

"I asked a question."

Bitch. How dare she tease me when I'm this hungry.

"I was with your mum," I say, and cackle. There's nothing like a mum joke.

She doesn't laugh. She lashes out, snatching the lime cutting knife from under the bar and slicing my crotch.

"Dammit, Octavia, I barely have any trousers left."

But she ignores me, shreds my underwear, taking her time to cut and dice my trousers until they're barely hanging on, then pushes my legs apart.

"I'm going to ask you one more time. Where. Were. You?"

Do I really want to do this? Keep secrets from Octavia? It's like I'm playing everyone on every side of this game. But Octavia would lose her shit if she found out, and the Chief did ask me to keep it secret. Besides, ultimately, that is what I'm here for. To spy on the vampires and find strategic leverage to put us in a better position. If Octavia is going to keep secrets from me, secrets that don't even belong to her, then I'm going to play her at her own game. And sex is the ultimate game.

"I told you. I was playing with your mum's p—"

Octavia's hand shoots out and slaps my cunt.

I squeal, swinging my legs shut. But her hands are already there, shoving them back open.

"Octavia," I pant.

"If you weren't behaving like a brat, I wouldn't have to do this. It's for your own good. Are you going to answer the question?"

My nostrils flare as I inhale a deep breath. "N—"

She slaps my pussy again. This time I moan. It's deep

and carnal to match the flogger-like sting against my clit, right on the line of pain and pleasure. My legs want to close, but I push them wider, giving her access.

"Fine, I wasn't with your mum. I was riding Xavier's c—" I laugh.

Her face flashes pink, a tremor jumps in her eye, and it earns me two slaps. When her hand pulls away the second time, she takes some of my glistening excitement with her.

She stares at it for a moment before looking at me. "I can see this punishment isn't working. Too much of a dirty little whore, aren't you, Red? Do you like it when I slap that filthy cunt of yours?"

"Fuck, yes, I do. You keep talking like that and I might tell you what you want."

She growls at me. Grabs my hips and yanks me down the bar until my arse is right on the lip edge. She bends to my pussy and bares her teeth at me. I hesitate and suck in a breath. She wouldn't actually hurt me, would she?

She plunges her mouth down on my clit, sucking it between her teeth. I gasp at the sudden pressure, the sharp graze of her teeth against my most sensitive nub. She keeps it between her teeth, barely grazing the flesh. I pant, adrenaline coursing through me. I hitch up to look her in the eye.

Her tongue licks against my swelling clit. I melt. Her teeth sink a little harder into my flesh. I hiss, but she resumes stroking my clit with her tongue. There's a strange pressure, a pooling, like she's drawing blood into my clit, but the pressure of her teeth holds it at bay. And then I remember she can control her blood, even if it's in my system.

Oh, she is playing games.

"Fuck," I cry out as her teeth bite down a little harder, her lips suck my clit a little more, and her tongue moves at a pace that has me moaning and my head dropping back.

Finally, she releases my clit, and the blood flows straight into it. I swear she draws more into my clit to make it a little extra sensitive. The sensation is a head rush, but it stays isolated in my cunt. I'm dizzy and panting and twitching as bolts of pleasure radiate out.

"Look how wet you are for me," she purrs. "Slaps hurt more when the skin is wet."

She says it like the threat it is. But I was never one to back down, especially not when in brat mode.

"This is your last chance, Red. Tell me where you were or I'm going to fuck you until you're a sopping mess and begging me to stop making you come."

Not the worst kind of punishment I've ever received.

I sigh, all dramatic. "Fine. You win. I went to the Whisper Club and fucked myself silly in front of the day drinkers."

The slap that lands on my pussy this time almost has me tipping over into orgasm. My clit is hypersensitive after what she did. The sting pulses out and down my legs.

Octavia leans in and slides her tongue right down the centre of my pussy, lapping up every drop of wetness I have. I buck on the bar. Electric pleasure throbs through me. I'm close. I'm gagging for her to tip me over.

She stops suddenly. It's such a violent halt that my orgasm dies instantly.

"What the fuck?" I whine.

"Oh, I see. You'd like that, wouldn't you? My filthy little blood slut would take all the orgasms she could get. Even if that means being fucked into a sopping mess. Hmm. Perhaps I'll spend all night denying you, then. Yes. I think that seems like a far more fitting punishment."

Ahh, fuckity fuck fuck. She is serious. This is going to be much less fun.

She picks up the knife and slices up my top. But I put

my hand on hers before she can ruin yet another sports bra. These things are expensive. I yank it off and lay back on the bar, naked.

"Wendell," Octavia calls.

"What the fu—" I shout, but Octavia shoves two fingers inside me, promptly shutting me up.

She glides in and out, her thumb skimming over my swollen clit. Then the bar door creaks open, Wendell's nose pokes inside, but he's careful not to enter.

My entire body sets alight. If he inched the door open, even a millimetre more, he would see everything. Witness her finger fucking me. The thought makes me so slick that I am certain Wendell can hear Octavia's fingers gliding in and out of me.

"Could you grab me the black bag at the entrance of my private sex room, please?"

"Certainly, Lady Beaumont." He disappears and Octavia bends and licks my sensitive clit. I jerk against her, but she just continues her relentless pumping inside me.

"Safe word," she trills.

"Elysium."

Wendell returns and drops the bag inside the door and then it clicks shut. She speeds over to collect it and returns to me.

Her hands dive into the bag and pull out cuffs. She leaps up, cuffing my hands to the beer optics.

"Erm..." I say.

"Something you wish to say?"

"Well—"

"Unless it's where you were, or your safe word, I'm not interested."

Next, she pulls out a length of rope and loops it around my thigh and shin, and tugs until my calf hits my hamstring. She knots and ties my other leg with another loop of rope. I am completely at her mercy.

Next, she reaches in and pulls out two devices, a plug and a vibe. This is where I realise I made a mistake. I should have just made up a lie. Told her whatever I could to get her off my back. She pulls out a bottle of lube and dribbles some on the plug.

"Have you ever had anything here?" she says, placing the cool pad of her finger against my arsehole.

I gasp and jerk, but the cuffs clatter and jar against my wrist, reminding me I'm restrained in place.

I shake my head.

"Even better." She leans down and licks from my pussy, past my centre and over my arsehole. I squeal, the sensation utterly alien. It feels illicit, taboo. Her tongue swirls over my hole and I buck and writhe against her.

"Gods," I breathe.

She lifts up, replacing her tongue with something hard and wet.

"Are you ready?"

I nod, and she applies a little pressure. "Fuck," I moan.

She pulls back and pushes again. "Relax, Red. What happened to my filthy whore? Tell me you want it..."

"I want it," I say and arch up, adding a little pressure to the plug. It slips a little further inside. Then she pulls it out.

"Tell me how much you want it," Octavia says.

"I want it. Please. I want you to use me like I'm your little fuck toy."

That makes her smile.

"That's right, Red. I'm going to fill all of your holes, and then I'm going to ride your face and make you swallow all my come. Because that's what blood sluts that keep secrets are good for."

She pushes the plug in harder this time. There's a

moment of resistance and then the strangest sensation as I draw it inside. It feels divine, filthy, wrong. It tingles, I'm too aware of its presence.

She walks around the bar, pours herself a Sangui Cupa, then she returns and pulls a strap-on out along with a harness. She undresses, her pierced nipples already erect as she pulls her bra off. Her legs slide into the harness and after she's done strapping in, she takes a swig from the tumbler.

Then she leans over and pours the rest over my cunt. I gasp as the cold liquid slips over my folds and dribbles around the plug. She lunges for me, lapping the drink up instead of lapping at me. It drives me wild, her tongue always skirting around my clit but never quite touching it.

"Octavia," I scream, "Please."

"Do you want to tell me where you were today?"

"NO," I cry.

"Then I think I'll continue as I am." She resumes lapping, though this time every third or fourth lick strokes the edge of my clit. Her fingers find my core, teasing the entrance. A bead of sweat forms on my brow. I'm still hungry, desperate for more blood. Desperate to come. But she gives me neither.

She slides her fingers inside my pussy, thrusting hard and deep. Her mouth descends to my clit, and fuck, I'm so sensitive. Every lick and thrust sends pulses of pleasure radiating around my body. I buck against the wrist cuffs, but all it does is make noise. I'm going nowhere. My legs heat where the ropes bind me.

My pussy tightens. Her knuckles knock against the plug in my arse and with every brush and movement, I'm certain I'm going to explode. My nipples are on fire, my skin alive with tingles and sensations. I float to the precipice of orgasm. Just need one. More. Lick.

She removes her mouth.

I scream in frustration. My cunt instantly cooling where before it was throbbing with delicious heat.

"Fuck YOU," I cry.

Octavia grins. It's wild, like midnight storms. She's getting high off of the control. Her tongue swipes around her fangs. She pulls a chair across and kneels on it, aligning the strap-on with my core. She notches the dildo at my entrance and teases my wet hole.

I bounce my back on the bar, desperate. For anything. Ready to beg. To get on my knees, to confess. But she doesn't give me a chance. She thrusts the cock into me. Over and over, she drives the cock into me. My tits bounce and rock with the movement until Octavia leans down and pinches one.

"Fuck," I moan as a climax rises again. As soon as she senses I'm close, she pulls out.

"Please, Octavia. I can't take it anymore."

She picks up the same knife she used to slice my clothes and cuts me out of the rope binding my legs. But she doesn't release my hands. Instead, she removes the strap-on and digs a different one out of the bag. This has little ears that, as she slides the shaft inside me, tickles my clit. She hits some buttons, and it bursts to life, sending waves of pleasure through my entire pussy.

"Octavia," I scream.

But she ignores me, instead climbing onto the bar herself and kneeling either side of my cheeks. She lowers her pussy to my mouth. No instruction needed. I ravage her because I am starved. The need for blood is incomprehensible. She rubs her pussy over my mouth, grinding my head into the bar. Her fingers thread through my hair, gripping and tugging as she rams herself into me.

Her moans fill the bar. She's getting off on riding me,

and by the way my cunt is clenching around this vibrator, so am I.

Finally, she inches up and I gasp for air. "Do you like being used as my personal fuck toy?"

"Yes. But if you don't feed me your blood soon, I'm going to pass out and then your little fuck toy won't be awake to play."

"So drink," she says and unclasps the handcuffs at last. I rub my wrists as she flips herself over. She yanks the vibrator out of me, letting it clatter to the floor. Then she presses her body against me and sinks her fangs into my groin.

A blinding white light flashes across my vision. When it clears, the pulling of hot threads of blood leaving my body rush through me. Octavia slides her fingers into my pussy, she's gentle at first, then as the fervour of her drinking increases, her fingers pump harder.

Oh, fuck me. Every inch, every cell of my body is vibrating with an explosive tingle.

She rocks back, lowering her cunt to my face. I lap at her pussy, feasting on her, drawing long, slow licks. But she bites down harder on my groin, and something in me snaps. Manoeuvring myself to free an arm, I push her legs apart. I thrust a finger inside her, draw my tongue over her arse the same way she did to me and then sink my teeth into her cheek.

There's a momentary pause, where she stops drinking from me to moan. And then she's sucking at my leg and driving her fingers inside me. And I am doing the same to her. Blood leaks from my mouth, covering my neck.

Just like on the rooftop, my world blurs. Bright colours and absolute darkness. My senses erupt into a thousand teeming sensations. Both of us moan, our mouths full of blood, our fingers covered in juices. We feed off each other like animals. I lift off, bite again, and again.

I cover her.

Mark her.

She does the same to me. Punctures my thighs over and over. The air stinks of the sweet alcoholic scent of Sangui Cupa. We're drunk off each other. Drugged and high on pleasure and liquid claret. My soul swells, my vision frays.

"I'm going to come," I moan into her arse cheek. She bites down hard, drawing a long mouthful of blood, and I explode. Stars splatter across my vision. I swear my heart stops beating. My pussy clenches, my muscles tensing. And that is what makes her spill over. She clamps down on me, a rushing liquid soaks my hand. I pull out, moving myself over her pussy and drink down whatever she gives me. Her come mixes with her blood in my mouth, and I think I must be dead because nothing should taste this exquisite.

The pair of us lie there, our pussies pulsing and relaxing as the aftershocks hit us. Slowly, we both remove our fingers and fangs, and she rolls off me.

I sit up, aching, sore, but utterly satiated.

I glance at Octavia and have to stifle a smirk. "Do I look as bad as you?" I point at her, and she nods.

"Gods, you look like you were in a fight."

Blood smears cover her face, and her hair is ridiculous. I glance down. I am covered in come, vampire whisky and a lot of blood. My thighs, while no longer cut, still bear her mouth markings.

"And you look like you've been royally fucked. But then, that's what you get for being a brat."

She holds her hand out to me, and we race through the mansion, stark bollock naked, giggling like teenagers.

CHAPTER 21

CORDELIA

One Thousand Years Ago

For three long days and three long nights, I stay by Eleanor's bedside. I couldn't stand the sight of her hair so lank and dry, so I apply moisturising creams and pastes to her waves to revive them. I take over rubbing the potions and pastes onto her burns and help the healers in any way I can.

It's on day three that the nurse pulls me aside and asks me whether I've taken a shower or rested anywhere other than the unforgiving wooden armchair beside Eleanor's bed.

I shake my head at her. Despite my protestations, she tugs me out of the room into the hallway. She tells me to stay put while she speaks to two hulking men in beige uniforms with a stripe down the side of their legs. She whispers behind her hand like a conspiratorial child to one of them. I frown at her, but she smiles and giggles.

One of the men raises an eyebrow at her. She responds

by slapping his arm playfully and pushing him off to do whatever she's bid him to do.

She scurries back to me and drags me across the other side of the hospital to where there are showers.

"Well, m'lady, I hate to be ill-mannered, but you ain't smelling too fresh. I'd really rather prefer it if you could wash yourself while I find you clean clothes."

I splutter in response, about to give her a mouthful, but I know she's only doing her best and wanting to help. And probably right. Reluctantly, I shuck off the dress and stand in my undergarments, which, now I get a closer smell of myself, aren't the freshest.

Her nose wrinkles. "Come on, miss, them too."

"But I'm... I'll be..."

"Look, I see bodies all day long, ain't nuffin' special about yours. No offence. Give me the clothes and I'll have 'em laundered for you."

I huff and turn my back on her, pulling my undergarments off too. I hand them to her, and she scoops them into her arms.

"Towels in the cupboard. Now scrub up."

With that, she scuttles away and closes the door behind her. I switch on the shower and let the water run warm before I climb under.

I slump to my bottom, wrapping my arms around my knees and letting the water soak my locks and wash the grime away. Several tears leak down my cheeks, not from any single emotion, but from all of them.

I'm exhausted and desperate for Eleanor to wake, and all I keep thinking is that I've come this far, and she still may not return to me.

I scrub the dirt from my hair, kneading the soap in until it froths. Then I start on my body and use the scourer to scrub my skin. I find a spare razor and raze the hair from all the places I hate to see it, and it's this action that finally feels restorative.

It's what makes me feel clean.

With my body smooth, my hair creamed and conditioned, I climb out of the shower and towel myself off.

The nurse must have popped back in because there are clean clothes waiting for me on a stool.

When I'm finally dressed and ready, I pull open the bathroom door and wonder if I'll be able to find my way back. This place is quite the warren of corridors and rooms. But to my surprise, the nurse is sitting on the floor waiting for me.

"Wow, that's quite the difference. You smell much better," she laughs.

"Thank you," I dip my head and curtsey at her, and she laughs again.

"Right then, ready?"

"I am."

As we walk back, she asks me. "How did you two meet, miss? If you don't mind my asking."

I smile, a soft chuckle escaping my lips. "Ahh, my mother was trying to marry me off to some hideous lord, and I injured my ankle at one of those equally hideous dance ball things. She sent me to a healer who ended up being Eleanor."

"But your families don't get on?" she asks.

"No, and that's the polite way of saying they're essentially mortal enemies. Our families have done awful things to each other and unfortunately, I believe they discovered we were together..."

I let the rest of that sentence hang in the air between us. Thick and malignant, like tar.

Slowly, her eyes widen as the realisation of what happens dawns on her.

"So... Miss Eleanor... it was..."

I nod, and she swallows hard.

"Gods," she breathes as we arrive back at Eleanor's bedroom.

As soon as she clocks the door, her expression morphs. She bobs up and down on her toes.

I examine her face, but she presses her lips together like she's holding a secret on her tongue.

"Hmm, what are you up to...?"

But she shrugs at me, a big grin peeling across her mouth. I open the door and gasp.

Eleanor is now in an enormous double-sized bed with plenty of space for me to sneak in and lie down next to her and, thank the gods, sleep.

I glance back at the nurse. "You did this?"

She shrugs again. "The boys helped, but yes."

I leap at her, bundling her up in my arms. "Thank you so much."

She startles and relaxes into my embrace. A smile that makes her entire face radiate warmth blooms across her countenance.

"You're most welcome, miss. Now, get some sleep."

She disentangles herself from me and disappears. I clamber onto the bed and lay myself next to Eleanor.

I tug the pillow until it enables me to be pressing against her body. I stroke my fingers down her arms and lace our hands together, and that's how I fall asleep.

For three more nights, I sleep there praying and hoping she will wake, but with each passing night, I lose a little piece of hope.

Time loses its sense of meaning. Days melt into nights, creams and pastes and potions into learning the physical movements they put Eleanor's body through to prevent muscle loss. I don't venture outside; the nurses sneak me food when they can, and I spend my idle hours reading healing manuals and books I find discarded around the ward.

I find it remarkable that time can elongate itself, an impossible elasticity that draws into weeks and months in the space of just a few days. But then ask anyone grown of a few decades and they'll tell you time has a strange stickiness. A duality that enables one to be old in body and young of mind, tired and full of memories with a heart desperate for adventure. If this stay has taught me anything, it's that time doesn't quite work the way it should. Moulding this way and that, sometimes it stays upright and daylight and other times you blink and find yourself in an evening two days later.

That's how, one morning, I peel my eyes open to the sensation of being stroked, of someone's thumb rubbing circles on the back of my hand.

It takes a moment for me to recognise it's not happening in my dream but in the now, in the here.

I sit bolt upright. "Eleanor?" I gasp.

"Hello, Cordelia," she says, her voice cracked and dry with lack of use.

"Oh, my gods, *Eleanor,*" I wail.

I break into the most unladylike tears. Giant heaving sobs that sound much like the women warbling and puffing on the birthing ward when it's their time, wrack my exhausted body. Giant tears plop onto the bed and splash Eleanor's arm.

She smiles at me. Her lips don't quite pull into the same smile she had before. She has a scar running through her top lip that makes her face even more radiant.

That's what I kiss first. The one tiny imperfection that is already my favourite part of her.

She kisses me back, gently at first, and then hungrier.

We lie back on the bed, our arms wrapped around each other. She strokes my hair back from my face and kisses my cheek, my eyelid, my brow, and finally my nose.

"What happened?" she asks.

It's funny how we can hope for something so desperately. And I assure you, I've prayed to the gods night after night, begging them to return me to her. And yet, now the moment has come, I find myself dreading the truth that lies between us.

I dread spilling the awful secrets that led us to this place, and yet I cannot lie to her. I cannot keep in what must be told.

For even though I have trekked across cities and villages, spent days searching for her, I'm no longer sure whether I made the right decision.

Not because I don't love her.

But because I do.

I take a deep breath and tell her everything, pouring all the awful moments out. I explain why her body was bruised, broken and burned.

"It was my family, Eleanor. It's all my fault," I say.

She shakes her head. "You are not your family."

"I know. And yet, if it weren't for me, my family wouldn't have done this to you. I love you more than anything, but I am wondering whether I made a mistake. Whether my being here has put you in further danger."

"Cordelia, if you have done as you said and travelled across cities for me, stayed by my bed and cared for me while I slept, why would you leave now? Why would you think that I would accept your leaving after you sacrificed so much for me?"

But before I can answer, the nurse who has always been kind to me flusters her way into the room.

"You need to leave, miss..."

"Pardon?" I say, pushing my still-wet locks out of my face.

"Now, m'lady. Please."

She's hopping from side to side. The urgency in her tone sets my alarms alight. Goosebumps fleck up and down my arms.

Eleanor glances at me, her expression wide and startled. She glances at the nurse. "Is it my family?"

The nurse nods. "Healers took you off the sleeping meds thinking you'd be healed up enough to wake up. They called for your family. They're here. And after what miss told me... I... Please, Cordelia..."

Eleanor grips my arm. "Go. Hide and don't come back until the nurse collects you and tells you it's safe."

I lurch out of the bed, and then halt, grabbing Eleanor by the neck and pulling her back in for one deep kiss filled with everything I love and everything I've missed about her.

She kisses me back like I'm her medicine and my lips are the only thing that will heal her.

She kisses me, hard, then soft, then hard all over again.

"Miiisss," the nurse hisses.

Eleanor breaks off. "Go."

So I do. After weeks of searching for her, I am forced to leave all over again. But not before I risk one last glance as I dash from her room and pray that one day we can stop living like we're nothing more than a filthy secret.

CHAPTER 22

OCTAVIA

Red and I are in my office. It's long past midnight, and we've cleaned ourselves up. She is in a soft hoodie and leggings now. But she's right, I owe her an entire wardrobe. Not that I give a damn. I can't stop fucking her even if I wanted to.

While we were busy, a book arrived from Gabriel; a gift he sent to each of the hunters. He found it in the library and thought it was the most comprehensive book on dhampirs that he'd found to date. Red has been absorbed in it since we sat down.

There's a knock on the door and Amelia's blonde hair peeks around its edge.

"Hey," she says.

"Evening," Red says and swings her legs off the arm of the chair to get up to hug her sister.

I swallow down the lump in my throat. My eyes flick to Amelia. When they meet, there's a ripple in the air. It's the heavy weight of the secret we share about the night I turned her. Red only knows part of the truth. A version we agreed was palatable. And then I forbade Amelia from telling Red the whole truth.

"You should sit down," Amelia says to Red.

She does, and Amelia pulls a large grimoire out of her bag and places it on a coffee table in front of Red's armchair.

Amelia pulls a chair up, and I move my office chair around to sit with them.

"What's going on?" I ask.

Amelia's eyes dance between Red and I.

"It's worse than we thought..." Amelia says, her fingers trailing to the book. "Or at least, I think it is."

"You're going to need to get to the point," I say, tension ebbing into my tone.

Amelia chews her lip, running her fingers over the grimoire's cover. "This is a book of predictions, all of them from blood monks. There's a lot of theoretical discussion in here about the dhampir. We're all already agreed that Red needs to embrace her vampire side in order to transition, right?" She looks up, her knee bouncing up and down, her fingers twisting and rubbing against each other.

"Amelia, what the hell is wrong?" Red says.

"There's a lot of conjecture, but they're all agreed on two things..."

"Which are?" I ask.

"The first is that, as Cordelia suggested, this is a new type of dhampir, a true hybrid form, unlike the witch-dhampirs of old. We know the original dhampirs only used blood in their magic, not that they consumed it or needed to feed on it like vampires. But when the witch-god created Cordelia, it required such an enormous amount of power that it severed all their magic. She literally slaughtered an entire species of dhampir, causing the extinction of magic."

Red and I both nod. Some of this we know.

"Right, but we're bringing it back," I say.

She shakes her head. "Not exactly. That's why they think you're a hybrid. The dhampirs of old are gone-gone. You are something new. My best guess is that blood was the dhampir's source of magic. Their blood made vampires. And now the cycle is being closed, the magic seeded in vampirism is going to make dhampir's reawaken."

"That doesn't sound too bad," I say.

Amelia swallows. "Right. But the second thing they're all agreed on is that in order to transition, the dhampir won't just have to drink human blood..."

Red frowns, clearly still putting the pieces together. Amelia meets my gaze because I understand the insinuation in her words. This time, it's me that swallows hard, and the pair of us wait while Red stares into the distance, her eyebrows flickering. Micro expressions play out across her features.

The frown disappears, her eyes widen and her nostrils flare as she pulls in a deep breath. Her hands claw at the armchair, her knuckles white.

Her words are scarcely audible as she whispers, "I have to drain someone, don't I?"

Amelia sags. "Yeah."

"But other vampires don't have to when they transition. They only have to drink a bit of human blood. Why the hell do I have to?"

"Because of the level of magic required to complete the transformation. I'm so sorry," Amelia says and falls to her knees to take Red's hand.

But she yanks it out of Amelia's grasp.

"I'm not doing it," Red snaps and stands.

"If you don't—" Amelia starts, but I touch her hand and silence her.

"I. Am. Not. Doing. It," Red barks. Then she marches out of the office, leaving Amelia and me in silence.

Amelia puts her head in her hands. "If she doesn't drain someone..."

"I know," I say, and I get off my chair and pull her into my arms. "She will. She has no choice." I hug Amelia tight, hoping that it's enough comfort. But deep in my gut, my tummy swirls as much as I imagine Amelia's is.

We are both far too familiar with how stubborn Red can be. This is a precarious position. Neither of us wants to be the one to push her into digging her heels in. That's why I stopped Amelia talking.

"We need to give her space and time to process. She's still human, and a hunter at that. The last thing I imagine she wants to do is to drain one of her own in order to gain a load of power that—if she's honest—she probably doesn't agree with having. Look at how much she disagrees with vampires and what they've done to your family."

Amelia pulls her head off my chest and wipes her face. "I can't lose her. She's all I have left."

"Then for now, we pray to the Mother of Blood that I can sustain her for long enough to let her process what she needs to do and come to terms with it."

Amelia gathers herself and then heads to find Red, but she returns a short while later saying that Red had passed out on her bed, her cheeks tear-streaked and surrounded by pillows. We agreed we should let her rest for the remainder of the night. Which is why, several hours later, I'm still sat at my desk signing off on castle salaries and order sheets for kitchen supplies. This is the dull work that no one recognises when you run a castle the size of mine. That's without including the pile of club paperwork on the other side of the desk.

I, thankfully, use my vampire speed to make my way

through the documents, staffing reviews, alcohol and blood order forms in a little over half an hour.

It's only as I finish the last couple of signature sign-offs that Wendell comes into the office.

"Yes?" I say.

"There's... well, I think it's best you come and see. There's someone at the front of the castle."

I sigh, push myself back from the desk, and follow him.

We meander through the castle. The stone corridors are cool, and growing colder as the last of the sun's warmth ebbs away. The flame lanterns hanging uniformly along the stone corridors flicker to life, showering us in a minuscule amount of heat. We pass the grand hall and make our way to the central staircase.

It's only as I reach the bottom of the stairs that I spot Red. She's standing next to Lennox, my resident vampire blood healer. I like to think of him as insurance should any of my staff get injured and need rapid healing. The pair of them wait by the front door.

Red's eyes are puffy, a result of the crying, I suspect. She's wearing a scowl that would put even Sadie's demeanour to shame. She hides her head under an over-sized jumper hood and bed shorts. Goosebumps fleck her legs.

Wendell's expression is severe. He touches my elbow. It's jarring. While he is caring towards me, and I sense that he's fond of me, he often averts his eyes like the other humans. But he has certainly never offered a touch before. At least not like this.

"Be careful," he says and rubs his finger along the inside of my elbow before disconnecting and standing back.

A shiver runs down my back. I'm not sure if it's Wendell's touch or the fact that Lennox pulls open the door and Red sucks in a sharp gasp.

Standing in the doorway is not one, but two blood monks.

Monks, that to my knowledge, once ordained, don't leave the church grounds. They dedicate their life in service to the church, worshipping and preparing for the return of the witch-god.

Red glances at me, her eyes as wide as I imagine mine are. What the hell are they doing here?

"What—" I start, but the monk's sudden movement stops me.

His eyes jerk up. They're a muted blue. Faded and washed out like an ancient watercolour. But there's a fervour buried deep within. I don't think he's happy to be here. Perhaps he feels it's a mockery of his service. The other monk is female, and she too seems furious. Deep wrinkles crinkle her lips where they're pursed together.

They're both wearing the long claret-coloured cloaks typical of the church. Their arms remain hidden beneath their sleeves, which they hold joined in front of their bodies.

I want to ask why they're here, how we've angered them, but I don't get the chance because in eerie synchronisation they each draw out a hand from their cloaks and present their palms out towards us.

Lennox jerks forward as if he's going to step in to protect us. But I touch his arm to stop him.

The female monk's eyes drift to meet Red's.

"I guess that's for me, then?" Red says and takes a step forward.

"Wait," I say, knowing full well if this is a trap, I stand a better chance of surviving. "Let me."

The male monk edges forward, lifting his palm up to me. It's only now that I examine what it is floating in his palm.

"A bead of blood?" I mumble, more to myself than everyone else.

"It's the spirit challenge," Red says.

"Of course. Mother said we would receive invitations, but how is a drop of blood an invitation?"

The monk lifts his hand up as if he wants me to consume it.

"I see," I say and glance at Red, who's quietly shaking her head, knowing that I don't want her to drink another vampire's blood, and she doesn't want to drink a human's.

"Is it blood?" I ask the monk.

His head sways side to side in an agonisingly slow movement. He lifts his hand right up to my mouth.

"Here goes nothing," I say and suck in the not-blood hovering above his palm.

The moment it hits my tongue, my mouth bursts with flavour. It's like every drop of claret from everyone I've drunk from over the last millennia all at once. My head kicks back, white fills my vision. My mind heats, chains lock onto my consciousness, dragging me wherever this entity wants me to go.

Through the white cloud, a mirage emerges. The Church of Blood. I'm standing in a room beneath the main structure of the building. Nine beds made of stone surround a glass structure filled with blood. The room is circular in structure and dim enough the hunters will struggle to see far.

I squint at the glass vial-like structure at the centre of the stone beds.

Mother of Blood, it's the sacred vial of witch-god blood. My ears roar, my chest tightens as I deduce what we are going to have to do. Surely Cordelia can't expect us to undergo this ritual? The attrition rate and number of catatonic monks or outright deaths as a result of this process is insane. She could kill half of us off in this one trial.

Perhaps that was her plan all along.

I'm dragged forward. I try to fight the tugging. But I'm unable to resist. The chains in my mind tighten.

Slowly, the bodies of my siblings appear: Sadie first, then Dahlia, Gabriel and last Xavier, who is half dressed—caught shagging then, I expect.

One by one, the hunters appear at the foot of the remaining beds. Lincoln next to Dahlia. Talulla next to Xavier, Keir next to Gabriel.

It takes another moment. My guess is Red was waiting for me to reemerge from whatever is happening to my body back in the castle before she took her drop.

So when she slowly materialises, I'm not sure if I'm pissed with her or impressed that she took the blood from the monk, knowing something was happening to me.

She catches my eye as the same invisible force drags her to the stone bed next to me.

It's then that a monk appears in the centre of the stone beds next to the vial of blood. A moment later, Mother materialises next to him.

She leans into his ear, and he nods, leaving the circle and standing at the edge. I suspect to protect the vial from Mother. It's not like she's ever shown any common decency to the monks or the church over the years. It's very much a mutual you-stay-out-of-our-business-and-we'll-stay-out-of-yours deal between Mother and the church. Which is why I'm surprised we're here and this is what she chose.

Finally, the Chief appears just outside the circle, her eyes focussed on Cordelia. They flick to the glass vial stretching up into the dimness and the higher she scans, the more her top lip curls. Finally, she gives Mother a nod of assent and Mother begins.

"Children, hunters, welcome. This is where your trial of spirit will be held. You have twelve hours to reconvene here, at which point you will endure the same trial that the hopefuls experience before ordination."

My stomach sinks. This is exactly what I feared. Xavier and Gabriel's mouths drop. I imagine they both gasped, but it appears we're unable to speak because despite their throats and lips bobbing and moving, no sound drifts across the atrium.

Unhindered, Mother continues. "Each of you will be given a single drop of sacred blood. What happens after that is unknown by anyone who hasn't partaken of the blood rite and unspoken of by anyone who has. Your experiences will differ."

Red catches my eye, and my lips press together. This isn't good. The only one of us who looks unfazed is Sadie. In fact, she looks distinctly smug. She folds her arms and despite the lack of light, her eyes still glimmer.

But of course, she would be smug because this trial was practically made for her. She's the most spiritual of us all, the strongest believer and the one most familiar with monks who have gone through this ancient rite.

Mother meets each of our gazes. "You will each be on your own during this trial. It is a test of mental fortitude and strength, not only a key skill for a leader, but one that will prepare you for what will come across the boundary. This will be a test of your greatest fears and darkest nightmares. You will experience everything in the confines of your own mind while your body remains here." She gestures to the stone beds. "The trial will last several hours for some and potentially several days for the weaker among us. If you do not complete it, your mind will be lost to the spiritual plane, and your body will either desiccate or starve to death."

Dahlia pales. She shares a look with Gabriel, and for once I don't need to be her twin to understand the fear trickling through her system.

"For each of you that successfully completes the test, the Mother of Blood will gift you a vision. It is this vision we believe will contain information that will help us across the boundary. For now, welcome to the spirit trial."

With that, she evaporates, and I'm yanked backwards through the white mist, landing back in my body at the entrance to Castle Beaumont. My stomach turns over on itself, and I swallow down the bitter taste of bile. My tongue burns like the aftertaste of puke.

Red appears back in her body a moment later. Stumbling forward, she trips straight out the door and hurls her guts up.

Wendell and Lennox rush to her side, helping her upright.

"Wendell, please fetch me some foods. Likewise, for Red. I'll need the richest blood, and she will need carbs. Lots of them."

He inclines his head and Lennox, once Red is sturdy on her feet, follows him.

Red pushes her hood down; her skin is pale and clammy.

"Well, that sounds fun," she says, her tone flat and dry.

I can't even muster sarcasm. "Hmm. This is a bad idea. The ordination process for the monks is severe. Who really wants to face their darkest fears?"

She wipes her face and stands a little straighter. "Then I'd say we have twelve hours to figure out how to kick our inner demons' arses."

CHAPTER 23

OCTAVIA

Red is in a foul mood. She needs to dose again. We're at the point that she needs blood almost every other hour. I'm keeping her rationed to a few drops each time and dosing little and often seems to be having an effect. For now. She's built a tolerance, and though it's also lowering the urge to fuck, I have to wonder if that's because we're already bonded or because her craving for human blood has increased and is offsetting the need for mine.

Dawn edges towards the horizon as our carriage arrives outside the Church of Blood.

She huffs again as she pulls the carriage curtain aside. "We're here, and by the looks of it, so is everyone else. I wonder if they found anything useful in the last twelve hours."

We tried researching the blood monk rituals and rites, but to no avail. All the useful texts were, unsurprisingly, in the church vaults.

"I highly doubt it. The only one with insider knowledge would be Sadie. I don't think anyone other than she will have a head start on this one. But remember, she didn't score in the first trial, and no one scored in the last, so she's still in last place. Even if she won this round, she won't be in the lead unless none of us makes it out."

"We have to win, Octavia. I want that cure for Amelia. And we're not going to unless we claw points back. And we won't do that if one of us dies."

I scan Red's face. Her words are potent, but her expression doesn't match.

"Do you still want to win?" I ask.

"Of course I do," she snaps.

But I'm not sure she still believes that. Or maybe she does consciously, but her subconscious says differently.

"What if we're ambushed? What if we lose our minds? What if the trial unleashes our worst nightmares and scares us to death?" She flings her arms in the air.

"Then I won't run this city, and you won't be getting a cure for your sister. So how about we lay off the negativity and focus on getting ourselves through this? Which you won't if you have a shred of doubt about your capabilities."

I lean forward and pull her chin around so she's facing me. "I believe in you, Verity Fairbanks. You're going to get through this. As am I. And when we're on the other side of it, we'll celebrate in style. And then we'll shape this city into something magnificent. Something we can both be proud of, and we'll do it by each other's side."

Her lips part, her breathing short and rapid. My focus drops to her mouth. I want to kiss it. I want to draw her lip between mine and suck it until she begs me to fuck her. But I can't. This love that we're holding between us is so fragile, I don't want to do anything that will risk what tenuous connection we have left. She hasn't forgiven me. I know by the space she holds between us. But I'll fight for every millimetre I can gain back.

It's why I refused to bite her the other night when her emotions were all over the place, and it's why I won't kiss her now. Because kissing her will lead to fucking her, which will lead to one or other of us biting each other. And we don't have time for any of it.

I pull the carriage curtain aside and glance at the sky. The first hints of burnt ochre simmer on the horizon.

"Time to go," I say.

Red grumbles but opens the carriage door and steps into the church courtyard.

We're welcomed by monks, one for each of us. These monks don't appear to have taken a vow of silence yet. They chatter away to each of us. The one chatting with Gabriel hands him a book and presses Gabe's hands against it. Gabriel about bursts with excitement.

The monk talking to Red seems to have lifted her mood already. She throws her head back, laughing. Her eyes are bright and smiling. There's a bite in my chest, a stab of something I'd rather not confess to. She seems delighted though, as they huddle closer and natter away to each other.

The church doors open as the sky brightens and my arms itch. My siblings and I all speed inside, eager to get the gnawing sensation off our skin. The hunters waltz in behind us, and last, the blood monks follow, closing the door and sealing us inside the church.

Red was fine outside, but as I scan her up and down, I can see she's trembling. I edge next to her. "Everything okay?" I ask.

"The scent is strong in here," she says.

The blood, of course. I hadn't even thought about it. But last time we were here, there were basins filled with blessed blood. Given the state of her addiction, she's got to be overwhelmed.

“Breathe through your mouth. It will reduce the severity.”

She nods and her lips part.

The nine monks stand in front of us and bow, indicating that we should follow them. Side by side, down the main aisle, we proceed through the church.

My eyes gaze up at the art that adorns the building. I’m impressed each time I see the stories told not with words but with images, and the memories painted and carved into the ceilings and windows.

It makes me wonder whether artists should really be called wizards, for the gift they have for translating meaning and emotion from one complex language into another.

We pass through a gate at the rear of the church and into an area I’ve never visited, down a narrow, twisting stone staircase and into the bowels of the building.

My body flecks with gooseflesh at the drastic drop in air temperature; Red and the hunters must be freezing. At the edges of my vision, the unyielding stone walls seem to pulse, and I can’t work out whether it’s in my head or if they’re really throbbing with some mystical force.

We reach an antechamber and the monks guide each of us to stand in a circle. Red is back chatting with her monk, and whatever he’s saying is engaging enough that she’s smiling again. All I can say is thank the Mother of Blood for him because the last thing I want is for her to go into this trial mentally distracted and riddled with doubt.

The monks vanish and return with bowls of water and washcloths. They make us cleanse our faces, brush our fangs and wash our hands.

We’re silent the whole time. The only sound is the slow, methodical beating of the blood monk’s hearts and the increasingly rapid beating of the hunters’.

Next, they bring us red cloaks identical to the ones they wear, though several shades lighter.

I reach to take it, but the monk pulls it away and points to my current clothing.

You have got to be kidding me. I clench my jaw but strip off anyway, snatching the cloak out of the monk's hand a little too aggressively. Dahlia is as unhappy about the situation as I am and snatches her cloak harder than I do. Lincoln, Talulla and Keir quietly do as they're told. Gabriel cops an eyeful of Keir while he's changing but slips his arms into the cloak on request.

Once we're all de-clothed and fully robed, the monk closest to the chamber door opens it. There's a hiss as the door creaks open, and white mist rolls out of the room beyond.

"What the hell?" Xavier says.

Sadie clicks her finger to make him look at her, and she signs, "If you weren't so ignorant, you'd know they keep the Chamber of Blood at a low temperature to help with the preservation of the witch-god's blood."

"I see," he says.

But Sadie isn't finished berating him and raises her hands to continue. "It's also why you're asked to strip and wear the cloak. It's fur-lined and imbued with the tiniest hint of magic to retain heat. The magic is weak, so it only works if it's next to the skin."

The monk guiding her nudges her. She pouts with her mouth, but the glare she gives him is vicious. Sadie is normally in charge as the head of the church, so to be bossed around by her underlings must sting.

We're led to our respective stone beds, the same ones we saw in our visions. Only this time there's an obsidian basin at the head of each bed filled with a shimmering silver liquid.

One of the monks heads to the enormous glass vial containing the blood from the witch-god, our holy Mother of Blood. He holds a bowl under a faucet attached to the bottom of the vial and twists the handle, allowing exactly nine drops to fall into the bowl he holds.

Then he makes his way around the room, using a syringe to draw up a single droplet of blood and deposit it in each obsidian basin. Sadie's is first. The liquid hisses and turns black. Dahlia next, then Lincoln. The monk makes his way around until he's stood in front of me and dropping the last bead of blood into my basin.

The Chief appears beside Mother. Together they enter the circle of stone beds.

"Sit," Mother says, her voice barely above a whisper.

In unison, all nine of us take our positions, sitting on our beds facing our monks. The blood monks tilt the basins, pouring the dark gloopy concoction into a chalice.

The beating of the four hunters' hearts ratchets up a notch. I'm sure my siblings can hear it. It thuds like an inevitable countdown.

Beat. Five.

Beat. Four.

Beat. Three.

Beat. Two.

Beat. One.

The monks raise the chalices to our lips. I glance at Red one last time.

Our eyes lock. She wears the same wide-eyed, pinched look I do.

I wonder if she wishes the same thing I do.

I wish I could tell her it will be all right. That we will get through this together. But I can't because we're doing this alone, and for the first time since these trials started, I can't help or support her. I can't protect her.

I want to tell her I love her, no matter what. And last, I wish those words were on her lips for me, too.

But they're not.

The monk tips the chalice up to my lips, and I tear my gaze away from her, swallowing the strange liquid.

It tastes like starlight and gold. Like the glistening of the moonlight on the ocean surface, and everywhere it touches, it tingles.

It slides down my throat, and as it does, I have a strange, disconnecting feeling as my body lowers to the stone bed, but I stay where I am.

I blink, and the room is gone. Instead, I'm in an ethereal landscape where the boundaries between reality and dreams blur.

I wave my hand through the fog. No one else is here. The dim-lit atrium, the stone beds and everyone in it have all vanished.

The white mist flows through my fingers like sand and silk, but eventually it clears enough I spot a ghostly figure standing in the distance.

"Who are you?" I call out, but the figure just stands there, immobile.

"I guess you're my trial guide? Or maybe my trial executioner. One or the other."

I make my way through the fog towards him, but the closer I get, the further away he seems. The air around me twists and undulates with a vibration that crawls over my skin.

I stop and glance back, wondering how far I've come, but behind me now lays a field of pasture. Daisies and poppies fill the landscape as the sky clears and the sun beams down.

I gasp. I've never seen the sun in the sky. Never seen so many flowers with open blooms, not unless they're moon flowers born of night. And there are many fewer night-born plants than day ones.

I immediately scream, patting my arms and searching for shelter, but my skin isn't burning. In fact, nothing hurts, nothing even stings. I am standing in the light, gawping toward the sun, and I am still alive.

Or trying to, but it hurts my eyes to stare too directly at it.

I turn back to find the ghostly figure and my blood freezes. He is right in front of me. There is a shrouded space where his face should be. A dark hood with a hollow void that is utterly endless.

I can't look away. The vastness of it holds me in place. I writhe on the spot, desperate to escape.

A hand reaches up to my chest.

"No," I say.

His fingers slowly dig into my cloak, piercing the fabric, and then press against my skin.

I try to grab at his hand, but my body is motionless. His nails slice my flesh.

I scream as the heat of his touch sears through my body. It's like he's pouring molten steel into my body as his hand sinks into my chest.

This is how I die. A thousand years and this, finally, is how it ends, and my only thought is of not having given Red a last kiss. Not pleading with her one more time to forgive me.

Not telling her I love her over and over until my lips chap and my throat runs hoarse.

Somewhere swirling around the mist, a voice screams. I think it's mine, but I'm no longer certain. He buries his hand in my chest cavity.

I'm certain he's going to rip my heart out, but he yanks

me forward and finally the pain ceases and everything goes black.

When I rouse, I am laid on stone cobbles in a strange place. The floor is dank and smells like iron and manure. The light casts a muted, dreary grey over the adjoining alleys. Like the sun ran out and spat the dregs of light out from the bottom of its fuel tank.

"Hello?" I call, but there's no answer.

I stand. The sky is burnt grey. Rain spatters against the cobbles. I glance around me and freeze.

"This is... This is impossible," I breathe.

I'm in Sangui City, but it doesn't appear like Sangui City. I stumble out of the alleyway I'm in and find myself in the main square near the Midnight Market.

In the distance, I can just make out the remnants of the market. I speed across the square and towards the stalls. The sellers are skeletal. Their skin stretches taut over their skeletal bodies.

Their eyes are gaunt and hollow.

The first stall I reach has a scant selection of items. Barely enough, if he sold them all, to feed a family for a week.

"What happened here?" I whisper.

"She happened," he says without even looking up. Instead, he raises his finger towards a statue in the middle of the market.

I glance at the statue, and my blood turns to ice. It's a porcelain figure of a face I recognise: mine.

"I don't understand," I say. But he's no longer responsive.

I speed around the market, and each stall I reach is more of the same. Starving humans and barely a passing trade, the market is still like death. The city seems drained of its life source. Drained of...

"No. It can't be. I would never."

I grab a woman shuffling past me. She, too, doesn't raise her eyes to peer up at me. At least the humans in my Sangui City glance up and then run away, horrified. These people are so... hopeless.

It's like someone has crushed their spirit.

"What. Happened?" I command.

She trembles against my grip but raises her other hand to the statue.

"Explain," I bark, and try to keep the anger out of my voice.

"She won the trials and became queen and then broke every promise. It was all lies. Everything she ever said was a lie. She is the monster we all feared she was."

"No. I... I mean, she wouldn't do that."

Somewhere in the recesses of my mind, I know this can't be real, that I don't belong in this city. But this city seems solid. The air is cool in my lungs, her arms wrinkled and leathery under my touch. Is this real? Did I fuck everything up?

I was certain the plans I had would help. We'd have a fair city that welcomed everyone. Where did I go wrong? Why can't I remember what I did?

The woman's gaunt face twists into a snarl.

"But you fucked up, Octavia. You ruined this city. You drained it of life and love and let your siblings drink us dry. Well now, we're all going to die because there isn't enough blood."

Her eyes widen. She grabs me and shakes me. "Are you listening, Octavia? There's never enough blood."

She screams, shaking me by the arms, gloopy spittle flecking my chest and face. She shakes and shakes until she shakes her skin away, and all that's left of her are her bones that clatter against the cobbles.

My skin prickles like I'm being watched. Every market seller has turned to face me.

"Monster," they whisper in unison.

Faster and faster, they repeat it until someone screams the word, and another follows.

Louder.

Louder.

Until I fall to my knees, clutching my ears.

"I'm not a monster." I rock myself forward and back, saying it over and over until a scream silences the market.

Then every single market seller and shopper runs. They all head out of the square. And I'm up and running and screaming at them to wait. To tell me what's going on. To beg them to tell what they are running from.

"She's coming," someone shrieks.

"The monster is coming."

"Demon."

More voices shriek until they're all running and pointing at me.

I'm running after them and shouting back that it's not me. I wouldn't do this. But they're leading me through a maze of streets and alleys. And none of it looks like my Sangui City.

Everything is derelict and broken. Bricks scatter the ground. The streets are narrow and dark. Everything smells like stagnant water and faeces. Windows are cracked or smashed. A layer of filth and grime covers the doors and curtains.

There are no children. Where are all the children?

The deeper I run into the city, the more lost I become. This isn't my city. I didn't do this.

Did I?

But the voices fill my head even as I lose sight of their figures. I hit a dead end, double back on myself only to reach another dead end.

Where am I? Is this really what will happen if I win? If I take over the city?

Am I just the monster they all think I am?

I wanted to protect the city, make it a space where everyone was welcome. What happened to me to destroy the thing I wanted to call home?

A tear falls down my cheek. I wipe it away as a piece of my heart wipes away with it.

Perhaps I should bow out now. Perhaps I shouldn't run this city, maybe I can't make it a better place after all.

I turn and catch sight of myself in a shard of broken mirror. My face is twisted and aged. The only signs of life are my blood-red eyes staring back at me. They burn hot and soulless. My fangs have elongated and sharpened to razor points.

I am a monster. That's all I ever was. All I'll ever be.

The ghostly figure who sent me here reappears at the end of the alley.

"You," I snarl. Ready for him this time.

"You did this," the faceless hood says.

"I did..." But my words falter as I catch my reflection in my periphery and it falters. For one brief moment, I see me the way Red sees me—not with eyes the colour of death, but the colour of love and life.

And that's when I remember. None of this is real. This is all just a test. One designed to try to break me. I run my fingers along the cobbles and through a grimy puddle. They come away wet.

A test that feels real. Perhaps in another universe this is what I did.

But I am better than this.

"No," I say, standing. "I did not."

The world around me dissolves and when it reforms, I'm in my bedroom. A figure lays in the shadows of my four-poster bed, a muslin layer shrouding them from view.

But I know that body. I know that figure.

It's Red.

"Did you win? Are we out of the spirit trial?" I ask.

"Yes," she says. "Come here."

So I do. I push the curtain aside and climb onto the bed. She's naked. Splayed ready for me to take her.

She beckons me forward with the curl of her index finger.

I climb up the bed until I am millimetres from her lips. "Gods, I've missed you," I breathe.

She brushes her lips against mine.

Something is off.

I slide my hand up the back of her neck and draw her to me until our mouths meet. She kisses me.

But it's forced. Cold. Empty.

The heat of our bodies nonexistent.

I pull back, frowning.

"What's—" I start, but she cuts me off, her face contorting. Her chiselled jawline becomes sharp and harsh. Her green eyes cold and icy.

I don't recognise her.

"I've seen the truth. I know who you are now, Octavia," she snarls.

"What do you mean? You've always known who I am."

"You're a liar. A thief. You ruin everything. You ruin me. Ruined my sister."

"No. I... I saved Amelia. She would have died. You know that."

"You're everything I hate. How many memories did you take? How many times did you take my free will away, Octavia? I'll never love you unless you let me go. Unless you let me be free. Unless you tell me what really happened that night."

"No. No. You made me promise. You begged me."

"So now this is my fault?"

"That's not what I..." I'm crawling back off the bed. I need to get away. I can't do this. This city is killing me. Everything is wrong and twisted and broken. And it's all my fault.

"Yes, Octavia. It's all your fault. You're a fucking monster, just like they all said you were."

I look up at her, my eyes welling as I scramble back.

"You don't mean that," I cry.

"I mean every word of it. You disgust me. You've always made my skin crawl. You will never be enough because you'll never be anything but a filthy fucking monster."

"No," I whisper, my voice cracking. "Please," I hold my hands out towards her. But she shoves me back.

I tip off the edge of the bed...

... and I land in a new room.

I stare up at the ceiling, recognising where I am. My mother's throne room. I roll onto my stomach and push myself to my feet only to stumble backwards until I hit Mother's throne and collapse down into it.

The seat is odd; not the soft, plush leather of normal but like I'm sat on someone's lap. I stand up, wrench around and scream.

Mother's body rests on the throne. Her skin is grey and

desiccating. Her mouth hangs slack, her eyes vacant and staring through me.

Pieces of her flesh flake off and drift into the air until a thick smog of decaying flesh swirls around me. The door swings open, and my siblings stumble through, each of them desiccating in the same way Mother is. Only they're still standing and walking.

Dahlia falls first. A long sword driven straight through her, front to back. She points a finger at me. "You did this."

"I didn't. It wasn't me, Dahlia, I swear."

Gabriel crawls on his hands and knees, his eyes already rotten to black orbs still stare at me like he can see. "Your fault. You ruined us."

Xavier appears now, stepping over Gabriel, but with each successive step he takes, his legs crumble more. His beautiful face is marred and shredded, scars gouge through his cheeks and mouth.

He opens his maw, his jaw disconnecting and hanging low as he chokes out gravelly words. "I thought you were better than this. You really are the freak everyone says you are."

My mouth falls slack, a silent scream ripping from my lungs.

Last, Sadie appears, only she is intact, the same Sadie I recognise. She floats up to me. He fingers caress my cheek. She tilts my forehead down to kiss it, like the sweet caress of a child to a doll.

"I just wanted you to realise," she says aloud. She speaks with words and not her hands. I don't understand.

And that's when I remember this isn't real. My Sadie can't speak. I desperately cling to the knowledge that this isn't real. But it looks real, it sounds real, it feels like home.

I wipe a hand over my face.

"Realise what?" I ask, gripping her by the shoulders.

But her eyes widen. Her mouth falls slack, and she tilts to look at her chest where the hilt of a blade protrudes, the shaft buried deep in her heart.

Her skin ripples, her hair trembles, a wash of black shivers through it and vanishes. Her veins darken beneath her skin, purple squiggles appearing all over her body.

"Why did you kill me?" she says and then she explodes in a burst of skin and bone and flaking life. The blade clatters to the floor at my feet.

"No," I scream. But no sound comes out.

I slide to the floor, wrapping my arms around my knees and rocking back and forth. All of my siblings are dead, their bodies rotting around me. My mother desiccating behind me.

How did I do this? Why did I kill them all? I love them, I didn't mean to make this happen. Whispers ricochet around the throne room, "Your fault. You're not enough. You ruin everything."

Over and over.

Louder and louder.

I don't want to hear it. I don't want to believe it. But maybe they're all right. Maybe I should desiccate myself. I reach forward, and my fingers skirt along the blade.

A single voice cuts through the noise of all the other accusations.

"Stop," it says.

The voice is familiar. I know it. It's like it's coming from deep inside me. It's like the voice is part of me. Or a part of who I was.

It's so faint I can hardly hear it.

I reach a little further forward, my fingers curling around the hilt as I bring the tip to my chest, right over the scar Red gave me. This time there will be no missing.

"Octavia. Stop. This isn't you. I'm here for you."

That's when I recognise who the voice belongs to. Red. Only not the Red from the bedroom a moment ago. The Red bonded to me. It's like the piece of her soul attached to mine is protecting me the way I always protect her.

Her words curl around me, wrapping me in comfort.

"They're the colour of love and life. I see you, Octavia. I love you for you. And you will always be enough. Now get out of here. I need you to come back to me," she says.

My fingers tighten around the blade, but instead of pushing it deeper, I pull it away and grip it like a weapon.

I will fight my way out of this because I AM ENOUGH.

I have always been enough, and now I'm ready to face anything this fucking challenge can throw at me.

I draw my body into a fighting stance, but the room is already dissolving.

The mist is sweeping back around my feet. My siblings' bodies dissolve, the throne behind me gone, and I am stood back at the beginning. The ghostly figure in the hood stands before me.

Only this time, he kneels on one leg and holds out a hand, palm up.

I glance at my hand holding the blade, but it too has vanished. So I lay my hand in his. There's a tingle between our palms as we grip each other.

"Congratulations, Octavia. And now, your reward. The gods have decided to bestow upon you a single piece of information. You've always wondered what happened to your birth mother. This is her story..."

The ghost vanishes, and instead I am standing in a quaint little cottage a thousand years ago, the sun setting, showering the cottage in beams of orange and burnt yellow. I try to move, but I'm pinned in place. The kettle simmers on the stove. A woman with long hair is facing away from me.

"Mum?" I say.

But before she can answer, dusk settles, and the light vanishes.

There's a knock at the door.

The vision drags me to the far side of the room. I try and step closer, but I'm stuck at the entrance to the living room. My birth mother moves constantly, so I can never quite see her face. I want to scream in frustration. What gift is this if I can't see her face, if I can't discover who she really is?

Her hand slides to the door handle, and she twists it open as a small whimper comes from behind me. I gasp, as I find a cot nestled just behind me in the entrance to the living room. It's a baby?

Not a baby.

Me. As a baby. I reach down to pick myself up but my hand brushes through my body as if I'm an apparition.

It doesn't matter. The door opens and the air cools to ice, gooseflesh prickles my birth mother's arms, and as I glance up, I gasp.

"Cordelia."

CHAPTER 24

CORDELIA

Present Day

I stand amongst the bodies of my unconscious children. I am not one for nerves, but as I stare down at their strangled expressions, my stomach churns and twists in on itself.

The blood monks hum and sing their chants, pacing around the outside of the stone beds, praying for my children's return.

The Chief appears at my side. "Wondering if this was such a good idea?" she asks, her blue eyes staring into mine.

My jaw flexes. Years of hatred seep into my bones, reminding me she is my enemy. Every hunter is. They always have been. They always will be.

"I still believe the Mother of Blood will reveal something of us to them. You forget, she too had power. She too was a dhampir. She would want magic returned."

"Perhaps."

"We must get through that border, Chief. Last night,

there was another attempt to break in. I lost three vampire guards."

"Was the boundary penetrated?"

"No. And the amulet is safe and under twenty-four-hour guard surveillance, too. I'm not concerned."

"More annoyed you didn't catch who was doing it?"

I nod. "If we were faster, I wouldn't have to put my children through these trials. Do you really think I want to put them through this kind of mental anguish?"

The Chief's eyebrow rises.

"Don't look at me like that. I am capable of love."

"Are you?"

I turn away. "I was. Once."

She sighs, a heavy breath full of unspoken words. She shifts her footing. "Is everything prepared?"

"Quiet. We're not to discuss that when there are others present."

"Fine," she huffs. "What would you face if you were in there?"

"You know exactly what I'd face," I say a little too sharply.

"The witch-god?"

I nod, bile licking up my throat.

This is the real reason I hate the church. The secret that plagues my soul. I would face the Mother of Blood herself. The biggest mistake of my life. And the only lie I've told for a thousand years.

This is the lie I tell:

Once upon a time, there were two families, the St Clairs and the Randalls. And like any respected families of nobility, they were at war. For petty things, land and property, the economy and legacy.

Those things are true. We were at war.

But here is where the lie begins. It wasn't a local witch

that took issue with our dealings. It wasn't a witch that cursed Eleanor and me to become mortal enemies.

It was our families.

They wove their secret betrayal in the depths of midnight. They spoke tales of curses and horror to the witch. Begged her in whispered promises and hapless lies to make our love stop.

Our families.

Our very own families.

How could they? All because their broken hearts were sick of our love, sick of the shame.

So, as midnight struck, they gathered together under the golden glow of candlelight.

As darkness enveloped the world, they forced a witch to sign a contract in bloody prints.

A scarred scroll thick with the fibrous rot of a curse.

And so it was that as the twelfth bell rang at midnight, all our fates—mine, Eleanor's and the witch's—were sealed together for eternity.

I think it's time to confess.

Let me tell you what really happened.

One Thousand Years Ago

Hope is an insidious little thing. It makes a mockery of reality. It makes you believe the impossible. Eleanor and I thrive on hope. For all the years we've tried and failed to stay together, it was always hope that kept us trying again. Kept us fighting for one more night, one more kiss. Despite the threats and warnings, hope made us ignorant.

It made us believe the impossible.

Tonight, we are finally free. Tonight, we fled our families for the last time.

That's how I find myself at midnight, curled under a blanket tucked into Eleanor's side.

Neither of us knows where we are, but it doesn't matter. We're leaving to find a new city. Perhaps the city with magicians, or perhaps one with the fae people. It matters not. What is important is that we're not going back. Not ever again.

Eleanor's breathing is heavy and deep beside me. The rhythmic exhalations lull me into a reverie. My eyes flutter shut, and that is when the pain wrecks my body.

I lurch out of her warm grip. The loss of her heat is instantaneous. I roll away, a strange sensation trickling through my body. Everything tingles and cools until I'm shivering.

It's a cold that leeches into bones and grows in graves. It creeps up my fingertips and crawls down my arms.

Inch by inch, my veins chill until they ache. I glance back at Eleanor, still sleeping sweetly under the stars. My eyes flick to her throat, the soft pulse of her blood through her arteries. My mouth fills with saliva. I frown, unsure why I have the urge to bend low and kiss her in the same spot where her skin flutters with the beat of her heart.

No, not kiss. Bite.

Bite. Bite. Bite.

Drink. Drink. Drink.

Drain her of life. Of magic. Of her blood. I want it.

Need it.

I slap my hand over my mouth and stagger back. What the hell is wrong with me?

I fall to my knees, my hand wrapped around my stomach as I lurch forward and throw up.

Eleanor's eyes shoot open.

"What's going on?" she says, her voice shrill.

"Stay back. There's something wrong with me," I say, putting my hand out to stop her from getting any closer.

I shake my head as a loud beating fills my ears. But it's not like the roaring of blood in my ears when I've run across the city. It goes ba-dum, ba-dum, ba-dum.

I glance at her neck. The sound moves with the same rhythm as the flutter in her neck. I'm hearing her heart.

I have to leave. Thoughts of consuming her fill my head. She's in danger, from me, and I'd rather leave and flee than see me hurt her.

"Cordelia, talk to me. What's wrong?" she pleads.

But my body is getting worse, the pain wracking my fingers and arms is flooding my entire system. It's like my insides are shrivelling, decaying, dying. And the awful knowing that the only thing that will cure it is her.

Not her.

Her blood.

There's no time to kiss her. No time to say goodbye.

She shakes her head at me, tears flowing down her cheeks. "Don't do this. Don't go. Not after everything."

But how can I explain what I feel in my bones: that I will hurt her if I don't leave? I can't explain what I don't understand.

So I turn and run.

I run to the screams and pleas of Eleanor begging me to stay. Not to leave her. That she will do anything.

And then, just as suddenly, her cries stop and the woods are silent as I stagger my way through them.

I trip and cut my knee on a stray branch, but as soon as

it bleeds, it heals. I scream in shock as I watch the skin knit together. What is happening to me?

My feet pound the dirt as I run and run, but after a time, I become aware that I'm not really running away. I'm being led. Drawn to the source of my pain. The magic that has bewitched my veins.

All night, I run until the sun rises, and my skin begins to itch and blister. I don't understand why my body is rejecting the sun. But as my skin starts to bleed, I find shelter in an abandoned property on the outskirts of Sangui City.

I pace the rooms all day, unable to sleep. Half the hours I lay on the floor screaming and writhing as my body contorts and twists like a dead spider. Sharp pains lance through my bones, hot then cold as the depths of the ocean. I throw up everything in my stomach. I sweat half the day away until I am sure I should have died from dehydration.

I eat my way through the stores. I consume everything, mouldy bread, jars of dried beans, grains, flours that crawl with bugs. But it matters not. I throw everything up and even the bits I keep down cannot satiate the hunger gnawing in my veins. It consumes me.

It makes my teeth ache and my tongue twitch. Nothing helps.

The pain ebbs away for a while, and I pace again. And then, as the sun sinks in the sky, I finally leave the building and make my way towards the source.

I take a week of searching, hunting. I live off rats and rabbits and scraps of meat, even drinking down their bloody fluids. My mind vomits everything, but my body keeps it down. I want to claw my skin off in disgust, and I consume the rodents like I consume the air. But still, nothing satiates the pains in my stomach.

Finally, after a week of seeking shelter in the day and

trudging on at night, I can feel I'm close now. I can sense the connection. Under the dark of night, I enter a small village on the edge of the city, a rather quaint gathering of bungalows and thatched cottages. There are no people around. It's like a ghost village. I steal fresh bread and milk, only to drink it all down and gobble it without tasting. But like all the other nights, I throw it up and hunt for a rat instead. I find some scraps of chicken in a bin behind a larger bungalow. But even that doesn't satiate the pain in my belly.

I continue on.

But the further I go, the sicker I feel. It's not only the hunger, but the bodies.

At first, it was only one. A young girl, dead in the street, a dhampir—a healer. Her hands have shrivelled as if someone sucked the magic out of them.

The deeper I travel into the village, the more bodies I find. They litter the streets and doorways. I peer into windows and find corpses riddled with maggots. It's a stark contrast to the herbs and planting troughs that fill the front gardens. Their windows have jars and jugs of picked flowers and herbs. Specimens and creatures.

The witch village.

Was I cursed? The realisation hits me hard as I peek through window after window. But nothing in there is what I seek. Then, I reach the last house in the village and warmth settles in my belly. I found it.

The door throbs with more magic than any other building in the village. It hums the same rhythmic beating that weaves its way through my veins. A beat that dies with ever successive pulse. And I have to wonder if this is where I meet my demise.

I knock on the door as another fresh wave of agony curls my stomach in on itself. The hunger now is like nothing I've ever experienced. It threads its way into my mind until the only thing I can think of is that I need to drink.

Drink blood.

The door opens, and a young woman stands before me. But I'm weak and I can barely see her face. Long raven-coloured locks covered much of it.

She gasps when she sees me.

"What did you do to me?" I rasp.

"It... it wasn't me," she says, "Your family. They made me."

"Made you what?" I bark, though it comes out as a choked cough. Blood splatters her white dress. I think my insides are disintegrating.

"They made me curse you and your lover, Eleanor. They didn't want you together."

"What did you do?"

"I..." her head hangs low. I want her to look at me. To stare into my eyes so I know the face of my killer. But she won't, she refuses. There's a rustling in the background, but I ignore it. I'm fully focussed on her.

"What did you do? Why am I hungry?"

"I'm sorry," she weeps. "Curses are fickle things, and the wording... I don't understand what you are. But I know what you need. The curse was wrought in blood magic. It ruined everything. We have paid the price because it destroyed all our magic. The dhampirs are dead. I am the only one left..."

"Then how do I survive?"

"I suspect unless you consume blood, you, too, will perish."

That is why Eleanor's neck, the pulsing of her heart, drew me in.

"Your family asked me to curse you, to make you hate each other, to never love one another again."

Something cracks inside me. We fought for so long to keep each other. Through beatings and burnings. Through the hate and betrayals, only to have this fucking witch take it all away, anyway.

My stomach screams, hunger consuming me. She took everything from me. Hot, putrid fury seeps into my chest. She needs to pay for what she's done.

I grab her neck and yank her to me and sink my teeth into the fleshy pulp of her throat.

As my teeth graze her skin, they sharpen and sink into her flesh. Her screams rend the air as the first drops of her blood kiss my tongue.

Sweet, sweet blood flows down my throat, and that is when everything changes.

The stars wink to life, as time stands still. The wind silences, the rustling of leaves and plants ceases.

There is nothing but the slowing beat of the witch's heart and the wet slurps of my tongue lapping against her neck. Blood pours down my dress, splattering and staining my chin, my jaw, my chest.

But with every gulp I swallow, my body relaxes a little more. The agony coursing through my body loosens. The itching in my veins ceases. Cold settles. No longer a burning ache, but a cooling peace that wraps my heart into a new rhythm.

Power floods my system as my muscles reform and reshape themselves. My eyes sting like they're pinching and sharpening.

I am becoming something else.

The witch weakens. She sags in my arms. She's a full-grown woman, but I find her weight to be that of a feather in my arms. That's when I glance down and notice her tummy is rounded.

The soft paunch of post birth.

I startle as I lay her down. She is not long for this world. I have drained her of almost all her blood. She will not survive the hour.

She glances up at me. "Please," she begs. Her voice is barely above a whisper and yet it is loud. It's like she shouts at me. "Don't hurt her."

"Hurt who?" I ask.

"Octavia." It's the last word she says.

I glance up at the kitchen door, and there, beyond the entrance, is a crib. I step over her body and make my way to it.

Cradled in a yellow blanket is a baby. It can't be more than a couple of days old. It cries, its eyes opening as it screams.

I gasp. It's the most beautiful and wretched thing I've ever seen. Staring back at me are crimson eyes unlike anything I've seen before. No human has eyes like this. And I realise that this was the witch's penance. Curses require dark magic. If she was pregnant when she cursed me, it was her baby who paid the price.

A curse made of blood.

A baby born of a curse.

This creature is like me. That she hungers for the same blood I do.

I cradle her to my chest. "It's okay, sweet thing. I will look after you, Octavia," I say. "Mother has you now."

I take her from the cottage and leave the body of her birth mother bleeding what little remained in her body onto the kitchen's stone slabs. Her lips mutter prayers to her gods. Her body is already pale and growing paler and more contorted as death consumes her. I don't wait around. What's the point? I've consumed her life force. Despite never turning around, the sting of her eyes boring into me as I stole her baby away still torments me a thousand years later. I step into the night, the fluttering and stuttering of her heartbeat slowing until it's faint and weak. Her fate sealed.

She had wrought hell upon me; I sent her to hell in kind.

Or so I thought.

It wasn't until many weeks later that I discovered she hadn't died. While I never had confirmation, I am certain that it was her. There were too many rumours that a monster ran through the woods of the territory on the western side of the city.

Too many bodies bled dry. And at that point, I hadn't worked out that I could turn others to become like us. That took another few years and happened by accident. There were no others, only Octavia and me. And it wasn't me bleeding the humans.

I loathed myself for years for not paying attention to the witch as her skin paled and her body morphed. I thought it was death coming for her. Not the hand of her gods saving her. And how would I find her now? I fear she wouldn't look as she did.

I don't know what magic the gods cast to save her life. But she became like me.

I spent weeks in fear that she would come for Octavia. My Octavia, who stole my heart.

She never did.

What kind of mother abandons her daughter?

Eventually, she disappeared. She formed the Montague territory and turned enough vampires to carry on her legacy. Her true origins never surfaced. No one ever discovered what I'd done. I decided to create history the way I saw fit.

Her story became a myth, she became a god.

And I became a monster.

CHAPTER 25

RED

The liquid tastes like shit. But I mean, of course it does. It's thousand-year-old god blood, what did I expect?

I lie down on the stone bed, or I think I do. Only I still seem to be sitting upright, so weird.

The atrium blurs, mist rising from the ground until it's thick enough I can't see in front of me. I swirl my arms through it, shout for Octavia, but she doesn't reach out to me.

The air cools and then warms until finally the mist clears, and I'm in a pasture full of daisies and poppies.

If this is the extent of the trial, I'm going to boss this. What was everyone worried about?

I get up off the stone bed, which disappears the minute I stand. I'm about to walk, but a black, amorphous shape appears a little way in front of me.

The blackness resolves into a strange creature. Almost demonic with it's unusual height and shroud so large when I try to catch its face, there's nothing but pitch black. It makes me think there is no head. Just a hollow void straight to the depths of hell.

It sends a shiver down my arms, goosebumps tracking over my skin.

"The fuck are you?" I breathe.

But it doesn't answer, instead it floats—though that seems like too gentle of a description. It's gracefully charging towards me, a gnarled arm leering out at me.

"Listen bitch, why don't we calm down, yeah?" I say.

I take a step back, except I don't move. Panic prickles its way up my arm. My stomach turns raw. I struggle against whatever the fuck invisible force is holding me in place. By the time shroud-thing reaches me, I'm fists clenched, ready to go out swinging.

But then, a force pins my arms in place. Its hand stretches out and plunges into my chest.

...I scream

and scream

and

scream,

and then I'm falling backwards into darkness.

When I wake, I find myself somewhere achingly familiar.

I'm in my childhood home. In the kitchen. A fire burns low in the hearth. On the sideboard are the remnants of cookie ingredients. It makes my chest ache.

"Mama?" I call.

I stand up and brush my arms down. Flour sprinkles

dust the red tallies on my arm. I've always worn those tallies with pride, killing the monsters, taking power from those who wield too much of it. Those who use it to hurt the weak.

But here, in my empty childhood kitchen, the tallies take on a different feeling. My skin crawls, the tallies itch, and I'm no longer sure what they mean. They vanish, dissolving one by one as my entire being shrinks.

Suddenly, I'm not Red the hunter, I am Red the child. I am Verity.

The air is warm and still and stale. Like no one has breathed it for weeks. I don't understand. Where's my mummy?

"Mummy?" I cry out.

A baby cries in the other room. "Amelia?" I race out of the room, searching for my little sister.

I cry out for her over and over again. Finally, I find her in a cot. But when I tiptoe and peer over the cot in the living room, the blood drains out of me. I stumble back and hit my head on a chair.

My little heart stutters and pounds against my ribs.

"No. No. No." I am sobbing. "MUMMY," I scream.

But no matter how many times I cry out for her, my mother doesn't come. I crawl back to Amelia's cot and dare to snatch one more glance. But it doesn't change what I see in there.

The image of her lifeless body, her skin greyed and swollen. Patches of purple and grey all over her chubby cheeks.

I run around the rest of the house screaming for my mummy. I skid back into the kitchen and that is where I find her. Still as death, perched on a chair.

"Mummy?" I say and slide my hand into her stiff fingers.

Her skin is ghost white; puncture marks pierce her neck.

She jerks forward, sitting up, her lifeless eyes staring me down. "It's your fault I'm dead, Verity. You should have been better. You should have trained harder, taken more power."

"No, Mummy. I didn't do it."

"Weakling. Pathetic. Too scared to protect your family. You were meant to be there that night. You should have brought a carriage to collect me. And now your baby sister is dead too, and it's all your fault."

"No. Please." I'm sobbing, my pudgy hands claw at my mother's chest. But with each successive swipe, more of her body flakes away, until even her bones have disintegrated, and I am left all alone.

The room shifts. I am an adult again as mist swirls in and curls around my legs and up my body, smothering me, the table, the ashes of my mother. Everything disappears.

When the fog falls away, I am in a vampire mansion.

In a ballroom, to be specific. People in sequined gowns and rich fabrics are dancing and twirling to music. Drinking, singing and playing cards. Everything plays out rapidly as if someone sped up time.

The room empties, until only a few remain. They crowd one vampire in particular, and it makes my toes prickle. This is Dahlia's house.

This is the night Amelia was turned.

My gut swims. The room moves. I'm dragged into a grand living room. There's a small group of vampires, Dahlia leading them.

They drink, and fuck, and drag humans into their game in order to drain them half to death before discarding them and throwing money in their laps.

I'm frozen to the spot, staring in horror as their party plays out.

Their bodies move as if sped up, swirling around me as I stay the only constant. The room dims and everything grinds back to normal speed.

Dahlia is furious. Her eyes darken as she storms towards me. She passes right through me and wrenches open the cupboard door behind me.

She drags Amelia out by the scruff of her neck. Dahlia beats my sister, shreds her clothes and makes her crawl through the blood of her friends. I'm hauled from corner to corner, forced to watch the horror unfold.

Finally, Octavia appears, holding Dahlia's friend. This has already happened. I know what comes next. The scene skitters forward, and Dahlia has gone.

I scream, desperately trying to reach Amelia. But it's futile. Octavia sinks her teeth into Amelia's neck.

Over.

And over.

And over again.

Until Amelia is limp in her arms and tears streak my face.

My sister is convulsing on the floor. Writhing and screaming in agony as her body contorts and dies, her heart slows and her insides reform themselves. Her skin pales further, veins popping up. Her teeth lengthen, sharpen.

Her eyes harden. She twists up to face me, her mouth curls into a snarl, "You."

"I'm sorry, Amelia."

"You're not sorry. If you were sorry, you would have stopped it."

"I wasn't here. I couldn't stop it. I tried."

"Why weren't you here, Red? You should have saved me. You should have been faster. If you were like them, you would have been here. Instead, she saved me because you abandoned me."

"I didn't. I swear I didn't abandon you."

"It's my fault you weren't here," Octavia says.

I frown. "No. I wasn't here because..." But words fail me. I don't know why I wasn't here. What happened after I argued with Amelia that night? Where was I?

"It's your fault," Amelia snaps. "You should have been strong enough. Fast enough. What's the point of being a hunter if you can't even protect the ones you love?"

She rears up, pacing in front of me, then she turns on me.

"You're such a disappointment. Even *I'm* stronger than you now, Red. What's the point of you? You couldn't save Mother. You didn't stop Father leaving, and you didn't even try to save me."

As she runs at me, I attempt to stagger back and get out of the way, but my feet remain frozen in place.

I hold my arms out, plead and beg with her, but she doesn't stop. I cover my face, but the impact never comes.

I stay holding my head for a moment longer, and when I'm sure she's not coming, I lower my arms and gawp.

Dahlia's house has vanished.

I'm safe. I'm home. I'm in the Hunter Academy's foyer. Lincoln, the Chief, all my favourite people are here, and I sag against the wall.

"Thank gods, I'm exhausted." I say. I kick off the wall and reach out to fist bump Lincoln.

His top lip curls, a sneer spreading over his expression. It's jarring and makes me falter.

"Wh—what?" I stutter.

But Lincoln steps away from me. "I thought you were better than this," he says.

"I don't understand. Better than what?"

He pinches his entire face and looks down his nose at me. "Blood slut."

The word cuts me. When Octavia says it, it's degrading, but in a sexy way. Lincoln said this to hurt. Wielded as a weapon, a slur.

"Lincoln. What the fuck?" I say. "Bro. It's me."

He recoils, turns his back on me. "You're fucking a drainer, Red. How could you?"

"It's worse than that," Winston, my favourite student says, "She's in love with one."

"Vile," Lincoln says. "There's no fate worse than falling for a fucking drainer."

A middle-aged woman appears, her brown curls scooped up into a neat bun, those familiar blue eyes boring into me. She's not in uniform; it takes me a minute to recognise her.

"Chief?" I say, scanning her dress. A dress? Is this a prank?

The Chief folds her arms. "You were meant for so much more. I really thought you'd take over from me one day, Red. You are the biggest disappointment of them all."

Keir appears. Talulla, and even Fenella. Fenella? I thought she died. Where am I? They all point, their fingers trained on me like arrows.

"Traitor." Their whispers sing the word like a lullaby. It worms its way into my mind, filling my head with poison.

"I'm not a traitor. The Academy is everything to me."

"TRAITOR. TRAITOR. TRAITOR." Their whispered words scream at me.

The accusation circling.

Repeating.

Blaming.

"Please, it wasn't like that. The Chief asked me to go undercover. This is all part of a job."

I can't breathe. My chest is so tight I'm hyperventilating. My fingers tingle. They can't abandon me too.

"Is *she* part of a job, too?" Lincoln asks, and I know he means Octavia. How can I answer that when I wasn't meant to fall for her? I am supposed to be undercover for the Academy, but somewhere along the line, I lost my heart.

I stare at him, opened-mouthed and unable to respond. I can't lie, the lie won't even leave my lips.

"I—" I start, my vision dappling with static.

He snorts. "Pathetic. You're just like Erin, another fallen hunter."

They all turn their backs to me, leaving me alone. I fall to my knees, the ache in my chest suffocating me, drowning me. This is where my heart crumbles. Broken from the loss of everyone I love and all because I couldn't save them.

I couldn't save anyone.

"You saved me," a familiar voice drifts through my mind.

"Octavia?" I whisper.

"Every time I lose you, you come back to me. You save me, Red. Your heart, your mind, your body. You were born for me."

"But I couldn't save them," I say, my voice cracking.

"Some people aren't meant to be saved. Some people need to save themselves."

"It should have been me. I should have been strong enough," I say.

"You weren't ready for the power then."

"What? And I am now?"

"You're the only one who can answer that. But you won't if you don't get up and save yourself first. Get the fuck up. Don't lose yourself here. Leave and return to me so we can finish this together."

I stand up and get off the cold tiles where I was ready to lie down and desiccate like many of the vampires I've killed.

I flash the other hunters one last look. Their backs still

face me, and I turn around. Leaving them and choosing me instead.

I choose to save myself this time.

I open the Academy doors and step out.

But instead of stepping into the courtyard, the mist reappears, and I'm dragged back to the beginning and the pasture I stood in before this all began.

The demonic creature with the head in the hood materialises to stand before me. This time, instead of plunging his clawed hand into my chest, he kneels on one leg and holds out a hand, palm up.

I hesitate. The fuck am I meant to do? I don't trust it. But he lowers his head and raises his hand. I assume I'm meant to hold it.

I sigh and place the palm of my hand over his.

There's a tingle between our skin. It itches, or maybe it tickles. I can't quite decide which.

"Congratulations, Red. And now, your reward. The Mother of Blood has decided to bestow upon you a single piece of information. You are being deceived by a woman close to you. This is the gift we give you."

The pasture moves, but doesn't disappear, instead I'm dragged to a river's edge. I'm stood across it, but on the other side is a stone arbour. Two women are inside, giggling and talking.

I can't see enough. But there's no way I can get closer without moving across the river and there's no bridge or boat in sight.

As if this dream knows my predicament, I'm propelled across the river and dropped outside of the stone arbour.

There's a cute little burner stove inside it. The women, to my shock, are making love. I avert my eyes. But as I turn away, I catch sight of the hair of the woman lying down.

It's raven black. I move, craning my head, and freeze as I catch sight of those dark eyes.

"Cordelia," I whisper. Even without the silver streak in her hair, I recognise her. But she's much younger, much more... I don't know? Human? She looks the same, only happier, content, pinker, and not just because she has a woman between her legs.

Her fingers grip the blanket beneath her, scrunching it as her mouth drops open and she cries out a name.

"Eleanor."

I gasp, realising this is the love of her life. The woman lays between Cordelia's legs. I can't see her face, only a mop of brown curls.

But something gnaws in my gut. A familiarity. I scoot around, expecting to be frozen in place, but I'm not. I move freely and head around the back of the arbour to get a better view of this woman.

I press my back to the arbour wall, the cool stone seeping into my back when I remember none of this is real. They can't see me or hear me, so I don't need to hide.

I step off the wall and to the side, getting a full-frontal view of the woman, her wavy curls and blue eyes.

And everything stops.

My mouth hangs slack as I gawp at a woman I've known nearly all my life.

"Mother of Blood," I breathe, and the vision dissolves.

CHAPTER 26

And so, the Mother of Blood spilled secrets. Each of the St Clairs, each of the hunters now wielding a piece of information like a weapon. But who will be the first to tell? Who will determine the course of this competition now?

It's a delight to witness the chaos. You think you're controlling, when all along, I'm the one pulling the strings. I'm the one in control of the secrets.

But this role I'm playing... gods. How did none of you catch me?

Are you all truly so fucking self-absorbed that you've not noticed me? Or perhaps the deception I've woven is too clever.

Hidden in plain sight, isn't that the old adage?

Well, soon enough, I won't have to hide anymore, and then you'll work out the real game we're playing, and who will come out the winner.

CHAPTER 27

OCTAVIA

My mother is a liar.

It becomes a mantra. I cannot say, or do, or think anything else other than my mother is a liar.

Of course, I recognised on a subconscious level that she had done awful things over the years. I am not naïve. Plus, she told me I was adopted.

But she told me she didn't know who my birth mother was. I lived a thousand years not knowing where I came from or how I came to be. Only that I was. It is the most isolating of experiences to not know why you exist, to not understand why you are the only one of your kind.

And she fucking knew the entire time.

All of us competitors were silent when we finally returned to the chamber after the spirit trial. No one spoke a word as we left the church. Each of us was pale and drawn. My siblings' eyes held a horror that made me shiver every time I looked at them. All of us, save Sadie, looked like ghosts. But then, Sadie was always going to be the most prepared.

The points-awarding ceremony was a muted affair. Red and I were the second out of the trial. We didn't win—predictably, Sadie did. The Mother of Blood gifted her the clue to the boundary. The amulet is to be placed in a lock somewhere on the southern exterior edge of the boundary. But the Mother of Blood also warned her that there would be demonic creatures waiting for us when we crossed the threshold, and fangs may not be enough weaponry. A useful warning if nothing else.

Mother distributed the points. We are in the lead, much to Dahlia's dismay.

The points stand as such:

Red and I are the lead with seven.

Sadie was out first, but she didn't score in the first trial. So, she's in second place with five points.

Dahlia and Lincoln were out third, and got three points, plus her one point from the first trial. Meaning they're on four.

Xavier came out next with Talulla, though she took her time rousing. They scored two plus their one from the map trial, meaning they're on three.

Gabriel came out last, and unfortunately, Keir had to be forcibly withdrawn. Cordelia was all for leaving him under, but the Chief made some vocal threats and Cordelia broke the rules and dragged him out, though none of us are sure exactly what the damage will do to him. Given the awful things we experienced, I imagine he's rather traumatised. They scored five in the first round, though. Technically, they're in joint second.

This, though, gives me no comfort. While we may be in the lead, we should have been considerably further ahead. These trials are tricky affairs and as has been demonstrated already, anything can happen, and everything can change. A two-point lead does not a confident Octavia make.

As we exit the ballroom in Castle St Clair, the blood stones now assigned to their rightful jars, we leave with whispers of discontent at our backs.

The nobles requested Mother stay behind for discussions, and many of the hunter elders also requested the same of the Chief, so they moved to a different room.

None of them looked happy. There were more protests outside the castle during this points ceremony than ever. The city is wavering. It's on the precipice of collapse. My heart sinks. The whole reason I'm in this competition is because I want to change the city. But not like this. I want to make it better, build it up so that I finally feel accepted. But it's not just about me. I don't want anyone else to experience what I have. It's a belief born from the marrow in my bones. This city has to change, and I have to make it a place where anyone on the periphery of our society still feels safe, wanted, and like they belong.

We all walk through these trials with our teeth on edge and our feet on eggshells. All it will take is one pissed-off citizen to lose it, and a lot of people will die.

I don't think we can come back from something like that.

The nine of us contenders stand outside the castle doors, all staring at each other and wearing the same harrowed expressions.

"I could do with a drink," Lincoln says.

"Me too," Red answers, along with a chorus of agreement from everyone.

"Let us drink at the Whisper Club," I say. "My offering to you all after whatever the fuck that trial was."

There's a murmured agreement, and I find myself shocked that not one of my siblings protests.

"Do I detect a moment of peace between us?" I say.

"I think that counts as shared trauma, but if you use it against us, I will knock you out," Dahlia says.

I roll my eyes, but there's a small smirk nipping at the corner of both our mouths. It's these moments that remind me that while we may have originated somewhere else, we are family because we choose to be. We choose to stand beside each other, whether that's bickering and competing, or having each other's backs.

A carriage large enough for us appears, and we all take a seat inside.

It's a strange thing when all of my siblings are together. Especially in the presence and company of others. Usually, we prefer to keep our distance until mother summons us for dinner.

We make it across the city, through the tunnels and to the Whisper Club in good time. There were barely any carriages out this evening. Perhaps because most of them had already done their travel to Mother's castle to deposit half the city's leaders along with protesters outside her castle walls.

At last, the nine of us stand in my bar with much-needed shots being distributed.

"Let's never do that again," Gabriel says and raises his glass. The rest of us follow suit and all down our shots.

Dancers fill the room; the music cranks up and members of the public drift in. The nine of us split up, each of us wandering off to have our own conversations and drown our sorrows in whatever way we need.

I'm sat watching Red dance with Lincoln. They flit from dancing to intense gesturing and conversations. This competition has driven more than a few rifts between people. I sense a presence at my shoulder.

"Dahlia," I say.

"Sister."

"Can I help you?" I ask.

"No. I..." Dahlia starts.

"Spit it out."

"Would you give me a second? Gods. Look. When I was under, I experienced... It was..."

"Your greatest fear?" I ask.

She nods.

"Let me guess, you were weak beyond measure."

"How did you—"

I prod her muscled biceps. "It doesn't take a genius to know you pride yourself on your strength more than anything else. You're the head of Mother's army, for goodness' sake. You're built like a bison. And you hate people who are weak of mind."

She folds her arms, as if I'm not spouting obvious facts.

"Right. Well. When I was under, I experienced being ousted and condemned for being weak, and it made me think that maybe some of the isolation and hatred you've experienced might be a bit like that. And sure, we don't exactly get on. But you are my sister, and I have defended you where I can. And—"

"Dahlia."

"Yes?"

"Are you giving me a peace offering? Are you trying to empathise?"

"Fucksake. It wasn't nice. And I guess I'm sorry if you deal with shit like that."

I raise an eyebrow at her. "Gods, that trial really screwed you up."

"Oh, fuck off, Octavia." She whacks me unnecessarily hard on the shoulder and I wince.

"Oww."

"You deserved that," she says.

I laugh because she's right. I made that extra painful for her.

"Does this mean you've seen the light and realised that I'm the best sibling to take over and you're going to stand down?"

She snort-laughs and swigs from her tumbler, which, if I'm not mistaken, has rum and blood with essence of hate in it. Interesting drink of choice.

"Not a fucking chance," she says.

"So this is still war?" I ask.

"Oh, absolutely. When is it not love and war?" She gives me a fang-filled grin.

"Then I guess I'll see you on the battlefield."

"That you will." She holds her glass up to me and we clink. And for the first time in the five hundred years I've known her, she smiles at me. Really, truly smiles. It softens her face, makes her eyes bright and her whole expression light up.

She inclines her head at me, a rare expression of deference I am not used to and then vanishes into the club's gloom. What the hell did she experience in there?

Xavier sidles up next to me. "Favourite."

"Good evening," I say and tilt my head up for him to kiss.

He places a soft peck on my cheekbone and then leans against the same pillar I am.

"You okay?" I ask.

"Not even slightly," he says.

"What happened?"

"You'll laugh."

"Try me," I say.

"Gods, it was awful. I was... The aesthetic healers... you know the ones that can do procedures that aren't really for healing... They couldn't help. I was... I was so..."

Mother of Blood, is he joking? I keep my mouth shut, but my lip is quirking as I try to suppress the urge to laugh.

"I was rotten to the core, Tave. I was ugly on the inside, too. The outside... I wasn't a good vampire."

I have to rub my mouth to wipe the smirk off my lips.

"I told you you'd laugh."

"I'm sorry, I'm being an arsehole. I understand why that would be traumatic for you, and I'm sorry you experienced it."

"I can't shake it. Every time I look in the mirror, it's like I can see the shadow of who I was in there. What the fuck was that trial?"

I take his face in mine. "Xavier, you are beautiful inside and out. You live in a beautiful city, with a beautiful sister and a beautiful home. You're safe now because you're with me. Okay? This is real." I tip his forehead down and kiss his brow.

He physically relaxes under my touch.

"Better?" I ask.

He nods. I didn't compel him, but sometimes the illusion of something is enough for us to believe it. Just like those trials, I suppose.

"What did you find out?" he asks.

I shake my head. I'm not ready to tell anyone that yet. How do I explain I am the daughter of a god? The daughter of the Mother of Blood herself? Or perhaps that's not what she is after all. We mythologised her into a god. She was just another witch trying her best, but because of one curse, she changed the face of our city and the trajectory of her fate.

Our entire city's foundation is based on her myth. What am I supposed to do with that information? I want to fix our city, not break it. If I tell anyone, then the church, our pillars of law, the very fibre of our beliefs, it all goes away.

And Mother, Cordelia, knows that.

She's also the one who killed her, or at least she tried to. Drained her and left her for dead.

Unfortunately for her, the witch-dhampir survived and became the last of the original three. Which begs the question, if she knew I'd survived and Cordelia had taken me, why did she never come for me?

And where the hell is she now? Cordelia says she vanished, lost to history. What if she wasn't? What if the woman who birthed me is still alive?

"Octavia?" Xavier says.

"Huh? What?" I say, springing back to attention. But I notice Red in the middle of the dance floor shaking her ass enough another woman has taken notice.

"Sorry, favourite. Another time. There's a woman about to lose her hand," I say and speed off to the middle of the dance floor right as the woman slides her hand close to Red's arse.

"Touch her and lose your hand."

"I... I... I'm sorry I didn't realise she was spoken for," she says, her hand freezing a millimetre from Red's body.

"Well, now you do." My eyes flick down to her hand, which is yet to move away from what is mine.

She yanks it back and scuttles off to another corner of the room.

"Was that really necessary?" Lincoln says. "We were having a much-needed giggle."

He places his hands out and then folds them over his body, touching one hip then the other, and then does the same movement only on his temples. Then jumps around and does the same sequences of movements.

"What are you... Do you know what? I really don't care. I came to ask for a dance." Red hesitates, but I hold out my hand. She huffs and then reluctantly slides hers into mine.

I sling it over my shoulder and put my hands around her waist. I glance up at the DJ, and the music shifts to a slower beat.

She rests her head on my chest. "I am still annoyed with you."

"I know," I say. "But I wanted to talk about the trial. In there... I'm not sure how to explain it, but I think you saved me."

"Weird," she says, lifting off my chest and frowning at me as we take mini steps side to side in a circle.

"I think the piece of you bonded to me is what pulled me out of there. It's like you were in my head right as I was ready to give up."

"This is too weird," she says.

"Explain."

"I was in the Hunter Academy, and everyone was calling me a traitor. I hated myself, I couldn't save the people I love, and then everyone left turned against me. All because I wasn't strong enough, because I rejected the chance to take power. But right as I was ready to quit, there you were. Whispering everything I needed to hear. Telling me I'd saved you."

She shakes her head like it's a lie.

"But, Verity... You have saved me."

She glances at the floor. "There was something else, too." A furrow forms between her brows. "But I can't quite remember it now. It was something off, something I wanted to ask you. But it's slipped my mind now."

The music shifts to an even slower beat that thumps around the club. A few more dancers join us, swaying and grinding against each other.

"Because you still harbour fury at me for keeping your memories, you might not believe this, but time and time again, you save me. You have saved me. My heart will always be yours."

"What did you learn?" she asks, pushing my hair behind my ear.

"I'll tell you, but not here in the open. It would compromise too much."

She nods, her eyes darting this way and that. "I need to tell you, too. It changes things. Actually, it changes everything. I think I've made a mistake."

"Do you want to leave now?" I ask.

She takes a deep breath but shakes her head. "While we're in here, we're safe. Once I tell you what I learnt, everything will change."

"You have no idea how much I understand," I say, kissing the top of her head. "But for a few short moments, while we hold our secrets, nothing changes..."

She looks up at me from beneath her lashes, her eyes deep and heady, lust swimming under her gaze. And I thank the Mother of Blood that she wants to take a minute to fuck the frustration out before we charge back into this chaos again...

Wait. Thank the Mother of Blood? Oh, fuck me. I cannot be saying that anymore, either. I don't want to think about it, though, so I force myself to focus on Red.

"I want to kiss you, but I don't want you to kiss me back unless you mean it," I say.

She looks away.

"I want to be enough for you, Red. No matter what I've done, what secrets we hold. I want you to love me and for me to be enough."

"Don't you get it?" she snaps. "I do, Octavia, and that's the fucking problem. I loved you and you hurt me."

"Loved. Past tense."

She flings a hand off my shoulder in frustration. "You're

infuriating." Then uses her free hand to grab my chin and tilt it down as she rises on tip toes. "You want me to kiss you with everything I feel? Fine."

Her fingers slip down my chin and graze my throat.

She twists until her hand grips my throat and digs in, creating just a little discomfort. Her eyes hold me, waiting. As if she expects me to say stop. But I won't. I want to see where this will go.

I want to feel everything because I need her to dig into our bond and let herself connect to me again. She needs to understand that what I did was for her.

She squeezes and yanks me to her mouth, crushing her lips against me. She moves her mouth over mine in a bruising kiss, her fingers gripping my throat the whole time like I'm hers. Like she's claiming me. She kisses hard and fast, her tongue pushing its way into my mouth.

Her other hand grips my back, her nails stinging just the right amount.

She releases me suddenly and tugs at my shoulders, leaping up into my arms. Her legs wrap around my waist, her hands around my neck. I grip her under her arse and thighs. She tilts her head down and this time when she kisses me, it's so much softer and sweeter.

Her lips are tender, the faintest hint of vodka and lust melded on her tongue. This time, the kiss is slow and deep and full of longing and something a little bitter. Regret? No, it's hurt, and that realisation makes my heart clench.

Her fingers trail my skin, my throat, my back, she's everywhere all at once. And I can't get enough. I want to drink everything she gives me. I want to drown in her. She kisses me like she owns me; she kisses me like I am a dream she's prayed for and not the nightmare I've been.

She kisses me like she loves me.

She steals my breath, my mind, and my heart. Everything disappears into the heat and electricity of our touch. This is a kiss like no other.

She pulls off my mouth and holds my gaze, frowning. Her thumb brushes against my cheek, wiping something wet away.

"You're crying," she says. Her words are soft under the beat of the music.

"I wasn't."

"Octavia," she growls.

"You have no idea how much I love you, Verity. That is all, and for the first time in a long time, I really felt like you loved me, too. That kiss... it was everything."

She smiles at me and inches closer, brushing her lips over mine. We share the same air, the same space, the same bond.

"Sometimes a kiss can ruin everything... And sometimes it can save it," she says.

"Are you telling me you're my knight in shining armour? Come to save me from the big, bad villain?" I smile.

She huffs, "I thought you were my villain. I'm certainly not a hero."

"What if you were meant to be?"

But she pouts and refuses to answer, so I pop her down on her feet, a grin spreading across my lips. "I have an idea."

"Okay..." she says.

I take her by the hand and guide her to a corner of the club on a raised platform. Rouge fabric covers the entire area. On the outside of the circular area, there is a black leather booth seat curved around the wall. In the middle is a table. But that table doesn't always live there. And tonight, it's going away.

I hit a button that is flat to the surface of the wall,

hidden so idiots or drunk club goers don't touch it accidentally.

The floor rumbles, and the table drops into an underground hole. Then I press the button above and the ceiling opens, an iron-barred cage dropping into the place of the table.

"Oh, my god," she says as it settles into place.

Dangling from the top of the cage are handcuffs and attached to the bottom of the bars are ankle cuffs.

"There's lots of people in here, Red," I purr.

She's already bouncing on her toes. "We could give them quite a show," she says, and she's practically vibrating with excitement.

I beckon a club server with a nod and whisper a request to him. He returns the nod and vanishes.

"Get in the cage," I say.

Her eyes widen, but she does as she's told, opening the iron bars and slipping inside.

I enter with her.

"What's your safe word?" I ask.

"Elysium," she says.

"And mine is villain. Now... Strip."

Her breath shortens as she obediently nods and takes off her boots, followed by unbuttoning her trousers and then her top until she's left standing in her underwear. I've already stripped out of my clothes, too.

"I've been thinking about how I can prove to you that I'm sorry."

"Oh? And what did you have in mind?" she asks, running a hand over her extremely muscled abs.

"I have taken something that's yours. Would you like everyone to have a piece of what's mine?" I ask.

Her eyes sparkle, a slow smirk crossing her lips.

"I'll take that as a yes. Now, be a good little blood slut and kneel for me."

Her mouth opens, a soft breath escaping. Her expression changes, heat flooding her face as she assumes the Nadu position, kneeling on her calves, her head lowered and her palms face-up on her knees.

I slice my underwear off, letting it fall to the ground. My skin prickles, confirming that we've already attracted an audience, just as I'd hoped.

My member of staff should be back any moment with the toys I requested.

In the meantime, I grab Red's hair and tilt her head until she's looking up at me.

"You're going to lick my clit until I come on your face. Do you understand?"

She nods, but winces as her hair tugs against the grip I've got on her. "Make it a good one, put on a show for everyone watching, and I'll reward you after."

"Yes, Octavia."

I thrust her head at my cunt. And her hands come up to grab my thighs as I open my legs to let her tongue slide between my folds.

I inch my feet apart a little further as several shadows flicker across the curved wall. More voyeurs. Excellent.

I rock her head, tilting her and my hips until her tongue is right where I want it on my clit.

She moans sounds of pleasure as she laps hungrily at my pussy, her saliva and my excitement soaking her chin and cheeks. But she doesn't care and laps harder and faster.

She releases one of my legs and slides a finger between my thighs and to my entrance, shoving inside me.

I moan, my head tipping back as I thrust against her face. Ramming my cunt into her mouth and forcing her fingers deeper.

"Fuck, Red, harder." I say as I grind myself against her wet mouth.

I rock my hips. She curls her fingers, stroking the sweetest spot, and then I come with the insistent flicking and furling of her tongue on my pussy.

It peels all the way around my body. I shiver as the orgasm rips from my toes to my scalp. I step back as she pulls her fingers out and discover we've attracted quite the audience.

"My, my, that was quite the orgasm," I say.

She grins at me.

"Well, good little blood sluts always get rewarded. Stand up."

She does. "Now lock me in place," I demand.

She locks my ankles into the straps. Then she tugs my arms up and locks those into the cuffs hanging from the top of the cage.

I'm splayed like a starfish.

She steps aside, revealing the audience we've attracted and gasps. I adjust my legs, making the chains rattle.

"Is this okay?" she says.

"Let's call it punishment... you could do anything right now... Make me watch while you pleasure yourself in front of all these people. Let these people have a piece of what is mine."

The words sting as I say them, but this is what I need to do. She needs to understand that I have always been on her team. And if punishing me a little helps her forgive me, then so be it.

Her hands twitch, and I can tell it's not from nerves or anxiety, but excitement. The server I sent off appears with a tray of toys. He stands at the corner of the cage like I told him to.

I gesture as much as I'm able to the crowd. "Red, here, is

giving you the pleasure of her orgasm. I think it's only fair you get to pick how she receives that pleasure."

Red's mouth drops open. Her chest rises and falls, her nipples already peaked with excitement.

The crowd around the cage murmurs, but no one steps forward. Red's face falls, and I swear I'm ready to rip the cage bars open and drain them all. They're all too nervous to hand her anything with me watching. This is a me problem and not a her problem.

I take a deep breath and decide to push the rage and rejection aside and ask humbly for what I want. "Please... as visitors of my club, will you do me the honour of playing my game tonight?"

There are a few surreptitious glances shared, but finally, a woman who must be in her late twenties and is practically drooling over Red's body, picks up a feather and hands it to her through the bars. Her fingers skim Red's hand. It takes every ounce of my strength not to rip the cuffs off and bite her hand off. But I promised to do this. This is my punishment.

"Thank you," I say, and I find myself smiling at her. To my surprise, the woman offers me a quick glance. It's barely eye contact, but the moment she catches my eyes warmth radiates over me. She inclines her head and I really, truly smile. It's not much. But it's not nothing either.

I lower my head back at her, sharing the deference, and she steps back into the crowd as Red switches the feather to her other hand and swipes it over my nipples and then down her own body.

I shiver. It makes Red grin. "I think I'm going to enjoy this," she says, cracking her neck.

She runs the feather over the bars, teasing and tempting the crowd. Then she drags it from my neck to my pussy and between my thighs and then mimics the same movements on herself.

I shut my eyes when a man, encouraged by the woman holding his hand, slides a vibrator through the bars to Red. I take a deep breath. When I open them, Red is accepting it and says, "Thank you."

I also incline my head at him. He holds my gaze a fleeting moment longer than the first woman and dips his head at me. His partner unfortunately does not. But two out of three isn't bad.

He turns to leave, but Red says, "Wait. Don't leave. I want your partner to tell me what to do."

My eyes widen.

Red switches the vibrator on and runs it over her nipples and between her legs. Then she slides to the floor.

"Touch yourself," the woman says.

My nostrils flare as Red does as she's told. My whole body is on alert, tense and tight, but this is what I asked for. It's what I wanted.

"Use your pussy to wet your fingers," the woman outside the cage says.

My teeth clench, but Red's cheeks are pink. Her body is flooded with a heat I can sense from here. And I understand, as wetness slips between my thighs, that even though every cell in my body burns with jealousy, the sight of her glistening pussy and the scent of her arousal are enough to drive me wild. I tug at the chains, testing how much brute force it would take to rip them off.

"What should I do now?" Red asks, her eyes on the woman.

"Fuck yourself with it. Rub your clit all while watching Octavia."

Red's mouth parts, her breathing heavy and fast. She slides the vibrator into her pussy, drawing it in and out. I yank on the chains. I want to touch her. Taste the sweetness of her pussy.

When the first moan slips from her lips, I find my hands suddenly at my sides. I've pulled the metal cuffs off the bar. They should have been silver.

Red's eyes slip shut. She leans her head against the bars, her hips rocking back and forth, where she masturbates in front of me. The woman outside the cage watches with delight. Her partner slips his hands beneath her clothes. One to massage her nipples, the other between her legs.

I'm done. I need to touch Red. The chains break easier than I expected. I snap the remaining two, pick up a strap-on from the bag the server brought us and slide into it. I yank Red up by the arm and turn her around. She drops the vibrator. I clasp her hands around the bars.

"Hold on tight."

And then I slide her hands a little lower, so she's bent over. I notch the dildo at her entrance, and I push inside. She arches up in surprise.

But I push her head back down and thrust. I pump into her hard. Driving and pumping until her knuckles are white on the bars.

"Octavia," she pants. "Fuck."

I slide my hand around her front and find her clit.

"You're mine, Red. Mine to do with as I please. Mine to fuck. Mine to love. Do you understand?"

"Yes," she screams as I pinch her clit, applying a little pressure.

"Oh gods, I'm going to come."

"Look at your audience first," I demand.

And she does. The woman who gave her instructions is flushed as pink as Red is. She sucks her bottom lip in as her partner's hand moves faster, stroking her pussy at a feverish pace. She's going to come too.

"Octavia, please," Red begs.

"Anything, for you." I pump harder. It's no longer sex, it's fucking. Deep and raw. I fuck her hard enough that she shrieks, her hands slip further down the bars and her arse pushes against me. But I am nothing if not relentless, so I keep rubbing her clit, varying the pace, driving her wild.

"Oh my gods, I'm going to... fuck. Octavia..." she screams and shivers against me as she spills into an orgasm. She stays bent, panting, and finally, when she pulls off the cock, she turns around and grips my chin.

Her eyes hold mine. "Beautiful," she breathes. "Like old roses and burning sunsets. Likewise, autumn leaves and the sweetest blood I've ever tasted."

And then she pulls me down and presses her lips to mine in a kiss that makes the world vanish.

It is soft like silken summer petals, warm like the roar of a winter fire, and so deep I know that it touches both of our souls.

CHAPTER 28

RED

Octavia is panting by the time I've finished coming and released her out of the broken restraints. Her eyes are harried rivers. They flow with a torrent of tumultuous emotion.

She's pissed and aroused in equal measure, and for the first time since she tried to take my memories, I'm less resentful towards her.

Who knew an eye for an eye has some merit after all. She rubs at her wrists, there's a patch of skin so raw I'm amazed it didn't break.

It must have, though; she heals fast enough for the wrist to be fixed already. She must have found it exceptionally hard to watch me take instruction from another. And that thought makes another smile spread across my lips. Perhaps I'm more of a sadist than I realised. Something ruffles against my skin. I hesitate as I unclip the broken ankle cuff. My finger hovers over her calf.

"What's wrong?" Octavia says, her voice strained.

I frown, looking up at her. “Do you feel everything a little... well, more, now?”

“It’s because of the bond, I think,” she replies.

“I see.” I close my eyes and concentrate until I can sense more of her, more of us. I think I’d been so cross I was trying to block it out. But in this focussed state, I detect another heartbeat under my skin. It’s an alien sensation, like a splinter, but it fits so naturally, the same way the last puzzle piece slides into the picture. And there’s something else. Further away, separate. Like it’s in the air.

I stand up and grip her arm.

“Red...?” Octavia asks, her tone dropping into a warning.

“Don’t you sense that? There’s something wrong. Like a tension in the atmosphere. It’s electric but not the good kind. I can’t explain it.”

I release her arm but wobble on my feet as I get dressed.

“You’re hungry again?” she asks.

“No.”

“Verity,” she snaps. “I know you’re hungry, you can’t hide it from me. Besides, your skin has paled.”

“I mean, yes, I am. But we don’t have time, I’ll eat later,” I say, turning to the room to locate the anomaly.

I scan the dim crowd, but my vision isn’t as good at Octavia’s and it’s really dark in here. My body starts moving without me consciously controlling it.

“Red,” Octavia barks. She must throw on her clothes behind me because she speeds up to me in a rush.

She scans the crowd and then a hiss escapes her lips. “Shit. I sense it now, too. Front door.”

She rushes off ahead of me to try to handle the situation. When I catch up to her, I see it’s a scuffle and some of the tension I was holding drops out of my shoulders.

“Find them!” a human shouts.

My head whips around as I process what he said. Who is he looking for?

"Mike's got one of them outside," another man shouts.

Prickles run up my arms. Something tells me this isn't a club fight. Whispers ripple around me. Layers and layers of words rushing and whistling until I find the kernel at the heart of the hubbub.

"Get the dhampir before the vampires claim her."

My blood runs cold.

Octavia has disappeared into the ruckus by the front door, and I'm suddenly very aware that I'm all on my own. I have to get out, I want to make sure Lincoln and the other two are okay. I sweep around to the other side of the club, through the staff corridors and out the back exit.

But the Whisper Club is either not on my side today or it's distracted with what's happening at its other entrance because it deposits me in the main fucking market area.

I bang on the door, and Broodmire appears. He grimaces at me.

"Sorry, Red," he says.

"Help a girl out next time," I say and dart into the crowded market as he's already vanishing back into the door to reappear no doubt on the other side where Octavia is.

"Fuck me," I say.

The market is crammed full of people, human and vampire alike. I don't see any hunters. But as soon as I think it, a squad appears at the far side of the market square.

Dozens of humans protest with placards, more vampires do the same. All are jostling and shouting at each other. I can't tell who is on whose side at this point. It's a jumbled mess of bodies and an undercurrent of seething rage that continues to bristle along my skin.

As I step down into the crowd, I notice Talulla being

manhandled. She's putting up an excellent fight, but she's completely overpowered. There are three vampires to herself, and Keir is right next to her, being dragged away by several hunter nobles.

The fuck?

I'm sprinting before I can question whether it's sensible. I pump my arms as my vision speckles, and I regret not having taken another dose of blood. It was a mistake.

But there's no time to worry about that. I shove people and vampires aside as I force my way through the growing crowd. Even as I make my way across the market, the mass of bodies seems to swell. This isn't good.

Talulla is throwing roundhouse after front kick; Keir is trying desperately not to injure the humans who are grabbing for his arms and legs. They manage to find purchase and he's lifted into the air.

What the ever-loving fuck?

There are as many protesters holding signs for the cure and dhampir as there are against it. But where they're usually in neat clusters either side of the square, they are now a seething mass of bodies slamming into each other. Fists and feet flying.

Talulla is screaming as a vampire pins her arms to her body and hoists her up.

That's when the real shit kicks off. The humans holding Keir and the vampires holding Talulla round on each other as I come careening into their area.

"Give the dhampir to us," a vampire I vaguely recognise says. And then it clicks. It's the noblewoman from Cordelia's, Lady Net-something.

"Give the dhampir to us," a human retorts, his hair slicked back and as greasy as his stare is potent.

"How do you know you're holding the dhampir?" Lady Netterley says.

"I don't. That's the point. We want all of them safe and in our protection," the human says.

"Your protection?" Lady Netterley scoffs. "You're what they need protecting from."

The human's eyes darken. "Us?" He throws his head back, laughing a dark, and ugly deep in his throat. "How fucking dare you. The dhampir is our birthright. They share our DNA."

The vampire rounds on him, shoving the still struggling Talulla into the arms of another vampire.

"Hunters may have once been dhampirs. But you're certainly not anymore. You're weak. Pathetic. This is a new dusk, a new night, and the new dhampir belongs to us. They will be half vampire. They have to turn, become one of us. Whether you like it or not, that means they have to *choose* us. And we will see to it that they are part of their rightful community."

The human nods at several of the other men around him. They drag Keir off in one direction as the space is filled with dozens of other humans. And this time, they're all drawing weapons.

"Over our dead bodies," he snarls.

Lady Netterley sneers, turning her elegant, beautiful features bestial and terrifying. "That can certainly be arranged."

She draws back her lips, her fangs descending.

"STOP," I bark, moving into the space between them. "In the name of the Chief, I command you to stop. There will be no bloodshed. Unhand Keir Thomas and Talulla Binx at once."

The vampire cocks her head at me, as a sinking intensity winds its way around my gut.

Fuck, she recognises me. Lincoln catches up and appears at the edge of the market square. Our eyes lock for one brief second, before one of the humans catches sight of him and nods at half his men.

Lady Netterley spots Lincoln a second later and then all hell breaks loose.

The market seethes like a hornet nest; there are humans and vampires everywhere.

Half the time I'm throwing kicks and punches and the rest of the time I'm ducking and diving and rolling out of the way to evade being captured.

The confusion is fraught because there appears to be no one dying and minimal bloodshed. This isn't vampire attacking human.

This is vampires and humans trying to kidnap potential dhampirs. I have to get out of here and get Talulla and Keir out too.

"Lincoln!" He's occupied fending off yet another assault. "LOOK OUT!" I scream as someone slings a lasso-type rope around his torso. My big friend and confidant crashes to the cobbles as both a hunter and a human pile on only to be ripped off by two vampires.

This is fucking madness. Someone grabs hold of my arm. "You're one of them too," she shrieks, followed by, "FATHER!"

"I'm so sorry," I say and pull my fist back. The punch lands square on her jaw, knocking her out cold. She drops like a stone to the ground, releasing me as I leap over a group of people brawling and reach Keir. I aim a kick to one man's knee from the side knowing full well the kneecap is going to dislocate. I feel bad for about half a second, but he is trying to kidnap Keir, so like... too fucking bad, mate.

It's enough of a dislodge for Keir to twist himself round and use the body of the man holding him to leap free.

"Talulla next," I shout and together we fight our way

through the crowd to the vampires trying to exit the square with her.

"I don't have any stakes, this is going to be messy," I say to Keir.

"I've only got one."

"Keep it, my fists are hungry." I dodge around two protesters fighting, both of them slamming their placards against each other like swords.

Fucking morons. It's like the square is possessed.

"You take the one on the right, I'll go left," I say. Keir fist bumps me, and we launch an attack.

I leap onto the back of the vampire holding Talulla's legs. He can't expect it because he unceremoniously drops Talulla's legs and her feet slam to the ground. It's enough of a dead weight that the torso of the vampire holding jerks. His grip slips and she crashes to the cobbles. Before he can re-grab her, she's rolling out of the way and swinging her legs around, taking him out where he stands.

It goes well. For about three seconds. And then another three vampires appear, and I know we're completely screwed.

Someone grabs both of my legs, locking their arms around me and tackling me to the ground. I can't get out because his grip around my feet is like concrete.

I land blow after blow to his head, but he laughs at me as blood splatters the ground and his wounds heal before my eyes.

"Fuck."

A rich iron scent drifts on the air. My head snaps up, searching for the source. While Talulla is defending herself, she too, is weaponless, and she's bleeding from her arm and cheek. The blood is making the vampires practically drool. They're not the only ones. My mouth fills with saliva.

Keir is throwing punches, but he too is injured, the arm

holding the stake is hanging limp and one of his legs is unstable.

Shit. We're not getting out of this alive if something doesn't shift.

There's a flash of blonde and a rushing sound and suddenly the vampire pinning me to the ground is flying through the air.

"What the fuck?" I try to catch sight of which vampire is helping. But they're moving too fast.

It's not Octavia. The hair is too blonde, the body too small. That's when the blood drains from my face.

"Amelia?" I shriek.

Oh gods, no. She's not trained. She'll get hurt. What if someone stakes her by accident, thinking it's a vampire against us?

I'm up and on my feet and desperate to intervene and fight and protect her when a strange realisation washes over me. She is fighting to protect *me*, and she's arguably faster and stronger than me. I stagger back, momentarily shaken by this truth when Amelia stops long enough to shriek at me, "Get them out of here, Octavia is coming..." There's a cut and a bruise under her eye, but by the time she's finished shouting at me, they're healed and she's a blur of frenzied fists and harried kicks.

I blink at the space she occupied, trying to compute the fact that my sister, Amelia, the one I spent most of my adult life looking after is here, now, in the middle of a fray and the one protecting me. It doesn't make sense.

But I'm shoved forwards, and the blow knocks me to my senses. I stumble but correct myself quickly and land a roundhouse kick to the head of the vampire who was lunging for Talulla again.

I grab her hand and haul Keir away from the fighting and back towards the club when I notice Lincoln is missing.

I glance back to the edge of the market, but he's vanished. My gut churns but I can't leave him. I won't.

I hold both Keir and Talulla's hands. "Listen to me, get to the tunnels. There's a private station beneath the club. Tell it to take you to Octavia's mansion. Castle Beaumont. You'll be safe there. Tell Wendell that I sent you and that Octavia and I will be right behind you. He'll look after you. Tell him not to let anyone but family in."

"Where are you going?" Keir says, wiping an arm over his mouth and smearing blood across his face.

"I'm not leaving Lincoln."

"I'll help," he says.

But I shake my head. "No. They're after all of us. The more of us in the market, the worse the chaos will get. We need to get all of us out of the sight of the public eye. The fewer there are of us out there the better. Get to the castle and I'll be right behind you. Send for the Chief and I guess Cordelia. If they want us to continue in this fucking charade, they need to get a handle on their people. This is getting ridiculous."

"Be safe," Keir says and pulls me into a hug. Talulla embraces me next and then together, they lean on each other and hobble back into the club towards the tunnels.

I bend down and pick up a cap from a man groaning and holding his stomach. He attempts to put up a fight, but he can go fuck himself. Human or not, he was trying to kidnap me and the rest of the hunters. I'm taking his hat. I sling it on over my head and pull the peak down to cover as much of my face as I can.

Then I find Amelia in the crowd and a smile washes over my face, a warmth fills my tummy and I decide that for once, I don't need to protect her from what's going on.

I don't need to hide things away, she's not a child anymore. She's a grown arse adult... okay vampire, but maybe instead of trying to protect her the entire time, perhaps we can work together.

I sprint into the crowd, calling her name. Her head snaps around. It takes her a second, but I wave from under the hat, and I gesture at the end of the market where I last saw Lincoln.

She nods to indicate she's understood and finishes grappling with the last vampire, then speeds off the direction I'm heading.

When I reach the spot where I last saw him, we're set a little way back from what's left of the brawling crowd.

I think I see Octavia outside the back of her club, but I'm not entirely sure, it's too far away.

Amelia must grasp what I'm trying to assess as she says, "It's her. She's fine, it's under control."

I laugh. "You'll miss those added benefits when you take the cure, huh? I guess not everything is bad about being a vampire."

I nudge her in the arm, and she gives me a smile that very definitely doesn't meet her eyes. A brief frown crosses my brow as I try to work out the issue. But she changes the subject and my focus shifts.

"What do you need?" she asks.

"Lincoln has been taken." Two bleeding men stumble past us, arguing and clutching injuries as we cross out of the market square and head in the direction I last saw Lincoln.

"Whose fucking idea was it to listen to information that came from Castle St Clair," one man spits. "This was fucking ridiculous! The healer bills are going to eat all our savings, and for what? We didn't even secure the dhampir."

"You idiot, we didn't need to secure her. We needed to make her kill someone. That's what the commission said."

My eyes widen, and Amelia steps in front of me to

protect me from sight. Her hand slides behind her back to grip mine. Her shoulders rise and fall in the same laboured way mine do.

When they're out of sight she turns to me. "Someone else knows."

"How?"

Amelia kneads her brow. "If I've been doing research, I can only assume that others have too. This has clearly spread across the city. We can't assume that anything we know is secret. Which means you really are in danger."

"As many people hate the cure as want it, it will be fine."

Amelia pouts and flings her arm out at the chaos behind us. "No part of this is fine, Red."

The words of the men who stumbled past us flit through my mind again. 'We need to make her kill someone.'

Amelia interrupts my thoughts. "Didn't those guys say their directive came from the castle?"

I feel my eyes go wide. "We knew Cordelia was up to something. I guess Octavia was right. Either she's trying to control the dhampir or force them to transition by making us accidentally slaughter a human."

"We don't know for sure it's Cordelia," Amelia says.

"Who else would it be?" I ask.

"That I don't know. I suppose we have no better suspect. But we can't deal with this now. Let's find Lincoln and get him back. Look, carriage tracks."

She points down a muddy path. Together, sisters in arms, we jog down the dark path, united as equals for the first time in our lives.

CHAPTER 29

RED

By the time we catch up to Lincoln, he's already escaped his restraints and killed one of the vampires.

But he's grappling with three others.

Amelia and I move in unison, charging the group. Amelia darts to the side as a fourth vampire holding a rope approaches. She's lightning quick, throwing a series of punches at him. She's not as coordinated as me, but she's never trained for combat. What she has at her disposal is speed.

And fuck, am I proud as I watch her land hit after hit.

Lincoln drops to his knees in front of his main assailant, clearly exhausted from his prolonged fight. But he doesn't get to quit on me. I dive in front of him, fending off a slew of attacks, then leap and land a flying kick to the head of the vampire attacking him.

He's fast though. He spins around, ducks under my turning kick and lands a hefty hit to my ribs. I collapse on the ground, puffing and sputtering. If a rib isn't cracked, it's sure as shit bruised to hell. Coughing and gasping for air, I scramble to my feet.

I manage to block a blow to the face, followed by an uppercut, and slam a mean front kick to the vampire's knee. He yelps and staggers back, but charges forward a split second later when his knee realigns. Motherfucker.

This time, he's too fast. He lands a mean blow to my jaw, making me bite down on my tongue as my teeth clatter together. Blood spills into my mouth. I spit it on the floor, but he doesn't let up. I stagger, my ribs now burning, my mouth stinging. I need to get control of this. I inhale and swing, finally landing a savage blow to the vampire's solar plexus. He stumbles back, wheezing and breathless. Good. I want him winded. It'll be easier to take him out.

But as soon as I get cocky, a fist collides with my spine, and I'm flung forward through the air and crash against a stone. The sting of gravel rips through my clothes so I know I'm cut and bleeding.

The vampire who hit me lands on my back. He yanks me around and lands a series of brutal blows to my body.

I'm beginning to think I won't be getting out of this melee in one piece, when thank the gods, Octavia catches up to us. The carriage she's driving skids as the horses rear up on their front legs to slow themselves down. She jumps down from the bench and spins around, searching.

"Thank fuck!" Octavia says as she catches sight of me and speeds to my side. "You're alive."

"Alive, yes, but not faring so well," I say as I struggle against the pain in my back and my ribs to stand.

To my surprise, Dahlia hops down from the carriage and immediately dives into the fight. She launches at the vampire I'm fighting, grabs his neck and snaps it in a quick, wrenching motion.

Then she punches into his chest and rips out his heart

for good measure. But she doesn't wait, she moves on to the next vampire. A short-lived fist fight ends in her ripping his heart out too. Followed by the heart of the unconscious vampire at Lincoln's feet. It's all but over as Dahlia busts the leg of the last vampire and wrenches it until it severs from his body. The screaming stops shortly after that.

"You okay there, partner?" she says to Lincoln, who nods from his bent-double knees, catching his breath.

Partner? It stings hearing that, as does Lincoln putting his hand into Dahlia's as she hauls him up. Octavia and I stand staring at each other. It feels like an eon since we were in the club. Since we shared that kiss. But in reality, it was more like two hours ago. That knowledge hits hard since I can't remember the last time I drank her blood.

"You okay?" she whispers, pulling me into her.

"Not really. My ribs might be cracked, but it's also been too long since..."

"Later. I promise," she says, cutting me off before I say something that gives us away.

Her fingers brush my bruised cheek and bleeding lip. I flinch. She hesitates but offers me her wrist. I want to take it, but I also know that is the only carriage we have, and I'm not about to drink from her or fuck her in front of Lincoln.

I wrap my hand around her wrist and shake my head. "When we're safe at Castle Beaumont. That's where I sent Keir and Talulla."

"I sent Xavier there too." Octavia brushes my hair back from my face. Her expression is tight.

"I'll be okay," I say, even though I wince as I take a step.

Octavia's lips remain tight until she glances at Dahlia. "Mother of Blood," she shouts and then pauses, shaking her head. She clears her throat and begins again. "They're dead, Dahlia. Stop torturing them. We need to get back to mine and regroup."

Dahlia relents, reluctantly it appears, and we all clamber inside the carriage, me a little slower than the rest and with the help of Amelia. The driver, who had apparently stubbornly refused to let Octavia commandeer his carriage without riding in it, swaps out and resumes his place at the reins.

Laboured breathing and the rustling of clothing envelopes the carriage for the first few moments of the journey. Octavia and I, Dahlia and Lincoln, and Amelia take stock of ourselves and each other without speaking. We're all covered in blood and dirt. Lincoln and I probe various limbs and injuries, wincing and hissing with pain, but the three vampires have already healed.

Octavia throws me a hesitant glance. We're both dying to talk about what we saw in the vision-gifts from the Mother of Blood, but thankfully, she thinks better of discussing anything in front of Dahlia. Because even though she helped this evening, I don't trust her as far as I can throw her. And given the idea to incite fights this evening came from Castle St Clair, there's nothing to say she wasn't involved.

Perhaps Dahlia helping was a red herring distraction to knock us off course? Or maybe she genuinely cares about keeping Lincoln alive so they can finish the trials.

"You guys should sleep," Dahlia says. "It will help your healing."

"She's right," Lincoln says and opens his arm for me to snuggle under. Octavia's expression twitches but only for a moment before she resigns herself to remembering Lincoln is one of my best friends and she doesn't need to be jealous. Though I suppose she's still smarting from the club tonight.

But that's the last thought I have before sleep sweeps me under, and I drift off against Lincoln's warm, familiar side.

We arrived at Castle Beaumont some time ago, but apparently, I'm the last to wake. I stretch and yawn, and immediately regret it, realising I still haven't had any blood to heal my injuries. I glance out the carriage window; it's long past dawn and the others are gone.

My stomach is griping at me, like I'm starving, and I am in every way, but not for anything I want to eat. I push the gnawing sensation down and open the door to find the courtyard full of other carriages. The Chief's is here too. Wendell smiles at me as he rises from the lip of the ornate fountain across from me.

"Ms Beaumont told me to stay here until you rose, and to let you know they're waiting for you in the living room."

"Thanks," I say. "Is the Chief here?"

His eyes flit to her carriage, and he nods. "I believe she was in discussions with Cordelia. They'd taken a private room and were going to reconvene with you all once you woke."

"Thanks," I say and head towards the door, my stomach twisting and this time not because of the hunger, but because of what I learnt at the end of the spirit trial. I need to speak to the Chief. I should confront her and find out whether what I saw was true. Because if it is... Fuck, I don't even know how I am supposed to process that.

"Ahem," Wendell coughs.

I stop and face him. "Something else?"

"She also gave me this... And insisted I make you drink it." He holds out a flask.

My eyes fall to it, but the way my mouth waters, I'm certain it's not alcohol in there.

"Thanks," I say, even though I'm anything but. Unfortunately, the minute my fingers brush the metal flask, my stomach cramps up. There's no way I'm getting away without drinking at least some of it, and that's not just because of the hunger, but the injuries too.

I flick open the top and sip. And then sip again. And again. And again. I can't stop. The sweet iron nectar hits my throat, and my entire body relaxes. Warmth floods my limbs and I slide into the golden haze of a blood-drunk stupor. By the time the flask is empty, I can breathe easier, my chest doesn't feel bruised and my back doesn't sting or itch like it's healing. I lean against the doorway, steadying myself until I can take a breath deep enough that I ground myself again. My pussy aches to be touched, but there isn't time for that now.

I head into Octavia's mansion and quickly get lost. "Fucksake," I grumble. I thought I'd learnt the hallways by now. But clearly not because I end up near the kitchen instead of the living room. I double back on myself and end up at a dead end full of staff offices.

"Going well, Red. Really well."

I make my way back towards the courtyard door. If I can start again, I'll be able to take the correct turn when I halt. Two voices drift out from one of the staff offices, and they do not fit with what I expect to hear down here.

The Chief... and Cordelia.

I have two choices: leave and confront the Chief later, or confront her now, despite the fact she's in the room with Cordelia.

Instead, I decide on a different course of action. I creep up to the door, which is cracked open, and I listen.

"This is serious," the Chief says.

"I'm not an idiot. I instigated these trials, or have you forgotten that?"

"Don't speak to me like that, Cordelia. I'm here working with you for one reason, and don't you forget it."

There's muffled talking. A piece of furniture scrapes along the floor. I jerk back, leaning against the wall, trying to control my breathing so I don't give myself away to Cordelia's vampire hearing. When I calm down, I chance another listen.

"Perhaps who we were wasn't so bad," Cordelia says.

"Oh, get real... we were dreaming. We hated each other then, and we hate each other now," the Chief says.

"Didn't stop you fucking me a thousand years ago... did it, *Eleanor*?"

My blood runs cold. There it is. Everything in my vision matches.

The Chief is Eleanor. The Chief is... was? The love of Cordelia's life. She's a thousand fucking years old. Pins and needles trickle into my fingers, my nostrils flare as I try to breathe deep enough not to pass out.

How could she keep that from us?

"Yes, well, we all make mistakes we regret, don't we..." the Chief says, and that hangs in the air for longer than I'm comfortable with. Long enough, I consider running out of the corridor and away in case one or both of them are about to exit the office room.

But they continue talking. I miss the first few words, but I strain my hearing until I latch onto what they're saying again.

It's the Chief talking, but I only catch the end of her sentence. "...someone else will."

"Mother of Blood, Eleanor, I don't see you bringing in any information on our mutual enemy."

"Fuck you. Even working with you is enough of a risk to

threaten my entire academy. We're both losing control of our people. And if someone else gets to—"

"Hush," Cordelia hisses. "Come on, be reasonable. We're two of the most powerful women in the city. We can defend ourselves against anything."

"You're not worried, then?"

Something slams down.

"Of course I am. You need to control the dhampir. That was your job. Your end of this fucking bargain."

"I get that. She's almost there. She needs a little push, and we'll have her," the Chief says.

If I thought my blood had turned cold, it freezes in my veins. I can't breathe.

It's Cordelia who speaks this time. "We need to step up the trials. We need to get her to..."

I strain but I can't make out the end of the sentence, dammit.

"No," the Chief snaps. "I can do this. I just need to isolate her a little more. Get her to trust me and me alone. Maybe another riot, perhaps put her sister in harm's way. If it weren't for you matching her with Octavia, we might have already won her around. We need her in a position where I'm the only one she can trust. Then she'll have no choice but to come to me and do as I say."

My eyes sting, I suck my lip in and bite down trying to make the words go away. Praying I'm hallucinating and none of this is real.

"And if you're wrong? What then?" Cordelia says.

"I'm not wrong." Another object slams into something.

"But if you are? Then what?"

"I don't know, MORE. We can incite more riots? The more danger her loved ones are in, the more chance we have of getting her to do what we want. She's already told me she's the dhampir. She may have already killed someone today and initiated the transition."

"If you're wrong about this, Eleanor."

"Don't fucking call me that. I'm the one putting my people in danger here."

"You are? Do you have any fucking idea how many vampires have died patrolling that border? We don't even know what's out there for fuck's sake. Sadie said the Mother of Blood showed her a vision of demons inside the boundary. We don't have the weaponry to deal with that. What if—"

But I've heard enough. I can't, I don't want to listen anymore. I'm running down the corridor, sprinting away as fast as I can.

I can't breathe.

Not only is the Chief Eleanor Randall, but she's colluding against me, trying to fucking control me, just like everyone else. She was meant to be my leader. My commander. The one person I could trust with my life. And she's the one trying to manipulate me this entire time.

And she knows who I am.

She knows because I fucking told her.

I am in a world of shit. This whole time, she was pushing me to dig up dirt, to spy on Octavia. The fucking manipulation. Forcing me closer and pulling me away all at the same time. How could she?

Tears streak my cheeks as my chest constricts. I've ruined everything. I've hidden the fact I told the Chief who I was from Octavia. And fucking Octavia... she still hasn't given me my memories back.

Who am I meant to trust when everyone betrays me?

CHAPTER 30

CORDELIA

One Thousand Years Ago

Two days the nurse kept me from Eleanor. While I'm certain that her family were desperate to find her after the fire, I was most displeased that I had to be separated from her.

Especially considering I was the one who had bothered to track her down and help care for her. Where was her family then? I was the one who gave the nurse the information to contact them in the first place.

And yes, I am acutely aware it was the right thing to do, but that doesn't make me any happier about it.

But such is the plight of families. They like to own us, treat us as commodities and then discard us when they've finished rolling us out as show pieces. Or perhaps that's just what it's like in my family.

I have never been a daughter; I am a trophy. A prized show piece to be lauded to the other nobles and rolled out when my mother and father deemed it appropriate.

And I have to wonder whether Eleanor experienced the same because when I return to her room two days later, she's looking far worse for wear than when I left her.

I stand in the doorway of her room, my hands balled on my hips. My teeth gnash on my bottom lip as I take in her appearance.

"How is it I can leave you looking like you're on the mend and I return, and you look hideous? Didn't they take care of you?"

She pats the bed and makes a space for me to sit down. But I don't move.

"Peopling, family, especially after a long time asleep, is hard."

"And?" I say, tapping my foot on the floor and then pacing over to sit on the edge of her bed.

"That is why I'm exhausted. And I suppose they were more interested in getting the facts clear so they could spin a story than they really were about my state of health and ensuring I took my daily medicines."

My teeth grind against each other hard enough that Eleanor rubs her thumb along my jawline until I relax.

"I have spent weeks searching for you, finding you and helping you heal, then two days with your family and you've taken back steps."

"Not back steps. I told them that I had more healing to do. Meaning I bought us some time..."

"Time for what, Eleanor? What exactly is it you think we're going to achieve? We're doomed, dammit. If it's not my family coming after you, it's your family coming after me. How are we ever supposed to actually live a free life together?"

She grins so wide she shows me all her teeth.

"I told them it would be at least a month before I'd return home. A month is a long time."

"It will be at least a week before you're ready to leave, and then what are we supposed to do with the three weeks?"

She leans back against her pillow, dragging me by the shoulder until I'm laid flat against her chest. She runs her hands over my raven locks, stroking my head until the huffing ceases.

"I told them at *least* a month. I'd put money on them not checking on or worrying about me for at least five to six weeks. That's an awful long time for us to run."

"Run?" I ask, shooting back up again.

"Yes, Cordelia. I'm done hiding us. We're going to run. We're going to make this work."

CHAPTER 31

RED

I find Octavia in Castle Beaumont bar, half cut with Xavier.

She knows the moment I walk into the bar because her head snaps to the door. Fucking bond. It's like she can sense the problem before I can even communicate it.

I can imagine I look quite the state. Xavier sits on the stool next to her, laughing, with his head thrown back. But as if he perceives the problem too, he stops quite suddenly and stares at me.

Sadie, Gabriel and Keir are missing. But Dahlia, Lincoln and Amelia sit in various spots around the room.

The tension in here is palpable. Most of us don't really like each other, and yet, tonight, we all fought as a team. A strange reality when we're meant to be fighting against each other for the city. But tonight, the city drove us to fight against it.

So here we are again, relegated to corners of the room. Dahlia and Lincoln are whispering to each other. Strategising, I suspect.

Xavier leans into Octavia's ear and whispers something. Both of them catch my eye and then Amelia's. They want to talk.

Dahlia catches sight of our shared glance and narrows her eyes.

Gabriel barges in behind me with Keir in tow. "These trials are a fucking shit show," he says, slumping down on a large chesterfield sofa in front of the fire.

"Quite agree," Xavier says and swivels to face Dahlia. "But you always were Mummy's favourite, so how's about you go have a word and sort it out before we all end up dead because the city's lost its fucking mind?"

Dahlia's jaw flexes but her eyes never leave her twin. "And where were you two tonight? Hmm? Not like you got your hands dirty fighting with us."

"Not all fights need to be with fists, Dah," Gabriel drawls.

Dahlia tuts like she wants to protest, but she also knows there's truth behind the words. She hesitates a moment longer, but finally marches out, scruffing the collar of an unhappy-looking Gabriel and tugging him along with her.

Xavier strides over to and kneels before a rather pale looking Talulla. "Why don't you get some rest," he says and kisses her knuckles.

"I'm fine," she says, though she looks anything but.

He drops his tone, the waves of compulsion licking out around the room. "I think you should go to bed."

Talulla's expression shifts, melting into a gooey complacence.

"Yeah, you're right," she says and stands up and leaves without looking back.

"You too, Lincoln," I say from the door.

He frowns at me, shakes his head, but makes for the

door. When he reaches me, he leans in and drops his voice. Not that it makes a blind bit of difference.

"I don't know what's going on with you, but we used to be friends. It used to be me you wanted to talk to."

"Linc—" I start, but he shoves past me into the hall, and I'm left gawping at the space he occupied.

Am I really a shit friend? Under normal circumstances, he would be the first person I'd go to, but since he's on Dahlia's team, and we are pitted against each other, how can I?

When the only ones left are Amelia, Octavia, and Xavier, I glance back down the hallway to make sure it's empty and I close the door.

"We need to talk," I say.

Octavia glances at Xavier and nods, "Us too."

"Me three," Amelia says. "Actually, no. I just felt left out. I think I told you everything I had in the office."

Xavier hops behind the bar and grabs two bottles. A vintage Sanguis Cupa and a bottle of blood for Octavia, Amelia, and him.

He pours out their blood and drops a shot of Sangui Cupa into each one. Then he pours a shot for me and digs up a bottle of wine and hands me a glass.

"I figured we'd need this," he says.

Octavia rearranges the sofas so that there's space for us all, and we nestle down in front of the fire with our drinks.

Then we all start talking at once.

Xavier wafts his hands at us. "One at a time. Amelia, you first."

She sighs, her shoulders sagging. "I've already told Red and Octavia. But to catch you up, I've been doing research. In order for Red to transition, she needs to kill someone. A human, specifically."

Xavier shifts in his seat. "Okay, that's a lot," he says.

I nod and sigh, preparing to chip in everything I've discovered. "When we were in the spirit trial, I passed the test and then witnessed a vision of the past. It was two women in love. At first, I couldn't see who they were, but the vision dragged me closer until I could make out their faces. It was Cordelia..."

"And?" Octavia says.

"And Eleanor. Only I recognised Eleanor's face. I mean... she's changed, like, a lot. It's hard to explain how much time and battles and scars inside and out can change the shape of a person's smile. But her eyes, they were the same. I knew it was her."

"Who, Red? Who was it?" Xavier says and even Amelia sits forward in her chair.

"I wanted confirmation before I told you, but there's no question, after the conversation I just overheard. It's the Chief. She's Eleanor."

Octavia's eyebrows try to climb off her brow.

Xavier's eyes widen. "How the fuck did I miss that? I thought I was good at reading people."

"Because someone cursed them. But forget the past for a second because it gets worse. They incited and coordinated the riots in the city tonight. I always suspected it was Cordelia, but I had no idea it was the Chief too."

"Why the hell are they colluding?" Amelia whispers.

I shrug. "It's to do with me. They want to control me for something."

"Something more than opening the door?" Octavia asks.

"I guess? I honestly don't have a clue."

Xavier swigs the entire rest of his goblet and starts pouring more drinks. An appropriate response. I glug several gulps of my glass. Amelia puts her head in her hands.

"That's not all, is it?" Octavia says.

I shake my head. This is the bit of information I've been dreading sharing.

"No. It's not," I mumble, pulling my eyes away from her. "I...Well, I fucked up."

"Red," Octavia says, her tone deeper.

"Define, fucked up," Xavier says and passes Amelia a top up.

"I told her. Before, I mean. The Chief knows I'm the dhampir," I say, and the three of them fall deathly quiet. Xavier swallows and pops the bottle of Sangui Cupa over the sofa arm and on the floor and then sheepishly glances at Octavia.

"What the fuck?" Octavia booms, standing up. Xavier grabs her by the wrist and pulls her back into the seat.

"Say more. Make it better," Amelia says.

"I was pissed with you, Octavia, you'd tried to take my memories... again—"

"To protect you," Octavia barks.

I glare at her, unimpressed, and then fire an equally pissy look at my sister.

"Point is, I didn't trust you, and let's be real. I am a hunter. The Chief sent me into these trials to spy on the St Clair's, so I assumed..."

"Hold on a minute, aren't we missing a really fucking important point? Aside from the fact hunters and vampires hate each other. If the Chief is really Eleanor, why the hell are they working together? They were cursed to hate each other," Amelia says, a furrow forming between her brows.

"Are you saying they don't hate each other?" Xavier asks.

I shake my head. "Oh, they hate each other, alright. At least, from what I overheard, anyway. But they seem to think they have a common enemy, and they want to use me for something. But that's the limit of what I've discovered."

We all fall silent for a while. Octavia's fingers knead her knuckles. When I can't take her fidgeting anymore, I'm about to say something, anything, when she pipes up.

"I know who my birth mother is," she says.

My eyes bug wide, Xavier's do too.

"She's the witch-god," she laughs. It's a short, sharp bark. "The Mother of fucking Blood. That's who my real mother is."

"Wait, what?" I breathe.

Xavier chokes on the mouthful of blood he drank, and Amelia outright gasps.

"Yeah, Cordelia's been lying this entire time. The only reason she adopted me is because she killed my birth mother. Or so she thought. She left her bleeding out on the tiles of her kitchen floor. But she was praying and praying. And the witch-gods saved her and turned her into one of the monsters she'd created. I can only imagine that was some kind of god-humour." Octavia is dry and monotone as she speaks as if she's already resigned to all of this.

"But... what was her name? The other original vampire?" I whisper.

But it's Amelia who answers. "Isabella. Her name was Isabella Montague."

"What happened to her?" I ask.

Octavia shrugs. "That's the thing. There's no clear answer. I couldn't see her face in the vision. But I can't let go of the idea that maybe she never really disappeared or died. What if she's alive and wasn't lost to history? What if she's been in hiding this entire time?"

"Fuck," I say. "Have you confronted Cordelia yet?"

Octavia shakes her head. "What am I supposed to say? Fuck you for lying to me for a thousand years? Oh, and I found out you killed my birth mother. Oh wait, no you didn't. You're just the reason she chose to become a fucking vampire."

"Right. Good point," I say, because what the fuck else am I supposed to say to that?

Amelia blinks into the void. Xavier leans back and necks the rest of his drink, then outright reaches for the bottle and starts drinking from that instead.

And I grip the arms of the chair, wondering how fucking deep this rabbit hole goes.

CHAPTER 32

RED

It's Wendell who breaks up our discussions. As dawn crests the horizon, little embers of light streak the bar. I get up from our seating area and close the curtains before either Amelia, Octavia or Xavier get crispy.

Wendell makes his way into the bar with a selection of envelopes in his hand. He offers them out to each of us and then takes his leave.

Amelia pushes the plate of food I barely touched towards me. I pick at it, hating that I'm the only one who actually needs to eat. Obviously, none of them touch it, though there are three empty goblets of blood left on the coffee table. But I mostly shove the food around the plate, none of it appealing or tasting the way food used to.

Octavia glances at her envelope and then sighs. "We've been invited to a casino night. Hardly appropriate, given the riots the other day."

"I do love a casino night, though," Xavier says.

Octavia glares at him. "No, you love the hot, half naked

people running around serving shots of Sanguis Cupa and bending over the card tables."

"Or is it the unnecessary violence from the fights they usually allow... oh," Xavier's voice trails off.

He glances at Octavia, who inhales and sighs again, deeper this time. Her nostrils flare. "They're going to pit us against each other, aren't they?" She kneads her temples, wiping a hand along her brow. "Fuck."

Xavier leans back on the sofa. "Listen, I didn't fight for the amulet, I'm not about to mess up this exquisite face fighting for Mother's entertainment. Not when I have a sister made of savagery to do it for me."

"Plus, she's going to give you a job after this is over, anyway," Amelia says, grinning and swiping her finger around the dregs of blood at the bottom of her goblet.

My nose wrinkles at her movement, my stomach turning at the prospect of her enjoying blood. It only makes the resolve in my gut harden. I have to win. We have to win so I can pull her back from the brink. I have to get the cure for her.

But what if Cordelia's prophecy is right? What if there is no other way to open that door without me becoming the dhampir and half the thing I hate so much?

"What do we do about everything we've discovered?" Xavier asks.

"Which is a good point. You never did tell us what you discovered in the trial." I say.

He sighs dramatically. "Nothing useful. At least not for the trials. The Mother of Blood gave me closure. Something I've needed to know for a long time about someone I lost... It was needed. But it's not useful for us."

I slump. I was hoping there would be more intel we could use.

Octavia pipes up. "In which case, we do nothing. We

keep everything we know under wraps. Tell absolutely no one. Trust no one. This is our safety circle. And we absolutely do not confront my mother or the Chief before the time is right. It will be hard, but for now, we play their game, bide our time until we can stack the deck in our favour."

"Okay, so we should reconvene after the next trial, then?" Amelia asks.

Octavia shakes her head. "That's too far away. Maybe after the casino night tomorrow? Let's see if we can dig anything up. Keep your ears to the ground. Xavier, do your compulsion thing, go wild. Amelia, keep researching and I will monitor Mother."

"We should rest," Amelia says, looking at me, her brows knitted as she scans my face. "You okay?" she mouths.

And suddenly I'm not. I'm a little faint. The last few hours, the revelations, they're all catching up with me. I've had more of Octavia's blood, albeit rationed. But I am still starving. The bloodied steaks on the plate in front of me aren't cutting it.

"Octavia," Amelia says.

She snaps to attention, her eyes flitting from Amelia to me. Her lips press shut, and she stands.

"We're done," she says, "Let's convene before the casino night." Then she's lifting me by the arm and dragging me out of the bar.

"Where are we going?" I say, yanking my arm out of her grip.

"To my private wing."

She marches faster. A speckling of grey spatters my vision, and I stumble. She halts, speeds back to me, and grabs my arm again.

"You're going to let me help you, or I swear on the Mother of Blood, I will spank your arse until it bleeds."

I grumble at her but relent, and she leads me through the castle and to her private wing.

The noise drops to nothing as we enter her section of the castle. No one comes down here save for Wendell. She leads me past my room, past her room and to the room I've only been in once.

"Why?" I ask.

No answer. She opens the door, pushes me inside, and then locks it shut behind us and pushes me against the door, the soft velvet caressing my back.

She places her hands on either side of my head. "When did you last feed exactly?"

I shrug. "I took the entire flask you gave Wendell as soon as I woke."

"The whole thing?" Octavia says, her eyes wide. "Fuck."

"And then you gave me a mouthful about ninety minutes ago."

"Then why is your skin grey? Why are you sweating? Why do you look like you're on the brink of death? Do you need to fuck because you've drunk so much?"

"You make it sound so appealing," I say, pushing her arm away so I can escape.

"Your blood is no longer working. I'm not sure what's wrong, but it's not satisfying me the way it was. I need more. More I fear than you can give me. But I don't think that's what we need to talk about, is it?"

"No," Octavia says and turns away from me, leaning against the chest of drawers and shelving unit filled with toys. "You don't trust me."

She paces back and forth, and I stay quiet because I know I fucked up here and hurt her. I went to the Chief instead of to Octavia when the Chief was the one scheming against me. I placed my trust in the wrong woman. She rests her hands against the drawers again, her head tilted down, her hair covering her face.

"I didn't, trust you then," I offer. "But you understand why I made the choice I did, right?"

She nods, even though I can't see her expression. "Because I took your memories."

"You see my problem. You're telling me I asked you to take them. But I'm asking for them back too. All I knew is that you were trying to control me."

"Except I wasn't."

"No. It was the Chief. Fuck. Eleanor. Gods, what I'm supposed to call her now? It's all a lie. It was stupid."

"You're hurting," she says.

I nod, trying to keep control. "Everything hurts. It's like my body is wasting away. My heart hurts for you, it hurts because of you, too. The Chief. I want it all to go away."

Finally, she turns to face me. Something has shifted in her expression. "Do you truly trust me now?"

My mouth falls open. Hurt lines her expression. And yet, she still holds my memories from me. Even though I'm asking for them back. I want to believe her that I was the one who asked her to keep them from me no matter what. But what could I have done that was so bad I'd ask her to take them away?

"You still don't," she says, her voice cracking.

Fuck. *Fuck.*

"Octavia..."

"No. Don't lie to me. I can tell you feel for me. But this... these fucking memories are always going to be between us. It doesn't matter what happens. I'm never going to get to keep you, am I?"

Her words drop to a whisper. Her eyes are glassy. It's like she's pulling back, fading away from me. Like I've pushed her too hard for too long, and she can't take it anymore. And I hate that it's come to this.

"I'm here right now, aren't I?"

"Your body is, your heart is stuck somewhere else. Wanting memories you gave to me."

I shake my head. "I want them back."

Octavia's eyes drop to the floor. "You have no idea what you're asking for. And even if I did give them back to you, what does that make me? Either I'm a liar to your past self, or I break the current you by giving them back. Either way, I lose you and my integrity."

She finally looks up at me, and I realise how I can make her understand that, even though I'm hurting, even though everything is fucked up, I am still here. Still fighting for her. She turns around and leans her hands against a dresser.

I unbutton my shirt. Tug it off my arms and let it drop to the floor. Next, I yank off my sports bra and throw that to the ground. Last, I pull my trousers and underwear off until I'm standing there naked.

"Octavia." She doesn't respond. But I'm not giving up. Not least because I need this. I am hurting alongside her.

I grit my teeth. "Please..."

She looks at me, and I drop to my knees for her.

She sucks in a breath, her nostrils flaring. This is what I wanted. I plead silently that she will take me. Make me hers.

I keep my eyes on her the whole time as I lower myself onto my calves. Spreading my knees. I rest my hands, palms up, on my knees. I tear my gaze away from her face, lowering my head in submission.

"I can't," Octavia says.

But I'm not giving up. I refuse to when I recognise that she needs this, too. She needs me to submit, to prove I am still here despite putting my trust in the wrong person.

And I need her to punish me, hurt me, and make me feel anything but the agony in my heart right now.

"You need to feed," she says. But I stay where I am, keep my palms up and my head lowered. Until I hear her switch into the dom she needs to be right now, I won't get up. I won't move.

We both need this.

"Don't..." she says, the energy in the room shifting. My skin tingles with it.

"Fuck, Verity."

It's coming. I'm pushing her hard enough her tone is changing. She paces the room fast. Her fist slams down on the chest of drawers. I don't flinch. I don't raise my head.

My heart rate climbs, slamming against my ribs as I wait patiently for her to come around.

"You have no idea what you do to me, do you?" she purrs.

There it is.

"Hello, Mistress Beaumont," I say, careful to keep my eyes lowered.

"Did I tell you to speak?"

I shut my mouth. Blood rushes around my system, heat pooling between my legs, and the first pulse of pleasure washes through my clit.

"Safe word," she says.

"Elysium," I respond instantly.

"Good. You're going to feed, as will I..." she lets the words hang in the air. "I think you need to be reminded of who you belong to, Verity."

She rummages in a drawer and returns with a rope. Kneels and lifts my hands off my knees to loop the rope around both my wrists and knot it. She gives it a tug to check the pressure and hauls me up by the rope until I'm standing.

"We're going to feed from each other because I don't think you have much time left. I'm hoping the bond will help stave off the real need here, which is for you to... transform."

She avoids saying the truth of it, which is that I need to feed from a human, and instead leads me across the room to a chain hanging from the ceiling. On the end of it is a hook.

"I am tired of you not trusting me. Tired of doing the right thing and constantly being hurt. I want you to desire me the way I desire you."

"I do," I say without thinking.

Her hand rears back and smacks me on my naked arse.

"I am speaking. You will talk only when I give you permission."

My skin tingles with the imprint of her hand. I can sense the shadow of every finger that touched my cheek. She lifts my hands and drops the rope over the hook. I'm short, which means I am more or less on my tiptoes.

Octavia steps back, admiring her work. She nods and painfully, slowly, she unbuttons her top. Each button pop, pop, popping as if to tease me.

She takes her time, making me watch every movement, every flick of her fingers.

I lick my lips, knowing exactly what those fingers can do, especially pressed against my skin, thrust inside me.

She knows it too, as her ruby-red eyes glimmer. Her shirt falls to the floor, discarded, followed by her trousers and her underwear. She's as naked as I am. Only I am hanging from the ceiling and unable to touch her.

She steps up to me. I wriggle as I pull away. But that only makes her smile deepen. She runs a finger from my chin down my throat, between my breasts and all the way to the tip of my pussy.

I jerk back as her finger brushes my clit. It makes her smile wider and I know I'm in a world of trouble tonight.

CHAPTER 33

OCTAVIA

When you spend a thousand years living amongst mortals, your patience wears thin, and I have been patient enough with Red. Tonight she will do as she's told.

I slide my finger between her folds. Her body jerks on the hook. Her mouth parts as she struggles on tiptoes to pull away.

"Do you need to use your safe word?" I ask.

She shakes her head. "Good."

I step close enough that I can inhale the scent of warm skin and the tang of her lust.

I pull my finger away from her pussy and up to her mouth. I push between her lips until she sucks my finger over her tongue, her excitement dripping over her tastebuds.

"Bite," I say.

She freezes, but her canines draw down, their sharp little points nipping at the side of my finger. Her eyes widen as if she can feel her teeth moving.

"Red, bite."

She pushes me into place with her tongue and sinks her teeth into the flesh of my index finger. There's a searing stab. Her eyes roll shut as her excitement and my blood fill her mouth. She moans against me. I pull my finger out and suck the end till it stops bleeding. There's a dribble of blood in the corner of her mouth. I bend over her and lick it up.

My hand winds its way around the back of her neck, and I yank her to me.

I flick my hair back and bare my throat. She jiggles against the hook and restraints, desperate to touch me. But not tonight. Tonight, I'm in charge.

My thumb curves around the front of her neck, and she swallows, making her throat bob against my thumb. I'm cross enough I could press down and cut off her air. But I don't. I pull her to me and make her lips meet my throat.

"Take your fill," I say, and she lunges for my carotid. There's a needle-like sensation and then the hot threading tug deep in my veins as my blood flows into her mouth.

My body instantly responds, my fangs dropping. "I'm going to bite you."

She pulls off my throat only long enough to scream, "YES."

I jerk her into position. I'm done being gentle with her. She moans against me as I angle our bodies so we can both drink, and then I sink my teeth into her neck.

She stiffens under me, pausing her drinking to gasp as I draw blood from her. The chains above rattle, and then she moans as the pleasure takes over.

She lowers her mouth to my neck again, and we both draw sweet claret nectar from each other. She laps hungrily at my neck. The more she takes, the more aroused I grow. But she grows greedy, drinking too fast. It's wasteful. Blood overflows and spills between her lips, dripping down my chest and coating my breasts.

Her heart rate increases, making her own blood do the same, tumbling down her throat and over her breasts. The exquisite pulse of mutual feeding drives right to my core. My clit throbs in time with my heartbeat, or maybe it's hers and I'm feeling myself shifting. Pleasure addles my mind.

I pull off. She does the same. Blood streaks both of our bodies.

"Fuck," I say as I take in the sight of her strung up for me. Hanging by her wrists, blood painting her tits and torso in the most elegant of patterns.

I lunge forward, licking a long swipe from her pussy all the way up her body and over her chest, where I sink my teeth into the flesh and draw another mouthful of blood. I let the remnants trickle over her skin and stomach, and then I lick an O shape between her breasts.

She glances down, confused at the bloody O over her heart.

"You have something to say?" I ask.

"O for Octavia?"

I shrug. "O for many things: Octavia, owned, and perhaps if you behave, all the orgasms I'll give you tonight."

She kicks against the restraints, moaning and gasping. I pull back, slide my hand between her thighs. The slick wetness coats both her inner legs.

"Good girl. Looks like you can behave, can't you?" I say.

She nods at me.

"Still, Red. You didn't trust me. Over and over again, you've failed to see how I have your best interests at heart."

She opens her mouth to respond, and I raise a single eyebrow. She stays quiet.

"What do you need?" I ask.

She pouts and looks away. She's sad?

I pull her chin around. "I asked you a question. You answer me when I ask."

"I want the hurt to go away," she says. "Loving you despite everything we've done to each other. The Chief's betrayal. All of it. The fact is, I'm going to face a choice really soon. And I don't want to make it. So for tonight, can you just make it all go away?"

I speed to the drawer and pick up a flogger and the strapless strap-on. I insert it inside myself and turn the vibration on. Then I flick the handle of the flogger, letting the leather threads twirl through the air. Faster and faster, I fling it until it's zinging through the air and Red is nearly panting.

I pull back and land the flogger on her arse. She flinches, squealing, but it instantly turns into a moan. I pull back and slap her again.

The chains jangle. Her head rolls forward and the noise that comes from her mouth makes my pussy clench around the vibrating strap-on.

"Do you need to use your safe word?"

"No. I want more."

I tilt my head at her back. Fine. I return to the drawer and select a paddle instead. I run my hand over her ass and then bring the paddle down on her cheek.

She squeals, leaning forward. "Fuck," she moans.

I bring it down on her other cheek, once, twice, three times. The noises she makes unleash something feral inside me. I'm now the one panting, and yet she's the one receiving the punishment. I no longer know who's in charge here, who really holds the power.

I hold the back of her neck and push down until she's bent so far forward that her arms strain against the restraints. I step up to her backside, pushing the dildo between her cheeks. She gasps and pushes up, but I grip her neck harder, pinning her in position.

She moans. It's incoherent, a mumbled fuck or yes, or a

mixture of both. She's hungry for everything I want to give her.

"I swear, Verity, if anything other than my name comes out of your mouth, I'm bringing that paddle back. Do you understand?"

She nods, though her head can scarcely move under my grip. I slip my fingers to her entrance and circle. She's nice and wet for me, so I position the head of the cock at her entrance, and she jerks against me.

I thrust inside her pussy in one hard motion. She moans, her body relaxing, letting the rope and chains take her weight.

I draw the cock out slowly. Her legs tremble beneath her, but I never let up. I keep her pushed down. Thrust hard. Pull out slow. Thrust hard.

The chains jingle and pull and rattle against each thrust. I reach around her with my other hand. Her nipples are tight little buds. I pinch one hard, and she yelps against me, pushing her arse back against the cock.

I pump in and out, bringing her body higher, winding her tighter and tighter until she throws my name from her lips like a whip.

"I'm going to—"

I pull out. Leaving her right on the edge but holding back the release she craves. She twists around, furious, as she glares at me.

"What the f—" she starts, but I reach for the paddle and slap it down on her arse.

She screams, her eyes rolling shut, her body drooping as the chains hold her in place.

"I told you, I don't want to hear anything but my name on your lips."

She screams in frustration as I re-enter her pussy. I drive in and out, over and over, taking her back up to the peak of pleasure. I shunt her forward until her body is taut against the restraints and slide a hand around to massage her clit.

"I can't take it. I ca—"

"Do you need to use your safe word?" I ask.

"No—"

She squeals as the paddle comes down on her cheek again. She will learn to trust me, or I will punish her.

She hisses and I know I'm taking her to the edge of what she can handle. Her body is pliant, relaxing into submission. I've no doubt the endorphins are dragging her into subspace. I push into her again and again, taking her to the brink of her climax.

"Octavia," she screams.

I pull out completely. Her arms have paled, and I know the blood has run out of them. She needs to come off the hook. So I lift her down and rest her on the floor. I keep her wrists tied, though.

"Beg," I say and pull her chin up so she looks at me.

"Please..."

"Please what, Red?"

"Please everything. Forgive me. Love me. Fuck me. Own me. Take me. Bite me. Make me fucking come."

I smile, honestly. It's a nasty little sneer, but she needs to know who she belongs to.

"Who do you belong to?"

Her eyes drop to the O, still smeared in blood between her breasts.

"Octavia owns me and my orgasms."

"Good." I drop her chin and pull the cock out of my pussy, letting it drop to the floor. I grab a fist full of her hair and pull her to my cunt.

"Make me come, and then I'll think about letting you orgasm."

I push her face over my pussy, and she laps hungrily at my clit. She licks and swipes her tongue until I'm rocking back and forth. But it's not enough, I want more.

I use the fist of hair I have to pull her off me. Then I reach down and use a nail to shred the restraints.

Her wrists are a little pink, so it was the right time to take them off.

"Two fingers."

She nods.

Her eyes are bright and hungry. "You're being a very good girl this evening, Verity. Your reward will be handsome."

She rubs her wrists, helping the blood flow back into her fingers, and then she looks up, signalling that she's ready. I lay on the edge of the bed, tugging her now normal-coloured wrist. She scrambles across the carpet to the edge of the bed and slides between my thighs.

Her tongue draws long, lavish licks over me. She sounds like a starved woman as she moans and laps and sucks at my pussy.

My head rocks back, my hair falling off my shoulders as I collapse to the bed and prop my feet up on the edge.

I stretch open, give her easier access. Her fingers slide up my legs and to my entrance. She wets the tips, circling my hole before she glides inside. I thought I wanted it hard, but she pushes soft and deep instead and takes me to another place.

I gasp. But she is relentless, pushing into me deeper. Her mouth devours me, her tongue flickering light and quick, dancing over every inch of my pussy. She moans as if she's the one receiving pleasure and the sound of her enjoying the taste of my cunt drives me wild.

One of her fingers curls inside me, the other stays long as she laps at my clit in time with her thrusts.

"Fuck," I hiss, as a trickle of pleasure rushes through my pussy, sending tingles outward like electricity around my body.

I pinch my nipples, panting as she continues to slide in and out of me. Her fingers wet with my excitement. The slick slide and her moans make my entire body shiver with pleasure. My muscles clamp around her fingers, but she doesn't relent. She laps faster, making the pressure on my clit lighter, then switches her movements. Her fingers stiffen and she fucks me hard.

I rock my hips, shifting my pussy and rubbing against her face, making her chin and lips glisten.

The sight of her covered in me, taking everything I throw at her, pushes me over the edge. I fall, as a shiver of bliss run from deep inside me right up to the tip of my scalp. She continues licking my clit, drinking down every drop of my orgasm. She pulls her fingers out and pops them into her mouth, sucking up my juices.

She bites down, just as I made her do earlier. When she pulls out, her fingers drip with her blood and what remains of my come.

She pushes them into my mouth. The dynamic between us changing. I suck her blood and my come until all that's left is clean flesh.

"I'm done playing," she barks, command lacing through her tone. It makes me wet all over again. I could do this all day. Fuck her until we're both spent. But she's right, I've teased her long enough.

She swaps positions and lies down, spreading her legs until her pussy is fully exposed. She's swollen and desperate for me to finish her.

"Octavia," she growls.

I speed across the room and nestle between her legs.

The stiffness in her body instantly loosens as my tongue draws up through her centre.

I start slowly, building her back up to where I had her. My tongue worships her core. She's the sweetest thing I've ever tasted.

If she's all I ate the rest of my days, I wouldn't desiccate. Her hips slowly rock against my mouth the more I build her up.

Her breath shortens, sharp little pants escaping her lips. I slide a finger inside her. I draw it in and out until she relaxes enough I can slide another in to join the first. That's when the first real carnal moan rushes from her lips.

"Fuck," she pants. "Harder, Octavia."

I oblige, my tongue flicking her clit quicker while my fingers pulse in and out of her, searching for her G-spot.

She tilts up, her eyes locked on me, and she grabs my hair, holding me in place as I continue ravishing her pussy.

She rocks against my mouth, panting my name, cursing and swearing. Her skin breaks out in goosebumps as her nipples tighten and her pussy clamps around my fingers.

"Octavia," she gasps before she shivers, jerks and collapses back onto the bed as her hips jolt against my mouth.

I tease her, licking once, twice, three times more until she hisses at me to get off her oversensitive clit.

It makes me smile. I place a kiss on her pussy and then crawl up the bed so I can lie next to her.

"Hey," I say.

"Hey," she says. "We're a mess, aren't we?"

"Yeah," I nod. "But I want to get through it with you. Right now, you should sleep."

She nods, and reaches for a blanket, pulling it over both of us.

"You look better," I say, drawing my thumb over her flushed cheeks.

"I think it worked. Maybe the bond gave me some of your energy or something? I definitely feel better."

"Good, sleep now, and tomorrow we can figure out how the hell we're going to get through this."

She curls her back into my chest, making me the big spoon. I close my eyes, soaking up the feel of her naked body pressed against me.

My fingers find their way to her chest circling the dried O between her breasts. And that is where I stay while day yawns its way above us, and I try to pull apart everything that's gone wrong, and how the hell we're going to figure out what's really going on.

CHAPTER 34

OCTAVIA

I have concerns.

Red saunters into Castle St Clair's casino on the other side of the grounds like she owns the place. She's wearing a tapered suit. It's blood-red and matches the corset and trousers I'm wearing tonight. There's a hanky with an embroidered red O sticking up from her jacket pocket.

To everyone else, she looks confident, assured and rather dapper, if I say so myself.

And yet. I am concerned.

The casino is full to the brim with vampire nobles. Both hunters and vampires share card tables. Bottles of blood and whisky line the table lips and dealers dish out cards. The air is alive with competition and tension. It buzzes with a faint static energy. This kind of hunger can only be slaked by a score of wins and losses and the exchange of money, pride and the sweet scent of spite-fuelled bets.

Lincoln rests against the far wall. It seems he, too, is the only other person to notice what I notice. He narrows his eyes at her and then glances at me. My lips press thin in response.

He sees the same fatigue I see. For all the time he's spent with Dahlia, he still knows his friend. And we both have concerns tonight.

It's dangerous. A tipping point from which we cannot return.

The casino consists of sections. In the heart of the building is a circular bar. A central meeting point of sorts. The far side of the building holds racetracks for demonic little hell dogs. Filling the rest of the expanse are tables with dealers ready to open any game players desire and screened-off areas where more contentious rounds are played. In each situation, vampires watch hunters with barely concealed suspicion and vice versa. The knife's edge of hostility is palpable. Through it all, Servers wearing little more than string wander with trays of drinks and goblets. There's a boxing ring here too, though tonight it sits quiet and empty.

I'm offered a goblet of blood by a server wearing nothing but a G-string and nipple tassels. She averts her gaze as I glance at her tray of goblets.

I sigh, frustrated with the way most humans treat me. It's worse now that I'm seeing progress. The more often someone decides to be brave and make eye contact with me, the more hope grows and the harder I find it when normality returns, and someone treats me with fear or disdain. I pause before selecting a goblet and tip her chin up to look at me. She trembles against my touch.

"I wish only to thank you, not hurt you, okay?" I say.

She nods, the smallest of smiles breaking across her lips. She dares to hold my gaze a moment longer and then bobs her head at me, dipping into a curtsey.

My back itches, like eyes are boring into me. Which is

when I spot Red. Her arms are folded, nostrils flared as her gaze shreds pieces of me from afar.

I sigh and make my way over. There was nothing in the touch. And yet, if she had done the same, I may well have severed the head of the server girl. A mistake, one I shan't commit again.

Verity's jaw clenches, and I swear I hear the crack of molars. "Red..." I say.

"You'll be punished for that later." Then she turns her back on me and marches to the bar, downing a shot of something before I can stop her.

She makes her way to the dog lanes, leaning over and watching the hounds run around the outside track. I down the goblet of blood and make my way over to her when Lincoln stops me.

"Yes?" I ask.

"What's wrong with her?" he says, standing in my way.

I don't even attempt to hide my irritation. "Move."

"I asked you a question."

"Just because you're in this competition, don't mistake the fact you're still breathing for patience. If you don't get out of my way, I will happily drain you where you stand."

He shakes his head at me. It amazes me he can sneer down his nose at me while not actually making eye contact.

"I am concerned about my friend, and you're the one that seems to spend the most time with her now," he says.

Much as I appreciate him showing care for his friend, I can't answer his questions. For one, I don't know what he's told Dahlia, and two, I'm not sure I can trust him. Besides, the fewer people that have knowledge of Red, the better.

"And you're in my way. Leave." It's cruel, but it keeps him safe and alive in the long run. Sometimes we have to do awful things for the right reason.

He huffs and meets my gaze at last. "Dahlia was right

about you. You're nothing but a scourge on this city. I hope she wins, and I hope Red sees you for what you are."

A little piece of me shatters. I am so tired of making enemies. All I want is for people to understand me. For me as me to be enough. One step forward with the server, one step back with Lincoln. Will I always be stuck in purgatory? Or will I find a way to win this city's love?

There is nothing I want more.

I want to feel like this city, this place I have called home for a thousand years, wants me. That I belong here as much as any other citizen. What must I do for them to accept me?

Everything I do is to protect them. I foster the economy in my territory because I want to see it prosper. I want to foster real peace, genuine acceptance so that everyone can belong.

Red's knuckles whiten where she grips the rail. I step up next to her but face forward as well.

"I thought the feed last night helped, yet you appear sick," I whisper.

"It did," she says, turning to me.

"Find a card table and take a seat. You shouldn't be standing if you're this weak."

"How am I meant to get through the rest of the trials if I am declining?"

"You know how, Red. You just don't want to do it."

Mother appears across the room, sweeping the crowd with her gaze. She ascends the small raised dais beside the central bar.

"Welcome, nobles, hunters, vampires and humans. Tonight is an evening of revelry. Of fun and games, of cards, and hounds and drinking. Let us forget the sorrows of yesterday and rejoice in what is to come."

My stomach turns, knowing there is more than that to this evening. Across the room, Xavier's eyes find mine. He wears tension like a jacket, all stiff across his shoulders and hard jawline.

Mother opens her arms as the Chief, or should I say Eleanor, strolls onto the small dais next to her.

I try to imagine them loving each other. Try to imagine them holding hands, kissing. The thought promptly makes me feel sick, so I stop imagining it. Even so, I want to see a romantic seed. Something to tell me that Red's vision was correct. They stand next to each other, an icy wasteland of space between them.

Was the story Cordelia told all a lie? Were they really lovers once? Did the same curse that made them also break their love?

I stare hard, desperate to find any shred of evidence that there was once an intimacy between them. But I find nothing.

It's the Chief who speaks next. "Tomorrow night, we will hold the penultimate trial."

She turns to Mother and smiles. It's forced.

Mother turns back to the crowd. "Tomorrow, our contestants will fight. This is the trial of strength. A preparation for what is inside the border."

My stomach sinks. Red's fists ball. She must recognise that she won't get through a fight without drinking human blood. Hell, I'm not even sure she's going to get through tonight.

She stares up at me, and for the first time since I've known her, I find fear buried in her gaze. The sight of that alone is enough to give me nightmares.

CHAPTER 35

CORDELIA

One Thousand Years Ago

I am sitting in a carriage as I pull out a scribing tool and journal. Before what comes next, I need to think.

To work out where it all went wrong.

So, I put pen to paper and begin to write.

The problem with running is that it doesn't actually solve the issue, it just delays it.

As we grow and age, there are many lessons we learn. Unfortunately for Eleanor and me, despite our combined fifty years between us, we had not considered the fact that running wouldn't really resolve our issues.

The worst—and by that I mean the most important—lessons are usually learnt through repetition. For want of a better analogy, these lessons are always death by a thousand paper cuts.

For two years, we ran.

Two years we spent hiding and hunting for a new place to call home.

And two years our families sent men to hunt us down like common vermin.

We never really found a home. Sure, we oft settled for a few weeks; once, we even spent five months in the same place. But the rumours would always find their way to us. A whispered comment, a note slipped past our threshold, an overheard conversation.

What both Eleanor and I failed to account for was the ruthless determination that our families possessed.

For we had stolen from them.

We were not free agents. We were not our own people. And according to them, we did not have the right to run free.

We were symbols. Heirs. Pawns.

Both of us belonged to, or perhaps I should say, were owned by our elders. The Matriarch and Patriarchs of our family.

We were duty bound, and our families did not take the responsibility of duty lightly.

We ran from the hospital gleefully. So full of hope and joy, and we genuinely thought we'd won.

Eleanor healed people for coin. I was her assistant. Sometimes I was a farmhand, sometimes I tended tables. It was a far cry from our lives of wealth and privilege. But we made do as much as we made love. We had nothing, but we wanted for nothing either.

It was joy.

It was bliss.

It was a little piece of paradise.

We skipped from town to town, village to suburb. Searching for a place to call home.

Except we never found it. We were searching for something that could not be.

One might have concluded that the reason we could never find that place to call home is because blood does not a family make.

It does, however, create a tie.

A bond.

A noose.

Of course, they came for us.

And perhaps if we hadn't been so young, so naïve, maybe we would have recognised our efforts as the idealistic dreams they were far sooner.

But like any young fools in love, we fought back. We tried disguises and hats. We cut our hair and wore men's clothes.

But in every village we encountered, we stuck out. We didn't belong anywhere. No matter how we tried, no matter how we ran or hid or plotted.

They just kept coming.

And eventually they began to catch up. At first, we had months together in peace. Months of bliss until the hairs on our arms would stand on end. Months before the first prickle of eyes on our backs, before gooseflesh would crawl over our skin as the eyes of our families' henchmen watched us.

We escaped by night, by day, by boat and by carriage and once in the bellies of a farmer's barrels.

We were industrious, and for a time, we were proud and filled with the glory of winning.

But even winning can wear a person down when there's no rest or recovery.

They were relentless, their slow inevitable march

towards us, our slow inevitable march towards capture. The months shrank to weeks. Then days.

Until we forgot how to dream, how to win, how to run.

We grew so tired that even clinging to each other by our fingertips felt wearying.

Oh, how we loved each other.

Oh, how we lost each other.

But I suppose that's the problem with dreams. They always come to an end...

CHAPTER 36

RED

"Stay here, stay seated," Octavia says as she deposits me at a table in the corner of the room and hands me a drink. Then she heads over to speak with Xavier.

The Chief finds me and slides into the seat next to me. My skin prickles. My blood simmering a million degrees beneath my skin. Fucking traitor.

How dare she come and sit next to me like nothing is wrong? I want to fling my drink at her. Smash the glass across her face.

I want to throw my uniform at her and forsake the entire Academy. How fucking could she?

"Hey," she says, her brow creasing as she takes in my appearance. "You don't look so hot."

"Thanks," I deadpan, grateful that I appear sick enough that my tone will come across as humour, rather than the seething fucking rage I'm actually harbouring.

"I'm sorry. But you're sweating and ghost white."

"Yeah," I say, unsure what else I can add. I am both of those things and there's not a lot I can do about it.

"Is the competition getting to you? Do you want me to take you back to the Academy? For a time out and refresh?" she asks.

"No," I bark, unable to tolerate the nicey-nicey bullshit. But then I remember to cool it. Octavia doesn't want me confronting the Chief, and she's not confronting her mother. Not yet, anyway. "Sorry, I'm fine. A bit tired."

The Chief puts her arm around my shoulders and rubs, like she's comforting me. But her touch is like acid: sharp, stinging, and full of poison. I force myself to be calm and touch her hand, patting it like I'm grateful for her affection. Lure her in. Make her believe I trust her. Then I can flip this deception on her arse.

"Don't worry, Chief. I've not told anyone. It's our little secret."

She beams at me.

Cunt.

I want to knock the smile off her face.

"I was wondering... Would you let me take you for dinner. Just me and you? Perhaps we could talk about your future, what happens after... How we can work together," the Chief says, her eyes glittery. Once upon a time, I'd have seen those eyes as of a mentor, a hero or an angel. Now they're the eyes of the devil, a traitor, a villain.

I'm distracted by the sight of Sadie creeping through the crowds. Her eyes meet mine, and she cocks her head towards the door. I wonder if she's finally decided to help give me my memories back.

I wonder what the price is.

I get up, leaving the stool I was sitting on and instantly feel light-headed.

"Nice catching up, Chief."

"Wait. The dinner—" she says.

"I got to go, sorry," I say and leave, without a backwards glance.

I stagger across the casino, realising I'm in trouble. Octavia is right, there's no way I'm going to make it through tomorrow's trial without drinking human blood and gaining some strength back, and I can't keep draining Octavia, without making her weak for the trial either.

There has to be another way than having to drink human blood. I refuse to believe there's no other way for me to survive this. But then my insides cramp up, and I'm not sure I buy the shit I'm selling.

Sadie grips the back of my arm and before I know what's happening, my feet have lifted off the floor and I'm being sped out of the room. I forget how strong vampires are.

The moment I'm out of the casino, I know Octavia senses it. There's a sharpness in my chest, a panic and prickle rushing through my system that doesn't belong to me.

Is our bond growing stronger? Is it weakening and allowing the connection to let emotions filter through?

Sadie deposits me in the shadow of a tree about fifty feet from the entrance. Then she lifts her hands to sign.

"Meet me tomorrow, in the Blood Woods, by the river."

"Why?"

"Because I'm going to give you what you want. And the strength trial will be in the heart of the woods. So meet me there, and we will discuss payment. Okay?"

I nod.

But she frowns at me. "What's wrong?"

"Nothing," I say and wipe my brow as my leg cramps in my suit trouser. My stomach folds in on itself, and I have to bite my tongue to prevent myself from reaching out and chomping down on her wrist.

Her head turns toward the casino. “Octavia is coming. Will you meet me?” she asks.

“Yes,” I say, but she’s gone before I finish speaking.

Octavia rushes across the grounds to the tree as my vision smatters.

“Verity,” she says, but I don’t hear the rest of the sentence. I collapse, hitting the ground, and everything goes black.

CHAPTER 37

Layers and layers of manipulation. But you're all too consumed with the details to see the bigger picture.

Who is really the liar?

Who is really in control?

It's not who you think.

An alliance isn't going to save you. Not now, it's far too late. This has been in motion so much longer than you realise.

Idiots.

I just wish someone would work it out. At least then it would be a challenge.

I suppose as long as I get what I want in the end, then the entertainment doesn't really matter. And trust me, watching you all scramble is entertainment enough.

Yes, that will do nicely.

CHAPTER 38

OCTAVIA

Xavier, Amelia, and I speed our way under the city, carrying Red between us. We're ultimately faster than the carriages, because we can dart in and out of traffic, and take it in turns to carry her.

I want to get her out of Castle St Clair's grounds and back to the sanctuary of mine before anyone notices there was something wrong with her.

Which is how we came to be here, with Red unconscious on her bed in my castle. Amelia, Xavier, and I all stood around her.

We're reaching the crunch point with what her mortal system can take, and I fear that if she doesn't heed our warnings, she won't make it to the trial tomorrow, let alone through the last and to the boundary.

But if she drinks, or at least if she drains someone, she'll transform.

"We're agreed then?" Xavier says.

Amelia nods. "We beg her to drink without draining for

now. There's no way she's going to agree to kill an innocent, so all we can do is get her to agree to stay alive."

"And if she doesn't agree, I'll compel her?" Xavier says, as if that wouldn't be a complete betrayal of everything she believes and all the trust I've worked for.

Amelia gives me the side eye.

"No. We can't. If we compel her now, she'll never choose to drain someone when the time comes. And we need her to choose to transition," I say.

Xavier huffs. But it's the right decision.

"You're going to have to pull the sister card, and pull it hard," I say to Amelia.

Her lips pinch, but she nods. "I feel bad, but I want her alive more than I care about causing a guilt trip."

Xavier bends to examine her. I bristle. "What is it?"

"Her breathing is shallow. We may have to take the decision out of her hands," he says.

But I shake my head. I've done enough controlling of her free will. It's time I gave her the space and freedom to make her own mind up. I hate that it's now that I choose to do this.

"Amelia, go find Wendell and ask him to bring a bag of warm, fresh human blood. Perhaps the scent would be enough to rouse her from sleep," I say.

Xavier claps his hands. "Good thinking."

I roll my eyes. "I'm not just a set of pretty eyes."

He smiles and comes to my side, lifting my knuckles to his lips. "The most beautiful in all the city." He kisses my hand, but I yank it back.

"Oh, piss off, Xavier, you have to say that. I'm your favourite."

He folds his arms, looking affronted. "I have to say nothing of the sort. I've told you on more than one occasion when you're being a giant cunt."

I bark a laugh, but he continues.

"Besides, you don't see what Red and I see. And one day, when you do, you really will make the best queen for this city."

I huff at him, but Amelia returns with Wendell in tow.

He rushes to Red's side and uncaps the blood bag, wafting it under her nose.

She sits bolt upright, gripping his wrist where he holds the bag. Her eyes glare like suns at him.

I step forward, ready to protect him if necessary. None of us understands what this transition is doing to her physiology, let alone to her mental state.

"Red."

Her gaze snaps up to me. Her breathing is ragged. "That's not your blood," she says and then has to wipe her chin, as if she's about to drool.

"No, it's not," I say.

"Then why is it in front of me, Octavia?" she snarls. I have to give her credit. Her body is literally decaying in front of us, and still, she comes out swinging.

Wendell glances at me with skittish movements. I can tell he's uncomfortable. I nod at Amelia to take over his position. She relieves him, and he races from the room.

"Amelia," Red says and then tilts her head at her sister.

Xavier leans against the wall, an amused expression on his face. But he won't be laughing when I make him have a go at convincing her without compulsion next. I pray for his sake that Amelia can convince her sister. Because while I want Red to choose to do this for herself, I find a piece of myself wanting her to stay alive more. And I wonder whether I really am above compulsion and making her drink it, or if I meant what I said to Xavier.

"What's going on?" Red says.

Amelia sits on the bed and strokes the back of Red's

hand, her eyes flitting between the blood bag and Red's grey pallor.

"You passed out at the Castle St Clair casino night. You'd gone outside, none of us know why. Especially as Octavia asked you to stay put."

"I..." she says, but her words fade.

There's a flicker of hesitation.

"Don't remember," she finishes.

The hesitation was enough. She's lying. She remembers, but she's choosing not to tell us. Oh Red, why must you continue to disobey me?

She pushes Amelia's hand away. "I don't want it."

"I know you don't. But the strengths trial starts after dusk, and if you don't drink, I'm not sure you're going to survive the trip, let alone be able to take part."

That same hesitation I saw wrapping around a lie washes through her expression again. She's wavering. Thank gods, keep going, Amelia.

"Of course I can compete. I can get there fine," she says, but as Amelia glances at me and then Xavier, it's clear none of us believe her. This is bravado in the face of the decision she's been avoiding.

"We're not judging you," Xavier says from the wall. "We just want you alive and healthy."

Red cocks her head at him as if trying to examine whether that's the truth.

It is. I can tell when Xavier is lying, and he isn't.

"You really think I'll die if I don't?" Red asks, her voice quiet.

"Yeah, Red, we really do," Amelia says and strokes her hand.

"I must look shit," Red tries to laugh, but it comes out more of a stifled sniffle.

Amelia holds the bag up again. "Please? I can't bear it if

you were to...” She looks away, her eyes filling with unshed tears.

Fuck, Amelia, you are a master manipulator. This performance is golden.

“I can’t...” Red says, her voice high and whiny.

“Tell her, Amelia,” I say.

“Tell me what?” she asks.

Amelia sighs. “The research I’ve been doing... this whole time... Your addiction was never your fault. It was always in you. It’s the transition calling because drinking blood is part of you and who you are... who you’re meant to be...”

Red bites her lip, worry lines crease her forehead. We’re close to convincing her, but it’s her expression that makes bile claw up my throat. Are we any better than the Chief? We’re all stood here, manipulating her to drink blood when she doesn’t want to. But is it still manipulation if she’ll die if we don’t convince her?

“Red, please, you’re all I have left... Don’t leave me alone,” Amelia finishes.

It’s the tipper for Red. Her expression softens, and she clasps Amelia’s hand. Knowing she’s going to drink and survive another day doesn’t wipe the tang of guilt off the back of my tongue.

“Fuck,” Red says. She pulls her hands over her face, trying to hide the frustration.

She snatches the bag from Amelia. “I’m not fucking killing anyone, do you hear me? I will take a sip. But if it’s my life or an innocent’s, we all know who I choose.”

My lips press together. We will see about that. But I figure now is not the time to contradict her when she’s willing to try the blood, at least. This is a perilous game that the three of us are desperate to win. And Red hates losing.

Her eyes meet mine from across the room, her brow wrinkles, and I hate how much she doesn't want to do this. How much she's desperate to not be like me, to not become anything like me.

Then I remind myself this isn't about me. This is about her, and it's not a reflection of how she feels about me or a judgement on my monstrousness. This is about Red and her need to come to terms with herself.

She needs to embrace this side of herself or risk losing herself entirely.

Red keeps her eyes on me the entire time as she brings the blood bag to her lips.

Her hand trembles where she grips the plastic. She tips it and a drizzle of blood touches her tongue.

I'm instantly wet watching her consume blood. Gods, how would I feel watching her drink from the source? Possession and ownership are funny things. I don't want anyone touching what's mine. But watching her drink? Or using her power and embracing herself to guzzle blood from the still-living body of a human?

That sight alone might make me come undone.

Red's eyes light up as the first drops hit her tongue. She drinks more, then a little more. Then puts the bag down, the light winking out entirely.

"Nothing is different," she says.

Amelia and Xavier glance at each other. Something passes between them.

"What is it?" I ask.

Xavier kicks off the wall and heads to the door. "We suspected that blood from a bag wouldn't cut it. At least not at the moment. Not while she's still in human form. The transition has weakened her too much. We think she needs a far more pure, more beautiful source of blood."

Amelia stands up, taking the bag off Red. She glances at me before turning to her sister. "You need to drink from the source."

"What? No. I'm not a fucking vampire. I agreed to the bag, not to hurting a human," she snaps, crashing back against her headboard.

"I think you'll find your teeth are amply sharp enough not to hurt them." I say, and that makes her cheeks heat.

"Xavier," I command, and he doesn't need to be prompted. He flies from the room at vampire speed.

"I'm not drinking from a fucking human, Octavia. Forget it. What would they think? I'm clearly not a vampire. They're going to know that I'm the dhampir, or about to be it. If that got out...?"

"We can compel them," Amelia says. "Don't put boundaries in your way. You need to do this. And if drinking from a bag won't work, then you have to try from the source. It's no different."

Red's fists ball, her jaw clenches. "It's very fucking different."

I need to get a handle on this before we lose her. "I know it's not fair. But do we ever ask for the hand we're dealt? Life is about how you handle what you have. Do you lie down and quit? Or do you stand and fight?"

"Fuck you, Octavia," she says, but there's no bite in her tone.

Xavier returns, a rather flustered man in his grip. Red glances from Xavier to the man and swings her legs out of the bed. She wobbles as she stands, and Amelia grabs her.

Red approaches him as Xavier forces him onto his knees.

"Look at me," she says. "Do you consent to be a donor?"

"I do," he says and nods.

"I really don't like this," Red says and fidgets with her hands.

"Leave," I say suddenly, surprising myself too.

"But," Amelia starts.

Xavier glances at me. My expression remains stoic. "She's not joking, Amelia. Come on, I've got someone I want you to meet."

The pair of them leave, and the man stays kneeling before Red, his hands trembling.

"We won't hurt you," I say. But he can't bring himself to look at me. It frustrates me. I can't console him, despite wanting this to be a painless experience for us all.

"I promise I'm going to make this as easy as I can for you. Honestly, I don't really want to do it," Red says.

"Then why are you? Who are you? You look human to me," he says, staring at her.

"I am."

"Then why—Oh." His eyes widen.

"While you consent to donating, you will have your memory of this evening wiped. I'm sure you understand the significance of the information you've heard, and the severity of punishment should it leak."

He opens his mouth but closes it again and nods. "I consent."

"Good boy," I say and despite the fact he's a fully grown man, that phrase alone makes the trembling cease.

See? Why can't all humans submit? They want it, really. Deep down, they covet the release of absolute vulnerability. The inevitability of their demise, their mortality. If they could learn to bend the knee a little earlier in life, there would be a lot less conflict.

I run my hand along the side of his head until I brush under his jawline.

"Red, come here."

She does.

"You need to bite harder on human flesh than you do mine. It's tougher and more rigid than vampire flesh. Because we heal, we don't need to have as thick a layer of skin as humans."

Her skin turns green. But I continue because time is running out, we're already past midnight and I want her ready to fight by dusk.

"Lean yourself over his neck, like this." I demonstrate everything twice and continue.

"Tilt your head to angle your teeth with the sharpest points over his carotid. You stand the best chance of penetrating if you do a sharp jerk of your head as you bite down. Okay?"

She nods. And steps into position. "I'm sorry," she says to him and opens her mouth.

Her whole body quakes. But every inch she moves closer, I find my panties growing wetter.

"Good," I say. "Now lean forward. That's it."

I guide her jaw. "And jerk."

She takes the instruction like an eager student and sinks her teeth into his neck. He sucks in a sharp breath and stiffens. Blood spills out from between her lips as it flows into her mouth. Ah yes, I forgot to mention that it pumps out considerably faster than vampire blood—what with humans and their beating hearts.

She detaches, leans to the side and retches, throwing up everything she drank.

But she also nicked his carotid. If she doesn't have vampire venom yet, then she won't make his platelets rapidly heal. Blood gushes out in rhythmic spurts. It sprays her face and neck as she rights herself and wipes her mouth. He screams and grabs his neck.

"Red. Drink," I say, and grab her by the scruff of the collar and push her head back onto his neck. At least this way we can salvage the blood he's losing rather than go through multiple donors and have to spend half the day wiping their memories.

She slides her mouth over the wound, blood now coating her face and clothes. Her fingers find the back of his head and curl over his shoulder as she guzzles and this time swallows. The bob of her throat is rhythmic, and it makes my clit pulse.

Watching her take his life source. Consume blood like she was a vampire, too. I could watch her do this all night. I've never fancied myself a voyeur. But this? I'd give the next thousand years to watch her drain a human dry.

The air in the room heats like static and molten sunshine. Goosebumps rise over her arms, over mine and finally his, too. What is going on? Is this magic? Is this part of her transition? Or perhaps this is what it would be like if she drained him.

The magic or power or whatever it is surges around the room and grazes my skin, setting my body alight, and I am now aware of how much potential she truly wields. She is power incarnate. She will change the face of this city, and I want to be at her feet when she does.

"Stop drinking now, Red."

She doesn't listen, she's in a fervour, lost in the pleasure of consumption.

"Red," I shout. This time, I grip her jaw and pull her from his throat.

She rears back, a growl or a scream or more like a little of both roars from her chest.

The man falls backwards.

"Lennox," I shout.

He's at the door in a millisecond. He takes one look at the man, who is pale as snow, and nods.

"Wipe his memory. I don't want him having any recollection of this night," I say.

He inclines his head, bowing slightly as he swings an arm around the man and carries him out of the room.

Red is still panting, her shoulders heaving up and down. I take her in, staring in awe at the sight of her smothered in fresh blood, her fangs, which I swear are a little longer, still descended. My pussy twitches.

"You don't realise the power you have over me, Verity. In a thousand years of life, I've never fallen to my knees for anyone. But for you, I'd be willing to fall hard enough to bleed."

She glances at me as I step in front of her and slowly, inch by inch, lower myself to the ground in front of her.

"You are magnificent. You are everything I have ever dreamed of, and I don't think I can run this city without you."

She brings her fingers to her lips, smearing the blood. Her eyes fall away from me.

"Do not carry the shame for what you have done. The man lives. And you are stronger now. You will fight tomorrow because of his sacrifice."

She turns away from me, leaving me on my knees waiting for her.

"No one should have to die in order for me to take my power. A power I don't even want. I don't want to be the one who opens the door. The one that unleashes magic. Why can't we do it together? Why does that decision have to rest in my hands? It shouldn't be any one person."

I sigh. "Because that is the way life works. You misunderstand power."

"How?" she says. And then she turns to kneel with me, as my equal.

She runs her hands up my body to my shirt buttons and unhooks the first. Then the second and continues as I speak.

"Weakness and power are misnomers. There aren't such things. Each of us is powerful beyond our comprehension," I say.

"Then why are there so many weak people in the world? Think of all the victims and awful leaders doing awful things?"

I purse my lips. "Everyone is powerful beyond their comprehension. But here..." I press a finger to her heart. "Is where their power lies. And not everyone is strong enough to use their power or wield it like a shield. Not everyone is brave enough to wear the armour their soul already possesses."

I let my words sink in. I can tell she's hearing me, that my words are finally taking root. So I answer her other question.

"And then there are those who are more than brave enough. Those who choose to wield their power not as a shield but as a weapon."

She moves forward, her fingers curling around my throat.

"You speak of power like it's meaningless. Like me stood here with my hand around your throat isn't a threat. As if I wield no power over you, and yet a slip of my fingers, and I could choke you."

That does something to me. A tingle of energy shoots from the press of her fingers down to my pussy.

"And yet, it is I who wield the power in this situation because with the snap of my hand, I could have you on the floor, bent over begging for me to let you come."

She smiles like it's a lie, and I grin like it's the truth.

We both know we're playing games.

"The blood is in your system. Your colour is back. There's an energy throbbing through you I want to consume."

"Then consume me, Octavia."

I don't need to be asked twice. My hands slide to her shirt, placing one on either side of the fabric, and I rip it apart, shredding it. I tear through her sports bra, and I leave her there, topless.

"Fuck, you are the most magnificent thing I have ever seen."

And in this moment, she truly is. Her skin glows golden. Not the pale wasteland from earlier. Her eyes glimmer with a hunger for the world. For me, and I hope eventually for the power that clearly pulses in her body.

I pull at her trousers next and unbutton them and let her slide them off as I rush to the toy drawer in my room. I'm back in a second and she's only just taken them off.

I slide into the harness, a grind pad in the bottom for me, and then I tug her by the arm, pushing her to the bed.

"Bend over," I say.

She looks like she's going to put up a fight. I narrow my eyes at her. "Red... don't be a brat. You won't like what happens if you misbehave."

She stays put. I sigh. But it's not real. I like the fight. I want her to fight because it gives me the hope that she won't give up. That maybe she will finally embrace who she is and choose to fight alongside me for the city. Fight her way to the door and unleash magic so that she can become who she is meant to be.

"Make me," she hisses.

I lunge for her, but she's faster than I expect and lurches out of the way, bouncing on her toes.

"Interesting," I say. Realising that the blood must have done more than pull her from the brink of death.

But she's not transitioned yet. And until she can truly embrace who she is, she won't be a match for me. I leap at her, grabbing her arm and twisting it behind her back. She jerks, trying to free her arm, but I've got her pinned in place. I use my height against her and push her on her tippy toes to the edge of the bed and bend her over the edge until her arse is plump and rounded and ready for smacking.

"What's your safe word?"

"Elysium."

"Good, mine is villain," I say and then I pull my hand back and smack her arse. She lurches forward with the pressure from the smack and groans against me.

I reach back for one of the other toys I brought with me, a flogger, and then I yank that back and slap it over her arse too.

"The first was for disobeying. That was because I felt like it. Now, are you going to do as you're told?"

"Not as long as I breathe," she says, and it lights another flicker of fire in my belly. There she is. Embrace it, Red. Fuel yourself, grab hold of that inner power.

I take the end of the cock and bring it to her entrance.

"Are you sure about that?" I ask.

To my surprise, she shunts back against me, making the dildo penetrate her pussy.

My eyes widen in surprise. I wasn't expecting that. The brat in her is strong today. It was a threat, not a promise. The blood truly has gone to her head. I like it. Want more of it. I want her to dig deep and find the pieces of her that only she can reach.

I pull the cock out, but she drives back again.

"Make me forget," she says.

The words cut through me. Carve right to the heart of the night I turned Amelia.

Make me forget, Octavia. Please, make me forget.

Those words laced in pain, in regret, and the ache of knowing that whatever decision I made that night, I was going to lose her eventually.

"What?" I say.

"I don't want to remember what I did to that man tonight. Fuck me until I forget."

And here is the same old Red. I sigh silently, the cool heat of frustration simmering in my chest. If I had her potential, I would change the face of the city. I'd make it a better place, more accepting and fair. But then I wonder whether that's really the problem—I want the power, and she doesn't. Perhaps that would make her better at wielding power than me.

I thrust deep and she moans. The grind pad between my legs brushes my clit with every thrust and glides over folds, making the motion of fucking her just as pleasurable as the motion inside her.

I drive deeper, harder.

"More," she says, and her words choke and crack, the emotion of what's happened tonight finally getting to her.

"Please, Octavia? Harder."

And I can only oblige. I drive into her over and over and over until sweat drips down my brow. But her body doesn't tighten, her shoulders don't stiffen the way they would if she were going to climax. So I pull out despite the tingle on my own pussy from the grind pad, unstrap the harness, and I let it drop to the floor.

I pull her legs toward me and flip her onto her back, chucking her around like a rag doll. She grins at me. I cock an eyebrow at her.

"Oh, you like it when I treat you like my fuck toy, do you?"

"Maybe."

I sigh again. "Maybe isn't yes or no, Red. If you behave like a brat, I'm going to edge you until you're begging for release."

"Fine. Yes. I like being your dirty little blood slut. I like being your fuck toy, and I like it when you call me a filthy whore. So, Octavia, do I get to come now?"

I grin and climb on the bed. "Oh, you get more than that. You get to eat me while you come."

Her face brightens as I scoot down her body and turn myself over so my belly presses against her torso. I slide my head between her legs as my pussy rests on her mouth.

And there I go to work. I lap at her clit like the starved woman I am. I want to devour her, consume every drop of excitement and pleasure that I can. I want to spend the rest of my days wringing pleasure out of her until she begs for me to stop, and then maybe one more lick, one more orgasm.

Her pussy is mine, and mine alone.

Her clit hardens beneath my tongue, and I know this is what her body wanted. I wrap my arm over the top of her thigh so I can slide a finger inside her.

I don't know how long we spend like this. We fuck until the birds begin to sing. We fuck long enough that Red gets up and pulls the curtains shut.

We fuck until we're spent and crash into sleep, only to wake again and slide ourselves between each other's legs, lapping and licking and drawing out orgasm after orgasm.

I find myself between her legs, mouth on her clit, two fingers buried deep in her pussy when there's a quiet cough. A clearing of the throat.

I glance up, crane my eyes to the door, but I don't stop fucking her, I don't stop the drive and thrust of my fingers.

In fact, I curl them around until I find her G-spot and then I look at Xavier, who folds his arms.

"Oh, am I interrupting?"

"No. Do go on. What can I do to help?" I say as Red gasps, realising that we now have an actual audience. Her eyes flit from me to Xavier and back again, her body now utterly frozen.

I thrust again and the tiniest of whimpers escapes her mouth.

"You were saying, Xavier?"

"Right. Yes. Well," he waves his hand at me, brushing off the fact I am clearly still fucking Red in front of him.

I lean down and lick her clit; it's even sweeter now, the arousal of her being so aggressively watched must be pushing her close to orgasm. I lick again. And again.

When I feel her pussy clamp my fingers, I stop.

"Xavier, you were saying?"

I drive a particularly vicious thrust into her pussy, rubbing against her G-spot to see if I can tip her over into bliss in front of Xavier. To see how far her need to be watched really goes.

"Yes, sorry. Rather distracting and all that." Xavier says. "Anyhoo. Mother has sent word that they're ready for us in the Blood Woods, so she's ex—"

Red moans, her back arching while I pump harder and continue my relentless lapping of her clit. Her pussy is throbbing against my fingers. Her hands scruff the bed sheets. She's going to blow.

It makes me smirk against her clit.

"Fuck," Red says. "Oh gods."

"Mother of Blood," Xavier exclaims, pulling a hand over his face. "I'm leaving. Please, for the love of gods, put Red out of her misery, get yourselves cleaned up and then get to the carriage. We'll be w—"

Red lifts off the bed, her pussy clamping like a vice around my fingers as she comes apart, ejaculating sweet come on my tongue. It's almost enough to make me come, but I hold on, not wanting to cross that boundary with Xavier in the room.

She lays flat on the bed, panting.

"Well, now that's done with, do you think you could hurry up?" Xavier says and promptly speeds out of the room.

CHAPTER 39

RED

There is a river of red that flows through the heart of the Blood Woods. I wonder whether it connects to the Lantis Ocean, the crimson colour reminiscent of the glittering rubies on the ocean's surface. I kneel and run my fingers through the cool ripples, letting it splash up my knuckles. It's clear when it touches my skin, and I wonder what kind of magical illusion it is that makes the water red in our city.

I don't want to do this. I don't want to fight Lincoln or Talulla. Let alone any of the vampires.

Since the riots in the market, and the spirit trial especially, we're not exactly peaceful, but there is a shared understanding for everything we've been through. This trial feels like it's shoving a blade between all the progress we've made.

But worse, given what Amelia has told me, what happens if I accidentally injure one of them or worse, kill them?

Then I transform? Become this thing everyone wants me to be?

What about what I want?

What if I don't want to step into this role? If I do, would I really be any different from the vampires who took my family? Would I be a monster like them?

I scold myself silently because Octavia is one of those people, and I don't see her as a monster. Perhaps I could find a way to see myself as something other than a monster?

I shake my head and stand up, brushing the river water off onto my trousers.

It doesn't matter. I don't want to become the dhampir because I don't want to be responsible for that kind of power.

I don't want to become one of them.

Even if that means sacrificing myself.

I knead my temples, attempting to stave off the headache brewing deep in my skull. This trial, more than any other, has us all rattled. Even Dahlia is behaving oddly. She was playing nice with Octavia as if they hadn't taken chunks out of each other at the partnering ceremony. Like they haven't spent centuries hating each other.

The trees rustle in with a nonexistent breeze, and several burnt ochre and red leaves drift to the ground.

I glance up, but there's nothing there. No person, no animal skittering through the canopy. I frown and turn back to the river, only to leap out of my skin.

"The fuck, Sadie? You sneak up on me like that, it's enough to give me a heart attack," I say, trying to bring my breathing back to normal.

She laughs. It's silent, but her open mouth and rocking shoulders are a giveaway. She raises her hands and signs at me. "I was trying to take the competition out early."

I tense up. Did I put myself in danger by meeting her? She pouts, her eyes glimmering in the dappled moonlight showering through the trees.

"Were you?" I ask.

She shakes her head, smiling. She was making a joke? The pressure gripping my shoulders eases away.

"Then why did you ask me here?" I ask.

Her lips press together. She glances over my shoulder and scans the surrounding area. When she's satisfied there's no one in the vicinity, she signs.

"You're ready."

"For wh—"

She tilts her head at me.

"You're offering to give me my memories back?"

She rubs her thumb over her middle and index fingers in the same way I remember my father doing as he proudly told us he'd secured a higher paying job.

I sigh. "You'll give them back for a price?"

She nods and signs, "And it won't come cheap. So how much do you want the memories, Red?"

"More than anything."

"Why is it you want them?"

"Because she took them. Octavia took them and even though she says it was by my request, she won't return them now despite my asking. She's controlling a piece of me, and that's the kind of behaviour I hate from people in power. I want to love her with my whole heart, but I can't. How am I supposed to love someone who keeps a piece of me that isn't theirs to have?"

"So it's about love?" she says.

"And power."

That makes her smile. "Is there a difference?"

I open my mouth to answer and find I cannot. Are love and power really the same? If I love her, does she have power over me? If she loves me, do I wield power over her? Are any of us really free? If we love another, do we sacrifice that freedom for them? Or perhaps we gift it to them. Maybe that is the true power of love—we gift our hearts, our souls and the freedom we breathe. We drop it into the hands of our lovers, praying they'll keep it safe. Keep us whole. Keep our freedom nestled alongside theirs.

"Perhaps not," I finally answer.

She nods at me as if she approves of my answer. "I'll give you what you want. But I'm certain this is one of those times where you should be careful what you wish for. Sometimes things leave us for a reason. Some secrets should stay hidden."

I take a moment to catch up with what she said. Replay the signs in my head, processing her words, and as I comprehend each one, my skin grows colder. Like her words are an omen, a warning filled with ice.

I shake it off. She hasn't seen my memories yet. Which makes me pause. What if she can go into any of my memories? What if she works out who I really am?

"If I share my mind with you, will you be able to access my other memories?"

"Yes, but if I did, you'd know about it and be able to throw me out of your head. I'll only access what has been lost to you."

"Then tell me, what is the price you require?" I ask.

"Mother is only going to make one of each pair fight this evening."

I frown. "What? Why? I figured we'd all have to fight each other."

She shrugs. "I don't pretend to understand her motives. But I request you fight in Octavia's place..."

She leaves her hands hanging as if there's more to that sentence.

"And?" I ask. "Because that's not the end of the sentence."

"No, it's not," she shakes her head, her eyes dropping away from mine, and that's when I understand whatever she's about to ask is going to be the price that will hurt.

Finally, she glances up again and holds my gaze. "I need you to let Dahlia win."

I snort out a laugh. "You're kidding?"

But her face remains expressionless as she holds my gaze.

"Fuck me, Sadie, you *are* kidding, right?"

But she continues to stare at me. The dull ache in my head roars back to a pulsing throb. "Mother of Blood. You're asking me to sacrifice our chance of winning the trials. That would kill Octavia emotionally and risk our shot at winning. And you forget, I want that cure as much as she does."

"Just because you win the trials, does not mean you'll win the race to the boundary," she signs.

"That's true. But it's beside the point. It would kill Octavia. It's a total betrayal of everything she wants."

"And she took your memories. Many more, I fear, than you're aware of... don't you want those memories? Don't you want to see what she took from you?" she signs and folds her arms.

I narrow my eyes at her. "Why do you want Dahlia to win?"

"Does the reason matter? If you're getting your memories, then you're getting what you want," she signs.

"Of course it matters. You're asking me to betray my teammate."

"If you want to keep your memories private, and me out of your head, then you'll let me keep my secrets about Dahlia..."

Interesting. Her expression is dark, seething heat billowing under her eyes.

"You hate her as much as Octavia does," I say, less of a question and more of a statement.

"She could have let me out. Of the cage, I mean."

"Couldn't any of them? Octavia and Gabriel too? Xavier?"

She shakes her head at me. "None of them had any idea where I was. But Dahlia sought me out. She wanted to know what her mother was doing, wanted to watch on as I drove myself insane trying to escape. Night after night she would come and dangle keys, blood, anything that she thought would torture me in front of the cage. And night after night, she would leave. So yes... If Gabriel and Xavier are out of the running and if I don't win, then there's no choice between Dahlia or Octavia. I choose Octavia every single time. Her heart is in the right place, at least."

That takes me a moment to process too, but I get there eventually. My heart is heavy.

"You hate her, and yet you want her to win," I say.

She tuts at me. "Don't be shortsighted. Lose a battle to win the war, Red. That's how the game is played."

I sigh. "Octavia won't forgive me if I jeopardise our potential to win," I say.

"Would you rather she lived and hated you? Or died fighting Dahlia because you loved her too much to let her go?"

I grit my teeth. What choice do I have? I stare at her, those dark eyes such a stark contrast to her white hair. I wonder what her birth parents were like.

"Fine. I agree."

"And you swear that you'll prevent her from competing?"

I take a deep breath. The human man's blood is still

coursing through my veins, and as much as that thought makes me sick, I cannot change the fact that it brought me back from the brink of death and has strengthened me in a way I'm struggling to define.

I can fight.

I can win.

I just need to believe it.

"Yes," I say.

"So be it," she signs and then she steps up to me.

She places her hands on either side of my head and stares into my eyes. Hers are dark pools, endless orbs that hold so much more than I can access. A vastness I dare not tread into. It's only now, this close to her, I notice that the perfume she wears is as cold as her personality. She smells like winter and frozen landscapes. A sharp scent that cuts through wind and water and makes my throat burn with the odour.

"Remember," she says, and I frown. I hear a voice. But I'm not sure if I'm making it up or if it's in my mind or if I actually heard it. I couldn't have. She has no voice.

"Remember," she says, stronger this time and definitely inside my mind. I relax now, letting her vampire magic undo what was done to me.

Her words wash over my consciousness like a blanket of silk, lulling me into a warm hug, a sense of safety, and then she rips something in my mind, and I am screaming.

I scream and scream and scream as my mind burns and sears as she tugs memories from lost places. I should have listened. These memories should have stayed hidden.

My vision whites, the pain spreads from the deep well of my brain outward, washing over my ears and down my neck.

I'm on the forest floor, leaf mould and detritus smothering me as a flood of memories tears through my mind.

I'm on my knees. We're in her castle. I have no recollection of this. I don't know what I did or said, but Octavia's eyes well with unshed tears. She whispers quietly, "You need me." Her words are in a tone I don't understand. She's never been like this with me. What led us here and why is she talking like that? She continues, her voice cold and callous.

"You need my blood. Without me, you're nothing. You're just another blood slut desperate for your next fix."

I don't know if it's my actual hand or my hand in my memory, but my fingers come to my cheeks, and they're wet. How could she say such awful things?

I sob, I wrap my arms around my legs. I cry out at her, "You don't understand. I can't leave. Or be what you want. I have a family. Responsibilities. I have to keep my job as a hunter."

"And yet you can't do that and keep me," she says. "Or you're not willing to. You're throwing me away like I'm nothing but a fix, Red. Don't you see?"

I'm screaming at her, my words fuzzy and muffled all at once.

Octavia sneers at me. "So be it."

Then she's towering over me, and once again, she tears the memories of her away, the memories of our love, our fights, our heartache. All of them stripped away.

I am now certain Octavia lied.

Not a small white lie. But a huge, cut-my-heart-in-two betrayal. She didn't take one or two memories.

She fucking took them all.

Hundreds.

Thousands.

She erased herself from my life like we meant nothing.

For what feels like forever, Sadie reveals memories of

the times Octavia removed little pieces and giant chunks of herself from my life, my heart. How fucking could she?

The night Amelia was turned comes flooding back. I'm laid on the floor of Dahlia's mansion, Amelia screaming something I can't hear, then she rushes toward me. Something is wrong. It doesn't fit the motions that Octavia and Amelia told me. It's like the night is slightly out of sync, a beat off. There's another lie here. Another truth hidden from me.

I'm covered in blood, Amelia is sobbing, drenched in my blood, but when Octavia rounds to face me, I realise she compelled Amelia, too.

Oh Octavia, what did you do?

When I try to pull the memory closer, to make the sounds, voices and conversations clear, they're yanked away.

Octavia rounds on me, and I glance behind her shoulder. Amelia is glassy-eyed and slack-mouthed. Everything they told me the other night was just another lie, another half-truth.

I don't even know her.

I snort in my mind as I wonder, is Octavia even capable of telling the truth? Betray her? I will gladly lose this round. Fuck Octavia, I'll get the cure for my sister no matter what. Even if I have to save for a lifetime to buy it once it's been manufactured.

I want this to stop. I want to scream out to Sadie and beg her to stop this, but once again, I'm dragged through my mind and this time Octavia and I are in a village.

Oh gods.

Elysium. The village is called Elysium.

I remember now. This is where I met her for the first time. The village flares to life, small bungalows popping up around me, a brick wall bordering the village that I was walking around patrolling. A local bar.

A hoard of angry men screaming at her, trying to kill her. A pitchfork stabbed into her gut.

It moves on. I'm injured now. A scar across my belly. The memory flits forward and backward.

Octavia saves me. This is why I've always loved the name Elysium. It was the first time we met. And she never fucking told me.

The memory shifts again. I am in her arms. She feeds me her blood. Why the hell is she feeding me blood?

I know in my gut that this is the first time I've drunk blood. The addiction might not be her fault, but it never would have started if it weren't for her. None of this would have happened if it weren't for her.

I harden against the memory.

It flashes forward. We spend the night fucking and making each other come, drunk on the blood lust of her blood filling my veins.

And then morning comes, and I rise from the blood-drunk reverie. I panic. I'm afraid that I've fucked up, that the Hunter Academy will fire me, that I'll lose everything and Amelia will starve because I've lost my job.

Octavia wants to see me again, but I'm stricken with guilt, and I tell her it was a mistake. That she was a mistake.

Her eyes flash. The pain in her expression breaks me. But what she does next hurts me even more.

Her expression hardens, and she rounds on me. "You don't get to treat me like meat. You don't get to take a piece of me and then leave. If you don't want me, then you can't have any of me."

"Please don't," I beg. "Don't hurt me."

"Hurt you?" she snorts. "Gods, I thought you were different. I thought because you looked at me, actually looked *at* me, that you were different. You're just like everyone else. How could I be so fucking stupid? You're never going to see me for who I am. So fine. You don't need to see me at all."

She grabs me by the scruff of my shirt, and she wipes the night out from my memory. Leaving me doe-eyed and confused as she races me back to Elysium and dumps me there to pick up the pieces from the incident that night.

She drops me in the heart of the bodies and blood and battle remnants. But I'm barely functional after having my memory wiped, and she discards me like I'm nothing but trash. When she races away, she doesn't look back.

So many betrayals.

How could she take the first time we met, the first time we fucked, and the first time I drank from her away? Why would she take that from me? But there's no time to dwell on this memory because Sadie unleashes more. One after the other, they come flooding into my head.

I thought Octavia was different.

I thought she was the only one who was on my side, the only one not manipulating me, and this whole time she's been controlling my narrative. Controlling what I know, controlling what I remember...

Controlling me.

It's time for that to stop.

Sadie releases my temples and raises her hands to sign. "Will you fulfil your end of the bargain?"

I nod. "Without exception."

"Good, then I will return the rest of your memories after the trial. I suspect you'll be needing these..." she says and uses the hem of her gown to pull out and drop a pair of silver cuffs and some rope on the ground.

And then she's gone, racing through the forest and into the night.

CHAPTER 40

OCTAVIA

Something is wrong. Not an 'I made an oopsie,' wrong. But fundamentally about-to-tear-everything-apart wrong. It starts in my chest, a needle-like pain that it blooms out, coursing through my system until I am buckled over and about to puke.

I glance up, scanning the Blood Woods for any sign of Red. She is my first thought. Now, yesterday and always.

I have to make sure she's okay. This lancing pain is deep, it has an almost detached quality to it. That's when I panic. It's not me feeling this, but her. I wondered how the bond would affect us, what would grow or fall away, and I've been sensing more and more of her as time has gone on. And this... It's not me. She's in trouble.

I don't spare a second look at the strength ring. I'm racing through the woods hunting for her. The bond between us is like a cord. An eternal thread connecting her to me and me to her. I will always be able to find her, always be able to help and support, and I hope stave off her hurts, her pain.

And that's what's happening right now. She's in pain. Not the sort of physical pain that would end her life. But until I see her, until I can hold her in my arms and see that she's okay, I won't be satisfied.

I skid to a halt; she's moving. I change course and bolt through the forest in a new direction. There I find her in a small clearing. I can see the strengths ring from here if I strain. I must have done a full circle in my haste.

I speed up to her, and then I stagger to a standstill.

Oh, fuck.

Her expression is like fire and stone and steel and death.

"What—" I start.

But she cuts me off. "You lied. Our entire relationship, all you have been doing is lying. You said you'd told me everything about the night Amelia was turned, and you hadn't. Once again, you've only given me part of a truth."

"It's not like—"

"Don't try to fucking twist it. You've been lying. Did you or did you not compel Amelia that night too?"

I'm silent. Fuck. What the hell? How did this happen?

She shakes her head at me. "You fucking did. I knew it. Sadie is the only one who even bothered to tell me the truth. The only one who bothered to give me back what was rightfully mine."

I frown. "If she gave you back your memories, then why—"

"Gods, Octavia. Stop. There's nothing you can say right now to make any of this better. Once again, you were controlling me. Controlling the narrative and removing what little fucking autonomy I had. And you thought by not giving back my memories you'd what? Keep screwing me? As if you can't get a thousand other vampires to shag. I'm just a fucking plaything to you, aren't I? A novelty."

I don't understand what's going on. Why doesn't she

understand the truth of what happened? If Sadie gave her all her memories back, then she should appreciate why I did it.

"Verity, please."

"Don't fucking call me that. In fact, don't even say my name again. Mother of Blood, Octavia. Even Elysium. Oh yes, I know about that, too. All this fucking time and you never told me the real reason I picked that safe word. Who are you?"

She flings her hands at me; her eyes wild, dark, full of a thick potency that screams like nightmares.

I grit my teeth, my jaw threatening to crack against the pressure. What the fuck, Sadie? I thought she was on my team. That we shared some kind of bond that our other siblings didn't.

Red steps up to me, into my personal space. The scent of leather, warm skin and fresh forests drifts in the air between us. It's clear now that she's crying, that her rage is actually pain, and that realisation carves out a piece of my heart.

I want to fix this. I need to understand exactly what's happened so that I can make it better. Make her mine again.

"Verity, please..."

She sniffs and wipes her face, shaking her head, and then she leans into me, her head on my chest.

"I'm not doing this to hurt you, but to save me. Because I need to take back control. I need to be in control of something."

"I don't under—"

Something cold and sharp and then burning hot clamps over my wrists.

"What the fuck?" I hiss, staggering back.

Her face is like cold, hard stone. There's no emotion. No remorse.

“What are you doing?” I mumble, my wrists burning as I shake the cuffs. But they’re attached to a tree. I’m literally chained in place.

I tug at the cuffs, trying to yank them off, but they’re made of silver. Every movement causes a white-hot lancing pain to shoot through my wrists and arms.

Fuck.

Fuck fuck fuck.

The fights.

“Red, listen. You need to release me so I can fight Dahlia. Whatever you think you know, you don’t.”

She huffs. “So, you didn’t take the first memories of us together? You didn’t hide the fact that the only reason I’m addicted to blood is because you gave me my first taste?”

I open my mouth to say no, but I can’t, can I? Because I did those things. That first time especially, I took her memories because she hurt me. I didn’t appreciate what she would be to me. What she would mean.

I shut my mouth, and she laughs. It’s a nasty sneer of a thing.

“I thought you were different.” Her eyes well and I’m not sure if it’s the bond or the fact that I understand her so well, but she throbs with pain and hurt, and I carry it in my chest like an anchor.

“Don’t do this,” I say, but the words are pathetic and limp. “If you fight alone, you’ll lose.”

“I’m not as weak as you assume, thanks to last night.”

“Red, come on, that’s not what I mean. You are still human. I need you for the final round. You’re the only one who can open the door.”

“You need me,” she taunts, shaking her head at me. “Cool. Octavia. Cool. Cool. Cool. Good to know that’s the only reason you keep me around.”

My breathing hitches, my stomach flutters to life,

dancing with panic. She's going to get herself killed, or she's going to lose.

"This round, of all of them, needs us both. Let me fight. I can't watch you get hurt."

"No," she says and then steps into my personal space. "You're going to watch me intentionally lose. From here."

"What?" I say, the word a whisper. My blood freezes. Gooseflesh ripples over my arms. Hot ice drips down my spine. "What the fuck do you mean you're going to lose intentionally?" I jerk forward, trying to catch hold of her. She steps back out of my reach.

"You heard me. That was the price for my memories. Sadie said she would give them back if I intentionally made us lose this round."

"You wouldn't dare. You WOULDN'T FUCKING DARE. After everything I've done for you."

I can't breathe. This is my one shot. This is the only chance I've had in a thousand years to make this city feel like home. To finally belong. She wouldn't do that to me. She can't take that from me.

She huffs a laugh. "Everything you've *done*? What, like control me, manipulate me like everyone else? Steal memories and create a narrative that suits you?"

"YOU ASKED ME TO TAKE THEM," I shriek. My throat is thick, pins and needles scratch at my fingers. I have to do something. Stop this madness. I don't understand what's going on or why the hell she's doing this, but it will ruin everything.

"Verity—"

"You knew how much I hated being controlled. How much I hate that vampires have all the power, that those in charge took my parents away. And still you manipulated me."

I run the math through my head and determine if she

does this and loses, there's no way to win. Not outright. Maybe we could draw, but if she does this, she takes away everything I've been working toward. She pisses away my one chance to change this city for the better.

She'll take away everything that means anything to me.

I get on my knees. I am not beneath begging, pleading. "We won't be able to win."

She throws her hands up. "Win? You figure that's the most important thing here? Fuck me, Octavia, I thought I knew you."

Something wet streaks my cheeks, but my hands are too heavy to lift and it's not just the silver that makes them ache, but a lance that bores through my body as well.

"This will ruin us. It will ruin me."

"It already has. You already have."

She shreds two strips of fabric from the bottom of her top. She balls the first and shoves the fabric in my mouth. Then she uses the other strip to wrap around my face tying it in place, leaving me voiceless. Then she leaves, marching off into the trees towards the ring as I stare after her, watching my world fall apart. How could she do this to me?

She was the one person who understood, the one who saw me for me. But I'm a monster to her, like I was to that girl's father when I was little. Like I am to every human I've ever met.

Well, fuck her.

If they think I'm a monster, if she wants me to play her villain... then I will.

And Mother of Blood help anyone who stands in my way.

CHAPTER 41

RED

My heart thuds in my chest. A beat with a shadow that aches and whines and pleads with me to turn back. To undo what I've done. But I won't.

Not after what Octavia's done.

I thought hurting her would make me feel better, but all I feel is sick. I don't even want to fight any more.

I step up to the ringside, as night mist curls around my feet. The moon is bright tonight, and the stars twinkle with the weight of a millennia's secrets.

"Good evening, hunters, vampires, I see we are one missing," Cordelia says.

"Octavia has opted out of the proceedings tonight. I will fight on behalf of our team," I say.

Dahlia sneers on the other side of the ring. She folds her arms like this is a done deal. Like she's already won. But if I lay down and let her beat me, is it really winning at all?

The Chief, *Eleanor,* I don't think I'm ever getting used to that, steps up. "Fighters, please enter the ring."

Around the ring, Keir, Talulla, and Lincoln all remain

motionless. A crowd of people builds. Vampire nobles, hunter elders all pour into the woods surrounding the ring. The chatter and hubbub of noise is enough to drown out the thudding in my chest. For now. Xavier glances at me, his eyes boring into me as if his stare alone is enough to pull the truth out of me.

He zips around the ring, pushing and shoving people out of the way. He reaches me and grips my elbow. "Where is she?"

"Safe."

"What is going on?"

"I'm sure she'll explain. I'll tell you where she is when this is over."

But he's already speeding through the forest looking for her. It's too late though. The woods are heaving with spectators and guards. Even if he finds her, she's still wearing silver cuffs, and he doesn't have gloves. By the time he gets her out of those restraints, the fight will be over.

Sadie steps into the ring. Then me. And last, Dahlia enters.

"Only three fighters?" Cordelia says, a nervous laugh bubbling out as she welcomes the audience. A poor showing for this trial. An embarrassment for Cordelia. She's losing control of the trials. Losing control of me.

She glances at the Chief, a flicker of worry threading through her forehead. But the Chief shakes her head.

"Fine. Welcome, vampire nobles, hunter elders, humans, friends. Tonight is the trial of strength."

There's a stilted round of applause that smatters around the audience. I glance at the faceless crowd, too many expressions, too many faces to determine one from another. But what they do all share is tension.

Even the people recognise this city is falling apart and these trials are all a ruse that's failing.

Cordelia claps her hands. Her black gown is elegant this evening. It matches the colour of her hair, a silver bustle at the back matching the swipe of grey in her bangs. "Sadie and Dahlia. You will fight first. Xavier and Talulla, Keir and Gabriel you score zero for this trial. Red, out of the ring while they spar it out."

I hop out of the ring and watch. Sadie is going to lose, though she will put up more of a fight than I will.

Around the ring, more spectators arrive. Dozens of vampire nobles appear from the shrubs and darkness of the forest. They're followed by hunter elders. More spectators pack into this tiny clearing and spill into the depths of the forest. And then, to my surprise, a veritable selection of blood monks from the church arrives. I spot the lovely monk who helped me and made me laugh away the nerves before the trial of spirit. He catches my eye and inclines his head.

It makes me uneasy, but I can't quite put my finger on why.

The Chief raises her hand for silence. "The rules are two-fold. There will be no death. If you knock your partner unconscious, that signals the end of the fight. Two, there will be no weapons save your fists, feet and fangs. Do not pick up a weapon or you will be disqualified. Understand?" the Chief says.

Sadie and Dahlia both nod and then draw back into fighting stances.

"Fight in three. Two. One. GO." The Chief leaps out of the ring and to the ground as Dahlia launches at Sadie.

Sadie dives out of the way. She's lightning quick as she spins in the air like a ribbon. She dives onto Dahlia's back, pummelling her head with savage blows.

But Dahlia is up and screaming as she hurls Sadie off and kicks her leg out, knocking Sadie over.

It goes on like this. One minute passes, then another. By minute three, I would be struggling. But on they fight. Blow after blow until the pair of them are panting and slick with sweat.

Sadie glances at me, and that moment of hesitation on her behalf is the instant Dahlia takes the upper hand. She lands a fist against Sadie's jaw that cracks through the night like a gunshot.

The crowd hisses and cringes as Sadie flies backward.

She staggers to her feet, albeit stumbling and dazed. Dahlia is relentless. She speeds across the ring, landing blow after blow on Sadie. Dahlia lurches forward and swings an uppercut with such force that it throws Sadie from the ring. She smashes into a tree, her head crunching against the trunk.

She slides to the ground with a squelch, part of her skull left embedded in the bark. If Dahlia did that to me, I wouldn't be getting back up. But Sadie will awaken in a few minutes.

I swallow hard, knowing that I'm not getting out of this without serious damage. But perhaps that's the best thing for everyone.

Dahlia roars in the centre of the ring and then she rounds on me, beckoning me to join her in the ring.

Cordelia steps up to the rope. "Dahlia, do you not need a rest?"

"For this pathetic scrap of a human? Not likely, Mother."

"So be it." Cordelia glances at the Chief again, those same worry lines carving deep ridges through her face. It ages her in a way I haven't seen before.

Not that I care. The only reason she's worried about me is because she doesn't want me to cop it before I open that fucking door for her. She's just another fucking person trying to control me.

"Then let the fight begin in three. Two. One," the Chief says.

Even though I knew it was coming, the speed with which Dahlia moves at me takes my breath away.

Despite what I said, I don't want to die. Not in this moment, anyway. I duck, leap and scramble out of her way. But she is unyielding. She thunders across the ring, her boots hammering into the ground as she stalks me like prey.

I laugh maniacally. Is this what Amelia experienced? Being Dahlia's prey? Gods, maybe I should have been more sympathetic.

I spin on my heel and jerk up, landing quite the blow to Dahlia's chin. It takes her by surprise, and she stumbles, her eyes wide.

"Yeah, Dahlia. I'm not going down without a fight," I snarl.

"I do hope so. I like it when my victims put up a fight."

She swings her leg at lightning speed, and it connects with my shoulder, knocking me off balance. I fly back, skidding to the floor. A good fighter would dive after me and make the most of me on the ground. But I've trained to fight, so I predict her movement and use the force of my momentum to roll out of the way. Then I spin around and kick my leg up and at her leg.

Her calf tears, her knee dislocating with a crunching pop that makes me want to gag.

"You little cunt," she bellows and then drags her floppy leg across the ring like a childhood horror. Her eyes are all wide and frenetic, her teeth bared.

I scramble until my back hits the rope. But I should have got up. That was my mistake. Suddenly, I don't want to lose. I don't want to get mashed to a pulp by Dahlia, but if I don't, all of this, hurting Octavia, was for nothing. So I close my eyes and wait for the blow to land.

Even though I know it's coming, the force with which her fist collides with my skull makes the world shudder.

I see black. Then I'm wrenched off the rope as another blow makes my jaw crunch against itself.

Blow after blow, she pummels me until my vision is bloody. Her teeth sink into my arms and tear chunks of flesh.

Her foot, now healed, stamps on my legs, shattering them in multiple places. And all I do is lie there taking it, knowing that this is how I die.

Colours fade to grey behind my eyelids. Octavia broke my heart, but now my body matches. Blood pools beneath me. I fade in and out of consciousness. I'm not sure whether I can take any more.

I am certain I am bleeding internally. Most of my bones are broken. It would take draining an entire vampire to survive this.

I am going to die.

"ENOUGH," the Chief's voice booms around the ring, as both she and Cordelia pull Dahlia back.

"Strength trial is awarded to Dahlia St Clair."

Dahlia whoops and fist pumps into the air. But the crowd is silent. I can just about make out the sea of slack jaws as they gaze upon me.

"COME ON," Dahlia jeers at the crowd. "I WON." She reaches out to Lincoln to pull him on stage, but he shrinks back, his eyes flitting between Dahlia and me.

I must be in bad shape because he wears the same slack, horrified expression as the rest of the crowd.

"Lincoln," Dahlia snaps. "We won..."

But the only response she gets is a silent crowd and the bubbling, haggard breaths of her dying victim.

CHAPTER 42

CORDELIA

One Thousand Years Ago

As I sit waiting for my mother, I realise it would be remiss of me not to address the darkness swirling about my heart.

This is the story of the worst night of my life. But what I need you to understand is that neither of us wanted this.

There is no magic, no curse, or argument that could tear my heart from Eleanor's. Regardless of what happens, I will find my way back to her.

If fate wills it, and she is not to be mine in this life, then I will forge my way through space and time until I find her heart anew. She belongs to me. Hers is the only love that twines with my soul and makes me complete.

No matter what happens with Mother, Eleanor will always have a place in my heart.

Let me begin with that fateful night.

Eleanor's sturdy frame sits at the kitchen table in the latest cottage we have commandeered.

She buries her head in her hands, her loose waves falling free and covering her face. The strain of the last few months is visible in the taut shape of her shoulders. I sigh as I sit next to her and pass her a cup of tea. A fire sings a symphony of crackles in the corner of the room.

She sits up, her hands sliding over my knees, the light press of her fingers against my skirts just enough to tell me I'm hers.

"We should talk," she says, pushing the tea aside.

This is the tension in her shoulders. We've been avoiding this, despite the fact we're both aware. For weeks, they've been gaining on us. Neither of us have wanted to confront it.

But we are exhausted.

"We should," I say. "But... Can we pretend? One more time before we face reality?"

"Anything for you." She slides her hands to my arse and pulls me up out of the kitchen chair and into her arms.

I swing my legs around her back and lock them. My lips find their way to hers, pressing a gentle kiss.

She kisses me, deep, intense pressure building between our caresses. It's as though our lips hold everything unsaid. Her hands roam my skin, heavy and wanting, and filled with a strange mix of sweet strawberry and something darker. Hungrier.

But more than anything, the kiss aches all the way to my heart.

It hurts like knives and blades and paper cuts. How can some kisses heal and some kisses hurt?

This kiss tears my heart in two.

My eyes well because I know what this is. That this isn't just a kiss, it isn't just making love.

It's saying goodbye.

"Eleanor," I gasp against her mouth. "Don't do this."

I kiss her again, my hands finding her neck, her jaw, tugging at her hair, like that will make her understand.

If I plead hard enough, maybe she'll stay.

"No talking," she says, as if that's enough to make me forget the way she's kissing me. The way her hands grip my body, tugging and pulling at my clothes, my skin.

She wants me. Owns me. Is still letting me go.

The tears fall, but I can't bring myself to stop them. I need this. Need her. All of us, even if this is the last time, I'll have it.

I want to carve her touch into my memory. Make the shape of her a scar on my heart, so I never forget.

She tugs my dress over my head and lays me on the makeshift bed we pulled together of sofa cushions and blankets.

I return the favour, yanking at her shirt buttons until they pop open and free her ample breasts.

Her nipples are tight, and I feast my eyes on them, like I feast on the rest of her. I commit every inch of skin, every cell in her body to memory.

Eleanor is crying too now, only her tears are silent. They make her ocean blue eyes bright, intoxicating.

She doesn't graze my skin with kisses the way she normally does. She doesn't waste time on making me excited. Instead, she dives between my legs, plunging her mouth over my most intimate parts.

She's rough, her hunger making her devour me. This isn't making love anymore. This is fucking.

Her mouth owns me the same way her hands did earlier. She swipes her tongue along my centre like she's marking me. Leaving trails of sensation between my legs that I know will never leave my body. She gifts me a shadow of her touch that I'll never forget.

She thrusts a thick finger inside me, filling me, making me moan. Everything about this is new and different, and I crave it. How can something feel so good and hurt so much all at once?

The tears run quicker as I absorb this is a side of Eleanor I'm never going to experience again. For so long, she's treated me as her queen, hers to protect and love and care for. And now she treats me like property, like I'm hers to do with as she sees fit. I like both sides.

The thought of the latter makes excitement pool between my legs. There's a moment of fear where I think Eleanor will be repulsed by how wet I've grown. But instead, she moans a delightful sound, and continues to kiss my intimate region.

She pushes a second finger inside me. It makes my head roll back, my eyes shut, and a curse fall from my lips.

"Fuck, Eleanor." My heart breaks over again. Why did she keep this side of her from me? Why did she protect me when she could have had every piece of me in this way and all the others she wanted?

And now this is the only memory I will keep of her.

Harder and harder, she glides inside me. I glance up to watch the rocking motion of her breasts as she leans over me, her trousers still on, shirt discarded.

My body tightens, ripples of pleasure pulse where she kisses me. It's a tide, a swelling ocean of pleasure. Her free hand reaches up and pinches my nipple, and I cry out.

It stings, and that little act of violence pushes me over the edge. I spill into an orgasm that rushes from between my thighs up to the tip of my head. It tingles across my nose, my lips, races through my mind until I'm soaring.

I'm no longer in my body. I am only pleasure, and soul, and all of me is all of hers.

When I return to my body, I'm panting. Something inside me has snapped. I'm not the innocent little Cordelia I was.

She has fucked something into me, or maybe out of me. I am angry. I am ruined.

Our families are coming. They have done this, and I am furious.

"Take your trousers off," I command. This is a tone I've never used before. I feared the words would come out strained. But they don't.

I'm deep and sultry and demanding. Eleanor is always in charge, but not right now. Not after that.

She does as I ask, although I can tell she's struggling to obey me. This isn't us.

But then, tonight shouldn't be happening to us, either. Strange nights call for strange actions. And I will make her mine the way she made me hers.

"Come here," I say when she's naked.

She places her feet on either side of my legs and steps up my body, one foot, then the other.

"Kneel," I say.

And she does until her knees are on either side of my cheeks. I slide my hands to her backside and lower her down until my favourite place on her body presses against my mouth.

"I want you to look at me, okay?" I say.

She nods and I open my mouth, drawing my tongue between her intimate parts.

She inhales, tips her head back. I take my tongue off her.

"Eyes on me, Eleanor, I want to watch you come apart."

She rocks back to face me, locking her gaze on mine, and I begin again. Slow at first, drawing my tongue everywhere, letting it mark her the way she marked me.

I focus on her bud, lapping and licking until her breaths are short and fast. She rocks her hips over my face. Leans down and loops my long hair around her wrist as if even now, she wants to hold a piece of me.

I dig my nails into her backside hard enough she hisses. But she also grows wet, soaking my chin, and I'm certain she likes this. I dig harder, hoping my nails cut her skin and scar her.

I've never wanted to hurt her before. I wonder if I should be ashamed. But I'm not. I want to keep her, and if I can't, then perhaps she can carry a piece of me with her instead.

She juts against my face, rocking her hips in sharp motions as she reaches the edge of pleasure. I lap faster, tasting every morsel she gives me.

She leans forward, grinding herself on me. But her eyes never leave mine, and as she tips over the edge of pleasure, they come alive.

The ocean burns in her gaze, as if she sets the waves alight, the clouds on fire and my heart ablaze.

I watch her shatter, the space between my legs soaking all over again. I want to spend the rest of my life watching this. Consuming her as her nipples tighten, the hardening bud of her apex against my tongue.

I want to taste the pleasure that trickles from between her legs.

I want to keep her.

But I can't.

I grip hold of her for a moment longer until I know this is it. She tears her gaze away, lying flat next to me on our makeshift bed. She runs her fingers along my stomach, drawing gentle circles.

"Our families," she says finally.

"I know."

"I don't think we have long. I'm not sure we can keep running..." her voice breaks, the words fracturing the same way my heart is.

Little pieces and fragments of it drifting into the space between us.

"We can continue to run, but I think it's going to break us. Look at how tired we are. We should not be hiding in the shadows. We should not be living in the breaths between days," she says.

Her hand comes to my cheek and wipes away the tears I didn't know had fallen.

"Then what if we truly leave? Change our names, our identities, leave this city and the next. Run far enough they can never find us?"

Eleanor's hand falls away. "I want that. Truly I do. But I also wonder whether we will ever be free. Won't we constantly look over our shoulders? Spend our days with one eye on the horizon?"

"Always wondering if this is the day they catch up?" I whisper.

She nods. "I would live that life if it meant I could keep you."

"Oh, Cordelia, you are my oxygen. You are my light and love, but I want to live my life free with you."

"What are you saying?" I ask.

She shakes her head. "Nothing. Today, I'm saying nothing. But I can't keep doing this. I'm exhausted. And if we keep running, nothing is going to change."

"So we have a decision to make?"

Eleanor nods, brushes a loose strand of hair behind my ears and kisses my forehead.

"I will always honour your wishes. If you want to keep running, we'll run. But we need a new plan. One that isn't exhausting."

"And if I don't?"

"Then if you don't, we turn back. We return to our families and try to fight from within our prison walls."

I pull my hands over my face. I know what my heart wants and what my head thinks we should do.

But as is the case with many of the important decisions, if you wait too long, the decision is taken from you.

A deafening roar booms around the living room, the front door in the kitchen explodes off the hinges and clatters over the table we were sitting at a moment ago.

I scream.

The back door does the same a second later, flying off and slamming against a bookcase on the wall.

Men flood the kitchen and the living room. Men that seem familiar, some that don't.

Shouts rent the air, the noise blisters. Words are indecipherable. I grab my dress, clutching it as I manage to half pull it over my head.

Eleanor grabs my hand. Her eyes are wild and harried. She squeezes so tight I fear my bones will crack.

"I was wrong," she pants. "We should have run. I never want to leave you." This time she cries, and clarity floods my mind.

I glance frantically around the rooms, searching for the familiarity I'm afraid of and yet I know I'll find.

The logos on their uniforms. My mother's house: St Clair, and on the others, the Randall family crest.

They found us.

I lurch forward and clutch Eleanor to me. She's put her trousers on and her shirt, though it's not done up. She doesn't even try to fix the buttons. Instead, we cling to each other, half naked and desperate.

Our hands dig into each other's skin, only this time my nails don't mark her as mine, but with a desperate plea: please don't let go.

The first man, a Randall, lunges for Eleanor and grabs her around the waist. She jerks back; the force tugging away one of her hands, leaving us connected by one hand. Her grip stays firm.

She lashes at the man. Throwing wild fists at his head, his neck. Her leg kicks out almost pulling me over.

"Eleanor," I shriek, as a second man grabs hold of her. I'm knocked forward, as a man, a St Clair, leaps at me.

"No!" Eleanor shrieks.

But I am not as strong as her. One of my fingers slips. The heat and sweat between our palms making it hard to hold on.

The man drags me up and yanks at me.

But I refuse to let go. My knuckles ache with the strain, the skin between my fingers stretching and splitting where I refuse to let go.

"Eleanor, please," I beg.

But I no longer know what I'm begging for. This is inevitable. It's too late to stop them. Too late to run.

A second man grabs hold of me, a third on Eleanor.

She is a force. Her shoulders and neck strain with the effort of not letting me go. Veins pulse in her face and down her throat while her muscles quiver and burn with the effort of maintaining her grip on me.

The same heat floods my shoulders, the strain feels like my joints will pop. But still I refuse to let go.

And then, two women walk through the front door and into the living room where Eleanor and I are now horizontal, being tugged apart like a rope across the living room.

Their faces are shadowed by the light behind them. But when they are revealed with their proximity, all the fight leaves me. I know we've lost.

"Mother," both Eleanor and I say simultaneously.

The two matriarchs of our families stand before us. Both wearing scowls that could freeze oceans, destroy cities and sever heads.

"Release her," my mother says.

"Mama, please."

"Eleanor," her mother says, her tone sharp enough to cut our wrists.

Our mothers look at each other and give each other a slight incline of the head.

But it's my mother who speaks for them both. "We will ask you once, to choose to let go..."

She turns to Eleanor's mother who says. "Or the consequence will start a war that will tear the city and both of our families apart. We are agreed. Our families cannot be joined. We will do whatever it takes to protect the integrity of this city's economy."

My mother nods. "There are scars that run too deep between us for one fleeting romance to change it. This is a phase, Cordelia. You will get over it."

"No," I breathe.

But Eleanor squeezes my hand, forcing me to look at her. Tears stain her cheeks like paint.

"They're giving us the choice, Cordelia. Choose to let go, or they'll hunt us. I can't let that happen. I can't let them kill you. I'd rather you live without me, than die because our families forbid our love."

“E-Eleanor,” I plead, her name cracked between sobs.

But her fingers are already loosening, the iron vice-like grip slipping.

“Please,” she begs this time. “Don’t make me be the one to let go.”

I hold her gaze, and in that moment, time slows to a stop. There is only her and me, and the weight of our love, thick and endless between us. I try to let my eyes tell her all the things I wish I’d said.

That even though I’ve told her a thousand times, I should have said it a thousand more. I want to explain how deeply I love her. That my heart will bleed for eternity.

That I will carry an open wound in my soul for the rest of time.

I want her to understand that the way she looks at me made me feel like a queen, a goddess, wanted. Loved. Owned. Like I was her everything and nothing else mattered.

I want to tell her that there can never be anyone else, that no matter how many lifetimes I have to search, I will always hunt for her.

That even though I’m letting go, I will never stop looking for a way to get her back.

But she’s right. I can’t live in a world where she’s gone because of me.

So my fingers loosen.

I hold her gaze and plead with the gods to let her hear my message. To let her know that no matter how many millennia it takes, I will find my way back to her.

“Cordelia,” she breathes. One precious word, a sound I’ll hold in my heart forever; its echoes carving sharp memories in my mind.

My lips part to say something, anything, but there’s nothing else that can be said or done.

With our mothers standing over us, men tugging and pulling us apart, tears streaking both of our cheeks, I do the one thing I thought I would never do.

I let go.

CHAPTER 43

RED

The Chief kneels at my feet, pulls a sticky, pale red thread of hair back from my face. Her expression is soft. Caring. But I don't trust her. Not anymore.

"Oh, Red, sweetie. I'm sorry this happened to you."

"Sorry?" I splutter and blood and spittle spray her chest. I shake my head, my vision blurring as one of my eyelids swells shut.

"You need to drink human blood, it's the only way," she says.

My one remaining eye widens. I'm such a fucking idiot. "You planned this," I say.

"Of course I did. All these trials were planned by Cordelia and I."

I must lose consciousness because I open my eyes to her stroking my cheek with someone new knelt next to her. A young girl who can't be more than seventeen.

"No," I say. "You knew what I was. You wanted me broken so that I would have no choice but to transform. To drain an innocent and become what you and everyone else want."

She mocks a gasp. That manipulative bitch.

"I won't do it."

Her face darkens. "You have to. Or you'll die."

"But at least dying will be my choice, for once. You've taken everything from me. My death is the one thing I can choose."

"Don't be stupid, Red. You have to drain her."

I smile and laugh, it's crackly and filled with bubbles of blood which splatter out in a pretty pattern. "I don't have to do shit."

Every word hurts. Hot pain, ice, wracking throbs that course and sear through my body. My legs, my face, my ribs and my back are all broken.

Sadie appears in my field of vision. She signs at Eleanor. "Give me a moment with her." The Chief narrows her eyes. "Trust me, I can convince her."

"Be quick, her heart rate is dropping. I do not want to lose her," the Chief says and backs away, exiting the ring.

Sadie inclines her head as she crouches down and places her hands either side of my shattered skull. I wince as more bolts of pain lance through me. I black out for a moment.

But it doesn't matter because her words filter through my subconscious. "It's your choice what you do, Red, but I made you a promise. And I always keep my promises. You were never good enough for Octavia. You should have chosen her. You're going to die knowing that all along this was your fault. You hurt the one woman who could have saved you, and now you've ruined her chances of winning the only thing she ever wanted."

"Why? Why are you doing this to me?"

"To you?" She huffs, it's a strange, silent sort of sound,

as if there should have been volume and it got sucked away. "So arrogant. So selfish. Even now you think this is about you. You're all the same. Everyone thinks Dahlia and Octavia are the only ones in this fight. That it's brains or brawn that will win. But it's the quiet ones you need to watch. Didn't you read fairytales as a kid?"

I cough, blood splattering the ground. But finally, I pull my eyes open again and take in her face as I ask, "What do you really want?"

"I want what's mine, Red. What I'm owed. And I want Cordelia to pay for what she's done."

"For locking you up? Caging you away for a hundred years? Until you screamed your own voice away?"

She smiles, her eyes razor sharp as they lock onto mine and I can see that this is all it was about. A poxy hundred years in an immortal vampire's life. Gods, could I have been more stupid?

My body relaxes the moment the compulsion slides over my consciousness. Like silk and velvet, it caresses the furthest depths of my brain.

And then my mind unlocks, and I am flooded with a tidal wave of memories.

Surge after surge. Because she did it too. Not only did Sadie only give me half my memories, but she intentionally only gave me half the story.

The night in Elysium rushes back to me. Octavia telling me I was the first human to ever truly look at her. The hours of making love, the way she cradled me and caressed my wound. The way she asked to see me again, the innocence and desperation in her voice.

The moment I awoke from the blood lust. I was awful.

"I've made a mistake. You're a mistake. This was a terrible idea," I say, panic-stricken and thinking only of my sister.

“What? No. We... I thought,” Octavia says, her beautiful red eyes filled with wet tears. Bile claws at my throat in real time as all the memories of everything I should have known wash over me.

Octavia has her arms wrapped around her legs as I crawl across the floor next to her. “I’m sorry,” I say. “I really am, but I have to look after my sister.”

But she can’t bring herself to look at me, “You’re like the rest of them. What was this, monster kink? Fuck the city villain and tell all your mates about it?”

“It wasn’t like that. But I can’t. We... Gods, Octavia. I’m not just any hunter. I’m the head of security and you’re... Mother of Blood, you’re one of the original three. Can you imagine what this would do to me? To my career?”

“To you?” She laughs and yanks her arm out of my grasp. I wasn’t even aware I’d touched her.

“Octavia, be reasonable. I saved you, you saved me. We had a good night.”

How could I say this to her? Of course it would hurt her.

“You don’t get to treat me like meat. You don’t get to take a piece of me and then leave. If you don’t want all of me, then you can’t have any of me.”

She rounds on me.

“Please, don’t,” I beg. “Don’t hurt me.” Those words ring like déjà vu in my mind, only this time, I have the context.

“Hurt you?” she snorts. “You were meant to be different. All because you looked at me, really, truly looked *at* me. I’m pathetic. You’re no better than anyone else. You’re never going to see me for who I am. So fine. You don’t need to see me at all.”

The memory plays again, just like before the trial. Octavia grabs me by the scruff of my shirt and wipes the night from my memory.

Only this time, I understand.

She's never felt like she was enough. Never felt like she was worthy of anything because no one ever loved her unconditionally.

Until me.

Until I fucked it all up.

Until I took the one thing that meant everything to her.

Memory after memory floods my mind and each one gives me another piece of the truth, the full narrative.

The one I should have always had.

But then the memory of the night Amelia was turned filters through my mind. Though this one plays in reverse, taking me back to early that evening.

To an argument between Amelia and me. I don't remember this.

"Amelia, see reason. I beg you not to go out tonight."

"Lighten up, Red. You're always so uptight. It's a party."

"I don't like him. I don't like his values. You always make bad calls when you're with him."

"Well, it's a good job I'm the one with him then, isn't it? Besides, if anything goes wrong, you're not far away. It's not like you've ever let me have a fucking night out by myself, is it? You always come find me at midnight, like the prisoner I am. It's already eight, how much trouble can I get into in four hours?"

But I'm tired. I'm weary in my bones and in my heart and I can't take it anymore. I've spent years looking after Amelia. I was always the sensible one so she didn't have to be, and tonight I'm exhausted. I want to be free for one night. Free of the worry.

I sigh. "If you go, I'm not coming after you, Amelia. I mean it. We're both adults now. You're the one who begs me to let you live free. So fine. Go. Make your own decisions."

She rolls her eyes at me. “Yeah, yeah. See you at midnight.”

And with that she skips out of the house, she doesn’t even kiss me goodbye. And I am so fucking tired. I uncork a bottle of whisky and I take it with me in a carriage to find Octavia.

The memory rushes on, we’re in the St Clair territory, in one of her mother’s spare properties. This one happens to be near Dahlia’s mansion. Of course, Octavia paces the cottage, livid that she can hear their antics and the music blaring.

But I decide to take her mind off it.

I distract her the best way I can—with sex and orgasms.

The memory plays on, tugging me closer, closer to the ending I fear is coming. My stomach swills and I’m not sure if it’s the fact I’ve lost too much blood or if it’s the anxiety I hold in the memory.

Octavia gets off the bed and pulls her clothes on, her brow creased.

“What’s wrong?” I say as she rushes to the window and peers at Dahlia’s mansion across the way.

“I... I’m not—” she freezes halfway to pulling on her shirt. “Oh, gods.”

I sit bolt upright, already hauling my clothes on. It’s then I notice the music has stopped. Only, Octavia has superhuman hearing. If there’s no music and she looks this worried, then she can hear something going on.

“Octavia, you’re scaring me. What the fuck is wrong?”

Her chest rises and falls, her eyes wider than I’ve ever seen them.

“OCTAVIA?” I bark.

“Amelia.”

One word, and it shatters my entire world.

Octavia is already gone; she’s speeding across the small

field between the cottage and Dahlia's house. I'm out the door, I don't even shut it, I leave it swinging behind me as I run faster than I've ever run. I pump my arms so hard that goosebumps fleck out over my skin.

Octavia has vanished inside the house, and I want to scream.

I want to pray to the gods to have her speed and strength. Because I swear I'll slaughter anyone who hurts Amelia.

I run harder, faster. I push my body until my throat dries and I'm convinced I'm going to suffocate. Still, I dig deeper, until my vision greys.

It's then that I reach the door, cursing my pathetic human heart for not being able to withstand a faster pace. For not being fitter and stronger. For not being more powerful.

This was the beat. The misalignment from the fragments that Sadie showed me and the altered version Octavia had given me.

This is the truth. I wasn't there for her because I was with Octavia.

I barge through the door. But it's too late. The me in the present recognises that Amelia is already mid-transition.

She rounds on me, screaming and shouting. "YOU SHOULD HAVE BEEN THERE. YOU SHOULD HAVE COME FOR ME. YOU ALWAYS COME FOR ME, RED."

She's hysterical, maniacal.

"It's the transition," Octavia says over Amelia's shrieking. "Red, get out. She might—"

"Transition? NO," I shriek.

I fall to my knees, sobbing and shaking as I realise what's happened.

"What the fuck did you do, Octavia?" I'm screaming, I

don't even recognise the shattered voice coming from me right now.

"I had no choice. I had to."

"YOU TURNED HER?" I scream.

And everything crashes down around me. I see stars. I lean forward and vomit. The one person I loved more than anything is gone from me.

All because of one stupid argument. One stupid night of sex meant I wasn't there for the one person who needed me. This is my mother all over again. I failed to save her. I failed to save Amelia.

"Amelia, I'm sorry. I'm fucking sorry."

But my sister grabs me by the shoulders.

"This is your fault," she says, and her nails dig into my back. Blood sprays my face as she shakes me and my heart shatters into tiny, jagged pieces.

"I'm sorry. I didn't mean to. I should have been there. I'm sorry. I'm fucking sorry. Please forgive me."

"Forgive you?" She laughs, high-pitched and shrieking. Then she bends over, dragging me down as she retches and throws up right next to where I did.

She snarls at me. "It's your fault. It was your fault Mum died. Your fault Dad abandoned us. You didn't make it to her that night, just like you didn't make it to me tonight. You're useless. You prance around on your high horse, making out like you're the responsible one, and you've never really looked after any of us."

"Amelia, please," I sob. Every word she says is like a knife to my gut. My heart is splintering as she screams in my face.

I can't take it, everything she says is true. I failed. I'm useless.

Amelia's face shifts and contorts. Her two incisors fall out as new fangs draw down. Her nose flares. She glares at me with nothing but hate. She's going to drain me; I'm going to be the human she drinks to complete her transition.

And I'm going to let it happen because she's better off without me.

Everyone is better off without me.

Amelia's fangs finish descending, and she sinks them into my neck. A blaze of pain so hot it blisters my core, courses through my body, as hot threads rush out of my neck. My sister is going to kill me and I deserve it.

I let it happen.

I want it to happen.

I don't want to be here knowing I ruined everything.

Octavia rips Amelia off me, throwing her backwards.

"Oh, Red," she says, cradling me. I'm weak. But I am also broken on a much deeper level than the blood loss.

I curl into her arms, and I break apart, sobbing. "I should have been there. I should have been there. I'm always there for her. This is my fault."

"No. Blame me. I am the one who turned her. I did this." But her voice is desperate, harried, and I don't believe everything she's saying.

"What happened?"

She explains. She tells me that Dahlia hunted her friends, drained Amelia. And with every word she says another piece of me withers.

I scramble out of her arms. Hysterical. I'm rocking. Screaming. "Make it go away. Make it go away."

"Red," Octavia pleads, desperately trying to get through to me. But I can't hear her, my mind is shattered. Hurt. Desperate.

"I killed them all. Everyone dies because of me, Octavia. I don't want to remember. Make it stop." I lunge for her. Grabbing her and pleading with her.

"I can't." She shakes her head. "I swore I'd never do it again."

"OCTAVIA. PLEASE. I can't live like this, I can't bear it. My sister is everything I despise because of me."

"You despise me?"

"That's... that's not what I meant."

But her eyes drop, the damage is already done.

She pulls away from me. "If I do this, if I take it away it's because you asked me to, not because I wanted to do it. This isn't the right thing to do."

But I'm sat rocking on the floor again. "I killed them. I killed them all. You have to take it all away. Please, take it away." It doesn't matter that I've hurt her. Nothing matters. I can't live with the knowledge of what I've done.

And then... Just like that, everything eases, and Octavia is whispering tales of hate and hurt, truth wrapped in lies. Tales of her betrayal. She played my villain. Gave me someone to hate because that was the only way to heal my mind. To stop the cataclysmic break that was my soul tearing in two.

She took it all away.

All because I asked.

And now, as I lay dying in the ring, Sadie walking away, the truth is finally mine.

And nothing is better because of it.

Everything is worse.

The truth is, I ruined everything, and now I've broken Octavia's heart as well as mine.

Sadie purposely manipulated the memories she gave me. Only showed me the worst bits in order to make me do her bidding. And I may never be able to get Octavia back because of it.

I want to laugh.

I want to cry.

But instead, I lie bleeding, the last vestiges of my life running free in the ring. I'll never get revenge; I'll never get Octavia back and everything was for nothing.

But that's the thing, isn't it. I've been full of moralistic vitriol while I've been in the background, letting everyone else control me. I wasn't in the trenches or fighting on the front lines of life.

I've been sat back, watching all of this play out while I refused to engage with what was happening to me. While I refused to fight back against those pulling my strings.

I was naïve.

I was a fool.

And now I'm going to die because of it.

My vision spatters with grey. What a joke I am.

How little any of us really know about ourselves until we're facing the ultimate choice: kill or be killed. It's only in that moment that we truly find out who we are.

And here I am.

An old man I recognise kneels beside me, his red cloak soaking with my blood. The kind monk.

Oh no.

No. No. No.

I understand what he's doing. What he's about to do. This is what they wanted. This is exactly where the Chief and Cordelia have engineered me to be.

In front of a crowd of nobles and hunter elders so there can be no doubt. If I drink, everyone will realise who I am. What I am.

I won't do it.

"You have a choice to make," he says.

But I don't want the choice. He offers his wrist to me, but I turn away. If I do nothing, I let my body bleed out. Give up on myself, on Octavia, on Amelia.

Or do I give in to the one thing I've been running from?

Do I embrace who I am?

Accept that this is my destiny.

"You'll die," I sputter.

"We all die someday," he brushes his hand over mine.

I stare at the old monk offering his life for mine. I have to choose:

Do I betray every value I've ever had, take the life of an innocent to fight for Octavia's love? Fight to fix what I've done? To get the cure for Amelia?

Or do I stand by my morals?

Lay down my life to save this believer? Sacrifice myself to make sure no one else dies in pursuit of this cure? Let the door crumble and end all the fighting?

Either way someone dies.

The old man kneels beside me, sliding a knife into his wrist, the sharp scent of iron filling the air as he raises his dripping arm towards my lips.

I grab it, holding it away and preventing it from getting any closer to me. A shooting pain rushes through my hand where I hold him back.

Think, Red.

Think.

But my mind is addled, confused, swirling with delirium and blood loss. My eyes flutter shut. The old man yanks me, forcing me back to consciousness.

I need to decide.

I need to do it now.

Who am I fighting for? This city, Octavia? My sister?

Or me and my morals, my beliefs?

What or who is worth sacrificing everything I believe for?

My body cramps, the blood loss and lack of oxygen making my muscles spasm and draw tight like a dead spider's.

"Red," the monk pleads. "I will die now, no matter your choice. Will you really sacrifice us both?"

I glance up at him, knowing that whichever way I go, this decision will fracture our city. He blinks at me, his skin paling where his wrist bleeds out. His eyes bore into mine, drawn tight and desperate. The same harried desperation screaming through my gut. But there's something else in his gaze, a set determination that I recognise. Because there's only one question left.

Who do I want to save more? Octavia and my sister or myself?

I let that question swirl around my gut, carve its way through my consciousness. It throbs its way through my memories making my head swell and swim as I try to decipher the answer.

"Red," he hisses, this time it's him who sways under my grip.

It's in that moment that I know what I am willing to do. How far I'm willing to push. And what I'm willing to sacrifice.

At last, I've made my decision, and even as the weight of it settles in my gut, and the fog of unconsciousness bears down on me, the repercussions of this moment will change everything.

Nothing is ever going to be the same.

My last thought is: will they forgive me?

If you'd like to read a free prequel to my *Girl Games* series, full of just as many lesbians and just as much spice, you can do that by signing up here: rubyroe.co.uk/signup.

Last, reviews are super important for authors, they help provide needed social proof that helps to sell more books. If you have a moment and you're able to leave a review on the store you bought the book from, I'd be really grateful.

About the Author

Ruby Roe is the pen name of Sacha Black. Ruby is the author of lesbian fantasy romance. She loves a bit of magic with her smut, but she'll read anything as long as the characters get down and dirty. When Ruby isn't writing romance, she can usually be found beasting herself in the gym, snuggling with her two pussy... cats, or spanking all her money on her next travel adventure. She lives in England with her wife, son and two devious rag doll cats.

The Girl Games Series

A Game of Hearts and Heists
A Game of Romance and Ruin
A Game of Deceit and Desire

instagram.com/sachablackauthor

tiktok.com/@rubyroeauthor

Printed in Great Britain
by Amazon